"I love it! Spectacular storytelling, vibrant prose, wonderful handling of multiple narrators, and genuinely gripping. I haven't read a historical novel this good for years: it's reminiscent of Rosemary Sutcliff at her peak."

JOANNE HARRIS, author of *The Gospel of Loki*

"Beautifully crafted and elegantly told, I was carried away to a world both familiar and unknown – *Inanna* has an enthralling magic all of its own."

CLAIRE NORTH, World Fantasy Award winner and author of *Ithaca*

"*Inanna* is a deft, mesmerising novel, with a cadence true to its epic roots and an entrancing blend of historic depth, intoxicating imagination and sheer heart. Emily H. Wilson is an author to watch, and *Inanna* is a gorgeous myth retelling with a very timely message about power and empowerment, and who gets to set our cultural narratives."

LORRAINE WILSON, British Fantasy Award winner, and author of *This is Our Undoing*

INANNA

A Novel

EMILY H. WILSON

TITAN BOOKS

Inanna
Print edition ISBN: 9781803364407
E-book edition ISBN: 9781803364414

Published by Titan Books
A division of Titan Publishing Group Ltd
144 Southwark Street, London SE1 0UP
www.titanbooks.com

First edition: August 2023
10 9 8 7 6 5 4 3 2 1

A CIP catalogue record for this title is available from the British Library.

Printed and bound by CPI (UK) Ltd, Croydon, CR0 4YY.

For Jon, Jack and Aldo

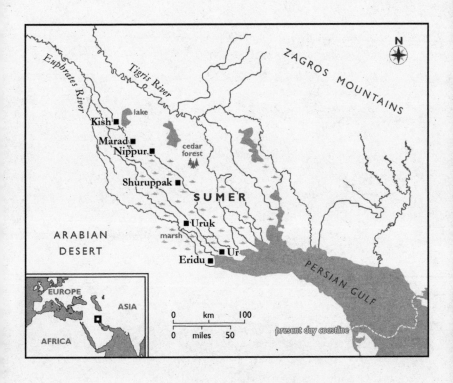

Ancient Sumer in 4001 BC

DRAMATIS PERSONAE

THE ANUNNAKI, HIGH GODS OF SUMER

An | king of the gods
Nammu | queen of the gods
Enki | lord of wisdom and water, son of An
Enlil | lord of the sky, son of An
Ninlil | child bride of Enlil
Ninhursag | former wife of Enki
Nanna | father of Inanna, god of the moon
Ningal | mother of Inanna, goddess of the moon
Ereshkigal | queen of the night, Inanna's sister
Utu | god of the sun, Inanna's brother
Lugalbanda | Gilgamesh's father, and chief minister to An
Ninsun | Gilgamesh's mother, goddess of cows
Inanna | goddess of love and war

THE HALF GODS
(Immortal children of Anunnaki and humans)

Dumuzi | god of sheep, son of Enki
Geshtinanna | daughter of Enki
Isimud | Enki's chief minister

The Humans

Gilgamesh | mortal son of Lugalbanda and Ninsun
Akka | king of Kish
Hedda | Akka's sister
Enmebaragesi | son of Akka
Inush | Akka's nephew
Enkidu | the wild man
Ninshubar | hero from the far south
The Potta | Ninshubar's adopted son
Amnut | Inanna's suitable friend
Harga | servant of Gilgamesh and Enlil
Della | mortal daughter of Enlil
Dulma | priestess at the Temple of the Waves
Shamhat | priestess in Shuruppak
Tomasin | elder of Marad
Lilith | priestess in Uruk
Uptu | leader of the scorpion men
Urshanabi | stone man
Shiduri | inn keeper
Uta-napishti | hero of the Great Flood, builder of arks

Demons and Other Creatures

Galatur | the black fly
Kurgurrah | the blue fly
The *gallas* | demon servants of Ereshkigal
Neti | gatekeeper to the underworld

PART I

"In the first days, in the very first days,
In the first nights, in the very first nights,
In the first years, in the very first years."

From the ancient Sumerian poem
"The Huluppu Tree"

CHAPTER ONE

INANNA

In Athens, they call me Aphrodite now. In Babylon, they call me Ishtar. But in the first days I had only one name: Inanna.

I was born in the city of Ur, in the springtime. In those days memories of the Great Flood were still raw, and everything was measured from it, so I can tell you that I was born six years after the deluge, when the land was dry and true again, but the dead were still every day missed.

It was in many ways an ordinary beginning. My mother screamed and raged, and then pushed me out, through bloodied thighs, onto linen sheets. She held me to her chest and wept. My father kneeled beside her all the while, his hands clenched tight before him.

The priestess laid me down in an ancient boxwood cradle. She counted my toes and fingers, and put her ear very gently to my heart. "She will live," the priestess said, and she smiled, very warm, at my parents.

My parents could not smile back at her.

They were high gods. They were Anunnaki. And yet this realm

almost killed them, when they first descended from Heaven. How could this child of their flesh, so very frail, survive Earth's blinding light, and choking air?

Oh, but I did survive.

Indeed, I thrived, in the scouring Earthlight.

I grew plump, beneath Earth's garish, cobalt sky.

In my first gasp I breathed in the cedars in the palace gardens and the salt coming in off the ocean. I breathed out for the first time to the music of the frogs upon the marsh. All of it was bliss to me. What had once been poison to my family was to me a strengthening balm.

The word went out from Ur to all the city states of Sumer. A new goddess was born: the thirteenth Anunnaki. The drums beat out from every temple.

My mother was exquisite when she was happy. She pressed the tiniest, softest kiss against the tip of my nose, and whispered: *"All hail Inanna."*

There was talk of taking me north. The king of the gods must see me. But my mother paced back and forth. Six days on a barge; how could it be safe for me?

As they talked, I lay on my back in my cot, stretching out my feet, and looking up and out at a square of clean blue sky. Without warning, the square was full of swifts. I must have made a noise at this extraordinary sight, at this waxing and waning of what had only been flat colour. I was not upset: I was amazed. But at once my mother picked me up and cradled me against her. "She is too young to travel," she said.

Seven days went by, and then a white-sailed boat appeared on the horizon, leaning over hard in the playful spring winds. It was a skiff from the White Temple. The punishment for delaying such a boat was death, and this one had come south down the river in two days and two nights, sweeping away all records before it.

Four men in black stepped off the skiff onto the marble quay at Ur, and a small object, wrapped in red velvet, was handed to my mother's chief priestess. This package was carried up through the griffin gates, past the ponds and palms of the temple precinct, and down long palace corridors, to be handed to my father as he stood beside my cradle.

Inside the velvet was a small clay tablet, raw orange in colour and covered on both sides with neatly pressed text. My father read it slowly.

"He is coming south," he said.

An, first amongst the Anunnaki, had not left his citadel since time out of mind. But now he was coming south to see me, with the lifegiving Euphrates surging beneath his helm.

The farmers stood in the fields, open-mouthed, to watch his oak-planked barge glide by.

It was an honour of the ages.

My mother said it was too windy for me to be taken outside, but I felt An's sandalled foot meet the marble of the quay as he was helped from his barge. I felt him drawing closer as he was carried through the walls of Ur, and set down at the door of the Palace of Light. I felt his slow and heavy tread along the corridors.

A muted disturbance outside our rooms, and An was with us.

The king of the Anunnaki embraced my father, and kissed my mother's round cheek, and then he came over to my cradle, blacking out my square of sky. As he put one heavy hand on my chest, I burst out with a noise, an animal bleat of fear.

My mother moved as if to pick me up, but my father touched her shoulder and she took a step back.

I lay quiet after that, with An's hand upon me, and the two of us looking upon each other, him so old, and me so new. He pushed his hand down a little heavier, smiling as he did it, but he could not make me bleat again.

"She's strong," he said, his eyes on me, "but strange too."

My father came closer. "I see the Earthlight working on her," he said. "Changing her."

"I cannot feed her," my mother said. "But she is greedy for human milk."

At this I stirred beneath An's hand, turning my head in hope of my nurse.

"A child of two realms," An said. "Two realms, and two peoples." He paused a moment and then he said: "What did you do, to have her?"

He was looking at me, but behind him, my mother became entirely still, a statue carved from soft flesh.

"What do you mean, Grandfather?" she said, her voice very natural. "We only did the rites in temple, as we always do."

"We have been in this realm for four hundred years, and produced no Anunnaki babies," An said. "We make mortal babies, and half gods, and babies we cannot find names for. But never an Anunnaki. And now suddenly here one is."

"We did nothing that we have not always done," my father said, most earnest.

An turned to my mother. "Is that true, Granddaughter?"

"Yes," she said. She looked very young in her plain white tunic, with her soft brown curls loose upon her back.

"Is that a promise?" An said. "The sacred promise of a goddess?"

"Yes," she said. "It is my promise."

An held her eye a moment, then turned back to my cradle. "Well, it is done now, whatever you did. And she is Anunnaki, there is no doubt of that. We will call her the goddess of love."

He leaned down, his beard scratching my cheek. "*Love and war*," he whispered. "*Do not forget the second part.*" The acrid smell of him filled my lungs: the stink of illness, and unimaginable old age.

"What does a goddess of love do?" my father asked.

An shrugged. "We will think of something."

He sat down heavily in the chair next to my cradle. "There are stories about her already. They say she is going to be a great goddess. Queen of Heaven and Earth. Greater even than me."

"Do we not control the stories?" my father said.

"Stories are sly things," An said. "They can be hard to catch and kill."

After that they let in the priestesses, and my parents' chief ministers, everyone in white, the colour of Ur. And behind them, crowding my mother's rooms, came the priests of An, sombre in their black.

"All hail Inanna, goddess of love," An said, and they all bent their heads to me.

An rummaged in his black robes, and from the depths of a pocket produced a grey-metal bracelet, small in his palm. This he slipped onto my fat left wrist. I felt the bracelet close upon my skin, hard and cold.

"This is the *mee* of love," An said, one huge finger resting on my bracelet. "This was once a great weapon of Heaven. And now it will be the *mee* of Inanna, goddess of love. Let her be entered onto the god lists, in every temple in Sumer."

I looked at my mother's face, at how smooth it was, and I could not tell if she was pleased.

My parents stood on the marble quay to watch An go, each with one palm raised. As the king of the gods slipped into the morning mist, my mother looked down at me as I lay in the crook of her arm. Her face was a brightness against the deep of the sky.

"My goddess of love," she said, dropping a kiss upon my forehead.

"We are truly blessed," my father said to her. He moved her curls aside, so that he could kiss her cheek.

It was only the smallest movement, but I felt my mother flinch.

My father seemed not to notice.

"My precious princess of Heaven," he said, smiling down at me. "May only good things happen to you."

CHAPTER TWO

GILGAMESH

I lay on my back on the muddy riverbank with two soldiers of Kish standing over me. One of them had a hard boot on my throat, and the other was prodding at the gaps in my armour with the nasty end of a spear. The warm rain fell, fat droplets of it, straight into my eyes and gasping mouth.

"I thought he'd be bigger," throat man said, pressing down harder on my windpipe. He had to shout over the roaring of the river.

"Gill-garrr-mehsh," the other man bellowed down at me, his spear piercing the skin on my belly. "Such a big name, for such a sorry creature."

"We could kill him and keep his armour. He's almost dead anyway."

"The king did want him alive."

"But who would ever know?"

At this they looked at each other, one hard and meaningful glance. And for the briefest moment, they did not have their eyes on me.

I immediately rolled with some violence to my left.
Straight into the raging Tigris.

For two or three long minutes I had cause to regret my decision.

First, it is hard to swim in bronze armour, and in a skirt sewn all over with pieces of thin-beaten copper. I hit the riverbed with force and was tumbled helpless along the rocky bottom.

Second, without the boot on my neck, I gulped for air, but found myself breathing water.

Moments into my newfound freedom, I was drowning.

My helmet hit something shatter-hard. Pain ricocheted through my skull. My neck was snapped backwards by my chin strap.

White bubbles, grey rock; a glimmer of heavy cloud through silver-capped water; rock again.

For a moment my face was in the air, but my lungs were full of water, and then I was hurtling along the river bottom face down and with my feet upriver.

Another moment, and I would have been lost to the Tigris, and no one would know the name Gilgamesh. But then I sensed something long and dark in the water and on a reflex, my left hand went out for it. My hand closed tight on rough, twisted wood, and at once every sinew in my body was working to keep a hold of it. In my panic I had inhuman strength, and as my body swung around with the river, I got my right hand onto the stick.

Legs, a man's legs.

Harga.

Of course, Harga.

The next moment he had his hands upon me, and he was dragging me up onto rough, wet sand. There I vomited up river water with shocking force.

My heart was hammering so hard I thought it might break from my chest.

When the vomiting had finally subsided, and I was breathing air again, I looked up, my vision clearing, to Harga's black curls, and creased, brown face.

"My lord Gilgamesh, we should hurry," he said, his voice raised over the noise of the river. "They are close behind. We would be wise not to linger."

I pushed myself onto all fours, but I had to stay there awhile, both hands flat on the sand, before I could find the strength to do more.

"How sorry I am to keep you waiting, Harga," I began to say, only to be convulsed by a fit of coughing, with yet more water streaming from my mouth and nose.

Harga pulled me up to my feet, and although I swayed from side to side, I found I could stand.

The great Tigris was to my back, a league wide and wildly powerful. All around us in the rain and mist lay thick bush and the reek of rotting vegetation. It was impossible to see more than a few cords from where we stood, but to my immediate left stood our two mules, looking thoroughly wet and miserable. To my right, upriver, I thought I could hear voices over the noise of the river and the rain.

"We should leave, my lord," Harga shouted.

"Let's kill them first," I tried to say, but my voice was not much more than a croak.

Harga tucked his wet hair behind his ears. "My lord, the whole of Akka's army will soon be upon us. There are times when it is wise to stand and fight, but this is not one of them."

I could happily have punched him at that moment, just for the pompousness of that small speech. But I was not sure I could lift my fists. "Very well," I whispered.

As Harga helped me up onto my mule, my whole left side felt strangely numb, and I could not close my left hand upon the reins.

We headed west, as best we could with no sun to guide us. The bush seemed only to grow more dense, and the rain more torrential.

I gripped on to my damp mule as hard as I could with my knees and one good hand, but I was struggling to breathe. Was my throat swelling?

I will tell you, I have felt better. My left shoulder was a molten mass of pain. My gut was bleeding heavily where the soldier had been poking at me. Indeed, I could not tell, as I looked down at myself, what was only wet with rain and river water, and what was wet with blood. My hand, when I put it to my belly, came away a brilliant red.

"Harga, where were you, when they had me?" I said, as loud as I could. "Did you have a plan to save me, or were you planning only to watch them kill me?"

"I was assessing, my lord." He did not bother to turn his head.

"Whether to save me or not?"

He rolled his shoulders. "I like to be sure of the outcome."

I felt myself listing off to the right, and then with no warning I was vomiting clear liquid over the front of my saddle. How could there still be river water in me?

Harga turned to scowl at me. "I will tie you to your saddle," he said. He seemed about to say more, but then his face changed, all expression dropping from it. At the same moment there was movement behind him: men in dark armour, on dark animals, coming at us through the scrub.

There must have been thirty of them thronging the bushes around us. Men of Akkadia, in their distinctive copper chainmail, and sitting upon the thick-headed wild asses that they like to ride to war on.

I pulled in my mule with my one good hand, and came to a stop against Harga and his mount, our wet thighs pressed hard together in the crush. He cast a glance at me, and then dropped his reins and lifted both his hands over his head. I would have done the same, but was not sure I could lift my hands without falling.

A flash of kingfisher azure through the rain and leaves, and a rider in brilliant blue came pushing through the press of dark riders. I had never seen King Akka before, but I did not need to be told that this was him. The azure he wore was of course famous everywhere, and he was as large and thickset as they said in the stories. His fabled black beard was immaculately crinkled, even in the heavy rain, and his long, wet hair was held back from his face by the thin gold band that the kings of the north have always worn.

"My lord Gilgamesh!" he roared. "Welcome to Akkadia!"

I woke up face down on what I knew immediately to be a good bed, and for a while I lay there luxuriating in the feel of clean sheets baked dry in sunshine.

How long had it been since I had woken up on a soft mattress? I counted backwards. Two weeks behind enemy lines, and before that three weeks sleeping rough in that wet field beside the Tigris. And before that the army camp, as our great leader agonised over whether to ride north against Akka. So, two months, probably, since I had lain face down and open-mouthed upon delicious softness.

The room was quiet, but for a while I lay and listened.

My breathing. The cat-like mewling of a buzzard, up high somewhere. Voices, cheerful, distant. Nothing threatening.

Then I turned my head to the right and opened my eyes: a white plastered wall.

With great caution, I eased myself over onto my back, but I was not cautious enough, and for a moment I was obliged to shut my eyes again. My head pounded most unpleasantly. My left shoulder: it felt like deep bruising. My neck was stiff with pain. Across my belly, a sharp agony.

My hands went to my gut. A wound, scabbed over, just beneath my navel. I realised I was naked.

I breathed in, breathed out.

My pain slowly settled into a bearable background throb.

I was in a small, simple room. My wooden bed, and a stool beside it. One small, high window, with a grid of wooden bars across. A pattern of sunshine upon the white wall opposite.

Nothing else. No sign of my clothes or armour, or Harga, for that matter. A plain white sheet had been tucked neatly over me.

I breathed in, breathed out.

Yes, it was good. After a while, I could not feel my shoulder; lying flat, my neck eased, and the rough and scraping feeling in my head began to fade away. It is my experience that the closer damage is to your head, the harder it is to ignore. Give me a foot injury, any day, over a head wound. But yes, it was good. I would survive.

A small scratch on the door, and a flare of hair appeared, then a pale face with two very bright eyes. "My lord, may I check on you?"

"Certainly," I said, throwing the boy a smile. He was perhaps fifteen years old, thin but tall.

Of course, I was unarmed: never pleasant. I kept up the strength of my smile as the boy came towards me, a clay jug and small glass in his hands, but as I did so I cast my eyes around the room. Nothing. The bed I lay on was made of wood, but it was solid and well made. There was my sheet. I could strangle him with it, if need be. Or I could use the jug or the glass. I had my hands and feet too, of course, and my forehead. If I could get close enough.

"Do you know how I got here?" I said.

"You passed out entirely, my lord," he said. "They had to carry you from your mule."

Yes, my forehead might easily be enough, against this boy. But what lay outside the door? Indeed, where was I? I could be in any city in Akka's empire. Should I act now, with maximum violence, or wait to know more?

The boy seemed to sense the general direction of my thoughts, and, instead of setting the jug and glass down next to me on my stool, took a step or two backwards.

"They thought you would be thirsty, my lord, after having slept so long," he said, "and I am to bring you a robe and to tell you that as soon as you are recovered, the king hopes to see you at dinner."

At this a vast hunger came upon me. How long was it since I had eaten? I could have eaten the jug. I could have eaten this beautiful boy for that matter.

"What does that mean, at dinner?"

"The king eats with all the court in the evenings, and you will join him there, sir."

"Does he eat well, King Akka?"

"Yes, my lord. They eat a lot. There is always meat."

"You can put the jug down," I said. "I will not hurt you."

"Very good, my lord," he said, edging past me, and putting down the jug and glass.

"Where am I?" I said.

"Kish, my lord." He was backing towards the door. "You are in the palace of King Akka."

"And do you know where my man is? Harga?"

"He has ridden south, sir, with the news of your capture and the details of the ransom they are asking for you. They told your man to take the tablet to your father."

"Ah, but of course," I said. "My father."

It seemed I would be in Kish for some time then.

That night I ate at King Akka's table: a strange experience, although as time went on it would become most ordinary.

The banquet room in the palace at Kish was truly splendid. The walls were painted iridescent purple, at what great cost I could not imagine. Upon them were hung the heads of giant boars, and the chest plates and swords of defeated enemies. There was room enough for all the royal family and all of Akka's generals, perhaps two hundred courtiers in all, and the royal table that the king sat at was carved whole from one giant huluppu tree. And the food and wine, it came and came.

I will tell you, I was not at my most splendid. I should have been in my bed, sipping thin soup, not sitting upon a hard wooden chair, trying to hide my injuries. And besides that, my grooming left something to be desired. I like to keep my hair and beard neatly trimmed, and I like good cloth against my skin. Now I sat in that splendid room in a plain robe of rough linen, and with hair and a beard that had not seen a barber in months.

All the same, the food, the wine and the company soon began to cheer me. The great table before me was made bright with enormous beeswax candles, and huge clay platters of roasted venison, baked radishes and dressed lettuce were passed between us as at a family feast. Indeed, all of Akka's female relatives were dotted amongst the men on the royal table. These women lifted hands to me, and gave me wide and heartfelt smiles, and you would have thought I was a welcome guest, rather than an enemy held hostage.

"It is good to have a Sumerian at court with us," Akka said, leaning over to pour me more of his sweet date wine. "I regret this war, Gilgamesh. To be fighting like peasants over scraps of fertile land... it should not have come to this."

"I have been told there is more to it than that," I said. "I have been told you have forgotten who the Anunnaki are, and what you owe them."

That he laughed at. "Indeed, I do not know what I owe the Anunnaki. But you should know that my grandfather loved your father, before he rode north to found his own city. He told me that your father was a good man, Anunnaki or not."

"I have not seen my father for four years," I said, draining my wine down in one gulp. "I am told you have sent a ransom message to him, but I think you will be waiting many weeks before my father agrees to help me. I left home at the age of fourteen, and I have not seen him since."

Akka smiled his generous smile, leaning back in his seat with his hands upon his silky beard. "I have told him we will execute you unless he sends me the prisoners of war I have asked for. If he does not do as I ask, I will send him one of your fingers, and then we will see whether he still loves you or not. My guess, Gilgamesh, is that gods love their children just as much as men do."

I heaped a fresh serving of venison onto my plate. "We will see, my lord," I said. It was hard to take Akka's threats too seriously, as I sat so welcomed at his table.

The young woman on Akka's left leaned forwards to me, and I took in the curve of her pink cheeks, and bright eyes, and the small, high breasts beneath her thin blue dress.

"This is my sister, Hedda," Akka said.

"I am so pleased to meet you," Hedda said. "I have grown up on the stories about you!"

"All heroic, I hope," I said. "All glorious."

She laughed, clapping her hands together. "I have so many questions for you!"

Akka looked at her fondly, and then said to me: "Gilgamesh, you will live with us as family while you are a hostage here, because of the love my grandfather had for your father, and I know no son of his will disrespect this house. Live with us gently and with honour and there is no reason why this cannot be a good and peaceful time for you, and a chance to get to know our ways here in Kish."

"That is generous of you, my lord," I said, my eyes on the shape of his sister's nipples.

"Well," he said. "I would like a prince of Sumer to see and understand how we live here. To understand that it is possible to live well, to rule fairly, without the Anunnaki in charge."

"Who do the people worship here, if not the Anunnaki?"

"They worship the Anunnaki, just as they do in Sumer," he said. "All the ceremonies are the same here, but the rites are done by humans. And you know, Gilgamesh, it all works. That is what you will see here. Distant gods are the best kind of gods."

"I look forward to learning my lessons, my lord," I said, most earnest, but I gave Hedda a little wink as I said it.

Hedda laughed again. "I will take you to temple tomorrow," she said. "And show you the city."

"I look forward to it," I said, and then I left my eyes upon her just for one moment too long, so that she would blush. Akka leaned over and kissed his sister's head, and looked back at me with what appeared to be great good humour.

It was astonishing to me, the idea that Akka might be planning to let me consort with his women. But then you meet fools everywhere, even in palaces, even seated upon thrones.

"To Gilgamesh," Akka said, raising his cup to me. The whole table lifted their cups to me in turn, and drank back their good date wine, a long line of smiles and warmth.

"To Gilgamesh!" Hedda said, looking prettier to me by the moment.

"To the royals of Kish!" I said, raising my cup to them. "May the gods smile kindly on you."

CHAPTER THREE

NINSHUBAR

There was no greater honour, in the tribe that I was raised in, than to run at the back of the hunt.

Normally it was a position that was only given out to boys. But sometimes there was a girl in the world who was faster, stronger, and more dangerous, and then she might be chosen, if the gods and the fates reached out to her.

Even when I was very young, I was marked out as a runner. My father would let me come out for the start of the long hunt, and then send me home with the old men.

"Only a little," he said, "until your bones are set."

From when I was ten, he let me run with them all day, only going back at the very end, while the final four runners went on. More and more, I was still strong at the end of the hunt. I was a runner, and one day soon I would be a great one.

Then one morning, I felt it. I felt it in the wind, and the way the branches moved in it. I felt it in the way my father looked back at me as we walked up onto the ridgeway in the early morning light.

I was dressed in my hunting strips, my small breasts bound down. My feet were bare: we run barefoot in my country. On my back I carried my bow and arrows; on one ankle my skinning knife; over one shoulder my waterskin. I felt strong and good, each toe sure upon the sandy path.

At the top of the ridge, we paused for a moment to scan the grass plains below. There were ten hunters there that morning, and with us four dogs, but we were one creature as we stood there, eyes sharp for distant movement.

My father turned to me and said: "Will you run at the back today, Ninshubar?"

I tipped my head to one side, careful to seem nonchalant.

"I will run at the back," I said. "If the gods will run with me."

It was the most glorious moment of my life.

We dropped down off the ridge onto the savannah as the sky above us lit up pink. The air was cool and sweet upon my face and in my lungs.

I was the first to see the kudu: dark shapes to the south. They like to stay close to bushland, but this group had wandered out onto the plain, greedy for the new grass.

I made a sign at my father and then all of us broke into a slow run, the dogs fanning out to the east and west.

For the first time in my life, I did not try to push to the front. Instead, I was careful to stay well back, running easy, soft and loose upon the earth.

It was my father who picked the animal. We would take the bull. He was magnificent, but in the last season of his life. The dogs carved him out from his herd, and he veered into a stand of acacia.

After that we were in thick bush, and dappled sunlight. We darted between trees and shrubs, thorns underfoot in the sandy earth.

For a long time, I lost sight of the hunting party, only following their tracks.

This was my job today: to stay back, to stay fresh.

When the sun had wheeled up into the sky, the two oldest hunters appeared before me; they were squatting under a tree, in a scrap of true shade. As I ran past, they handed me the last of their water, and small strips of dried meat. "One step and then the next!" they called to me.

One step and then the next.

I drank their water, tying the empty skins to my belt as I ran, and I ate their dried meat. I felt the gods in my belly and my bones, the ancient owners of this sandy path I ran upon, and the low green trees I ran through, and the blue above.

One by one, the men ahead fell out, and I would find them standing on the track before me, holding out to me the last of whatever supplies they had. I handed over the empty waterskins I was carrying, and took what they had, and ran on, never coming to a stop.

As the heat faded from the day, the leader of the dogs, a lean-boned female, dropped back to look at me, one hard eye upon me, and then ran on between the trees and out of my sight.

One step and then the next.

Not long after I saw my father standing ahead in the trees, with the last of the hunters beside him. "It is only you now," he said. "We will follow on slowly."

"I am strong," I said, and ran straight past them without slowing.

∽

Now it was only the hoof marks of the kudu: no human prints ahead on the path. His steps were shortening; he was slowing. The dogs were exhausted, after running their pincer movement upon the kudu for so many hours, and they began to drop back to run alongside me. Their leader kept her hard eye upon me, which made me smile.

"Have some faith in me!" I called to her.

For the first time, I thought I heard the kudu, a low rumbling sound in the gathering dusk. I slowed to a walk and made the sign to the dogs, to stay where they were. Then I walked on alone.

In a glade, upon spring grass, stood the kudu, his sides heaving.

He was a huge animal: as tall as me at the shoulder. His striped coat, up close, was of a grey that was almost blue, with flashes of deep black and a bright russet.

When he sensed me walking in on him, he lay down, first his forelegs, and then his hind. Finally, he put his snow-white chin down upon the grass.

I walked carefully around him, and kneeled. How huge and black his eyes were, and how brilliantly white the streak below them. We were so close, I could smell his musky scent.

We looked at each other a while, and then I laid down my bow and arrows, and said the death prayers to see him well in the heavens. He breathed very slowly, seeming to settle into the earth.

I stood then, fixing an arrow to my bow, and I shot him in the soft skin that hung from his neck. He seemed not to feel it.

As his blood flowed down into the earth, I said again the death prayers, for a life well lived, and well given. When the light went out of his gorgeous black eyes, I put my hand to his neck and dabbed blood onto my cheeks.

Then I sat there for a while as the light went out of the day, sad to my bones for the end of this beautiful creature's life.

Only the dogs creeping up broke my meditation. Behind them came my father. He leaned down, and kissed me on the head.

"The runner at the back," he said.

That was the second most glorious moment of my life.

There was a great feast the next day, at our dry season camp. My father drank the sacred sap, and afterwards, before all the tribe, he said to me: "Ninshubar, when I am gone, you will be leader here."

I felt pride at the idea of this, but also sadness, at the idea of my father being gone. But then I caught my mother's eyes upon me, and felt something else.

I had always been the strongest and most able of her daughters. I was exceptionally tall, which is valued highly in my country. I was clever, and kind. I was a superb linguist. And I was beautiful, too. All the boys liked to put their eyes on me, and then slowly slide them off. There was no girl with whiter teeth, or brighter eyes, or blacker skin, within four days' walk.

My reward, for my beauty and wide-ranging excellence, had been the unremitting hatred of my mother and my sisters. They spat up feathers of jealousy as I grew more wonderful and powerful with age. But what was that to me? I learned to brush the feathers off me.

Now, by the light of the campfire, I saw something else in my mother's eyes.

She wanted to *hurt* me.

There was no mistaking it.

I wondered for the first time what that might mean for me.

CHAPTER FOUR

INANNA

Ur is an oven in the summer, and on the hottest days I was allowed to go up onto the roof of the moon temple. They would set up a shade and chair ready for me, so that I could sit in what breeze there was and watch for dolphins. Sometimes there would be a ship coming in, and I would be eager to see what came off it, if only to tell my parents about it at dinner. But on this day, as soon as I came out on the roof I heard a strange noise, rising up from the gardens, and instead of sitting I went straight to the balustrade.

There they were, far below me, three children, laughing and running, in and out of the cedar trees. They were perhaps about my age, although I was too high up to see their faces. A moment later a woman emerged from the palace buildings, holding a wooden spoon up in one hand, and the children ran past her and out of sight.

"Oh," I said, although I had not meant to speak.

My guard was standing in the narrow doorway behind me.

"Little goddess, are you well?" he said.

At first, I could only nod.

"I would like to see my mother," I said.

As we climbed slowly down the twisting staircase, my guard kept glancing back at me in the gloom.

"What was it that you saw, Inanna?"

They were meant to call me Lady Inanna, but they dropped that when no one else was listening.

"I am quite well," I said.

I made a show of concentrating on the steps, one hand on the cool wall.

I had seen children before. In pretty costumes, in temple, their faces plain, their eyes cast down. I had seen them lining the route into the holy precinct. I had seen them at table, when our chief ministers joined us for dinner, although even at table I had never heard one speak. And I knew of the concept of children playing, from temple stories, from things I had overheard. Yet I had not grasped what it would look like, or sound like, or how it would knock the insides out of me. The *wildness* of it, striking at my soul.

"Did you have too much sun, Princess?"

"I am quite well," I said again. "I only need to see my mother."

I knew where to find her; I felt the familiar pull. And there she was, in the long south-facing room at the back of her temple. The shutters onto the courtyard had been thrown open wide so that the scribes, sitting cross-legged upon dusty rugs, could see to do their work.

My mother had a taste for finery, but for the scribes she wore only a plain linen smock, because she was certain to come away with clay on her. She lifted her luminous face to me in greeting, but then went on with what she was saying to the scribes. "Read it all back to me," she said.

A scribe stood, head bent, and read out a list of grains and other goods, and the amount of each, and the price paid.

When I saw that I must wait for my mother's attention, I lifted up my skirts and sat down next to her. She patted my right knee with one hand as she listened with great intensity to the list of goods being read out.

"What is it, my love?" she said, when the scribe's story of barley, and silver ore, and the best saffron, was finally over.

"Mother, I would like a friend," I said.

She gave me her most playful smile. "Am I not your friend? Am I not the best friend anyone could hope for?"

I crinkled up my face. "I do not mean an adult friend."

My mother's smile faded. "My darling, we will talk about this at dinner."

We three moon gods ate outside in the summer, on the terrace that looked out over the river. I saw at once, from my parents' set faces, that they had been arguing.

My father took the lead. "Inanna, there is no one suitable to be the friend of the princess of the moon."

"Who would be suitable, father?"

My mother leaned forwards. "An immortal, Inanna, would be suitable. Someone who will live a lifetime alongside you, not die in a handful of decades. But the only children in this city are mortal."

"You cannot get attached to them," my father said. "It will break your heart, over and over. I have told you this before, but I do not think you listen to me."

"We have worked so hard to protect you from this," my mother said. "You are so precious to us. We only want to keep you from the pain that this will cause you."

I looked from one to the other of them, silent.

I had never been refused something before. But perhaps I had never asked for anything.

I began to see children everywhere. Four boys lying together on the grass in the palace gardens, throwing something between them. A little girl with her hand in her mother's, walking with great seriousness along the street that traced the outer wall of the temple complex. I watched one small boy walk brave as an eagle along the top of the city walls, six cables high.

I went back to my mother, and I asked again. But she only grew firmer.

Then I stopped speaking to her.

"Inanna, this is beneath you," my mother said. "We do this because we love you."

I only lifted my eyes to her, and then looked back down at my lap.

After this, I began to push my food away at mealtimes, and I spent long hours with my chin upon the windowsill in my mother's bedroom, looking north towards the marshes.

In the end they could not withstand me.

The moon gods met in council with their priests and chief ministers, and finally they settled upon Amnut.

She was not suitable. She was a mortal.

But she was the least unsuitable child in the city. She was after all a royal princess: her father had been king of Ur for forty years. And although her family served my family, as every family in Ur did, they were deemed fit to eat at our table, at least on feast days. I was by this time eleven; Amnut was twelve. It would have to do.

The great day finally came, and I was led into the smaller state room in my mother's temple, the one with ochre-painted walls and a smooth granite floor. They had lit the fire and set out games there on a little ebony table, and sitting at this table, with her hands flat in front of her, was a small girl with long black hair.

"They will bring in some cakes," my mother said. And then she left us.

My parents had never left me anywhere without a guard to stand over me. But now it was just me and the girl.

Amnut was wearing a crimson dress and matching cape, and white kidskin boots. She stood, and smoothed her cape. She held her chin high as she did so, and I saw how delicate her nose and mouth were, and how sulphurous yellow her eyes.

I found I could not think of one single thing to say to her.

This was nothing, though, to Amnut.

"I am collecting ants," she said. "They fight each other."

"Oh," I said.

"I collect different kinds, and then watch what they do when I put them all in a box together."

There was a pause.

"You can see them if you want," she said. "But I was not allowed to bring them. We will have to go back to my palace."

"I adore ants," I said.

But then, feeling that only complete honesty would do on such an historic day, I said: "Although I am not sure perhaps that I have ever seen an ant."

Attempts were made to keep some distance between us. But only one Inanna had conquered two moon gods, and now Amnut and I combined were too powerful for the gods and their priests and the heaving ranks of the royal family. Soon enough we girls lived a life where we were only separated at bedtime, and for official business in temple. Outside those bleak hours we were allowed to roam together as much as we saw fit.

Each morning, from daybreak, the two of us could be found outside the soaring clay-brick walls of the city, in the grasslands that led to the marshes. I had become a passionate collector of crawling things, not just ants but also beetles and spiders. We had grown also to love flowers and trees, but it was the creeping things that were our first shared love, and these we continued to insist upon entrapping, and bringing back with us into our palaces.

These excursions beyond the city walls had at first been flatly refused, then furiously refused, and then just one expedition had been allowed, as an exception.

Now we went out through the griffin gates of Ur each day as if by ancient right, and our guards, long-suffering, rambled out after us carrying with them with our collecting boxes and nets.

On the morning of my twelfth birthday, Amnut and I were out even before dawn.

My brother Utu, the god of the sun, was born in Heaven; he was centuries older than me, and had his own city in the north.

But once a year, on my birthday, he would visit us in Ur. So today there would be a state dinner, much fuss, much bathing, and formal dressing, and Amnut and I were determined to enjoy some freedom early, while we could.

As the spring sun rose full above the marshes, we abandoned our observation of a funnel-web spider, and sat down upon a rock to eat our figs and cheese. Our guards made a camp on a sandy bank nearby and doled out their barley mash.

Careful to keep our voices low, Amnut and I turned to the grave and private subject of our shared bloodline.

My eyes were black, not yellow, but that one thing aside we two girls might have been twins. We had the same long, black hair, falling like water down our backs, and the same skin, sickly olive in winter, but already in the early spring a deep brown, and we were both fine-boned, and unusually short. The idea had come to us that my father might also be Amnut's father.

It would not be so unusual if he was. It was my father's sacred duty to spread the godseed in the people, to raise them up with his Anunnaki blood. Very often he would take a bride to temple, before she went to her husband.

Oh, how wonderful if we were sisters!

"So did you ask her?" I said.

"I felt awkward asking my mother," Amnut said. "But I asked my grandmother."

"And?"

"Your father did take my mother to his temple on her wedding morning, and they did the rites, but she cannot be sure whose child I am."

I let this sink in. "I wonder how one can even tell."

I stretched out my feet, to look at them next to Amnut's. I have never been vain, but I have always liked the look of my feet.

They are little triangles, wide at the toes and narrow at the ankle, and each toe neatly formed, and very evenly placed. I saw that Amnut's feet were longer and thinner than mine, and her toes less neatly arranged. I tucked my feet back into my skirts.

I was about to say more about my father, but then the captain of my guard approached us, tugging briefly at his copper-covered cap. "They'll be looking for you now," he said, addressing himself to me. Behind him, the soldiers had finished their breakfasts and were preparing to go. "My lady," he added.

I stood up and looked out north along the great river. I felt upon the horizon a point that was heavier than all the other points, that seemed to tip in on itself, and I knew it to be my brother.

"Yes, he's coming," I said. "Time to go in, Amnut."

At midday, when the spring sun had real heat in it, and the rolling chorus of the cicadas had begun, I stood out on the dock in all my finery. On state occasions, we moon gods wore snow-white linen robes, embroidered with countless pearls, and over our smocks the bronze chest plates of Ur. On our backs we wore wings fashioned from white eagle feathers.

Oh, we were the vision of Heaven, we three, with all our priests and priestesses standing behind us, also in the white of Ur, and behind them, lining the walls of the docks, the people of the city.

A shadow amidst the reeds on the shimmering horizon, and then one barge came into focus, and then another, and another. Eight great barges in all, each with a vast sail of saffron yellow aloft, and each with a hundred rowers lining its decks. As they drew close, the oars rising and dipping in perfect unison, we saw that Utu's fleet was decked in palm fronds and lotus flowers, as for a triumph. He had been in the far north, in the war against the barbarian king.

"I wonder that he thinks it a triumph, his progress in the north," my father said. "He killed a few camp followers, and retreated, is how I heard it. Is that a triumph?"

My mother frowned at that, but said nothing.

Utu's gleaming barge of state touched to, and after its coiled ropes had been strung around the bollards along the quay, and pulled taut, two hefty slaves helped my brother clamber up onto the marble, careful he did not stumble.

The sun god wore a dress in saffron yellow, the colour of his temple. Over this he wore many gold necklaces, and on his head, a gold crown in the shape of a rising sun. After he had kissed our mother, and nodded to our father, he tipped his face to me.

"Inanna."

"Hello, brother," I said, my smile wide.

"Twelve today."

"Yes."

"I'm told you spend your days grubbing around for insects."

"Yes," I said, my smile fixing in place.

"I do wonder that they allow it," he said.

The big banquet table, carved from one enormous slice of a cedar tree, was carried out onto the terrace, and we four gods ate our dinner in a pool of candlelight, with a half-moon overhead. I was made to wear my leopard-skin cloak over my dinner dress, in case the spring evening grew too cold.

We were served lamb, roasted whole and carried into the light on a huge platter, and also buttered samphire, and little fish, fried and then tossed in salt. Afterwards, the first of the apricots, grown in the palace gardens.

In the first days, Utu lived with my parents in Ur. He helped them build the city, and dig out the canals. For a hundred years, its business had been his business. Yet now he seemed to have no interest at all in it. He spoke at length about his city, Sippur, and about the war, but had no questions for my parents.

I was seated upon his right at dinner, and to me he said: "Is the *mee* working yet?"

"No, brother." My right hand moved to cover it.

"Why would An give you something that didn't work?"

"I do not know, brother."

After that he had no more questions for me, and I retreated into my own thoughts, very grim.

It was a constant source of worry and embarrassment to me, that my *mee*, the great weapon of my godhead, only sat upon my wrist, drinking in the light, good for nothing else. It was said that my father could strike down men dead with his *mee*. I knew that my mother could settle great disputes with hers, that people walked many leagues for her to end vendettas that had lasted generations.

Yet my *mee* did nothing. My mother's priestesses had scratched at it, and pulled at it, hurting my wrist, but it could not be made to come alive. What sort of a goddess would I be, with no *mee* to give me power?

And then: a name.

Gilgamesh.

The name pulled me back into the flow of talk around the table.

I had never met my cousin Gilgamesh, but I loved to hear stories of him. As did everyone; he was famous up and down the land. Was there a table in Sumer where he would not be spoken of this night?

"Any news we get of him comes in scraps, from ordinary men," my brother said.

"Gilgamesh?" I said. "Is he safe?"

"Undoubtedly not," Utu said.

"Why do you sound so disapproving of him, brother," I said, "when he bears arms against our enemy?"

My parents and Utu cast glances at each other but did not answer me.

"Time and time again, he breaks his father's heart," Utu said.

"It's hard for Gilgamesh," my mother said, taking an apricot.

"Why?" I said. "Why?"

"Because his parents are gods, and he is not."

I looked at her, at how bright and young she was, with the sacred *melam* glittering through her veins. I tried to imagine how it would feel if I myself was soon to wither, while my mother went on, strong, glowing, constantly renewed by the magical blood of the Anunnaki.

"Everybody makes excuses for Gilgamesh," Utu said. "But I for one have run out of patience with him."

I had a moment alone with my brother as he was helped back onto his litter. "My brother," I said. "I wish you were here more often. That we might know each other better."

Utu's men at that moment heaved him up to shoulder height, so I found myself looking up at his round face, framed by turquoise sky.

He frowned down at me. "They coddle you."

"What do you mean, brother?"

He shook his head. "They do you no favours by it. This is a hard world to be a young girl in, and they ought to be better preparing you for it."

After only the briefest pause, I said: "But I am not a girl, brother. I am a priestess of Heaven."

Utu raised one finely arched eyebrow. "Do you think that will make a difference, Inanna?"

Despite myself, I found myself swallowing. "I suppose I do think it will make a difference."

"Did it make a difference for our sister?" he said. "You should think about that, Inanna, as you collect your insects and act out your games in this world of fantasy that our parents have built for you. You should think about Ereshkigal."

As my brother's barges pulled out in the late morning, I did think about my sister, Ereshkigal. She was only a child when the Anunnaki descended, and she grew up in Ur. But she had been taken away many years before I was born, never to return.

The priests said she was queen of the underworld now. They said she had a palace in the Dark City. They said it was her decision not to come home. But who would choose to give up this world of brightness, for the screams and unending dark?

"Inanna?"

I blinked up at my mother.

"Do you want to see Amnut this afternoon?"

"Yes," I said. "Thank you, Mother."

And then we made our way back inside the great clay walls of Ur, that had withstood barbarian armies, and even the Great Flood, and I thought then could withstand anything.

CHAPTER FIVE

GILGAMESH

My weeks as a hostage in the court of King Akka were in many ways delightful.

Kish was an elegant city, cradled by low green hills and overlooking a turquoise lake, and its people were hospitable and slow to take offence. King Akka was at home for the first week of my captivity, and although I was too injured to ride out with him, he would talk over his day's hunting with me every evening. He took obvious joy in the talking over of even the smallest points of the hunt, and I took almost equal joy in listening to them. Sometimes we would also speak, most peaceably, of the war.

"Gilgamesh, I am not a warlike man," he said over dinner. "I would gladly only hunt, and worry for my people, and play with my son. But every year the Anunnaki creep closer to Kish, taking land that is ours. Pushing me and my people north. We honour them in our temples, and we seek only to keep the land that is ours. But that is not enough for them. They have forced me to make a stand. They have forced this war. And for what? So that young men like you can die upon the river plains and have your names read out in temple."

"The Anunnaki say that all the land between the two great rivers has always been theirs," I said. "And that it was your grandfather who stole this land from them, when he came here to build Kish."

"There are always excuses," Akka said. "But the Anunnaki will not be happy until they have taken Kish and all that it has. The very idea of Akkadia is a threat to them, that is the truth of it. A land without Anunnaki, where the cattle are fat, and the barley is golden, and the sky does not fall in without a living god in every temple. That is why they nibble away at our lands, and force me into battle. But they forget that there are more of us than there are of you. And my men do not rely on gods with toys on their arms to help them win."

"The toys you speak of can kill," I said, but was careful to keep my voice pleasant.

He sat back, smiling. "How old are you, Gilgamesh?"

"Eighteen."

"A young man still."

"I do not reckon it so young, when most men I know are dead by thirty."

"Trust an old man," he said. "You are a young man still."

The threats of violence, should my father not reply quickly enough to news of my capture, were never repeated. I found myself feeling very much a guest, with no thought of harming these enemies I found myself living amongst. I could possibly have run; they watched me less closely than they ought to have. Yet I was in no hurry to be running.

Indeed, any thoughts I had of hurrying, at that time, lay solely in regard to my growing friendship with Hedda, the king's sister.

Hedda had partially succumbed to my charms. There had been kisses, quickly snatched. On one memorable occasion I had had my fingers inside her, before her mother sat back down between us. But that was as far as it had gone.

My problems were twofold. First, Hedda was constantly surrounded with female relatives. She travelled everywhere with a swirl of them about her.

Second, Akka had appointed his beloved nephew, Inush, as my assigned guard.

Inush was a young man, thin and slightly built, with dark feathers of hair lying soft about his face. He had a prominent, well-cut nose, and high cheekbones. No doubt, on a battlefield, he would have made a deadly adversary, but as the keeper of a hostage, and chaperone to female relatives, he was at best indifferent. He seemed oblivious to my growing closeness to Hedda, and, indeed, to all of the day-to-day dramas of the court.

"I just can't stand it here," he said to me, plucking at his high collar. "It bores me rigid. I know I ought to pretend better, but I can't."

Inush was, however, largely *present* in every room that I stepped into, and that did present a significant obstacle to my plans.

When Akka left Kish to return to the front, I thought my chances of success would increase, but it was not to be. If anything, Inush, sad to be left behind, paid me more attention than he had before.

It came to me that perhaps some sort of excursion, outside the crowded palace, might offer me better opportunities.

Akka had been gone almost three weeks when a suitable scheme presented itself. The ladies of the court woke up to the most perfect summer day, and after a long breakfast of discussions, and some nostalgic talk from me about swimming in the ponds of Uruk, it was decided that a swim in the lake, and a picnic there, were in order.

By the time the heat of the day had begun in earnest, our large and straggling group was already in motion. The party consisted of me; my guard, Inush; my quarry, Hedda; eight other royal ladies of the palace, aged between six and twenty; and finally one bright four-year-old boy, the king's only son, Enmebaragesi.

I made sure that Hedda and I were the last of the group to get underway.

As I helped her up onto her donkey outside the royal stables, my hands skimmed over the linen that covered her buttocks, and then I stood there with both hands on her left thigh as she giggled at me by way of a telling-off.

"There is no harm in hands," I said, since all the others were already out of earshot. "No harm in hands or mouths. These things will not get us into trouble. There are other things that will get us in trouble, but you have nothing to fear from me there. I will always treat you with honour and respect." As I said this, I leaned over and put my teeth very gently on her inner thigh.

Hedda blushed deep scarlet as she squeezed her donkey to start walking. "Gilgamesh!" she said.

I mounted and pushed my mule on, winking back at Hedda as I passed her, to ride next to Inush at the front of the group. We were following the sandy, palm-lined avenue that led down to the lake.

"What an absolute chore," Inush said to me. "How can you bear them all?"

"I find them charming," I said. "They are wholesome young women. And I do not think I have ever met a finer young boy."

"I just want to be back at the front," he said. "I have nothing personally against you, Gilgamesh. If I must guard a hostage, better it be you. But what a chore."

"I am sorry for it," I said. "Although glad that my comrades are safe from you."

He laughed. "I wonder if we will ever meet in battle, Gilgamesh. And how it would be if we did."

"I hope we never do," I said, earnest for a moment.

The beach, backed by willows, was a narrow strip of white with rocks at either end. The water was achingly clear.

"Is that a crocodile?" I said as our party stood along the edge of the water to look out. All of the women and girls screamed and scurried backwards.

"I was joking," I said, and they all laughed.

Good humoured as it was, there was no further opportunity to get close to Hedda, and perhaps push a little more firmly at the limits of what might count as honour and respect.

Inush shook out a rug for us men, and sat down upon it with his back against a rock. The women meanwhile made camp at the far end of the beach, taking turns to go behind the rocks to change into their swimming robes.

"Will you not swim, Inush?" I said.

"My uncle wouldn't like it," he said. "To hear we'd swum with all the women. Even if we were forty leagues in distance from them, he wouldn't like us being in the lake with them. He's as old-fashioned as they come."

"Is he?" I said, trying to sound casual.

"Yes indeed," Inush said. "Be warned about that, Gilgamesh. He would kill a man for looking at those girls. Not that I think you ever would."

"No, of course not."

"But I have heard you had a bit of a reputation when you were younger."

I sat down beside him, and took the cup of water he was offering up to me. "I did act the fool when I was younger," I said. "My father was in despair at times, with everything I got up to."

"I heard you ran away when you were fourteen," Inush said, closing his eyes.

I took the opportunity to look over at Hedda as she picked her way into the lake water in her swimming robes.

"I suppose it must have been strange for you," Inush went on, "to be the child of gods, but human yourself."

"Yes, it was odd," I said. "It is odd still."

I would have said nothing more but there was something about Inush that made me want to explain myself. "As soon as my father realised that I was mortal, that I would live no longer than any other man, he went into mourning. He mourned me every moment of my childhood, even as he heaped love on me. His grief was bottomless. Everything I did was for him for the last time, and imbued with deep tragedy."

"What a bore," Inush said, opening his eyes, and raising one dark eyebrow at me.

"Yes."

"And your mother?" he said. "Did she not mourn you?"

"My mother's not the mourning type," I said.

"I see now why you ran away," Inush said. "I'd have done the same thing. Just to get some air."

"That's kind of you to say."

He gave me his slow and lopsided smile.

"It's a shame we're enemies," he said.

∽

I went to sleep that night thinking about Hedda, and how she'd looked as she came out of the lake, with her wet robe clinging to her. In my dreams I became confused. I was in bed with Hedda, but my parents were standing over me, in the black robes of An's temple, and my father was saying: "Gilgamesh, how can you live with yourself?" He leaned over and grabbed my arm, pulling me out of bed, and only then did I wake up and realise that my small room was full of men.

Armed men, some with lanterns, all with their swords unsheathed. Inush entered behind them, holding up an oil lamp, his face pale and drawn. "You were seen, Gilgamesh," he said. "By a stable boy. With your hands upon Hedda."

He came close to my bed, holding the lamp high. "Akka is going to kill you, but he will start by cutting small pieces off you, and forcing you to eat each piece as he goes."

I was going to say something to him, I am not sure what, but then I was hit hard in the head, and knocked into blank darkness.

CHAPTER SIX

NINSHUBAR

I will spare you the long story of what I did to my mother, and what she did to me, because all of that has been washed away now, by distance and by time. But I should tell you about the Potta, the first forever-love of my life.

The Potta was brought into our wet season camp when I was about ten. This camp was a stunning place: a tall rock shelter with views out onto thick forest. When the hot rain fell hard all day long, what joy it was to have a place to return to that was truly dry. The shelter turned into dark caves further in, and those were the places where we did our sacred dances and kept the secret objects. Everyone loved the wet season camp.

One day a whole tribe came up along the old path from the south. They were carrying their sacred objects with them, as a people do when they have no home to go back to.

These people were from the edge of our world. They had been pushed out of their land and had already walked for a season. They did not know how much longer they would need to walk.

My father and our shaman were away on men's business, but my mother went out alone into the rain to greet the strangers. "You are welcome here," she said to them. And then she said the names of the old gods, so that they would know they were safe with us.

These strangers came in to the dry, making the caves a lot smaller, and I helped light extra fires for them.

That was when I noticed the beast creature. He was like a boy in shape, but with skin the colour of a maggot and hair the colour of ochre. We children all gathered around him, some of my sisters poking him with sticks. He was holding his bony fists up to them, but my sisters were much bigger than him, and they had him surrounded.

I said to my sisters: "You leave him alone, you evil witches, or I will beat you." Which they did because they were scared of me. And then the creature and I looked at each other. His eyes were the blue of the deep ocean.

The shaman who walked with the strangers said the boy was a Potta, a different kind of human, they could not say where from. They had found him injured and abandoned, and had kept him as a pet, but they regretted keeping him, when one extra mouth could bring them down.

"What is his spirit clan?" I said.

"He does not have one," the shaman said. "He lives outside our law."

My mother said: "When we've eaten, we should call up the gods tonight. I believe this creature's blood will bring them."

The shaman nodded, and all the other elders nodded too, friend and stranger alike, although I thought the strangers looked sorry.

I planted myself between the beast boy and my mother.

"No," I said, my chin down. "You leave the creature alone."

My mother turned, looked down at me, assessed.

"Ninshubar. This is not for you to decide on. This is adult business."

I saw that she expected that to be the end of it. But my plan had already come to me, springing whole into my mind. I had made my calculations and I knew, even so young, that when you are going to do something, it is better to do it quick.

"Then I am adopting him," I said.

Everyone fell quiet, stranger and neighbour alike.

I turned to the Potta boy: "I am adopting you." I wanted it to be done properly.

In my country, anyone can adopt an outsider, and from the moment someone is adopted, they are kin and they live in the law. It is a vastly sacred thing, and it is irrevocable. As I said the words, the little Potta boy joined my spirit clan. It did not matter that we were the same age, or that he might not understand me: he was my spirit son now. In less than a breath he had become a child of the red moon and the cheetah, a creature of war. Now his roots stretched back with mine to the very beginning of the world.

My mother came over to me, as angry as I had ever seen her. "Ninshubar, you are a girl. The law is not meant to be used by you. You are meant to live in the law and abide by it." But her voice faltered as she spoke; she was not as sure in what she was saying as she might have been. She could see the faces of those around her, and she could see what they were thinking. "He's not human," she said then. "You cannot adopt an animal."

The shaman took a step towards her; he looked uneasy. My mother looked at him, and then all about her. There were more of them than there were of us, and anyone could see what they were thinking: that the law is the law. It cannot be undone with talking and excuses.

That first night the Potta would not stop crying. "Shut him up," my mother hissed over at us. "No one can sleep with his whining."

I put my hand out onto the Potta in the dark of the cave, and in the end, his chest still heaving, he slept.

The next day, when the strangers had gone, I looked at him all over. He had scars everywhere, and every kind of worm and burrowing creature in him. Everything that could be done to a child, that is bad, I think had happened to him. But he stood bravely to be examined, his chin held high, his mouth flat.

"Let me just pick off the lice and the fleas," I said. "And the things that I can scrape out with my knife. But the other things we will have to wait for the shaman to look at."

"He will not survive," my mother said. "He is full up to his eyes with bad luck."

"We will see," I said.

I gave him the best of my food, and never left him alone. I slept with both hands on his back, to make sure that he kept on breathing. And when we went down to the coast after the rains, the Potta walked with us. I gave him his own flint knife, to wear around his neck. I taught him to find shellfish, and how to tip them back into your mouth when you eat them. I was a wonderful mother to the Potta, and he grew into a wonderful son.

So that is how I came to have a beast-creature son about the same age as me. I kept on calling him the Potta, but his proper name, until he became a man, would be Ninshubar-son. This he could not pronounce properly, and he called himself Shub-son, and me Shuba.

It became clear to me that my mother would never forgive me, but I grew to love the Potta so dearly that to me it seemed a reasonable trade.

CHAPTER SEVEN

INANNA

When I was very young, my friend Amnut's father was the king of Ur and already an old man. And when I was twelve years old, he was still king, and still old. He was to me as unchanging as the soaring walls around our city.

How many times did my parents warn me? But there is the being told, and there is the knowing.

On the day that it happened I was sitting before a heaped-up fire with Amnut, playing the game of twenty squares. I was saying to her: "What a terrible loser you are, Amnut, how completely foul!"

"Inanna, you are a horrible cheat and always have been," she said.

I laughed at this, angry as it made me, but then I saw my mother coming at us, her priestesses behind. We both got up from our chairs, our faces plain.

My mother was wearing her temple dress.

"Amnut, you are needed in the palace," she said. "You stay here with me, Inanna."

My mother and I watched from the roof of the moon temple as the people poured out into the streets. They had never known another king. No one in the city had, except my parents. Now they rang bells and beat drums, and the roar of it rose up past us into the darkening sky.

A rare autumn storm was coming at us across the marshes, and my mother let me into her bearskin.

"I should be with Amnut," I said.

"This is a private time for them," she said. "We must let them mourn."

The first of the rain began to fall on us.

All the everyday business of Ur was set aside. Every man, woman and child was now caught up in the great endeavour: to dig out the grave pit for the dead king, even with the hard ground turning to mud beneath the pickaxes.

My father made himself captain of the preparations, concerned with every aspect of the pit. He worked from beneath a leather canopy in the royal graveyard and I was allowed to sit on a camp chair beside him, on condition that I wore my otter-skin cloak, and I kept my feet tucked up beneath me, to keep them from the filth and the splashing of the rain.

Occasionally my father would remember that I was there. "You have seen one of these before. A royal burial."

"No, Father."

"They're different from a normal funeral. Make sure your mother talks to you about it."

The chiefs of my father's household were assembled before

us, hunched over in their dripping cloaks. My father turned to this damp assembly and raised his voice. "I said I wanted it square, and three cords deep, and I wanted the ramp coming down from the east and running due west. I was very clear. And yet what I see you digging is a rectangle, and with a ramp coming in from the northeast."

The chief priest stepped forwards, pulling his wet hood back from his face. "My lord, we are worried about older tombs."

"I am not worried," my father said. "This is not about old tombs; it is about this tomb."

The chief priest shifted his muddy feet, his hands clasped together before him in the rain. "We are bringing up a lot of bone."

"Then put it somewhere safe and we will rebury it later. This graveyard is four hundred years old. You cannot put a pickaxe in the earth here without hitting bone. This mud is made of ground-up bone. Now give me my perfect square."

I wondered how many royal burials my father had presided over, since first he came to Ur.

Young farmers came in from the villages to do the hard digging and I watched the rain run down their bare backs as they worked. City men filled up buckets with the damp and claggy earth, carrying it up the ramp to the spoil heaps that lined the graveyard. Women and children threaded their way through the diggers, scooping up water to stop the pit becoming a lake.

"I could help," I said to my father.

"Don't be so foolish," he said.

∞

My mother and I went to the royal palace, each carrying a tray of honey cakes. The women and the girls of the household were gathered in the main hall, a long, elegant room decorated with mountain hunting scenes: an archer letting fly at a gazelle, a mountain lion about to leap upon some wild goats, a young boy skinning a hare. Near the fire, a table stood heavy with cakes and dried fruit.

Amnut was sitting between two of her aunts on a low couch along one wall. She was wearing the red of mourning, a new dress, and she had dark grey circles beneath her eyes. The crowd opened up to let me and my mother through, and when I had offered my commiserations to the queen and the other wives, I went over to Amnut and kneeled down in front of her.

I kissed her hands. "I am so sorry, Amnut. He was such a wonderful man."

She leaned forwards and kissed me on each cheek. She smelled of the lavender oil her mother sprinkled on all their clothes.

"I love you, Inanna," she said.

"I love you too, dearest friend. I have been desperate to see you, but they all said I should leave you alone."

"I've been desperate to see you too."

She was about to say something more. But then my mother's hand was on my shoulder.

"I will see you soon, Amnut," I said.

We pressed our cheeks together, warm and smooth.

When the digging was done, we went out into the drizzle to look down into the pit. My father gave out instructions for the tombstones to be brought out of storage.

"You know I will miss him," he said to me. "One doesn't often get so close to one's kings."

"Because he lived so long?"

"Yes, I suppose," my father said. "But also because of the man he was. He would have loved to see this day – the hard work, the planning."

The next morning it was still raining, but the king's tomb now stood. It had been fashioned in the shape of a temple, and amidst the sea of trampled mud at the bottom of the pit, it looked like a playhouse built for a child.

Something small and sharp began to jab at my heart.

"We will make it festive now," my father said. "I want all of it covered in reed matting. And I want everything clean: no mud."

"Tomorrow, then, for the ceremony?" the chief priest said. "I believe everything else is ready."

"Tomorrow," my father said. "Send out word."

I said: "Father, why is the pit so big, for this tiny tomb?"

He looked at me; I could not read his face. "It needs to be big for the household, Inanna. You know how royal burials are. Do you not remember how it was for the old queen?"

"I was told about it."

"It is a great honour for those who are chosen. Make sure you speak to your mother about it."

In the morning I got dressed for the ceremony in my mother's rooms, in front of the slatted window that looked out onto the Euphrates. At night they would cover the window with a wall hanging to keep out moths and mosquitoes, but now with the hanging taken down I could put my nose to the wooden slats and watch the bands of rain sweep dark and mottled across the surface of the great river.

The feeling of dread inside me had grown so large that I could barely breathe.

My mother helped dress me in the undyed linen we Anunnaki wear for mourning.

Then she sat down upon the bed, her hands tight upon her knees.

"Inanna, you do know that Amnut is going with her father today?"

I sat down on the bed next to her. Without warning, I could hardly see for tears.

"Mother, you must stop it."

She took both of my hands in hers. "Her father asked for her especially."

"Amnut did not say."

My mother wiped the tears from my cheeks, but more kept coming, rolling down one upon the other. "This is the honour of her life," she said. "You must do your duty today."

"There must be something you can do, Mother."

"My precious love, I should not have let you get so close to her," she said. "I knew I should not have allowed it."

"But, Mother, please stop it."

"Inanna, she has chosen. They have all chosen. Do not make this harder for them."

I stood up, taking my hands from her. "Mother, you must do something."

"Inanna," she said, "I have already tried."

I made my way, in the pouring rain, out of our precinct and along the royal way. With my dress soaking wet against my skin, I stood outside the door to the royal palace and knocked upon it with my fists. The captain of my guard stood anxiously behind me.

The king's chief of staff came to the door, dressed for mourning, and looked at me.

"I am here to see Amnut," I said.

"She does not want to see you, my lady."

"I do not believe it."

"I am so sorry, Lady Inanna," he said. "But it is true. She told me to tell you that she will not see you because she knows that you will not understand. But she loves you."

A thousand times since, more, I have gone over it, and wondered, *Could I have done more?* But the truth is that I did not.

We mourners gathered along the top edges of the pit as the sharp rain turned to hail.

The new king, the eldest son of the old, stood between my father and mother, and he seemed to me to be full of good cheer behind the blank face he gave us for the ceremony.

All around us stood our household, the priests of the moon temple and our guards. Beyond, on every memorial stone, on walls, on scraps of mud or grass, stood the people of Ur, wrapped up against the cold and wet. Near the gates a group of marsh men, so tall, and wreathed in black, stood apart from the rest.

A great beating of the drums, and the dead king's priests gathered at the top of the ramp. They wore red felt robes and close-fitting caps, and between them, slowly, they carried a large bronze cauldron down to the centre of the pit. This they set to hang there, beneath a heavy tripod.

My mother leaned down to me and said: "Strength, Inanna."

I watched the dead king carried down through blurred eyes, my mouth clamped shut so that no noise could escape me.

When the body had been laid down inside the tomb, I heard my father say to my mother: "Put her in her room, if she is going to make a fuss."

"No," I said. "If it is going to happen, I will see it happen."

Through what was now sleet came the king's senior wife, the queen, and his youngest wife, Amnut's mother, wearing glorious sprays of gold-wrought flowers around their heads. Their robes, a brilliant red, trailed behind them through the mud.

A priest stood waiting for them down in the pit, the cauldron before him. He handed each a small cup, and these they each dipped into the cauldron.

I felt my mother reaching for my hand, but I did not give it to her. Instead, I stood with both my hands pressed together before me, pointing together towards the grave.

The queens carried their cups inside the tomb, being careful not to spill what was in them. Very quickly the soldiers came to seal the tomb shut with bitumen and a piece of marble. As they did this, the drumming swelled up at us from the pit, above the hubbub of the household gathering and the keening of the crowds.

They brought the animals next: four oxen, four donkeys, four goats, four sheep. These were killed quickly, although the drums could not drown out their screaming. A slow, scarlet tide ebbed out across the reed matting.

Next the pit began to fill with the householders. Each came to take a cup of the liquid from the bronze cauldron, and then went to their prescribed place and sat down carefully, not drinking yet. They were all women and girls, except the eight soldiers chosen for the honour.

The pit was filling up, but I could not see Amnut.

I was going to ask my mother if there had been a change of plan, but then I saw the princess making her way to the top of the ramp, with her sisters and aunts behind her. As I moved to go to her, my mother grasped at me, but I wriggled away. As I did I saw Amnut moving to me, and moments later we stood face to face, oblivious to the crowds around us.

She was wet, her hair and red dress clinging to her; she had been crying.

"I haven't done my hair yet." She held out her metal hair ribbon to me – a curled-up strip of silver, beaten thin.

"It doesn't matter," I said. "You look beautiful as you are."

"I suppose it doesn't matter." She put the silver ribbon back into her pocket.

We kissed, one cheek then the other, our faces wet and cold.

"I did not expect you to be going." I had not meant to say more than that, but then I found I could not help it: "Amnut, do you have to go?"

We looked at each other in the rain. Her eyes were so lustrous, so very full of life.

"I had hoped to have longer here," she said. "But I promised my father, from the time I could talk. So let us try to part with smiles, Inanna. Do not make me cross with you."

"Amnut, please," I said, pressing her hands between my own.

"I have loved our time together, Inanna."

That was all.

I went back to my parents, and I looked up at my mother. "Is this right?" I said. She showed no sign that she heard me.

Below us, Amnut took her cup, and then went to take her place amongst the household.

And then it was time. I watched a harpist as she sipped from her cup, and laid herself down as if to sleep, clutching her harp to her chest. I could not see Amnut's face, only the back of her head, and one shoulder, as she settled herself.

As the mourners began to throw down earth onto the sleepers, my mother finally looked at me, and bent close. "You know, Inanna, the people here did this before we came. They have always done this for their kings. Since before there were cities here. These stories came from the old gods."

"But do you think it's right? Is it right?"

She straightened up, her face closed to me.

I said: "I do not think this is right."

In the pit below, my friend's body disappeared beneath the earth. First handfuls, then buckets of it. It would take hours, but when the first layer was down, there would be a feast over the bodies before the next layer of earth went down.

I was so sorry now that I had not helped Amnut with her ribbon.

That she had had to die with it still in her pocket.

CHAPTER EIGHT

GILGAMESH

My final days in Kish were not as pleasant as my first days in the city.

I spent them in a dark, half-flooded prison cell, with no bed or chair to sit on. I was obliged to prop myself up in one corner, to try to keep out of the muddy water that pooled upon the floor. I tried to think of some trick that would save me. But the days passed, and no ideas came to me. My head hurt, almost constantly, and indeed I found it hard to think clearly.

The door was heavy, and locked from the outside. There was one window, but it was small and with metal bars across, and it was too high up to get my hands to.

Once, Inush came in to look at me. He said: "If you are wondering why you are alive, it is because Akka is not yet back, and he will certainly want to kill you himself."

He looked even thinner than he had before, and even more angry.

"I wonder if he will blame you for this," I said. "You were meant to be guarding me."

Inush gave a grim sort of smile. "No man of Kish would treat a princess like some slave girl. The king will not blame me for how low you have sunk."

That night, no one came in with my food, or to fill up my waterskin, and I went to sleep, jammed upright in my corner, with despair welling up in me.

The next thing I knew it was hard dark, and someone was hissing my name.

"Gilgamesh."

It was Harga.

"Harga?"

"Quiet," he hissed.

I stood up, my hands on the damp clay walls, but could see nothing at all beyond the faint light around the edge of the doorway.

"Where are you?" I whispered.

"I'm at the window, you fool."

I spun around and looked up.

I could see a small square of stars, now and again obscured by the black and twisting outline of Harga's wild curls.

"It's too high," I whispered.

"Just put your hands up, and I will pull you."

There was then a short and ugly scene, as with much scrabbling and the loss of a great deal of skin, Harga pulled me up out of the window, and then without any ceremony, let me fall a full cable to the ground.

Lying on my back on the grass, winded, I watched Harga climb down from the roof of the prison. Even by starlight, I could tell that he was scowling at me.

"Who would have thought it, my lord, that you would get into some kind of trouble here," he said.

That I ignored.

"How are you here, Harga?" I said, clambering to my feet.

"Let us remove ourselves from this city," he said, "and then we can take time to swap our stories."

I followed Harga through the dark streets. He had a way of moving with such confidence that no one would ever think him out of place.

At the edge of the city, he led us off the pathway and up small steps cut into the city wall. To our right I could see a guard's fire burning, perhaps six cords away.

"We'll have to jump down," Harga whispered. "Try not to break anything." A moment later he was gone off the side. I heard him land and move off, and jumped after him, landing hard and painfully on my bare heels. Then the two of us were running through low forest, barely able to see before us but for the dim light from the stars.

When we had been going perhaps half an hour, and my bare feet were much cut about from twigs and thorns on the forest floor, I said: "Harga, I am battered. Let me sit down, just for a few moments."

He stood over me, dark against the sky, as I sat down on the leafy floor of the forest and leaned back in great relief against a tree. All my ribs seemed to be cracked, and perhaps the right side of my jaw, and I was finding it hard to separate out the different parts of the pain.

"I am going to tell you something funny now," Harga said. "Although it is not making me laugh."

"Tell me, then."

"I could not find your father in Uruk but then I followed the path of the Sumerian army north and I found him at peace talks with Akka."

"Is that so?" I said.

"Yes, I came upon the two of them clapping each other on the back and talking about their wonderful Gilgamesh. And Akka talking about how fond he was of you, and how glad he was that now there was peace, but he would be sad to say goodbye to you, having no grown sons of his own and having come to love you in only a matter of days."

"Interesting," I said.

"So, then I thought I would leave that scene undisturbed and come north to check on you. I could have just ridden in here, demanding to see you. But call me what you will, there was a part of me that wondered, *Has Gilgamesh made a mess of it already?* And I decided to come into the city quietly, just to get the lay of it before declaring myself."

"Ah."

"Ah indeed," he said.

"I myself blame Akka," I said. "What was he doing, leaving a wolf tucked up with his sheep?"

"I suppose he thought you a prince," Harga said. "And he thought that meant something."

"He knows better now," I said.

Harga pulled me to my feet again. "The peace will not hold, after what you have done. So, I suggest we keep moving before someone discovers our mules."

We rode south from Kish to what was then our home, in Shuruppak, in a somewhat roundabout manner. A journey that might have taken a week, we stretched out into two weeks. It would be wrong to say that we crept home, but we were certainly careful to avoid our own forces, as well as Akka's men, as we made our way across the river plains.

As we rode at last into the town square at Shuruppak, the old steward came out to greet us in a state of half-dress.

"My lord Gilgamesh! We did not expect you. We were told you were a hostage, in the court of Akka."

"No more, I am glad to say," I said. "Akka has settled with my father and the sky gods, and allowed me to ride free." I was unpleasantly aware of how dirty, and blood-stained, my clothing was.

The steward looked confused. "Is the war over then, my lord?"

"For now," I said.

As I turned to ride off, the steward said: "But they kept your armour, Lord Gilgamesh?"

I turned back to him. "They are barbarians," I said. "What can one expect?"

We made for the house, Harga riding alongside me. Behind us, someone began ringing the temple bell in celebration.

"I wonder how long that story will hold," Harga said.

"Long enough for us to open some wine."

When I had drunk away a few days, all gone and entirely lost, I called Harga through to my bedchamber.

"I feel a dangerous urge to know how much trouble I am in," I said. "Although I know I will regret the knowing of it."

Harga leaned against the door frame, looking down on me in my sheets in that supercilious way he had. He was clean and freshly shaven. No self-respecting Sumerian man would shave his face, but Harga kept to his own backcountry ways.

"I could send word north that you are here and safe," he said. "See what comes back."

"Very well," I said. "Do it."

"Who should I send the message to?"

This I thought over. I had not sent word to my mother and father since I'd left home at the age of fourteen, and found my way north to my uncle Enlil. Now, though, I had the image of my father embracing Akka, and talking fondly of me to him. Perhaps it was finally the time to send a message to my parents. But then in military terms my duty was to my uncle Enlil, the lord of the sky, and the leader of the Sumerian forces in the war against Akka.

"Send two messages," I said. "One to my father, telling him I am well. And one to my lord god Enlil, asking for fresh orders, and telling him where I am."

"All right." He was fiddling with the pebbles he kept in a pouch upon his belt.

"What is it?" I said.

"Nothing, my lord."

"Harga, speak."

"Akka may come after you if it becomes known where you are. He may come for you."

"Let him come," I said. "And we will deal with him when he does."

I put my throbbing head back under my pillow.

That evening I went out drinking in the town square. I was sitting there in the street with my chair tipped back and some good date wine in one hand, and suddenly there was Harga again, looming over me. He had two raggedy strangers with him.

"My lord Gilgamesh." He looked about rather rudely at my drinking companions.

"Did you send the messages?"

"Yes, my lord, but I am here about a local matter."

"Harga, speak!"

He paused, as if considering my response from every angle, and then said: "My lord Gilgamesh, some shepherds have come into town to tell us that there is a wild boy living up in the oak woods. They say he is hairy like an animal, and he is feeding on their sheep."

Harga waved one thumb at the two men behind him. The men wore the felt cloaks that shepherds favour, and each carried a long crook. Two ancient sheep hounds were frozen in crouched positions at their feet. "These are the shepherds," Harga said.

I raised one eyebrow and took a drink of wine.

"They want us to go and kill the hairy boy. They say he may be a demon. They think he may put a curse on their flock." Harga used the local word for "curse" since nothing similar existed in Sumerian.

The shepherds nodded at this dreadful word.

I had been looking forward to more wine, a game, maybe a visit to Shamhat in the temple. But when people asked me what I liked to hunt, I did like to say: "Everything." And more pertinently, I did feel rather in debt to Harga, after everything that had happened in Kish.

"Very well," I said, draining my cup in one. "Fetch up the dogs."

∞

We walked west out of Shuruppak towards the setting sun. Time out of mind, Shuruppak was a rich town, sitting full upon the river. This was where the ancient kings came to have their ships built. It was here that Uta-napishti, ever-hero of the Great Flood, put a thousand people and all their animals onto his arks, and took them away to safety.

When the floodwaters went down, though, the river never came back, and now only desert scrub grew in the dusty fields of Shuruppak, where once had stood grain.

I took the left flank on the way out, with two of Harga's boys following on behind, and my otter hounds out in front. The two shepherds followed behind Harga, and kept on shouting ahead to him in the nasty old patois that they spoke.

"My lord Gilgamesh, they say he is armed," Harga called over to me. "They say he has axes."

I pulled up short. "Harga, I only have my fig knife." I held it out to him. "You said nothing before about axes."

"The dogs will get him." He kept on walking, fiddling with his slingshot.

It was a gorgeous evening. Just growing cool, but only so cool that you could still delight in feeling warm in it. The evening lit up the bushes in orange, and the air was sweet with the scent of wild thyme trampled underfoot.

At the bottom of the hill, I saw footprints: bare footprints that disappeared where the earth turned to rock.

I signalled to Harga and the shepherds: a short whistle. They came over, quiet, and nodded at the footprints. We spread out again, in silence.

Only a few minutes of steady climbing and the dogs started up somewhere ahead of us, making the horrible noise they made when they had cornered something. I broke into a run, picking my way quickly up the rugged slope. The boys tried to keep up; Harga and the shepherds seemed happy to fall behind.

The dogs had found the boy lying in a narrow gully, about a cable down from where I stood. The six dogs were crouched at the edge of the ravine, growling down at him, their manes raised along their backs.

Down in the gully, in a mess of rags and sheep hides, was the wild boy.

"Haroop!" I said.

The dogs backed off most reluctantly to let me through.

I dropped down carefully onto a rocky ledge just above the boy.

What a sight he was. He had skin the colour of long-polished oak, and long silky hair, mottled brown and cream like a wolf's, with a wild beard to match.

His eyes were shut and for a moment I wondered if he was only sleeping, but then the smell hit me: flesh rot. The boy was sick, maybe dying.

"Careful, sir," Harga said, from above. "He could be faking."

"He's injured," I said, but as I climbed down off my rock, I was careful to kick the boy's stone axes well out of his reach. He looked young, but he was man-sized, and even unconscious, he looked strong enough to kill any of us. The smell close up was dreadful: not just the rotting smell of his flesh, but who knows what else. There was something badly wrong with the boy's right leg. He had bound it with what looked like some sort of poultice, but it was a foul mess.

"We should take him to the temple," I said.

"Are you sure?" Harga said. "Might be kinder to finish it." The rest of the hunting party had joined him now, all peering down into the gully.

"He has the look of a marsh man," Harga said. "Although that's a shepherd's coat."

That was when the wild boy opened his eyes.

His eyes were the colour of the sea over white sand.

The wheel of my life: I felt it turn.

"We will take him to the temple," I said.

We took him to Shamhat, the chief priestess at the city temple. The boy weighed far more than any of us had guessed, and we had to take turns carrying him, two men at a time. We all itched with fleas the whole way back across the brushland.

It was full dark by the time we reached the gate to the temple. I banged on the oak and shouted: "Shamhat!"

"I'm done now, Gilgamesh," she called from inside the compound. "Leave me alone."

"It's not that. We have a sick boy for you."

The gate bar lifted, and Shamhat came out into the street, severe in her temple black, a torch held high in one hand. "Who is this?" she said, peering down at him.

"We don't know."

"And you want me to take him?"

"As a temple orphan. I have gold. I'll have some sent over."

Shamhat turned her famous almond eyes upon me. "Why? Who is he?"

"What does it matter?" I said. "Let him be a temple boy. Take him."

"This doesn't seem like you," she said, looking back down at the boy.

∽

When we got back to the house that night, tired and hungry, we found a messenger waiting, dressed in black, and with four soldiers behind him, also in black, but with bronze chest plates and helmets over.

I thought the messenger might hand me a tablet, but instead he spoke out in a formal tone: "Lord Gilgamesh. I come to you from Nippur, under the god's seal. My lord god Enlil requires your presence in the Holy City. I have orders to take you back with me."

Harga and I exchanged weary glances.

"Now?" I said.

"Now," said the messenger.

"Would it not be better to wait for morning?" Harga said.

The messenger slowly and firmly shook his head. "My orders are to lose no time in fetching you."

I was glum indeed on the ride north that night, with only moonlight to pick out the dusty road before us. Harga and I, huddled up in our cloaks, rode some paces behind the messenger, and perhaps a cord in front of the soldiers, allowing us a small amount of room to whisper together in.

"I wonder how he knew I was here, when we have only just sent out a message," I said.

"No doubt the steward wrote to him," Harga said.

"I wonder if this time he is actually going to kill me."

"I would not be surprised if he was."

That I scowled at. "If Enlil wanted to kill me, surely he would have just sent someone to kill me? There would be no need to march me north, don't you think?"

"Unless he wants to execute you in public in Nippur, my lord."

"Thank you, Harga, that is cheering. But perhaps the war has started up again, after what I did with Hedda, and he wants to berate me. Or perhaps he wants to hear from me about my inside knowledge of Kish, because he wants to attack it."

"If he wanted intelligence, he would have sent for me, and would have no need for you."

"You are absolutely no help at all, Harga."

Sometime past midnight, the messenger allowed us to stop, so that we might snatch a few hours' sleep behind a wall around some date palms. As I lay down and closed my eyes, I found myself remembering the face of the wild boy as he lay there in the gully. It felt as if it had been days, instead of only hours, since I had found him there on the rocky hillside.

"I wonder if I'll ever seen him again," I whispered to Harga, who lay only an arm's length from me.

"Akka?"

"No! The boy from the woods."

"I doubt it. Now sleep because you are going to need it."

I boiled in annoyance for a few minutes about how it was that Harga, my so-called servant, had come to rule over me so imperiously. Enlil had put Harga with me when he gave me my first command, and he had said to me, in front of Harga: "This man will be useful to you." And he had indeed been useful to me. Yet he was also very rude and very often disapproving. Then I thought again about the wild boy's pale green eyes, and how I had felt when they opened, and my irritation with Harga faded.

In the earliest of the morning, I woke with a jolt. Something, half-buried, had burst back into my mind.

Something terrible.

I stood up, feeling nauseous, my belly flipping over, my skin cold with sweat.

"What is it?" Harga said. He was over with his mule, repacking his blanket.

"Nothing," I said. I stretched, and breathed in the cold morning air, looking out over the green plains to the pink and gold sky in the east. The soldiers were already up, I saw, and drawing water from a well.

Harga came and stood very close to me. "Tell me what it is."

I said: "I think I may know why I'm being called to Nippur."

"Yes."

I breathed in, breathed out. "Before we set out on campaign, I got very drunk at the leaving feast."

There I paused.

"Gilgamesh?"

"And I ended up in bed with Della."

Harga's mouth became a hard flat line. Then he nodded. "You lay with Della."

"Yes, I think so. I was fall-over drunk. But I woke up with her, in the Blue House."

"You woke up with Enlil's daughter."

"Yes, as I have just said, Harga. But I crept out, and afterwards she said nothing about it. She looked at me just as she always did. So I came to think that she did not remember the night, and that the danger had passed, and I had stopped letting it worry me. But now I feel it in my gut that this is the reason for me being summoned."

Harga made both his hands into fists, and then nodded at me for a second time. "You are going to be executed. Tortured and then executed. I should have left you in Kish, for Akka to work on. Because it would have gone easier for you there than it will with Enlil."

"Yes," I said miserably. "I know that to be true."

"In all my life," Harga said, spitting out the words, "I have known no greater fool, no man with more of a death wish."

He stalked back to his mule.

"No greater fool," I said to myself, in sad agreement, looking up at the glory of the sunrise. I thought for the smallest moment about making a run for it, but even as I did, Enlil's soldiers were at my side, urging me to hurry myself.

We rode into Nippur on the third evening.

The sunset had lit up the ziggurat in pink, and the Holy City looked very beautiful as we made our way to the palace, even for a man weighed down with dread.

The messenger led us, weary and dusty, into Enlil's temple compound, and I was left to sit alone in a corridor, on a stone bench, while word of my arrival was taken to the god.

After a long while, long enough for me to consider lying down on my bench and getting some sleep, Enlil appeared before me. He had come from temple; his wings were gone, but he still wore his ivory chest plate. Was there more granite grey in his hair now?

"Follow me," he said. He neither smiled at me nor met my eye. So: it was as I had thought.

I followed him into a formal room of the sort he met his functionaries in. He sat down there beside a fire, and poured himself a small glass of water. He made no move to offer me any, and did not ask me to sit.

"My daughter Della is pregnant," he said, looking only at the fire. "I should be angrier, and more surprised, but then I only have myself to blame for this. Everyone warned me about you, but I chose to love you, protect you, treat you as a son. And this is what I get from it."

"Yes."

"I should kill you. But then where would that leave Della and the child? And where would that leave me with your parents? What is going to happen is that you are going to marry her tomorrow. You will be cleaned up, and put into good clothes, and you will consecrate your marriage in my temple at dawn. Is that all clear?"

"Yes."

"Afterwards you will go back to Shuruppak and retrieve your men. I have reports of a fine cedar forest on a massif to the east. That you will inspect. After that I want you in Marad. There are rumours Akka may be moved to take it, and I cannot have that road in his hands. Details of all this have been passed to Harga, and you will take his advice at every step. I cannot have any more failures or drunken disasters."

He seemed to have finished talking, and he took a sip of his wine, his dark eyes still on the flames.

"And what about Della, my lord, and the baby?" I said, when it seemed clear he would not speak again.

"They will live here with me in Nippur; I have given her the Blue House as hers. Whether I will ever allow you to see them, that I will decide later."

"Yes, my lord."

"You should go now."

I looked at the darkness of his face – a face that had once shone so brightly on me.

"I am sorry, my lord."

I saw his hand tightening on his cup, but he said nothing more to me.

Harga was waiting for me out in the gloom of the flag-stoned corridor.

"He didn't kill you, then."

"Not today. But I'm getting married at dawn."

"Congratulations, my lord."

"This is no time for your humour, Harga."

We stood there a while, looking at each other.

"She's pregnant," I said. "And since it's five months since we left this place, I'm guessing she is five months pregnant."

"Ah," he said. "Congratulations again, my lord."

In the early morning, Harga helped tie me into my bridegroom clothes. They are designed to be pulled off in one piece in the temple, when it is time for the rites, so you must be careful how you knot the ties.

"You were so drunk that night," he said. "I'm amazed you had it in you to make a child."

"I have always been a gifted drunk."

"That is true enough, my lord."

He poured me out a huge tankard of wine. I drank it down in one.

"Are you sure about this, my lord?"

"If I am going to lie with Della again, but this time in front of her father, I need to be drunk."

He filled up my tankard to the brim again.

"For what I have to do now," I said, "there cannot be too much wine."

Afterwards I walked, as if to my execution, through the ancient palace that I knew so well, towards Enlil's temple, the temple of the sky. As I did, I remembered dancing with Della, and giggling with her in a corridor on the night of the feast. I remembered Della's chaperone passed out on the floor of what must have been Della's bedchamber.

I did not remember much else.

"I did not imagine my wedding day like this," I said to Harga.

"This is exactly how I imagined your wedding day," he said.

In the temple, the fire bowls had all been lit. As I entered, the drums began. The central colonnade was packed with priests in black; my uncle had always kept his father's colour. I looked up at the gorgeous paintings of Enlil upon the walls. They showed him separating Heaven from Earth, and making the world fit for humans, and I felt very sad for a moment, to have lost his love as I had. Then the priests stood aside for me and for my escort, Harga, and there, at the far end of the temple, was Della.

She was standing with her hands clasped before her, in the simple white dress that brides wear. Behind her, soft and white, was the sacred marriage bed, and behind that the altar. Two priestesses flanked Della, ready to take off her robe.

Della was beautiful. She had always been the most beautiful. As they slipped her dress off her, and I walked slowly towards her, I saw that her breasts were bigger than they had been, and her belly more rounded.

Even at some distance, I could tell how angry she was.

A fragment of memory returned to me. My mouth against her ear, me whispering: "*I will not let anything bad happen to you.*"

Even with the wine in me, I had to force myself to keep walking. "Just do the rite," Harga said. "Ignore the crowd. Ignore how she is feeling. Just do it."

I walked to her, and stood before her, so close I could have reached out and touched one of her naked breasts. Harga took my robe off me, rather less elegantly than the priestesses had done it for Della.

When the priests had said the sacred words of binding, I stepped forwards at once to take her in my arms, just as you are meant to. Everything must be as it has always been for the rites, everything in the same order.

"You stink of wine," she whispered to me, as I took one of her nipples in my mouth. "You stink of sweat. You disgust me, Gilgamesh."

"Just let me do my work," I said.

CHAPTER NINE

NINSHUBAR

When the Potta had been with me for almost three full years, my father and brothers went out hunting wildebeest and did not come back.

I was at the front of the search party, following their tracks along a dried-up creek bed, and so I was the first to come upon them.

What was left was scattered, ripped, coated in dust. A mess and smell of stray bones, one skull – but also, undeniably, the precious things that could not be mistaken. Things of no worth to the lions and hyenas, but of agonising value to me. My father's flint knife. My eldest brother's arrows, so distinctive, tipped with chert and fletched with eagle feathers.

I sat on a rock, holding these proofs of what was lost, dumbstruck by the finality of it. My father was a good man, and when I did something foolish, he would say: "Ninshubar, you are only learning; forgive yourself." No girl could have had a better father. My brothers had taught me to fish, and to set traps. I could not have had better brothers.

The Potta came up beside me, and put one warm hand on my back.

After that, things went badly for me.

My father had been leader of our clan, since before I was born. I was too young now to stand in his place, and after the funeral feast, my mother was voted the new leader. She was brave, strong, clever: I saw why they did it. But for me a fire was put out. I could no longer hope for protection from above. It was a cold feeling for me, while it was new.

In my tribe, there were men and women, and their initiations, but there had always been a third way, for those who were gifted hunters, warriors, or shamans: a way to live outside the world of family. That was the path I had always been walking.

Now my mother said she had seen a vision, and I must come into the women's enclosure. That I must be prepared for my cutting and for marriage. She had an idea, she said, of a great tribe leader I could be given to.

As soon as she told me, I said: "Mother, I will not submit."

She said: "You will do it, Ninshubar, or you will die."

The Potta woke me when it was still dark. "Shuba, the elders are meeting about you," he said, very quiet. "To decide how you must be punished."

I sat up and saw that my mother was missing from the sleeping mats.

"They're down on the beach," he said.

We prepared for what was coming in the first glooming of the light. I had no hunger, but I made myself ready in the old-fashioned way, just as if it was an ordinary hunt I was going on, eating the right amount, tying up my straps around my tools so that they wouldn't rub against me, binding my breasts with my lion-skin straps. The Potta watched me in silence.

"They will kill you if they see you," I said.

"They will kill me if they catch me. But they are not going to catch me."

I pressed my mouth to his forehead. "I will see you very soon. Just do as we planned."

And then I picked my way up onto the ridgeway to wait.

When they come to kill you, you are meant to kneel and accept it gently. That is what the gazelle does at the end of the long hunt. She sets herself down onto the earth, and she waits for you to come up with your arrow. And that is what I was meant to do now.

They came up over the brow of the ridge with the wind behind them, heads down, looking for my trail. The sweat and the smoke lifted off them. My mother was out in front, a battle axe in each hand, face and arms painted red. Our shaman, close behind, was carrying the sacred spear that he kept back for sacrifices.

I saw that they were surprised to see me as I was, in my running straps, all ready for a long run. For a moment, they hesitated. But then my mother stepped forwards, her face hard.

"Kneel," she said.

For a heartbeat I felt how easy it would be. To kneel, to let it end. In the same moment I thought, *If I do it quickly, I could cut her throat.* I could see it: the blood spraying from my mother's neck. But if I got to her, I would not get away again.

"The elders have found you guilty," my mother said. "This is the day you die."

The shaman nodded.

My mother began on the death prayer. "May all the spirits look kindly on you. May they nourish you, may they guide you, in the darkness on the other side."

I looked about at my executioners. They had not even bothered to surround me.

They should have remembered that sometimes, at the end of the long hunt, the gazelle does not lie down. Sometimes, when you think she has nothing left, she springs back into life.

Well, I had made my calculations, and if you are going to do something, it is always better to do it quick.

As my mother took a breath, to begin her final words, I turned on my heels and took off.

Hard south.

Slowly I geared down into the hunter's run, strong and light. I pulled in the cool air through my nostrils, filling out the bottom of my lungs.

In the first moment of confusion, the shaman had thrown his spear, and it had clattered along the rock somewhere near me. Now they were well behind, running slow. They knew what their task was now and they were planning what to do next. When I flicked my head back, I saw the shaman, the slowest runner, veering off down the slope to the east. He would be heading back to tell the others.

It's better to be the hunter than the hunted. I could feel the truth of that now. But my would-be executioners had not expected to run. They had not drunk their fill or bound their breasts or eaten just the right amount. They did not have water with them. They had come armed for murder, and now they were carrying heavy weapons that, so far at least, still felt too precious to drop.

This knowledge put the strength in my legs and helped me smooth out my fear.

On I ran, growing stronger and calmer as I ate up the ridgeway. The early sky blazed crimson, and in my mind, I said the running words: *One step and then the next.*

At the end of the ridge, the path dipped through low trees before passing out onto the plain. I loped down towards a sea of yellow grass studded with near-black tree clusters.

Gradually, my followers slipped back. They had a plan now.

As the sun moved high into the sky, the animal track I had been following widened out into the main track south: better running, with red sand underfoot. But this was a long haul now. My mother would be suffering.

On I ran, along the red path through the grassland. Time yawned, contracted, yawned wide again. One breath would last forever and then a moment later I would think: *Did half a day just go by in a heartbeat?* Again, and again, I said the running words: *One step and then the next.*

As the light began to fail, I looked round and saw a fire spark. I knew this for the trick it was. Some of them would be pushing on in the darkness, hoping to catch me out.

They say that when you have been running for long enough, it doesn't make any difference if you are a man or a woman, old or young. All that matters is your will. It had not come to that yet: this was not life or death. But soon it would begin to matter and I ran faster now, down towards the wetlands, to prove that I still could.

Between the plains and the marshland there is the crocodile river. I drank like a dog from it, the water shockingly cold on my face. I had seen buffalo die in that river in great and terrible eruptions. But there was no point in thinking about it. I drank my fill, filled my waterskin, and then ploughed straight into the hard water, leaning into the current, feeling my way across the slippery rocks, one questing foot at a time.

In the marsh I was forced to slow down, jumping from one clump of sharp grass to the next. Soon after, in the last of the light, I stopped, and sat down.

What perfect relief. I put my feet out in front of me in the black mud, resting them on their heels, luxuriating in the not-running. The grass was sharp to sit on, but it was very good to sit.

The sky above gleamed gold and lilac, and I sat and listened. It was strange to be just sitting, after running and running for so long.

I listened.

Nothing.

Nothing except swamp birds going home for the night, and the annoying buzz of the mosquitoes.

I waited just a few heartbeats longer, reluctant to stand again, then I heaved myself up with a grunt of effort.

This time I went north. Straight towards my pursuers.

I walked just to the left of the path, quiet as a ghost. I listened with every hair on my body for the sound of someone coming the other way.

Once, in the darkness, just after I had crossed back through the river, I thought I heard my mother's voice. For a long moment, I froze mid-step. But the voice moved on, somewhere to the south and east.

A long time after, in the true night, I moved back into the hunter's run, keeping west of the path, and trying to keep myself straight north by the soft light of the stars. Slower and slower. At times in the night, I found myself standing still, about to lie down.

At the first signs of dawn, I saw a shape ahead of me. It was a young man, sitting on a rock, his arms over his knees. I stopped dead, about to turn, but then he moved his head, a flash of fire, and I saw it was my Potta.

He was in his running straps too, with his old flint knife tied neatly to his left arm. I pulled myself up straight as I got close.

"You took your time, Shuba," he said, getting up. I noticed for the first time that he was taller than me. He held out some dried meat to me.

"Are they following you?" I said, stuffing the meat into my mouth. "Did they see you go?"

He rolled his eyes at me. "Do you see them here, Shuba?"

I nodded, kept chewing, fought the instinct to sink down upon the earth and sleep.

He said: "We could hide for a bit. Your feet are bleeding."

I shook my head. "Just keep up."

I lurched off again, slow, but moving.

A heartbeat later, the Potta fell in behind me.

I said to myself the running words: *One step and then the next.*

CHAPTER TEN

INANNA

Enki came floating across the bay to us on the boat they called the Barge of Heaven.

The barge was ten cables long, and it flew three blood-red sails against the grey of the winter sky. The oars that dipped into the white-flecked sea flashed bronze as they cleared the water.

We three moon gods stood on the quay in in our full temple finery. I was thirteen.

When An, the king of the gods, first came down from Heaven, he brought with him his two sons, Enki and Enlil. Enki was the youngest of them, and he was also my grandfather. I felt the drag of him, the sink-well of his enormous power, long before we could make him out by eye.

Enki had been away in the far south since before I was born. Yet as he drew close, he was instantly and completely recognisable to me, as if he had just stepped, seething with vigour, from the paintings in my mother's temple.

Here was the great god Enki, lord of wisdom, lord of writing, lord of the canals – here he was. A man who raped four of his own daughters when his wife Ninhursag left him, to show her what it meant to cross him.

I lifted my chin, to show that I was not afraid.

Enki stood on the edge of the boat, leaning out a little, his right hand wrapped around a rope. He shone like aged bronze when the sunlight caught him.

As the barge touched the wharf, Enki dropped down onto the quay, soft as a leopard. A moment later his chief minister, Isimud, unfolded from the barge behind him. It was said that when Enki wanted people tortured, Isimud liked to do it himself. Now here the famous *sukkal* was, thin and dark as a deer hound. His glance grazed across me as he took in the sweep of the scene.

Enki ignored my mother and father. Instead, he spread out his hands to me. "Inanna!" he said. "The miracle Anunnaki! I have something for you."

In an instant, a reed basket was being handed to him and in two steps he was kneeling on the quay before me and gently lifting something up: a scrabbling lion cub. And in the basket: another cub.

He had brought me two lions.

"My lord," I said, in that moment entirely undone.

I was wearing my best dress. It had taken three women a year to embroider. Now, without a thought for it, I sank down to my knees upon the damp stones of the quay. Enki passed me a cub and our hands touched as I took it. The wriggling lion hissed at me and flung a claw out towards my face. "Oh," I said, suffused with delight. "I hope they are not too cold in this weather."

"You must keep them warm," he said.

I became aware of my mother standing over us, in her moon-shaped crown, and beyond, the hush of the crowds.

"A present worthy of a high goddess," Enki said to me, leaning in, his voice low. "I am glad to finally meet you." He was so close I could smell him: olive soap, and the warm scent of a grown man. His eyes were brown but flecked with gold.

Before I could think how to thank him, he leaped up to kiss my mother.

The next day, Enki was out with my father all day, looking at the canals. That night the adults ate without me, which might have been nothing. But the next day, the doors were still shut against me. When they went to temple, I was put into my mother's room.

On the third evening, my father came to me very solemn. He sat at the end of my mother's bed and tried to hold my feet through my blankets. I kicked myself free of him.

"Enki is thinking you will be a match for his son Dumuzi," he said.

"The sheep god," I said. "A half god."

"My love," he said. "Dumuzi is good-looking and well-mannered, from what I remember of him as a boy. They will value you in Enki's court, because you will lift Dumuzi up. You will only be over the river from us, so close."

"No," I said.

My father had no smile with him. "Little goddess," he said. "Enki means to take you back with him to his temple at Eridu. We cannot refuse him."

"And that's it?" I pushed myself up against the wooden bedhead and crossed my arms over my chest. "I have no say?"

"Inanna," he said. "This is not a kidnap. This is an alliance, a grand marriage."

I got off the bed to stand facing him, my hands in tight fists.

"Father," I said. "Say no to him. Tell him he cannot have me."

My father's face grew hard. "Inanna, if we say no, he will punish us. We are subject to him, all of us in the south."

My lion cubs were at my feet now, looking up at me nervously, hissing at my father.

"All this talk of me being so precious," I said. "Yet this is what I am worth."

My father got up to leave. "You go too far, Inanna," he said. "I am doing my best for you. This is painful for me too."

I almost laughed. "For you!"

As I packed, my mother said: "He will not kill you." She was crying. "You must remember that I am alive," she said, "and I am well, even though I lived with him for years and years."

"I am not afraid," I said, very cold. "I will have my lions with me."

My mother wiped her cheeks with her dress. "It was clever of him, the lions."

I picked out the best of my summer dresses to take with me, although, on this cold winter day, they seemed too flimsy to ever be of use again.

"You could not save Amnut," I said. "And now you cannot save me. How very useless we moon gods are."

She stopped me packing, kneeled down before me, and put her arms around me, unyielding as I was. "My precious love," she said, her damp face pressed against my chest. "I have a *mee* of peace. Your father has one *mee* of battle. Your *mee* does not work. Enki has an entire arsenal of *mees*. He has been trading for them or stealing them or going to battle for them for two hundred years."

"I know that," I said.

"I know you are angry, but I need two promises from you."

I shrugged very slightly against her, my mouth turned hard down.

"The first is: you must submit. Do not fight Enki. Only submit. Whatever he asks, do it."

"And the second thing?"

"You must trust no one. Listen to me, Inanna. In Eridu, everyone serves Enki. Everyone. You will not meet one person who will lift a finger to help you. Whatever they may say. Promise me. On both things."

"Yes," I said, but icy still, my eyes on my chest of furs.

"Say the words, Inanna. You must say the words."

"I promise," I said.

"Say it."

"I give you my sacred promise, Mother. The sacred promise of a goddess, which will never be broken."

She nodded, and kissed my forehead.

"I know what no one knows," she said, "and that is that you have the heart of a general. More than that – the heart of a god of war."

I said nothing.

"But, Inanna, you do not yet understand what it is to fear."

"I feel fear."

"Not as you should. That is my doing. I have so wanted you to be happy. But right now, it puts you in danger."

I shrugged at her. "Well, I am not happy, if that is a comfort."

"Inanna, please. This is not the time for gods of war. This is not when we fight Enki. This is the time for submitting. That is your duty now."

"So, you and Father both say."

She was angry with me then. "Inanna, do not think the *melam* in your blood can protect you from what Enki can do. The pain is real, even if the flesh heals. And he will find new ways to hurt you if pain is not enough. You must go to your grandfather as a goddess of love, and be all that that means, but nothing more."

I softened, just very slightly. "I have already said that I will do as you ask."

She nodded, kissed the top of my head, kissed my hands, kissed the *mee* on my wrist.

"Inanna, I love you more than anyone or anything."

We stood there for a moment, cheeks touching.

Then came the knock: Enki was waiting for me on his ship, and the lions were already onboard.

"Say a kind word to your father before you go."

"Why should I?"

"He is no more useless than me."

"I disagree," I said.

The Barge of Heaven kept close to the reed beds, the blood-red sails billowing, a hundred oars dipping, through the land of ten thousand islands. We sat in leather chairs, with furs heaped upon us, beneath the blood-red shade. Enki's colour.

Four of the deck servants were occupied with my lions; the last brought warm mountain tea, and dried figs.

All of Enki's manners were pleasing, never over-done. He ate neatly and served me everything first. He never raised his voice. He always waited a moment before answering, so that I felt he was truly listening. Sometimes he would touch me, to give me this or give me that, with his firm fingers, but always it would be neat and polite, never lingering.

I had been dreading the journey, but sitting with him, watching the flamingos lift up off the salt marshes, I felt relieved to be underway.

"I know they have filled your head with stories about me," he said. "Of Enki the monster, who eats babies, and ravages little girls."

"No," I said.

I was thinking about him raping his daughters, as the priests said he had, and whether it could really be true.

Enki looked me in the eye for a moment, smiling. "Inanna, when you are a great goddess, whatever you do, however hard you try, they will tell lies about you – terrible lies, stupid lies. And worse, everyone will believe them, and add to them, and the lies will grow bigger and bigger. And it is the lies you will be remembered for. It doesn't matter that I brought canals to these people, and writing, and running water, and the wheel. That it was me who saved the Anunnaki from starvation in the first days. None of that matters, only the lies that have been told, and the lies that are believed."

He offered me another fig. "You must learn not to mind too much. Because it is not such a bad thing to be feared."

I took the fig, and we looked out together at a passing heron, trailing its legs as it flew over the reedbeds.

I thought about asking about my sister.

Before I had had time to form my words, Enki said: "If you are thinking about your sister, Ereshkigal, you should ask your father about that. People say it was me who forced her down into the underworld. That's not how it was. But I am glad she is down there. What everyone likes to forget is that it was *her turn*. We all agreed that we would take turns in the underworld. One of us has to be there. But your sister refused to go."

He paused, looking irritated. "So, about all that, you should ask your father. He will say, *she was mad, she was not fit for it, she had a child in her belly, it was cruel to send her,* but... But. What difference if she is mad here or mad there? An Anunnaki must man the Dark City, and it was her turn."

"A child?"

"It died, I think," he said, watching the lions.

"You do not know for sure?"

"She doesn't talk to us now," he said. "And she won't come out, although her time is long since up."

A lion cub, escaping, pounced on one of his feet. He scooped it up onto his lap and kissed it. "Inanna, I can tell that maybe in a hundred years or so, when you have seen something of this realm, you may be quite the goddess."

"Thank you, my lord," I said, very prim, and he laughed, a full-bellied laugh.

"Now listen, Inanna, I have been honest with you; will you tell me one thing in return? I am wondering how your parents did it. Hundreds of years we have been here, and no new Anunnaki babies. And then, suddenly, you. Have they talked about it to you?"

"I believe they did the rites, my lord. In temple, in the usual way."

He smiled at this, and winked at me. "No special medicine, though, no special *mees*?"

"I don't think so."

"I'm told you have special powers. That you can sense an Anunnaki coming. That you always know where your family are."

"Is that a special power?"

"Interesting," he said, watching my face, but he let the subject go.

CHAPTER ELEVEN

GILGAMESH

And so I returned to Shuruppak a married man.

I had only just arrived back at the house, and was pulling off my boots before the unlit fireplace, when Harga appeared. "It's the wild boy," he said. "That you made us carry to the temple. He is filling up our doorway, and he says his name is Enkidu."

I felt my insides turning over. "He lived, then." I paused, careful to keep my face blank. "Oh, send him in. Why not?"

The wild boy who called himself Enkidu soon appeared, much cleaner and sweeter-smelling than when I had seen him last, but very stern. He was a big man, standing on his own two feet: a powerful man.

"Sit," I said, waving at a chair.

Enkidu seemed reluctant to take the chair I was offering him. Once sitting, he seemed unwilling to open his mouth, even to say hello.

For a short time, then, we sat in silence. Was he from the marshlands, as Harga had suspected? The men of the marshes are a proud and formal race of the sort one dreads dealing with. They are happy to sit in silence for many hours if custom dictates – a terrifying prospect for any city-born Sumerian. I remembered that the marsh men always greeted guests with wine or hot tea. "Bring us through some wine," I called to Harga, even though I knew how much he hated to fetch things for me.

Silence fell upon us once more. I wished I had my boots on; this felt like a formal scene, and for reasons I did not care to examine, I felt that Enkidu had the upper hand. Finally, defeated, I said: "It is good to see you well, although I suppose you may not remember me at all. Are you well?"

"Yes," he said.

Silence again.

Harga did not reappear, but instead my house man came in with wine. I saw that Harga had made him bring the good wine, made from special dates, that had been sent south to me by Enlil, the lord of the sky, when I was in favour. In a time of even greater favour, the lord of the sky had sent me two fine conical cups fashioned from solid silver, which came with a pretty stand to rest the cups in. These silver cones had also been sent out with my houseman, by way of secondary punishment. But ah well, why not treat the marsh man? I filled the silver cones to the brim with the good wine, and passed one to my guest.

The cone looked very small and awkward in Enkidu's hand. He took a tentative sip at it.

"Do you like the wine?"

"No," he said. It seemed marsh men were too good to lie.

My house man came in to light the fire, and as he did, I let the silence go on, sometimes smiling at Enkidu, who sat there straight-backed, unsmiling, his wine undrunk in his hand. I drained my own cup, and offered him more, but he refused, so I only helped myself to some.

The guest hall in my house in Shuruppak was small, but the walls were carefully painted. Along one, oxen grazed in a lush pasture; on another a group of boys and dogs hunted duck through some marshland. The painter had offered to do scenes from my father's life, the thunderbird landing, the story of the wild bull, that sort of thing, but I had said I wanted something more anonymous, less scripture, and this is what I'd got.

"Do you like the paintings?" I said.

Enkidu looked about him, careful to see it all. "No."

I felt then that the preamble, however amusing, had gone on long enough. "Enkidu, tell me why you are here."

"I am here to serve you," he said. "To pay back the blood debt I owe you. Shamhat has told me that you saved my life. I will stay with you until I have done the same for you."

"There is no need for any of that. I release you from any debt to me."

Enkidu said nothing, although he put down his silver cup, still with wine in it, fumbling a little as he tried to set it neatly in the cup stand.

"Enkidu, I have enough people serving me; that is the only reason I say no to you. But I do thank you nonetheless."

"This is not something I can be released from," he said.

"All the same, I release you. You can go now. Live your life."

In the morning, as I lay in bed still trying to sleep, my head splitting, my house man came in and said: "That marsh man is sleeping outside the gate."

I went out into the dusty street, in the cold morning air, still in my nightshirt. Enkidu was sitting upright against the outer wall of the house. He stood up when I appeared, pulling his clothes straight.

"Enkidu, go back to Shamhat. The temple is your home now."

"I serve you," he said. "Until the debt is paid." Again, those crystal green eyes, unblinking.

For a moment I felt that I might fall, and did not know what would break my fall.

"I beg you to just go," I said.

Then I went back inside and tried to go back to sleep.

Harga came in while I was eating my breakfast: fruit and cheese, and some leftover lamb stew, and beer. He had one of his pebbles in his right hand, and this he rubbed between his fingers as we talked, even though he knew how much the habit infuriated me.

I said: "Is he still out there?"

Harga paused, as if mulling over who I might be referring to.

"Yes," he said finally, with a solemn nod.

"Could you get rid of him for me, do you think?"

"I could. But I did that earlier, and he only came back."

He began throwing his round pebble from one hand to the next.

"You could lock him up," I said, watching the pebble go back and forth.

"Might that seem somewhat harsh, my lord, for a temple boy who has only offered to serve you, and in payment of a blood debt, in accordance with the traditions of his people?"

"I can't have him sleeping out in the street."

Harga shrugged. He put his pebble back into the pouch he kept hanging from his belt. Then he tucked his curls behind his ears, as he always did when he was trying to get his way.

"You could accept his offer," he said. "I'm not really sure why you don't."

I did not know what to say to that. The idea of having the boy around filled me with a kind of terror. But I could not explain that to myself, never mind Harga.

"I have given you my orders," I said. Despite myself, I found my voice was raised.

"The marsh men don't give up," he said, unmoved by my show of emotion.

After Harga had left, I called for some wine, to properly clear my head, and to block out the strange shapes that were starting to form there.

The town of Shuruppak and all its lands were given to me by Enlil, in the days when I had not yet got his daughter with child, and he still sent me wine and silver cups in the shape of cones. I was perhaps only there about half of the time, but when I was, I made sure to take full advantage of what was due to me in that town, that being all that was due to a god.

My rights included the first night with every bride in town. No one could argue it.

That night, though, the family of the bride made a fuss of it. The father of the bride got down on his knees and begged me not to enter their house. I stood with one foot in the door and said: "I have a god's right here; I was given this city by Enlil to treat as my own. This is my right."

Tears rolled down the man's face. "But you are not a god, my lord Gilgamesh," he said. "That is the point."

"I'm god enough for you," I said, angry then, and pushed him backwards.

I was in the act of stepping over the threshold when someone came at me from the alley, shoving me hard aside.

I stumbled, righted myself, and came up with my knives in my hands.

But I pulled up short. It was Enkidu.

We stood there, almost nose to nose, while I reassessed. He smelled strangely sweet close up, of cloves, and cinnamon: of temple. But he was dressed in fighting leathers, and he had a flint axe in each hand. He was not on temple business.

I wished to the gods I had not drunk so much. I was not as steady on my feet as I should have been.

"Not here," Enkidu said. "Not tonight. Let this one go."

"I have a god's right here," I said, taking in the crowd clustered behind Enkidu in the dark, and behind them in the square, my men forming up, carrying torches.

"Maybe you do and maybe you don't," said Enkidu. "But you're not going in."

I stood there, swaying a little, watching to see what he did. He stood there like a bull does when it has already decided to charge.

"What's it to you?" I said. "Out of interest."

"A lady of this family has asked me to step in."

That I snorted at.

"Hear me," I said. "I may not be an immortal. But I am the son of Lugalbanda and Ninsun, two of the Twelve. And you know it was Enlil himself who sent me to serve here, and as high priest not just as steward. And the girl wanted me to come. I wouldn't have known it was her wedding night if she hadn't told me."

I heard how meagre that sounded, even as I was saying it.

"Everyone here is angry with you, Gilgamesh," he said. "But they do not dare say it, because of who you are."

"All except you."

"It's my duty to tell you. Because of the blood debt I owe you."

"Marsh man, I'm going in. And then my boys are going to beat you to death."

"Gilgamesh, you are drunk."

"Enkidu, move aside."

"Gilgamesh, the girl doesn't want you here. Her family don't want you here. Come away with me."

"Very well," I said. I put my knives away, one then the other. I kept up eye contact with him, smiling.

Then I punched him very hard in the gut.

He had not been expecting it but instantly he brought his head down on me, smashing my nose.

I felt blood spurt, and shooting pain.

We staggered together for a moment in a tight hug, then both of us went over hard onto the ground.

I couldn't get my knives out again because he had his arms locked tight around me. We were rolling around on the ground in the dark, with people shouting all around us.

Men pulled us apart: my men.

They propped me up. Someone clubbed Enkidu to the ground.

Harga was there. "You want him dead?"

"Just lock him up."

I made my way back into the town square. I was angry and I had blood all down me, my nose was agony, and I was humiliated. The town folk stepped back into the shadows as I made my way through the streets and home. Two of Harga's boys followed on closely behind me, although I tried to wave them away.

I felt much drunker than I had before. I had to concentrate on my steps, and where I was going. I'd been knocked out with a blow to the head in Kish, and I had thought it was getting better, but now it felt worse again. Just outside my house, I stopped, leaned against a wall, and vomited all over my sandals.

A demon stalked my dreams, and I woke up feeling sick, my head splitting, my nose throbbing, my mouth desert-dry. My pillow was dark with blood.

Harga came in as I was sitting useless over my breakfast. "Gilgamesh, your nose is broken. I know you heal faster than most men, but I will send my man over. It would be a shame to ruin your looks over something like this."

I grunted. "It's only bruised."

"So, we have this wild man of yours. Locked up, as you asked. Not dead, as requested."

"What of it?" I felt like putting my head down onto the table in front of me, but I did not want to do it with Harga there. "I am not in the mood for you, Harga."

"It is only to say to you, my lord, that I have the priestess Shamhat outside the jail. She is unhappy about us having her boy, and calling all kinds of bad luck down on us all, in the name of the god An. It is creating something of a scene and many of the town people have come out to watch. I thought you would like to hear about it, given that this is Anunnaki business now, at least the way Shamhat is telling it."

I did then put my forehead on the table, careful not to knock my nose on it as I did so. "Let her take him, then, if that is what it will take to make you leave."

I sat there alone after that, feeling unreasonably perturbed, not just because of the pain and the hangover, but unwilling to pick at the why of it.

Enlil's new orders for me, involving a cedar forest and a move north to Marad, had been couched in terms vague enough, in the matter of timing, that I had so far seen fit to ignore them.

Now, with my battered nose, and hungover, and with the shame of a street fight hanging over me, I found my lord's commands could be ignored no longer. They were in fact a matter of urgency.

The next day the steward of Shuruppak found Harga and I in the open market, buying supplies for the expedition. The merchants had piled up their dried fish and their onions on reed mats, and Harga and I were pointing at what we wanted, and then waiting for our boys to scoop it up.

"Lord Gilgamesh," the steward said. "I hear you are taking the city guard and going up country to inspect some forestry, and then deserting us for the city of Marad."

"What a spy you would make for King Akka," I said, "with such detailed knowledge of troop movements."

"I hope the steward of this town might be trusted with the news that we are to be deserted by you."

"I am being sent to look at a cedar forest, certainly. And then after that to Marad. Yes. We are told it is a matter of some urgency."

"Leaving us here without soldiers on the front line."

"This is hardly the front line," I said, leaning down to look at some beans. "The armies of Kish will need to get through the armies of the sky god Enlil to get to you here in Shuruppak. And why indeed should they bother, when our land here would not be of much interest to them."

"My lord, the talk now is of them pushing further south. And if they came the long way round the mountains, then we will indeed be the front line. Can Enlil really mean you to take every man we have with you?"

I stopped beside a large reed mat covered with figs and turned to him. "Take your case to the god Enlil. Because these are the orders he has given me. Is it useful work, urgent work? Are we so desperate for lumber that this must be done now? Is Marad more important than Shuruppak? That is not for me to decide. It is the work I have been given."

The steward shifted from foot to foot. "I cannot imagine that Enlil would want us left unprotected."

I felt less patient of him then. "I think I know better than you do what my father-in-law would or wouldn't want."

As I left the market, I passed the wild man, Enkidu, standing there, one foot up against a wall behind him. He did not seem any worse off for our scuffle, or from the treatment my men had handed out to him. "I'm coming with you," he called over to me. "On this expedition you are going on."

I kept on walking, but threw an irritated look at Harga. "Is there a man in this town who doesn't know about our mission?"

Harga was looking at me sideways. "What is it this man has done, to make you so very angry?"

"Is it not enough that he attacked me in the street?"

Harga rolled his shoulders in what might have been a shrug. "We will need all the men we can get, in Marad," he said.

In the evening, an unexpected guest: the priestess Shamhat. I sat with her in my visitor's room, our chairs before the fire. There was no friendliness in her.

"Gilgamesh," she said. "Let him go."

She took a silver cone from me and sipped. "You are going to get him killed."

I sighed out, rather hard. "Shamhat, firstly, I am the only reason this boy is alive. I am the one who rescued him and paid you to nurse him and shelter him. How has this been forgotten? And I do not hold this man. I have refused his debt to me. I have begged him to leave me alone. I do not want him following me about when I do my duty for Enlil. I would be glad if you could intervene for me, and talk some sense into him."

"He won't listen to me," she said. "He says it is his life's path to follow you."

I put down my wine cone in my little wine stand; my hand was shaking. "I locked him up to stop him following me, and you didn't like that, and made a fool of me in front of the whole town. What is it you want from me now?"

"I don't know," she said. "I feel dread, that is all, that I am losing him, although I have known him such a short time."

"That's as may be but hand on my heart, Shamhat, I wish this marsh man would leave me alone."

We went out two abreast well before dawn, forty soldiers, plus me and Harga. We left behind only a few boys to help in any sort of emergency. Some girls turned out with flowers for their soldier sweethearts, but as soon as we were out of the city, we heard them bolting the gates behind us.

Enkidu was following us, wrapped in a large, poorly sewn sheepskin coat. On his back he had a small pack, and also his two enormous stone axes. Harga raised two eyebrows at me.

Something in me gave way.

"I don't care," I said. "Let him join us. Let him march with us if he can keep up."

It turned out that Enkidu could keep up very easily with the soldiers of the sky god, and soon he was loping along next to me. He seemed a different man: softer, throwing out beams of good cheer. "This is the coat you found me in that day. Do you not remember it? Shamhat has mended it for this trip."

"No, I don't remember it," I said, pacing on to get away from him. But then I felt obscurely churlish for not being kind about his coat.

We camped the first night close to a lake, and while the men cooked and set up camp, I swam out, looking out at the first of the stars. For the first time in a long time, I had had nothing to drink. The sky above me was alive with bats, but the water was limpid, a soft smooth black.

"There are hippos here," Enkidu shouted out to me. "I know this lake."

"Just leave me alone," I said, but not loud enough for him to hear.

In the morning we saw the cedar forest, still a long way off. The great trees grew on the highest reaches of a huge massif; clouds clung to the treetops. The walls of the massif looked to me to be sheer rock, rising up two or three leagues into the sky.

"It's a climb, then," I said to Harga. "You didn't mention a climb."

"I'm quite certain that I did," he said.

All day Harga and Enkidu walked together, exchanging stories, and laughing. I had never known Harga to be so friendly to anyone. The men took their lead from this, and by dusk you might have thought Enkidu one of the boys, had it not been for his strange outfit.

It was too late to start the climb that day, so we decided to camp on the flat ground, and then scale the massif in the fresh of the morning.

We camped so close to the mountain that we could hear the myriad tinkling waterfalls, tumbling down its cliffs, as we prepared our supper.

It was colder that night, and so we built up the fire after we had eaten. I saw the men were twitchy, turning their ears to every noise in the black. "This is very near my country," Enkidu told them as they were climbing into their blankets. "All these sounds and smells are very familiar to me."

"What happened to your people?" Harga said.

"The Great Flood happened." Enkidu looked around at us. "And then men like you."

"Do you know this place?" Harga said. "This massif?"

"I've seen it many times, but I've never been up it," Enkidu said, "because of the monster."

The men had all been lying down to sleep. Now they stood up, apparently with no tiredness at all in them, and came to crouch around Enkidu.

"His name is Humbaba," Enkidu said to all gathered. "I thought you all knew about him. Everyone knows he guards the cedars."

"There's always a monster," Harga said, nodding grimly. He had his slingshot in his hand.

In the face of Harga's implacable certainty, and Enkidu's plain talking, I found myself, for a moment, sitting there wide-eyed, with my mouth hanging open. But then I remembered that I was in command, and that it was my job to keep the men together.

"This is nonsense, Enkidu," I said. "What are you doing, scaring everyone like this? We are here to look at the cedars, and how easy it will be to get the wood off and away. There are no monsters here, just a forest."

"A man should know what he is going into," Enkidu said.

"All of you turn in," I said. "Enough of this."

In the night I woke, shockingly upset. Even wrapped in my camel-hair cloak, and lying so close to the fire, I was cold to my bones. I remembered my dream: a giant monster, clawing at me.

I saw that Enkidu had his eyes open, gleaming at me in the dark. He was lying wrapped up in a blanket near my feet. "Bad dream?" he whispered.

"Yes."

"What was it?"

"Does it matter?"

"Dreams have meaning, for my people."

"It was you, putting ideas in my head. I dreamed of a monster. Of course I did." I swallowed. "It had fire coming out of its mouth, and it rose up in the sky. It looked like a man, but its shape was strange. It seemed very real."

"It's a good omen," he said. "It sounds like your god Utu. Maybe he is here with you, following you. Maybe he will help you when the time comes."

"I don't believe in omens, and I happen to know Utu. I can tell you that he doesn't creep about at night, and he is not interested in helping mortals. He'll be in his soft bed right now, sleeping soundly, just like all the other gods."

But already the fear was draining from me, and I felt tiredness creeping back in.

"In this country, we believe in omens, and demons too," Enkidu said.

We were quiet a while, and then he said: "Gilgamesh?"

"Yes?"

"Thank you for letting me join you. It's right that I am here by your side. I feel it."

"You're a madman," I said, smiling at him. "I should have left you there in the crevasse."

I felt his bright eyes on me still as I closed mine to let the sleep in.

The next day, early, we began the climb. Close up you could see the cliffs were not in fact sheer: there were paths up, albeit steep ones, and the climb was studded with small terraces of grass, and tumbling streams. As we climbed, all around us we could hear the drip, drip, drip of water on the moss-cloaked rock.

It was a hard climb. Our thighs burned with the effort, our lungs heaved, and the sun scalded our necks. But we crossed several streams and I don't think I'd ever had water so clean and sweet.

Even before we were halfway up, we began to catch wafts of the most glorious scent: the deep and musky smell of the cedars.

It took us six hours to reach the plateau, and then we sat there in the blessed shade, just inside the edge of the cedar forest, looking up at the gigantic trees. We ate white cheese and onions, sitting on fern-clad boulders, with the smell of the sacred trees filling up our lungs and heads. "It's beautiful," I said.

"It's big," Harga said. "It's going to take us at least a week to get round it."

"Maybe more," Enkidu said. "This is not easy walking up here. And there is Humbaba. I think we should look around, and then go down quickly, before the monster comes."

All of the men edged closer to Enkidu, even Harga. Enkidu had no official authority, far from it, but then authority rarely flows in straight lines.

"There's no monster," I said.

Harga, who ought to have spoken up, said nothing.

I saw that, as often happens in the army, I was now obliged to abandon my position and side with the men, and this I did most promptly. "I do not think we need to go all the way around the massif," I said. "That was only talk, before we realised how big it was. I think we should head inwards, find the highest point, have a good look over the place, and then come back. If we are quick about it, perhaps we can even be down again by dusk. We can leave our packs here."

This was met with approval, and everyone was then keen to strike inwards immediately.

I led the way at first, following what looked like an animal track through the russet of the fallen pine needles. Then in a pool of sunshine we came upon a mess of broken branches, churned up with mud. Harga and Enkidu, following close behind me, exchanged a look.

"There isn't a monster," I said, but very quiet, given all the circumstances. "It will be just some kind of animal."

The path grew wider, and more worn.

"No talking," Enkidu said, as if he was the leader of us and entitled to give orders. Everyone fell silent.

We came to a broken-down tree, the branches smashed, lying awkward and surreal over our path. Something seemed to have gouged out great chunks of bark. Enkidu went and put his hand to a gouge, and then raised his eyebrows to Harga.

"Just move on," I whispered.

Soon enough we passed more smashed trees with huge

scratches gouged from them. I looked up and the sky had clouded over.

"They say Humbaba is the last of his kind," Enkidu said, turning his head to us. "They say that once there were many just like him."

"I thought you said no talking," I said. "No talking!"

We were now walking on a smooth bed of needles, the path no longer visible. I became aware that I could not be sure that we were holding our direction. Harga and I both looked up for the sun, but it was impossible even to guess at where it was.

"We came from the west, straight in," I said. "We went towards the middle of the massif. And it's been... I don't know. An hour?"

"I don't know," he said. "It's hard to keep track up here."

It was unusual to hear Harga sounding so human.

All of us kept on craning our necks up to get proper sight of the sun in the sky.

"This way," I said, veering off to the left, since someone had to decide.

"I just cannot tell," Harga said, plunging after me.

After a long while we were still walking on smooth needles, still more and more unsure of which way we were heading and which way we had come from.

"Maybe if we climbed a tree," I said. "It might help us get our bearings."

We all looked up at the distant canopy; the first branches were at least a cable high.

Every way I looked now, the forest and its giant cedars looked exactly the same.

Enkidu came forwards. "Let me lead," he said. "I will keep us going straight from here, at least."

Annoying as this was, I let him take the lead, and so we walked on, in air thick with the aroma of the cedars, my sandals leaving no prints on the forest floor.

Ah, but there was light ahead; the trees were thinning: we were there!

"Oh," I said. I had expected to find myself at some outcrop in the centre of the massif. But instead we had reached the edge of the escarpment once more. Below us lay the plains; was that the Euphrates in the distance, or a lake?

"Can we have walked all the way across, right through the middle?" I said.

"No, I don't think so," Enkidu said. "I think we've been spun around."

I looked around. Was this where we'd come up? The clouded sky made it hard to tell. Our packs weren't there. Yet it was so familiar. "Did we double back on ourselves?"

Harga had a nervous look on him, like he'd heard something. "Might be well to keep to the edge now," he said. "Work along the edge of the escarpment until we find our packs."

Enkidu was peering back into the trees. "Did you hear something?"

We all stood root still. I thought I had heard something too: a muffled thud, crashing maybe, branches breaking. Very close. Harga and I locked eyes.

"Let's go with your plan," I whispered. He nodded, and we turned—

It was Humbaba.

He was a shaggy brown giant. Like an elephant, but bigger, and with a huge and heavy pelt reaching almost to the ground.

He breathed white smoke in the cool mountain air, and he had great curving tusks, very ancient and yellow. He towered over us.

Humbaba stamped his front right foot, and the ground shook beneath us. He rolled one yellow eye at me, then he stamped his great foot again, and jays lifted out of the trees behind us, crying their alarm.

For these long moments, all of us stood frozen.

Then with no further warning, Humbaba came straight at us, sending everyone screaming and running.

With the stinking breath of the monster upon me, I leaped out into empty air.

I woke up lying on my back. I could see vultures circling overhead, their feathered wing tips black against the blue.

It took a moment for the pain to hit me. I was about to try to sit up, and then realised I was lying on a narrow ledge and if I moved at all, I might fall to my death. Above me: cliff, studded with ferns and damp plants. I could not see how I had got to where I was, but it seemed to me, even lying still, that I might be badly hurt. I could feel my right leg – a shooting pain in the knee. But I could not feel my left leg at all. It was the strangest sensation.

Movement just above me. A sort of fat mouse. She and I looked at each other, each of us frowning, and then she disappeared. I would have felt my head, to see if my skull was broken, or if there was blood, but I was scared to move my arms, in case I tipped myself off the cliff.

"Do not be afraid," I said out loud. Perhaps to myself. Perhaps to the mouse. "There is nothing to fear."

Darkness came. If I tipped my head just a little to the left, I could see the sun setting.

I passed water where I lay, unable to do anything but briefly enjoy the warmth of it spreading between my thighs and up my back.

I thought, *What will my father think, of me dying like this, on a cliff, all alone?* So pointlessly. Had I had the *melam* in my veins, I would be sitting up right now, strong again, looking for a way to climb. But instead, I lay still, terrified that I might fall if I fell asleep.

In my dream that night, the demon came to me again. He had a great yellow eye; snakes slithered in and out of it.

In his huge claws he cradled heaps of bodies, here or there a child's head or hand lolling out.

"You need to choose, Gilgamesh," the demon said. "Will you live your life as a whole man, or as half a god?"

PART 2

"He put his hand in her hand.
He put his hand to her heart.
Sweet is the sleep of hand-to-hand.
Sweeter still the sleep of heart-to-heart."

From the ancient poem known as "The Courtship
of Inanna and Dumuzi"

CHAPTER ONE

NINSHUBAR

We walked north towards unknown country. The land dried out; the trees thinned. The first night we slept, unfed, in a crack in a rock face in a sandy ravine, back to back, our feet touching. He said to me in the night: "Do you regret it?"

I said: "I will never regret it. How could I?" I pressed the raw soles of my feet into his.

All night I was listening for my mother's voice, in and out of sleep. I dreamed of her standing over me, in the wet season camp, and her saying: "You must live in the law, Ninshubar, not twist it for yourself." But when I woke, cold, hungry and thirsty, in the earliest light, I saw we were still alone, just the two of us, in the same narrow ravine we had gone to sleep in.

That day I turned us east and west and east again, zigzagging over the half-known land of neighbours. Before dusk I had to stop. I was leaving footprints of blood in the dirt. The Potta found me berries and one small blue egg.

"For you, Mother," he said, smiling. I took the food gratefully.

While he watched me eat, he said: "You have done nothing wrong, Shuba."

"I know that," I said. "I know. Yet it is a thing to cast the law aside."

"It is the law that was wrong," he said.

We crossed grassland, here or there studded with forest. In the night we lay together in a hollow of dark trees, our foreheads pressed together.

"The law is the law," I said. "And under the law, she had a right to tell me where to put my bed."

"Your law," he said. "Not the law of my people. Not the law even two days' walk north of here."

I kissed his cheek. "It is the law of the gods I grew up with."

"Those gods are behind us now," he said. "Stuck in their caves. Far away from us. We will have new gods to worry about soon! Stranger gods!"

That made me laugh.

The next day my feet were worse not better, and I began limping badly, favouring the sides of my feet, or my heels, going slower and slower although I was very brave, and said nothing to the Potta.

The secret signs of my people's law, the twisted twigs and special marks upon the earth, were gone from the land. This was stranger country. Everything looked different: the grasses, the trees, the shapes of the mountains beyond. Even the earth was different, a strange, staining orange.

One step and then the next.

For six days we climbed, with mountains ahead and to the left of us. After that we began to see the signs of a new people.

Sometimes we would spend a whole day only hiding, because we heard people passing too close. For a long time after, the path we followed sloped gently downwards, following the course of interlinking valleys.

For one long moon, we followed the course of a great river, and then one morning the distant horizon resolved into the magical blue of the ocean.

My spirits rose up inside me.

"Maybe we will stop down here," I said. "Make a camp for a while."

"Maybe," said the Potta.

"I'm going to swim at least," I said. "And I will help you to do so also."

He laughed. "I may not be a dolphin in human form, as you are, but I think I am safe to go swimming now."

We paced out down grassy terraces, winding between outcrops of dark grey rock. I thought, *The sea water will be good for both of us, but especially for his burned skin.*

Near dusk we had not yet reached the sea, so we found a crook in some rocks, and began to light a fire. As I twisted the fire stick, the Potta said to me, "How are your feet?"

I was looking up at him when his face changed.

"Shuba…" he said.

Everything I would remember after, I remembered as if it had happened in silence.

The men were standing all around us in the dusk-light, as if they had somehow sprung up whole from the earth.

Strange men with hard faces and long greasy hair.

I was already on my knees; now I put my hands above my head, looking at the Potta, willing him to do nothing except copy me.

As I looked up into the Potta's face, time froze for a moment as one of the men swung something at him.

Now he was on the ground, my pale-skinned Potta, with blood surging from a wound at the side of his head, and the orange of his hair growing dark with it.

In the silence that is all I have left of it, I stayed kneeling, not looking around me at the men, just looking at the Potta, until they pulled a bag down over my head.

For a very long time after, I tried to remember, anything, something, anything at all, about that last sight of the Potta. Was he breathing still? Did I see him move?

I woke up with sacking over my face, lying on my back with numb arms beneath me, my legs twisted agonisingly to one side. There was an overpowering smell of dried fish.

I was in a boat, and we were underway.

I could see through the sack, although not perfectly. There were four men in the boat, but no Potta. I was thinking about what to do about my arms, when one of the men clambered over some sacks to get to me.

Even with the bag over my head, there was no mistaking what he planned to do to me.

When these men had come at me on the land, I had made a calculation. Part of that calculation, then, was that I did not want the Potta to get hurt. Also, at that time, I had been clear that I did not want to die.

But that was then. Now the calculation came out differently.

Well, if you are going to do something, it is better to do it quick.

I lay limp as he untied my ankles. Then with one giant wrench of my body, with everything I had, I wrested myself up into a sitting position and in the same movement brought my forehead down, as hard as I could, into where I thought the man's head was.

I hit skull, a piece of luck. Then I tipped my head back a little and bit down hard on him, through the sack, on whatever I could get of him, knowing it might knock my teeth out.

I got his ear – and it crunched between my teeth.

A moment later my mouth was full of salty sweet blood and ear and sack, and he was screaming like a devil spirit. He reared back from me in the muddle of it and as he did, I managed to twist up onto my knees, then feet, the boat lurching, and I smashed my head down again on top of him. Again, the old gods were with me, and I hit bone.

And then something unexpected happened: suddenly there was only emptiness where the man had been.

He had gone.

A splash.

A scream.

I sat back down into the boat, falling painfully against my bound arms, and spitting ear and sacking out of my mouth. My forehead was bleeding into my eyes, and I had wrenched my right shoulder badly, but it was my teeth and lips that hurt the most.

A pause, another scream, further away now, and the boat rocked as everyone moved. And something else unexpected: the men in the boat began laughing, great shrieks of laugher.

I sat back against the edge of the boat, waiting for what would happen next.

For a while anyway, the next did not involve me. There was a melee as they pulled down the sail and got out oars, shouting back to my would-be rapist. But even in the midst of their efforts, they were panting with laughter.

I stayed still and quiet, trying to understand what was happening through the pinprick holes in my sack. My forehead burned, and the bleeding seemed to be getting worse. I had bruised my mouth, split both lips. One of my front teeth was wobbling.

They pulled my attacker back on board, with him screaming what could only be abuse at me.

For a while after they left me alone.

Later the man who was the leader of these men came over and beat me, but carefully and deliberately, with a heavy stick.

He hit me wherever he could without getting too close to me: shoulders, shins, the top of my head. I tried to duck my head down, but I let him do it. There are always repercussions when you refuse to submit to others.

Afterwards he pulled the sack off my head, and then, having gestured for me to twist round, he cut the cord that was tying my wrists. I did not understand the words he spoke to me, but I hoped that I understood his message: *No more trouble and we will leave you alone.*

It was a small boat, old but of good oak, and with three stained sails, and oars for when we needed them. It was small for the five of us, but I had my own scrap of space. When the sea or the weather got rough, they would shout at each other about what to do next, and at the end of the shouting, we would either head to shore, to hide from the worst of it, or head out to sea, to avoid plunging catastrophically into the shore.

At first, I felt quite unlike myself, with a churning sort of sickness in my belly, and this sickness, for a few days, pressed out all other matters from my mind. But when I thought that only death would be my salvation, the sickness began to pass, and then, miraculously, was gone. For all of this, the leader of the men, the shortest and most powerful of them, who had given me my beating, was often kind, passing me water, or a cloth to wipe myself with if I was sick.

We were at sea for one full passing of the moon. There were days when we kept close to the shore, and I sat mesmerised by the yellow cliffs, the wheeling gulls, and the swell crashing up and over the rocks at the base of the cliffs. There were many more days when we were too far out to see more than the dark of land upon the horizon. My world then was shrunk to the sea, the sky, and to our colourful, overloaded boat, and my stinking companions. In the sky there were the signs of all the weather to come, and I learned to watch each cloud, and eddy upon the water, with great interest. The sea beneath us was sometimes gentle as milk, and at other times threatened to kill us all. Sometimes it boiled with fish, or produced dolphins from its sparkling depths, marvellous and powerful.

We only went ashore at beaches with rivers or springs. The men would fill their water jars and settle their legs, and I was allowed to ramble about as long as I stayed in sight. Sometimes there was forest pressing down upon the beach, and huge and unfamiliar birds, sometimes food to forage: eggs, nuts, coconuts, fruit. Sometimes they let me fish, although I was only given a net and never a spear.

When we were at sea they gave me water every day and dried fish, sometimes fruit if they had it. They kept well back from me whenever they could and there was no more violence between us. Most of the sacks onboard contained dried fish. But also there were animal skins tied up in wedges at the back of the boat, and small chests containing other treasures, tightly strapped down to the floor of the boat. And finally, there was me, a trophy that I do not believe they had planned for.

Trophy that I was, I cannot have looked like much of a prize. I was in a kind of shock, like a fledgling bird that had fallen from its nest. I was in pain from my beating, although my feet were healing. My Potta was gone, and I did not believe I would ever find him again. But over and above that, I struggled to know if what I was seeing and feeling now was real and true. Was this the real world or a terrible dream sent by the gods?

I had always been told that if you go off your own country, you will shrivel and die of the sadness that is not belonging. I knew what that meant now. What was a world without law, without the land that my family had cared for since the dawn of time? What was a world that I had no living connection to? But the days went by, sometimes like a dream that was really not so terrible, when the wind was behind us and I had a full belly, and the sun was bright in a dark sky, and dolphins rushed alongside us, casting at me their holy eye.

And somehow I did live, heartbroken and cast out as I was.

One morning in the distance... the most astonishing thing. A growth upon the shoreline: mountains of a sort I had never seen. Termite mounds, but made by great giants, and all wrong, with sharp lines where there should have been curves. As we got close, I saw there were people all around these mounds, more people than I knew existed in the world. Dozens of boats, just like the one I was in, jostled in and out of the beaches and the long stone structures that snaked out from the land.

I was so astonished that, for a few heartbeats, I forgot to breathe.

The leader of my captors rummaged in the string bag he carried, and produced a piece of cloth, very white and bright.

This he passed to me, and he gestured for me to put it on.

It is nothing to me, what people choose to drape themselves in, but all the same how I did admire that cloth as I tied it across my chest. How gloriously black and lustrous my skin did look against the chalky white.

Soon enough, we were close enough to hear it; the roiling hubbub that these great mounds gave out. On the big stone steps ahead, there was a scene of great activity: people jostling, baskets and pots being passed up.

As our boat came flush with the stone, the leader of my captors took my left arm in one hard hand, and pulled me off the boat with him. My legs seemed all at once to have no strength in them, but he pulled me on. Another man followed us up; the other two stayed with the boat. I found I could not make my calculations. What was the right thing to do here, and what was the wrong? I looked back at the men on the boat, and if I could have, in my alarm then, I might have run back to them.

Instead I was taken up the steps and through a hole in the side of a giant termite mound. Inside there were so many people, all in pieces of dyed cloth of very many colours, and all of them looking so strange to me, like no people I had ever seen. The unfamiliar stink of them hit me hard in the back of my throat.

Pushing through, my captors took me to a large open space inside the mound. Here there were many people shouting, and others tied up to posts. My captors held me out in front of them, and began shouting too. People turned to look at me.

We were there a handful of heartbeats when an old woman came through the crowd to stand before us. She was wrapped from head to foot in black cloth, and she was holding out a small, shining object, that later I knew to be a silver shekel.

I felt my captors let go of me.

What I did not know then, amongst so many things, was that in this new land, here in Sumer, the temples had first choice in the slave markets, by ancient right, and the price they offered, one standard piece of silver, could not be refused.

The old woman crooked one finger at me, turned, and walked off. For a heartbeat I stood just where I was, then slowly, then more quickly, I followed on behind the old woman.

She did not look back at me, but kept on going, and I followed the black hem of the old woman's dress through the shouting, sweating, heaving crowd.

I knew that along that thin line, my life thread ran.

One foot in front of another, I followed on behind the woman.

One step and then the next.

CHAPTER TWO

INANNA

Eight hours, full across the mouth of the estuary, and we were at Eridu, the first city. This is where the king of the gods put up the first temple, when the Anunnaki descended from Heaven.

"Welcome to Eridu," said Enki as he lifted me onto the quay, his face close to mine, his hard hands gripping my ribs.

My grandfather was put on his litter. I followed on behind on a donkey, with Enki's chief minister, Isimud, walking next to me, one hand on my bridle. Isimud kept his hard eyes turned away from me. Four soldiers, carrying between them my basket of lions, followed on behind.

The people of Eridu lined the paved road from the royal wharf up towards the city. They dipped their knees and tipped their faces as our procession passed by, but here or there I caught the flash of an eye as my donkey picked its way past.

Enki gave me a small set of rooms in the Palace of the Aquifer, looking out over the lakes and marshes to the north. It was small but each room was a gem, exquisitely painted with peacocks and pomegranate trees. One room contained a copper bath big enough for me to sit up to my neck in.

On that first afternoon two girls came, eyes down, with water, soap and towels for me. My chests of clothes arrived. The lions fell asleep in their basket.

And then it was only me, sitting on my bed.

Absolutely and truly alone, for the first time in my life.

I went to stand by the bedroom window. It was a small rectangular window, with neat wooden shutters, each hooked back against the inside walls. In the far distance, I could see three canoes, black lines cutting across the marshlands. If I stood on tiptoe and looked down, I could see a neat roof of square red tiles, and a large clay-brick wall beyond. I shut my eyes, searching in my mind's eye for my parents, but I could only tell that they were east of me, and far away.

For a while I watched a luminous praying mantis, very green, her head so elegant, sitting quietly upon one wooden shutter. I had not seen one, up close, since one morning in Ur, with Amnut.

Tears began to tumble from my eyes. For Amnut. For my mother, angry as I was with her. And for myself, and how lost I felt.

A knock at the door. I knew his pull now: Enki.

He had changed into an undyed smock, with a thin crimson rope tied around his waist, and a crimson cloak thrown over.

"Inanna, I thought you would like to see the palace."

"I would love to!" I had only been alone half an hour, and yet I felt so relieved I could have kissed him.

"Shall we bring the lions?" he said. "I could carry one, if you carry the other."

"Oh, yes!" I forgot, in the moment, even to feel nervous of him.

He swept us along the corridor. Long, thin rugs ran along the clay-brick floor; the walls were plastered and painted, white ceilings overhead. The corridor floor undulated a little, rising and then falling, as we made our way along it.

"The palace is so old," Enki said. "Over time it's started to sag a little. But I love it still. You know this is the first building of any significance that we built here. Really it is the oldest building on Earth, at least of any note."

"It is much bigger than our palace in Ur."

"We all lived here, you know, in the first days. The place was thick with Anunnaki. We acted like a family then, although it is hard to believe now."

We turned right, and then left through wide cedar doors into a long hall. The floor was covered in huge wool carpets, all brilliant with colour. "I have collected these from all over the world," he said. "These really, well, you will not find finer weaving anywhere on earth. This one here is from the high steppes." We stood together and looked down at a crimson and blue rug, shot through with white. "Come and see this, though."

We went through another set of doors, and in another long hall there were dozens of tables and upon them clay pots of extraordinary colours, patterns and sheens.

"This one is my favourite," he said.

It was a small marble table, held up by a ram fashioned from gold and lapis lazuli. The ram had its front hooves up on a small, golden huluppu tree.

"I adore it," I said.

"Yes, it's wonderful, isn't it?"

He led me up to huge oak doors that opened out onto a grand terrace. The Palace of the Aquifer was made of the same neat bricks as the rest of the city, but here they were laid down so wonderfully and thoughtfully that each space and each new view felt like a gift. "It's a pleasure just to be in this building," I said to him.

"Yes!" he said. "That's what I intended."

Outside on the terrace the wind had a bite to it, but he took me over to the western side of the balcony to look down at the city. From high you could see the city houses were laid out in squares, with an open courtyard in the middle that you could never have guessed at from the narrow streets. Many had shallow stone pools in these secret places, and little gardens of palms.

"That way, to the west, there is good farmland, but then, if you go far enough, desert." He swung around and pointed north. "That way marshes, vast marshes. We hunt boar there, and hippo, sometimes crocodiles. Also sometimes we hunt the men there. They are a dangerous people. Then if you go far, far to the north, you get to Uruk, where my father An rules. And then east of here is the finest farmland in the world, and the river."

"And Ur beyond."

"Yes, your blessed Ur! Now I am going to show you your favourite place in the palace."

I laughed. "How can you when I do not know what it is yet?"

"I know already what it will be."

We went back past the tables and the rugs, left down a long flight of stairs, and then out through more wide doors. "Not far," he said.

He led me across a damp and muddy courtyard to a high brick wall with a small blue door in it. Enki opened this little door, and let me go through first.

"Oh," I said.

It was a green heaven, thick with trees and flowers, cut through with paths like green tunnels. At the heart of it, in the green shade, was a mosaic-bottomed pool, set about with stone benches. We put down the lions and they at once made their way into the shallow water, one brave paw at a time.

"Oh," I said again. "My favourite place in the palace."

"It's yours," he said. "You can spend as much time here as you like. And I tell you it is much more glorious in the summer; it is a haven."

"Thank you, Grandfather," I said.

He stood looking at me with his head tipped to one side. "Inanna, I know you are going to miss your mother and father very much."

"Perhaps less than you might think," I said.

"Ah. I do not think that will last. So, I say to you now, if you want to see them, tell me, and we will make an expedition of it. We can be there and back in two days if you really need to see them."

"Thank you, Grandfather," I said again, and against my better judgement, I felt a rush of gratitude towards him.

Every night Enki brought the palace together for a grand dinner, and his love of these huge occasions, never waning, drew us all into the dance of the court. Sometimes we ate outside, if it was warm enough, but often we ate in his grand dining hall, decorated all around with the captured chest plates of his enemies, and the heads of giraffes, leopards and zebra, killed in the hunt and stuffed.

From the first night I was put to sit at his left hand. As the plates came round, he served me food from each. Leeks in butter, grilled lamb, boiled greens with lemon juice and salt, all perfectly cooked.

"When will I meet him?" I said.

Enki looked sweetly baffled for a moment. "Who?" he said, leaning an ear to me.

"Your son Dumuzi," I said. "Who I'm to marry."

"Ah!" He sat up straight and ate a piece of lamb. "He's away. He'll be back soon."

I had seen Enki always open and smiling; now he was neither.

It is strange to say now, but in those first weeks in Eridu, Enki was my best friend, and my lions our shared passion. I had no set servants: it was rarely the same girl who dressed me two days in a row. Dumuzi, my husband to be, was away, his absence unexplained. My relatives gave me a wide berth. I knew they were out there; I felt their pull as they moved around the city. But no word came to me from them. I had no occupation, no temple of my own.

All I had was my lions and our magical garden to play in, and almost every day, I had Enki. I was wary of him; how could I not be? Yet I learned to look forward to him arriving at my door.

Who had been his friend before me? I could not work it out. His current wife, a water goddess, was the child of a mortal priestess, although the *melam* ran in her. She was beautiful, you could not say otherwise, yet she seemed like a stranger to him.

Enki seemed to have all the room in the world for me.

My lions were lionesses, and I named them Crocus and Saffron. "Pretty names," Enki said. "For two very deadly creatures."

The lions constantly scratched me and nipped me, until they grew big enough to be more careful of me. I did not like the pain, but I liked to watch how quickly my hands and shins healed.

"What a strange child you are," Enki said. "But I remember doing the same, you know, when I was young: watching myself heal, being interested in it."

Crocus and Saffron slept with me in my bed. If you have not slept with lions, then I recommend it: they are excellent, civilised bed mates, never stirring too early, or taking up too much space.

Everywhere we went, Enki would let the lions ramble along behind us.

I said: "I'm worried that they might hurt someone, even if only in play."

He laughed. "These are not my first lions. As long as you take them very early from their mother, and hand raise them, and then include them in everything, then normally you are all right."

First thing in the morning, Enki would meet in private with his *sukkal* Isimud. I had heard that Isimud was a son of Enki, by a kitchen girl; certainly they were very close. But after that, whatever Enki's business, in the fields, on the canals, in the treasury, in the markets, in temple, my lions and I would be there, trailing after him. "It is a pleasure to teach you the business of this land," he said. "It is a long time since I had a young Anunnaki underfoot."

My lions loved him. After me, he was their most beloved. Enki fed them meat from his plate and gave them collars studded with carnelians. "My beautiful, terrifying girls," he said, and then he would wink at me, to show me that he meant to include me in that.

An invitation came on a small clay tablet, carried to me by a servant on a tray.

Ninhursag, Enki's former wife, was inviting me to come and drink tea with her. Ninhursag had been my mother's stepmother, after my maternal grandmother died in Heaven, and I knew that Ninhursag had been very kind to my mother. But this was also the famous Ninhursag from the stories, Ninhursag of the Anunnaki. Whose girls Enki had punished by raping them.

I said to Enki: "Ninhursag has invited me to her compound."

"Do you want to go?"

"Yes."

"Then go," he said. "You are not my prisoner here."

He ruffled my hair. "Go. I will not be angry. Just come home with some stories and make me laugh later."

"Who should I ask to take me?"

"Ask Isimud. He will be happy to take you."

Isimud, Enki's chief minister, the holy *sukkal*, who commanded the army of Eridu, did not seem happy to take me. All the same, he did it. A phalanx of his personal guard paced out in front of us through the cobbled streets, and I brought along my lions on long leather leads. I had not been outside the palace without Enki, and our expedition, down streets lined with clay-brick houses, had the thrill of an adventure.

Ninhursag lived in a separate compound from the palace; she had her own temple there. In the stories they said Ninhursag had tried to leave Enki, and in return he had meted out brutal violence against her and her girls. Now she stayed in the city, but never came to court. They taught her story in Enki's temples, as a lesson for all the wives.

As we made our way up to the compound gates, servants came rushing to open the woven-willow gates. Inside there was a lush garden of lemon, fig and pomegranate trees, cascading flowering bushes, bougainvillea. Strange palms that I did not recognise, and stone-lined pools of orange fish. The compound servants led us along a cobbled stone path through the vegetation, and then there was Ninhursag, sitting in a chair in the shade, her feet tucked under a blanket. She was dressed in dark grey: her colour.

Ninhursag said to Isimud: "For decency's sake, perhaps you and your killers could wait in the street."

Isimud only stood there, his face impossible to read.

"Go on, Isimud," I said. "You can wait outside for me."

I thought for a moment that he might hit me.

But instead he gestured to his men and retreated.

So here was Ninhursag.

I recognised her from the temple paintings, but she was very changed. I had never seen a god look old before. Ninhursag's dark skin was criss-crossed with lines, like a fishnet, and her long hair was white, and very bright, against the dark grey velvet of her dress.

"I loved your mother," she said, gesturing for me to sit. "I was sorry to see her go, and I am unhappy how rarely she comes back. But I am happy that she has got away from Enki."

"All hail him," I said.

Ninhursag waved the hail away. "I wish I could go and see her, but I am not allowed out now, lest anyone see me and work out that the Anunnaki are not quite as immortal as we are meant to be. I would have liked to have come and seen you, too, after you were born, and to have helped your mother then."

The tea came, and we were quiet until the man had gone.

"Anyway," she said, "I am glad to meet you at last, the famous hostage."

"I'm glad to meet you too," I said, absorbing the word "hostage".

"You should know he has taken all my *mees*. He said he would kill the children otherwise. So, I cannot protect you from him. But we have herbs here, the right medicines. I can help you keep pregnancy at bay."

"Thank you, goddess, but I have no need of protection."

"Inanna, I have invited you to give you these herbs." She looked over her shoulder, and a priestess came forwards with a small parcel, wrapped up in linen, and tied neatly in string. This I accepted, not knowing what else to do.

"You put a pinch of it in your tea, or in your water, first thing in the mornings. It will stop the babies sticking to you. Anunnaki babies don't tend to stick for long, but believe me, you will not enjoy miscarrying them."

I looked down at the parcel in my lap. Might it be poison?

"Tell me about yourself, little goddess."

"I am a goddess of love," I said. I put my hands onto my parcel.

"I never thought I would see another Anunnaki, a new one," she said. "Not here in this realm. This ghastly world is brighter for you, Inanna. Will you try to stay alive?"

"Yes."

"Then take the herbs."

At dinner that evening, without preface, Enki leaned in close to me and said: "You know those girls aren't my daughters. Ninhursag's girls. We found we could not breed together in this realm, and although I did raise them as my children, they were fathered by other men. Everyone says I raped my daughters, but it's a lie. I had sex with *her* daughters, to punish them and to punish her, but I did it in temple; it was all proper. And I did it to keep this family together."

He gave me a look then, out of the side of his eye, that for the first time made me truly afraid of him.

I am a goddess of love, I said to myself, breathing in deep. *A goddess of love.*

"You look very stupid when you look like that," Enki said.

I shut my mouth and said nothing.

I think then he was sorry for snapping at me.

"Inanna, you must understand how young you seem to me. It is difficult for me to take young people seriously. But I should try harder, now we have a young Anunnaki. I will try harder, I promise."

Every evening after dinner, I would go back to Enki's rooms, part of his inner circle. He would sit in his sheepskin-covered chair, right in front of the fire, and the chosen few would sit in a half-circle around him. These half gods and high priests were his most favoured courtiers: the men who ran his city for him. But he always kept a cosy leather chair for me, on his left-hand side. He told funny stories. He talked about the secrets of the gods, about their battles on Earth, and when he was drunk, he would talk about them all arriving here in Eridu, or even about their time in Heaven.

"Do you know the story of my brother Enlil, and his wife Ninlil?" he said that night. "Of when they first met, in Heaven?"

We were six of us in his rooms, but the question was directed at me.

"I only know he first saw her beside a stream, and fell at once in love with her."

Enki bent his head to the right, and to the left, his mouth turned down. "That's sort of true. What your parents and the temple texts have missed out from that, though, is that Ninlil was six years old."

"I did not know that."

He laughed. "Six years old, and my brother conceived such a lust for her that he kidnapped her, then and there. And brought down the fury of the girl's family upon us, then and forever more. These days Enlil is too good to sit at my table, but it was not always so."

He raised a wine glass to us. "To the sky gods in the north," he said. "And their foul predilections!"

That we all laughed at.

Oh, how he made me laugh at first, big open laughs. I felt I had not laughed for an age, until Enki brought it out of me.

At the end of the night, it was often just the two of us beside the fire.

"What did you think of Ninhursag?" he said that night.

"I thought she looked old, for a god."

"Yes." He leaned over to kiss the lion that was sprawling out of my lap. "Do you feel in danger here, little moonbeam?"

"No."

He stood up, took the cubs up by the scruffs of their necks, and put them out in the corridor.

"I've got a new game I would like to play with you," he said.

"What is it, Grandfather?" I kept my hands soft in my lap.

"Come into my bedroom and I will show you," he said.

For some long moments, we looked at each other.

"What are you thinking?" he said, his leopard eyes gleaming in the firelight.

"That I am a goddess of love," I said.

I lifted my chin to him, to show that I was not afraid.

"Come and love me, then," he said, and put out his hand to me.

CHAPTER THREE

GILGAMESH

I lay very still, there on my sliver of a cliff edge, on the side of the great massif, and I thought something I had never thought before: *It would be good to see my father.* Not like this, with me lying in my own filth, shaking with fright that I might fall – no, with us in front of a fire, over wine. To tell him I loved him, and that I was sorry, looking back now, for all the pain I had caused him, when he had done me no wrong other than to love me with all his heart.

And, of course, to be an Anunnaki.

Ask me about the Anunnaki, and I will tell you, having been raised amongst them, and smelled their farts, that they are not quite the gleaming god-creatures you might imagine, had you only seen them in temple. If you took away their ancient weapons, and scraped the *melam* from their veins, they would not be so different from you or me. But that does not mean they are all bad.

My parents came down to this muddy realm with no children,

and my father longed to have one. All he got was me, a weedling mortal, although at first, in my cradle, they thought I might be something more. What a sight I would be to them now, lying here on my back on this slip of a ledge, very cold, in the early dawn. A cliff above me, and, I was fairly certain, a deadly cliff below, although I was reluctant to turn my head to make sure of it.

If my party had been looking for me, I would have seen them by now, or heard them. And so I lay still on my ledge. The vultures, which had been gone in the dusk, now soared overhead again, black against the sky. Three of them. I thought about what a huge and rich meal I would be when the time came. Although the rest of me was a sea of dull pain, I could still not feel my left leg. I crept my hand around on it; it was still there. Only lumpen and numb.

The mouse thing reappeared, looking at me very intently.

"Hello, friend," I said.

Had I been asleep again? I saw a shape above me, very large. A head hanging over. It was Enkidu. Those very bright eyes, sunlit water on sand.

He was climbing down slowly to me, with a rope tied around his waist, although it was hanging slack, and this he kept moving, to stop it catching on the rock face. I could see that he had climbed before, and that he was strong. But I said nothing, for fear I might distract him.

Agonisingly slowly, he made his way to my ledge, touching down about half a cord along from my feet.

"Please tell me now that we are equal," I said, trying to lift up my head to look at him, also trying to smile, although now for the first time I realised that my face was swollen.

"If I get you off here alive," he said, "then I promise you that we will be equal. But not before."

I watched him cautiously untie the rope around his waist, leaning in as much as he could to the cliff.

"Was that a mammoth?" I said. "Humbaba. Was he a mammoth? I did not think there were any left, this far south."

"Well, they're all gone now," he said. "We drove him off the edge."

"I'm sorry for that," I said.

Lying there on my back, but with Enkidu there with me, I felt a rush of sadness, for the monster, for how glorious he had looked for a moment up there on the massif, with his breath white on the air. But also I felt the strangest thing: of intense and unfamiliar happiness, to be just where I was, just there with Enkidu, on this narrow ledge halfway up to the sky.

They felled a mighty cedar, so that they could fashion a proper litter for me. I had to lie there uselessly, watching them.

Harga, who knew something of fixing bones, strapped up my legs. "Can you feel that foot now?"

"A bit now."

"You'll mend," he said. "You always mend quickly. Although you've had your share of bumps and scrapes this month, I will grant you."

"We should keep some cedar for Enlil," I said. "As a gift for his temple."

"And drag it all the way to Marad?"

"Harga, I need to win his favour back!"

"It will take more than cedar," Harga said.

∽

While the men worked on fashioning some planks of wood, Enkidu came and sat with me. He tore me up some dried venison for me to chew on.

"What will you do now that you are free of your blood debt to me?" I said.

"I could go back to Shamhat. But I am not sure that I was born to serve in a temple. For a god who is not mine, you understand. I could go back to the marshes, but I think everyone I know there is dead. Also, I have not sat in a canoe since I was ten years old. And on the marshes, you are always in a canoe."

I ate my meat, watching his face.

He went on, not looking at me: "And I think it might be strange there, living outside this world. Now that I have seen brick houses and tasted good wine. Drunk from silver cups, and seen walls with birds painted on them."

I smiled.

"You know," I said. "You could come with us on to Marad. We are always looking for good men, in the army. I need a body man, as it happens."

"Is it a fine town, Marad?"

I laughed. "I do not believe so. But we go where we are ordered to go. Why not come and see for yourself what it's like? See something of this world. You might even meet the god whose temple you serve in."

"Have you met An? Is he not the king of the gods?"

"Strange as it may sound to you, I grew up with An, in his temple precinct at Uruk. He is as real to me as you are."

I was suddenly desperate that Enkidu would say yes, that he would come with us. But I said nothing more.

Finally, he nodded, slow and serious. "I will come with you."

I had a rush of feeling, a jolt of cleanest joy.

I thought, *Perhaps I can bear it, living only one short life, if this man is here to live it with me.*

As we made our way slowly down the escarpment, the men taking turns to carry me, we passed the mountainous body of the demon Humbaba, the last of his kind, sprawled out on a scree slope, a huge, useless heap of hair and flesh.

Some of the men talked about cutting his tusks off him, if they could get across the scree to where he lay.

"It would be unlucky," I said, raising my voice. "It is unlucky to disturb the bodies of demons."

They seemed happy to believe me, and there was no more talk of disturbing the body.

"He was too big for this world," Enkidu said.

CHAPTER FOUR

NINSHUBAR

And so my life as a temple slave began. I could have shrivelled like a sea-plum in the hot sun, but instead I thrived. We in my spirit clan are hard to kill, when we insist upon living.

The strange and crowded place I found myself in had a name: Eridu.

Many people lived in this city, so many people that I would never know all their names. I had to learn to walk past each new person, when all my instincts told me to stop and ask who they were.

The high walls all around the city protected these people from storms and invaders, and the people grew their food, and hunted, on the river plains outside the walls. This was a camp that they lived in all year round, although it took me a while to understand that.

Indeed, for three full moons I walked everywhere with my mouth hanging open. I was a fool, but I could not be ashamed of it. Chariots, wheeled carts, potteries, kilns, metal making, great factories churning out clay bricks, rivers carved out by human hands: it was a city of wonders. I wanted to know how everything worked, and how everything was done. It is always best to know how to do things.

My new home in this city was a holy place called the Temple of the Waves. Although at first it struck me as a grand and awe-inspiring place, it was in fact an old and simple temple, built a very long time before from clay bricks and roof tiles.

There was one room for the congregation, and behind that a small room for the most secret ceremonies. That secret back room led out into a small yard, with high walls all around. At one end there was an ancient vine, thick and green and trained over a wooden frame, providing shelter for a cooking fire and a few cushioned seats. Along one side of the yard there were four sleeping cells, one of which was given to me.

Yes, it was a simple place, by the standards of Sumer, and yet it had its jewels, which might bear comparison anywhere.

First the paintings, in the main room of the temple. The gods, in these very ancient paintings, looked so real that you felt they might reach out and touch you. Beneath these paintings were the strange patterns, pressed into the wall plaster, that the people of Sumer used to record their most holy secrets.

And then there was the statue. I do not think there was ever a finer statue in all of Sumer. The body was carved from wood, the face from clay, and she had been painted with such vivid realism that she might have been a living woman.

It was a likeness of the goddess who once lived here: the goddess Nammu, queen of the Anunnaki, which is the name the people of Sumer give to the highest gods of their land.

The statue had hair of a kind I had never seen before: golden curls, heaped up high onto her head. The skin was painted a golden brown, the colour of a cheetah, and the eyes, inset with huge gems, were the blue of a midday summer sky. Could Nammu have really looked like that?

It was said that the goddess once slept in one of the cells out in the courtyard at the back of the temple, and in those days, there were many priestesses. But no one expected the goddess to return, and now there was only one priestess here: the woman in black, who had bought me for one shekel. Her name was Dulma.

Dulma was a good woman, but she was infuriated, in the early days, by what she saw as my stupidity. Why did I not know how to use a bath house? Why did I insist on sleeping outside? Why could I not be trusted to make a simple pot of tea? And why, above all things, was I so slow to learn Sumerian?

I did struggle with the language. In my own country, I was known to be a superb linguist. I spoke fourteen languages, some of them known to only a handful of people. All the same, the Sumerian came quite slowly to me at first. The names of some plants and animals, and some foods, were familiar. Everything else made no sense to me until I had forced myself to learn it. It was an ugly language.

"When you hear the gods speak it," Dulma said, "you will not think it ugly."

Dulma told me that the gods of Sumer walked about on the streets, just as men did, even in the heat of the day. They did not hide in dark caves, as the gods did in my own country. Here they were more like tribal leaders than gods. They spoke to people, face to face. Therefore, I must speak their language: that first over everything.

Dulma had bought me from the market to be the temple orphan, which meant cleaning, cooking and fetching water. But when I had been there a handful of moons, a man came in off the front steps of the temple with a look of ready violence in him. I thought, *Better do it quick.* So I shoved him, kicked his legs out from him, and put him down hard on the ground.

After that Dulma gave me an eight-pointed star, the sign of Nammu, carved out of hippo ivory. She tied it to my neck with a thin piece of leather.

"Now you are the protector of the temple."

I was still a slave, but a better sort of slave.

"I will need knives also, if I am to protect this place," I said. "I will make my own if I can find the right stone. I am a master flintknapper."

"No doubt you are," said Dulma.

In the afternoon ceremonies, beneath Nammu's exquisite statue, Dulma would kill a cat, or a pigeon, on the little clay-brick altar, and say the prayers that were sacred to the goddess. Then she would daub the animal blood on the foreheads of the small band of worshippers who still came to the temple. Most were old fishermen and their wives, praying for sons who were out on the water.

"You know if we had a real god to cut, then many more would come," Dulma said.

"Would a god let you cut them?" I said, very surprised.

"Yes, it is a common rite. They heal quickly, because of the *melam* they have in them."

"I should like some *melam*," I said. "I would like to heal quicker."

Dulma laughed. "Not only you, Ninshubar."

So I had been told of the gods. But they were not real to me, until one day I came out with my broom to sweep around the altar and there was a man there, kneeling down in front of Nammu's statue.

A man, but not a man.

He had rich brown hair, very straight, a beard close cut, and dark brown skin, with a strange green sheen to it, which lay thin and tight over his muscles.

The man looked up at me with the eyes of a leopard, and I felt the power ripple off him, wave after wave.

On the wall directly behind him was the painting of a man who looked just like him.

Enki.

Nammu's son.

His bare arms were strung with many heavy bracelets, made of some ancient metal. His clothes were a thing of quite extraordinary beauty. He was dressed in a cloth that had been dyed blood red, and then beautifully, intricately stitched into panels and layered skirts that moved over each other so seamlessly and elegantly as he stood to look at me. How many people had it taken, and how long, to make these clothes?

"You're new," Enki said. It was the first time I had heard an Anunnaki speak, the strange accent they had. "And you are tall. Quite something."

He was tall, too, and I could see that he was dangerous.

My hands moved, involuntarily, to my knives.

"Handsome, too," he said, "if one doesn't mind a scar or two."

I heard Dulma behind me.

"No one is going to call *you* new," Enki said to the priestess.

"No, my lord," Dulma said.

"No sign of my mother, then?" he said.

"No, my lord," Dulma said.

"I'm joking," he said, laughing. "I imagine that you might have told someone if the mother of the Anunnaki suddenly appeared!"

"Yes, my lord," Dulma said, doing an awkward bow, but with her eyes still on him.

Enki looked up at the statue of Nammu, her sapphire eyes very bright in the dark gold of her face, and around at the small clean room with its stamped-earth floor. Then his eyes settled at last upon me.

"You've looked after this place well," he said.

"Thank you, my lord," Dulma said.

"I did not intend to be away so long," he said, looking up again at the statue of his mother.

"No, my lord," she said.

"I will be in temple tomorrow," Enki said. "For the full rites. I will send a priest for you both, and you will have seats at the front."

"We are honoured, my lord," Dulma said.

When Enki had gone, Dulma said to me: "Perhaps we will see the moon goddess that they call Inanna."

"Who is Inanna?"

"She is the new Anunnaki. Born in Ur, now brought here to marry Enki's son."

"And why do we want to see her?"

"They say she is destined for greatness," Dulma said. "I would like to put my eyes on her, that is all. There might be luck in it."

When I saw the inside of the Temple of the Aquifer, with its army of priests, in blood-red robes, and its great arching ceilings, then I saw that I had not yet understood the scale of the city that I lived in. As we pressed forwards through the crowds, the smoke and the incense, I walked with my head tipped back, trying to take in all the paintings on the walls and columns.

At the front of the temple, before the altar, someone had set up what looked like a bed. It was covered in rich, red cloth, and with many shining pillows.

A priest pointed us to a wooden bench right there in the front, and Dulma and I found ourselves sitting only an arm's length from the bed.

"What is going to happen?" I whispered to her.

"You will see," she said, with a knowing arch of one eyebrow.

Well, I did see. The god Enki appeared from behind the altar, and a heartbeat later, a woman appeared beside him. A thin, dark woman, with jewels tied into her long, straight hair.

Heartbeats later, priests appeared around each, and then the two gods stood there naked.

When I saw what they were going to do next, I nearly laughed out loud.

Then I only stared.

I had never seen anyone have sex before, only heard people doing it in the dark.

Now these two gods had sex before me on a bed that I could have leaned out and touched. They were so close I could smell the heavy oils they had been daubed in, and, later, the smell of their sex.

At first a sexual thrill went through me, but after a while, I only felt awkward, and bored. Then came the shock again.

Once a month, when he was in the city, the great god Enki lay with his wife in the Temple of the Aquifer, with all the gods of the city, and all the priests, and as many others as could cram into the temple, all watching. He did this so that the sun and the moon would continue to rise over the Earth; so that the crops would come; so that the river would flood: this was the law in this country.

Sometimes it was his wife, sometimes one of her priestesses; sometimes instead he would pull out a woman from the congregation, and she would be honoured. Sometimes young brides would be brought to him, before they went to their new husbands. But today it was the turn of his wife and she lay before me receiving his attentions with no expression at all upon her face.

It did remind me of the secret places, of the ceremonies that only the elders are meant to ever see, and I saw that it was holy work to these people. For his part Enki appeared to do it with relish, and endless patience, and all the while I could have reached out one hand and touched the cloth of the great bed they were lying on. At one point, I found myself looking straight into Enki's eyes. Again, I had to stifle shocked laughter.

Enki warmed to his task. Drums began; the priests began chanting. The crowd shouted encouragement, even breaking into applause.

At one point a group of women came forwards to sing a hymn.

"Our lord is the honey man," they sang, their hands held aloft. "He is the one her womb loves best. He who ploughs her, ploughs her well!"

Enki entwined himself around the goddess. I looked up amidst the huge columns; all over the temple walls, there were paintings of him doing exactly this.

Dulma whispered to me, and pointed: there was Inanna, the little moon goddess that everyone was so eager to see. Inanna sat unsmiling on the benches to our right, with two young lions sitting neatly in front of her. She was very small compared to the soldiers who sat either side of her. As I looked, she turned her eyes to me.

Her eyes were the black of a night sky that had been robbed of all its stars.

They gave out no light at all.

A great shudder went through me, of fear, but also of a high emotion I could not yet name. I looked away quickly.

Afterwards I said to Dulma: "These gods are not like the gods in my country."

Dulma stifled a yawn. "I can tell you they are not."

"Do you think his wife enjoyed it?" I said. "She seemed so limp, like a dead rabbit."

"This is their duty," the priestess said.

As we walked back to the Temple of the Waves, through the crowded, dusty streets, she said: "Ninshubar, he may call you to temple. You should be prepared for that."

"Why?"

"He likes strangeness. He likes to mix up new blood in his stock. If he picks you, Ninshubar, you must go with him."

I heard what she said, but I already knew: I would never submit to that.

In the afternoon, I went down to the slave market.

Dulma sent me out at this time every day to buy food for our dinner. Normally she would send me for vegetables and some lentils, but after the Temple of the Aquifer, she seemed to be in the mood for a celebration, and she said: "Tonight we will eat fish. Get some small ones and make sure they are fresh. And some mountain greens, fill up a basket, and get two lemons and some salt."

So I went out into the streets with a round basket over one arm, and a pot tucked inside that for the fish, and my temple chits in my pocket to pay for it all.

Dulma often said to me: "Why don't you run away from me, if you are such a good runner? What is holding you here when you can run like the wind? When you are the greatest runner the world has ever seen?"

I would say nothing. Now I went down to the slave market, on my way to the food market, just as I did every day. I crouched on a wall, and began my process. I would look at the face of every merchant, as carefully as I could, looking for a face that I recognised. And then when I had finished looking at the slavers, when I was sure I had seen every one of them, I would look at the face of every slave. I must not miss a face. Most of the slaves were captured soldiers and villagers from the north: spoils of the war against King Akka. But some, you could see, were not from the north. They had been snatched from further away. These were slaves I looked at most closely.

Because what if the men came through again, and I was not there to ask them: what became of my Potta? Did you kill him, or is he still in the world?

Or what if the Potta was brought through this market, and I was not there to find him and save him?

That day, as every day, the men from the boat were not there. My Potta was not there. So, I walked on with the basket, to buy some fish, and greens, and some salt and two lemons.

CHAPTER FIVE

INANNA

Finally, without warning or fanfare, Dumuzi, my future husband, was at court. I felt a strange sensation of the new, two unfamiliar pulls upon my bones. And then I arrived on the dinner terrace one early spring evening, and there he was, in the seat to the left of mine. Behind his chair, in the moonlight, his two famous sheep hounds sat, black sentinels, with their knife-sharp ears and long, thin noses. I was glad I did not have my lions with me.

Dumuzi was even taller than his father, very fine looking. His skin was a burnished bronze. He had a small black mole near his mouth, and dark freckles across his nose.

Oh, he was as handsome as people said he was. But there was no cheer in him.

On his left sat his sister, Geshtinanna. I did not need to be told who she was: she was almost exactly like him, the same height even, and very elegant in how she held herself. They were the half-god offspring of two different priestesses, but they shared a father in Enki.

"Has he hurt you?" Dumuzi asked as I sat down. Those were his first words to me. "My father. Has he hurt you?"

"No. He hasn't hurt me."

A servant leaned between us with a plate of fried fish.

"The man has habits," said Dumuzi. "Tastes."

"Well," I said. "They have not yet extended to me."

Dumuzi shook his head, flicking his eyes at me; they were darker than his father's. "Sometimes he likes to wait, until you really think you're safe."

Geshtinanna, hidden from me behind her brother, snorted with laughter.

Around the fire, in the evenings, Enki was different.

"So what do you think of Inanna?" he said, on the night Dumuzi first appeared.

Dumuzi looked at his father and said: "She is the beauty of the Earth and Heaven."

"Yes, isn't she," said Enki. "The moon and the sun in one."

I could tell that he had already been drinking.

"Maybe I should keep her for myself," Enki said to Dumuzi. "And you could have her mother. She is after all a sister to you, and you do like sisters, don't you?"

Enki turned to me. "Would you like that, Inanna? Would you like to marry me instead?"

"Whatever you think best, Grandfather," I said.

Despite everything, despite myself, I could not suppress some sort of feeling of pride.

Enki smiled, and put a hand out to the top of my head.

"You're a good girl really, Inanna," he said.

All the warmth that had been in him was gone.

I looked over at Dumuzi, but he kept on looking straight into the fire.

Dumuzi's sister, Geshtinanna, my future sister-in-law, came to look at me being dressed.

My dressing chamber was tiny, and Geshtinanna filled up the doorway as she watched me, her head on one side.

"He could marry me, you know. It would be quite proper. We are not even full siblings."

"Go ahead, marry him. If that is what Enki wants, and what Dumuzi wants."

Geshtinanna looked a little sly then. "Enki thinks you are a strange one and a snake. He doesn't want you as his daughter-in-law."

I lifted my chin so that my servant could fasten a string of gold beech leaves around my neck. "Geshtinanna, who do you think you are fighting here? I am thirteen years old. I am entirely powerless. If you want Dumuzi, you must ask Enki for him. What can I do to change what is going to happen?"

I turned to look at her full on. "I am not much of an enemy, Geshtinanna."

"Oh, I know that," she said, her lovely shoulders slumping. "I know you are nothing in this."

Enki no longer called for me to come about with him on his business, and I spent my days alone. But then Ninhursag invited me to tea for a second time.

I said to Isimud: "Let others walk me there. You are a *sukkal*. Why should you be waiting in the streets for me?"

But he took me there himself.

In the luscious garden, two of Ninhursag's servants brought us trays of wild mountain tea, and sweet almond biscuits. She was dressed in dark grey again, but this time in a dress made from silk, and stitched with small pearls. From the corner of one eye, I watched a stag beetle make her way across the path towards the pond, and I felt a flood of sadness that Amnut could not be there with me to see it.

When the servants were well clear of us, Ninhursag said: "I am speaking out of turn here, and I am foolish to do so, but you prick at my conscience."

"How so?"

She did not answer that directly. "I want to know if you have a plan, or if you are only a passenger."

"I am a boat upon the sea. I go where Enki's waters take me."

I held Ninhursag's eyes.

"I am submitting," I said. "I am a goddess of love, and I submit. That's all."

"Well, little love goddess in a boat," Ninhursag said, "you sound hardly worth saving, if what you say is true. I will nonetheless give you an old-fashioned warning, because of the love I have for your mother, who was my daughter for many years, after Enki's first wife died."

"I know."

"What you do not know is that something has happened. I don't know what. But something has happened to make Enki desperate, and desperation makes him dangerous. I warn you because your mother was good to me after my fall from grace, when there was nothing in it for her."

I sipped her sweet green tea. I had a mouthful of questions, but I knew that questions did not count as submission. Would this woman go straight back to Enki with stories about me?

In the end the lust to know more was too much for me. "Lady Ninhursag, these gods here, Dumuzi now, Enki before, they are always coming and going. Not just now. It has been happening for years." I leaned forwards in my chair. "Why do they keep coming and going as they do? Where has Dumuzi just been, for so long, with his sister? Where was Enki for so many years? Where is Nammu now?"

"The passenger at least has her eyes open, then." The ancient goddess nodded. "Yes, they come and go because Enki is looking for things. Things that we lost in the first days. Several things. But the problem they have now is that they are short of *melam*."

"We are born with our *melam*," I said, my hand going to my belly.

"But it doesn't last forever. Look at me. We used to have supplies, ample supplies, for when the *melam* in our veins began to run out. But they've wasted it, on half gods, on mortals, on trying to make Anunnaki babies – babies like you. The sky gods in the north ran out years ago, but here in the south there were scraps left. Now there is this ugly squabble for the last of it, and it is going to lead us down into another war."

She looked very tired then. "You know your mother should have told you all this. Even you, one day, will need more *melam*. Or you will have to accept going the way of the humans."

I drew myself upright. "My mother did not tell me."

I am a goddess of love.

"Are you angry with her for that?"

"She must have had her reasons."

"I see a lot of anger in you, goddess, flickering there beneath the surface."

"No, no." I sat very still, my hands soft in my lap, and gave her my warmest smile.

"Are you angry with your parents because they let Enki take you?"

"I am a goddess of love," I said. "I have only love in my heart."

She looked at me hard, but then blinked her eyes away, shrugging.

"Thank you for my warning," I said. "I am grateful to you for it, although I do not know what to do with it."

She stretched out her crooked hands. "Soon there will only be our statues left, and all the real gods will be gone. Except you. You will have a few hundred years on us, before you too start to fade." She nodded at me, as if dismissing me; I could see that she had had enough.

But then she said: "You know, in the first days, it was Enlil we were worried about, after the thing with the little girl. But then he became all duty, and since then it has been Enki who has been the trouble."

I did not know how to answer that. I stood, sat down again. "What does *melam* look like," I said, "if I should ever happen to find some?"

"It's a black powder, like kohl. You only need to eat a spoon of it, and *boof*. It has demons in it that cut away the old age inside you. So, if you find it, keep some for me!"

"I will keep an eye out for some."

"You do that, little goddess. It's the most precious stuff in the world."

I almost ran into Dumuzi as I made my way back to my rooms. We stood and looked at each other a moment, me with Isimud and my guards behind me, my lions baring their teeth at him. It was unnerving to me sometimes, how handsome Dumuzi looked.

"I hear you have been visiting," he said.

"What of it?"

"He likes to give people the chance to destroy themselves. And it seems you are stupid enough not to see it."

I put my hands onto my hips. "Thank you for your counsel, lord of the sheep."

"At least one can eat a sheep. What can one do with love?"

"Perhaps your sister can tell you," I said.

As I made my way past him in the corridor, I made a little lamb noise, a small bleat. I did not look back to see if he had heard it, but I smiled to myself as I walked on.

At my door, Isimud said to me: "I wonder at you, making a mockery of him, a man who may soon have so much power over you."

I gave him a little shrug, my mouth turned down. "I will take my admonishments from Enki," I said, "but I do not believe I have to take them from you."

Then I shut the door on him.

I should not have spoken to Dumuzi as I had. I should not have bleated at him. I should not have spoken sharply to Isimud. I was breaking my sacred promise to my mother.

Sometimes it was hard, though, to keep so much anger hidden.

CHAPTER SIX

GILGAMESH

"Gilgamesh?" It was Enkidu, just his head around my door. "Wake up. They're here. It's begun."

"I am coming," I said, turning my face back into my pillow.

"I can see you are doing nothing of the sort."

I was so comfortable, and sleep was still so close. "Give me one minute."

"Gilgamesh, the enemy is here! We are under siege!"

I turned to look at him. "What on earth are you wearing, Enkidu?"

He had on his head something not much unlike a saucepan, made from what looked like beaten copper.

"It's a helmet," he said. "Harga said my leather cap wouldn't do, for real battle."

"Harga is having fun with you," I said. "All right, go, I will be there in two minutes."

∽

I wrapped a strip of linen around my waist, and I made my way barefoot out of the barracks, the men politely stepping aside for me. My left leg was still stiff and painful from my fall in the cedar forest, but it eased out as I walked.

Marad was a small city, and poor. It had one claim to fame and one only: that it squatted, like an ugly yellow toad, upon the main road from Kish to Nippur. To get into the heart of Sumer, you must either pass close enough to Marad to be picked off by arrows, or track many leagues out of your way. And so Marad, in theory, commanded a trade route.

But there was theory, and there was Marad. Its battlements were sunken and undulating, although topped, in an uneven loop, with a thin line of clay-brick wall. Not many arrows flew out over the road from Marad, whether the caravans stopped to pay their taxes or simply trundled past.

Rather wishing I had brought a cloak, I made my way up the eastern embankment. I had a table and three stools up there, under a cloth shade, and that was my command post.

The embankment was about a cord wide there, and I could sit and look out most comfortably over the track that led out of Marad and then intersected with the main north–south road.

The sun was just coming up over the hills as I looked out at the valley. Straight away I could see movement. There were men dropping down out of the rocks on the far edge of the main road. More men were coming south down the road from Kish, and over to the west, on the other side of the river, I could see a small force moving into position along the banks. I wondered how they'd made the crossing, and where.

Akka, my old friend from Kish, had brought every man he had against us, and as the sun gained power I saw columns of his soldiers snaking dark across the home farms.

Enkidu came climbing up the bank to me, in his ludicrous saucepan-hat. He had his two enormous stone battle-axes slung across his back.

"Stop laughing," he said. "There is nothing wrong with it."

"We should eat," I said. "Before something more dramatic happens. Something more dramatic than that cap, I mean."

"Ho, ho," he said.

We both stopped to look up as three swans flew over them, their wings beating such a loud *woomf woomf woomf* into the morning air. "A good omen," I said. "Since you like omens so much. Swans are sacred to my father."

"Do you really want food?" Enkidu said. "What if they attack?"

"Then I will fight like this," I said, straightening my piece of cloth. He shook his head at me.

As we ate our porridge, and drank our morning beer, we watched as Akka's men began unloading wagons just to the north. Meanwhile the frontline soldiers were taking up their positions below us, settling along the edge of a disused barley field.

It was curiously intimate, peaceful too, despite the overtly warlike nature of the occasion. There was something magical about the quality of the sound in the morning air. Marad was rammed full, with every last farmer for a league crammed inside its walls. And yet I felt I could hear everything that was happening out in the valley. I heard crows giving the alarm in a distant field, and thought, *Oh, the army of Kish is putting birds up before it*. I could hear dogs barking, far off: I'd been told they brought their dogs to battle. Now and again, I thought I could hear an enemy soldier shouting out an order.

"Remarkable," I said out loud, shaking my head at the strangeness of it. "It's my first siege," I said, turning to Enkidu. "Have you been in one before?"

"I've been surrounded and attacked, a few times now, but it was always over quick."

"No, I don't think that counts. I think there need to be walls involved, and some sort of formal standoff, for it to be a siege."

I had barely finished my porridge when I saw a mule trotting southwards down the high road, and then turning right onto the short stretch of track into Marad. The man on the mule was wrapped in scarlet, the colour of an envoy, and to make the point even clearer, he was holding a stick with a scarlet flag tied to it.

There was something oddly familiar about the listless way in which the man was holding his stick. I had a burst of recognition: it was Akka's nephew, Inush.

It made me smile, the way he sat on his mule, as if he was out for a picnic, but a very boring one. I wondered if he was still angry with me over what had happened with Hedda.

Three priests rode behind him on asses, and they were also cloaked in scarlet. They were shaking rods and flails and singing what sounded like a hymn to the holy An, which was a bit much, really, given that it was An's city, strictly speaking, that they were in the midst of besieging.

"The boy on that mule is Inush. He was my guard in Kish."

"He looks young to be sent to us as an envoy."

"No, he's our age, I think. Eighteen or nineteen."

As Inush drew close enough for us to admire his saddle cloth, the gate opened below us with a creak. I peered over the wall: Tomasin, the chief priest of Marad, was going out to meet the envoys of Akka.

Tomasin walked huddled over in his black robes, with his under-priests and a gaggle of assorted city elders following on behind him.

It was really the most unforgivable affront imaginable, a gargantuan insult, for them to be going out there without consulting with me. But I could not feel too annoyed, having told my men, just the evening before, that Tomasin would try to surrender the very minute the enemy crept into view. I had even offered to bet on it.

"You did say," said Enkidu, who knew how much I liked to be right.

The two parties drew up in front of each other, about a quarter of a league from the city walls, each fanning out into a small semi-circle. The details of the diplomatic discussion were lost to the morning air, but it looked to me as if Inush had the best of it. He stayed on his mule and seemed palpably unmoved by the discussion; meanwhile, Tomasin waved his arms, and at one point got down on his knees.

"Do you think you could hit one of them with an arrow?" I asked.

"I might just get one into Tomasin."

We both chuckled.

Moments later Inush turned his animal around and, giving it a bit of kick, trotted off. His priests were quick to follow him. The esteemed priests and elders of Marad, after a moment looking out after the retreating envoys, crept back into the city.

I watched the envoys of Akka as they trotted north towards what was rapidly becoming the enemy camp. "How many, do you think?"

"I would say two full banners," said Enkidu. "And maybe another half-banner of followers in the camp. Too many for us."

"I was thinking we could arm the boys, and the farmers."

"We will struggle to put three hundred men out, even if we make the priests fight. Even if we put a sword in Tomasin's hand."

We both smiled at the thought of Tomasin with a sword in his hand.

"They are too many for us," Enkidu repeated.

The gate below opened up for the elders, then closed again on their heels.

"Do you think they have actually surrendered?" asked Enkidu.

"I think they will have had a good stab at it. But they will not have liked Akka's terms. You know in some ways, Akka and I did not part quite as friends."

"Is that so?" said Enkidu. "How you astonish me."

"I see Harga has been gossiping to you, then."

"Everyone in this city knows the story of you and Akka!" he said. "I am forever being told of your exploits. Harga has no need to tell tales."

"Well, I am happy to entertain you all so," I said.

As I finished my breakfast-beer I kept one eye on the enemy without, and the other on Tomasin and his henchmen as they made their way, with some difficulty, up to my command post. Having gained the top of the walls, they were prevented by the narrow and crumbling nature of the embankment from standing abreast, and were instead forced to form a queue in front of us, leaning heavily on the outer wall for their own safety.

"Gilgamesh," said Tomasin – he broke off for a moment as it became clear to him that I wasn't dressed yet, and also that I was sharing my food with my servant – "Gilgamesh, out of respect for your father, the lord god Lugalbanda, I am here to tell you that we are going to settle."

"Settle?"

"Surrender," he said. "The envoys of Akka have promised to spare all our lives if we will open the gates."

"And what else?"

Tomasin wiped his hands on his black skirts. "And we must hand you over."

"Me?"

Tomasin held my eye quite manfully. "They intend to execute you. For crimes you committed as a hostage in Kish."

I looked down, as if considering this deeply, and then said: "No surrender."

"Gilgamesh," said Tomasin, in his most pompous voice. "This is not up to you. As chief priest, I am in charge here. I have been steward of this city for fifteen years, and it is my decision."

"No."

"You cannot stop us."

"Tomasin." I stood up. I regretted not being in my armour now. "Tomasin. I am the steward. Enlil sent me to take command here, and on the day he sent me here, Enlil said to me: 'Do not on any count surrender to that man Akka.' Those were his exact words. And hot-headed as you may think me, I am in the habit of obeying the holy Anunnaki."

Tomasin's hands seemed to spasm into fists. "We have four hundred extra souls to feed – because of you. If you wanted to win this, you should have left the farmers to their fate in the fields."

"All the same, though, we will not be surrendering. Setting aside, just for a moment, my direct orders from the lord of the sky, I do not believe in this promise of all lives spared that Akka has made to you. And most importantly, nor will my men when they get to hear about it. Everywhere he goes, Akka kills the fighting men when he takes them captive, as is very well known." My voice was raised now.

"Gilgamesh!" He was almost shouting. "Gilgamesh, with every day that passes, the terms will get worse. You know how he does things. And if you really need another reason, think about this: Enlil could just as well kill you for refusing to surrender. One cannot predict the whims of the gods!"

He was right about that, but ah well.

"Tomasin. Hear me. We are not going to bend our knee to the house of Kish. That is not going to happen. We are not going to spend one moment with our heads bent to that donkey's arse of a king. The great gods protect us," I added, with a devout nod.

"The great gods are not here to do anything!" Tomasin stormed. "If they were, I would not be standing here, begging you not to throw away all of our lives on some impulsive plan! I know you were sent here as punishment for your carousing and drinking, and now we are all going to be punished in our turn!"

I looked around for Harga, and found him watching the scene from below, his black curls tucked behind his ears. "Harga," I called down, "arrest this man."

"Yes, my lord." He stood up from his camp chair in a tolerably brisk manner, whistling for his boys.

I climbed up onto the wall, and looked out to see Inush, thinking maybe I would try to wave hello to him, but the envoys of Akka had already disappeared from view.

For three days Akka's men came at us, always in the morning but sometimes again when the afternoon was cool. For three days we threw rocks, spears, pots, whatever we had, down at the men of Akka, and slashed at every arm that popped through or over the wall. And for three days our supplies of rocks, spears and pots dwindled. The city began to get hungry. There were no more breakfasts on the walls.

"They are holding back," Enkidu said. "Is it to save their men?"

"They didn't expect us to be here," I said. "They are still feeling us out."

On the fourth day, the Akkadians managed to get men over the wall, and they were almost at the main city gates before they were hacked down. Their bodies were tipped off the western walls, straight down into the Euphrates.

Harga said to me: "Presuming you have a plan, sir, it might be time to put it into action."

"You are quite right, Harga," I said, ignoring the rudeness of that word "presuming". "It is time we negotiated. But this time let's send a soldier, not Tomasin. I will need a volunteer – an envoy to send out."

Enkidu stepped forwards at once. "I'll go and talk to Akka," he said.

"No," I said.

But at the same moment Harga said: "Bravely done, Enkidu. Thank you."

In that moment, in front of Harga and the men, I could not find the words to stop it happening. "Find him something scarlet to wear," I said, looking away.

Out Enkidu went, large and heavy on a donkey. "That is not a happy ass," said Harga.

They had fashioned him a cape, of sorts, out of some sort of scarlet cloth.

"Could he not have walked?" I said.

"It was felt it was more envoy-like, my lord, for him to be mounted," said Harga.

I saw them letting him through the front line, and watched his agonisingly slow progress as his donkey trotted north along the road and up onto the plateau towards the now familiar landmark of Akka's royal tent.

Akka himself came forwards to greet our envoy: I saw the flash of his azure blue. Then the distant patch of scarlet that was Enkidu was swallowed up by a swirl of Akka's men.

Oh my lord Enlil, in your divine mercy, please protect him.

"They wouldn't hurt an envoy, would they?" I said to Harga, keeping my voice light.

Harga shrugged. "I would, if I was told to."

I turned on him in some fury.

"He was not the man for this," I said. "It is your fault he is out there."

Harga waited a moment, his face expressionless, and then said: "He stepped forwards very bravely, sir."

"Why are you still here?" I said. "You should be gone by now."

In the afternoon they brought Enkidu down onto the track into Marad. When they were sure I was watching, they battered him from head to foot. Akka did it himself, with Inush. They took turns to kick him and hit him with clubs, and the sound of their assault on him, of the crack of their weapons against his precious bone and flesh, and their grunts as they swung at him, and Enkidu's cries, forced out of him, were carried to me very clearly upon the afternoon air. The ground beneath them grew dark with blood, but they did not stop.

Every now and again, Akka would break off, and look up at Marad, searching for me on the walls.

"Can you hear what he's saying?" I said to the men behind me. I realised I'd been holding my breath.

One of Harga's boys stepped forwards, swallowing. "My lord, I think he's saying, 'I'm going to fucking kill you, Gilgamesh.'"

"Ah," I said. "Thank you."

When it had gone on so long that Enkidu must surely be dead, they dropped him in the dust, and retreated.

CHAPTER SEVEN

INANNA

Isimud brought me the news.

Enki had decided: Dumuzi would marry me now, and we would go north, and rule Uruk together. The city at the centre of the earth.

"But Uruk belongs to An," I said.

"That's all over," he said. "An has left the city. Uruk goes to Dumuzi now."

"And you, I mean," he added, but I took no offence.

There was to be a formal betrothal ceremony, in Enki's own temple, with all of the Eridu gods there, even Ninhursag and her daughters.

"You will marry here, and then travel north, to set up your temple," Enki said. He did not mention his father, An, whose city it was.

"Yes, my lord," I said, smiling up at him.

"Yes, Father," said Dumuzi, his face a blank.

Dual preparations went on. Firstly, I must be dressed for a holy wedding. On my head I would wear the famous *shugurra*, the gold crown that had been Nammu's, in the first days. I would wear a chest plate moulded from bronze, and etched with the famous wild bull of Heaven. I would wear a great necklace of lapis lazuli that I had brought with me from Ur. I would carry a quiver carved from ivory. My wings would be fashioned from the feathers of giant eagles. The thinnest cloth must be found, the finest turquoise, the softest leather. My lions would wear special headdresses, studded with carnelians. It is not every day an Anunnaki gets married.

Secondly, I must be prepared for the sacred marriage bed. This was done in private, in Enki's temple. Two priestesses were tasked with ensuring that I did not disgrace myself on the day. The senior priestess supervised; the younger priestess took the part of Dumuzi, with a stick tied round her waist, as a pretend penis.

"You need to show emotion," the older priestess said. "They won't know what to expect, whether you will be nervous, overwhelmed, excited. But they will expect something."

"I will give them something," I said.

"And when he enters you, you should shout out," the young priestess said, climbing off me to better make her point. "Scream, moan, make a big fuss."

"Yes, scream out," said the senior priestess. "As if you are going to die from pleasure. You cannot be too loud. You must shout and shout, scream all you like. No one will ever think it is too much."

"I was raised for this," I said. "I know what my duty is. I have seen the sacred rites done, perhaps a thousand times."

"But it is different when it is you," the priestess said. "It's easy to forget your part. That is why we practise."

I climbed on top of the younger girl. "Oh, my gorgeous vulva!" I roared. "Oh, my tiny breasts!"

The priestesses both burst into laughter. "But that is very good," the older priestess said, wiping away a tear. "Very good. Do it just like that but push your chest out more."

"You will do well," the young one said.

"I know that," I said. "I am not afraid."

My brother the sun god came south for the wedding. He had some business first with Enki. But afterwards he came to look at me in my green garden in the palace.

Utu had grown even more grand since I had last seen him in Ur.

"I think this is a good match for you," he said, "as good as we could expect."

"Kind words, brother. I thank you."

He looked down at my lions, both now long-legged and half grown. They were trying to nip at his ankles, but found themselves clawing at empty air, and tipping backwards, each time they leaped towards him.

"Is that one of your *mees*, protecting you?" I said. "Is that why they can't bite you?"

"Of course it is," Utu said. "One would think you were brought up in the wilds."

"I have never seen a *mee* doing that before," I said.

"And yet every god in this city wears a *mee* that can do this. Enki must have roomfuls of them. You might try asking for one."

"I do not need protection from my lions."

186 EMILY H. WILSON

He shook his head. "Inanna, there are other dangers in this world, far more dangerous than lions."

Utu came back to Enki's rooms after dinner that night. They seemed to know each other well. Enki pressed Utu for news of the war in the north, and Utu told us that Akka continued to put out farmers onto land that was Anunnaki, and that violence continued to flare in towns along the front.

"Akka no longer believes in the supremacy of the Anunnaki," Utu said. "He believes that if he is clever about it, he can absorb all of Sumer into his empire."

I waited as long as I could bear to, and then I asked after my cousin Gilgamesh.

My brother frowned at me. "He was always a hero to you, that awful boy."

"I heard he was taken hostage," I said.

"She has sympathy now with hostages," Enki said, laughing.

My brother watched Enki laughing, but did not laugh himself. "He's no longer a hostage. The last I heard he was at Marad, with King Akka almost at the gates. I imagine he's dead. Akka has sworn to kill him."

"That's a shame," Enki said. "He had a flair that one does not often see in a mortal."

"And how your brother Enlil does love him," Utu said.

Enki put on the face that he always put on when anyone mentioned his brother: a polite half smile, one eyebrow raised. "Yes, my brother does love him," he said.

I saw him weighing up whether to say more, and then giving in to the impulse. He said to me: "One day you will meet your grandfather Enlil and think him a very fine man, Inanna. But when you do, try to remember that it is only because of Enlil that we are all here."

"Here in Eridu, Grandfather?"

"No, here on Earth, of course." He sat back in his chair. "You still see him, don't you, Utu?"

Utu took a deep swig of wine. "I keep close to all my family. There are so few of us left."

The great day dawned: the wedding of Inanna and Dumuzi, goddess of love and the shepherd prince. The drums began before dawn. Across the water, I felt the old and familiar pull of my parents, drawing ever closer.

Dumuzi and I were carried down to the quay on a litter to meet them. Dumuzi was obliged to put up with my lions leaning up against his knees. "You should have left them in your rooms," he said.

"They have special headdresses," I said. "They are part of the ceremony."

I found it difficult to think of anything except my crown; it seemed to push my neck down into my spine. But I dreaded the moment of seeing my mother again after so many months apart. I felt shame, for how angry I had been when we said goodbye, but I also still felt angry, for what had happened. Would she be angry with me now in turn?

But as soon as my parents came off their barge, so resplendent, and so full of false smiles, I saw at once that there was something wrong. My mother and father were upset and angry, but with each other, not with me.

My mother, the moon goddess Ningal, was in the full costume of the moon gods: cloud-white linen and her bronze chest plate, ornately carved with reed knots, the symbol of her temple. On her left arm, she wore her ancient *mee*. She tried to put warmth into her greeting to me, despite her upset.

My father, behind her, was equally glorious, but he had no warmth at all for me and did not try to pretend. I had never known him so cold.

My parents were carried up to the Temple of the Aquifer on a huge litter bedecked with jasmine, and Dumuzi and I followed on together in our smaller litter. We each held on tightly to a lion, for fear they might jump out into the crowds.

I tried to shake off the gloom that had descended on me. "I hope you enjoy ploughing me today," I said to Dumuzi, very quiet, and all the while smiling out at the crowds. "I hope you make my vulva very happy."

Dumuzi only grimaced at that. "I suppose someone might as well enjoy this."

I looked around for his sister, Geshtinanna, but could not see her in the royal procession. "You are my honey-man," I said, leaning into him with a grin. "You are the one my womb likes best."

"Laugh away," he said.

Enki's enormous temple was lit up bright with candles and bowls of fire. I saw Enki was already there, most awe-inspiring with all his *mees* of death and violence on display. He gave me a friendly wink.

A bed had been set up in front of the altar: a huluppu frame, a straw-stuffed mattress, the whitest bedding. I saw my mother and father being seated beside Enki, right out in front. A priest came to take my lions from me.

The drums beat faster, and the *sukkal* Isimud read the marriage rite.

The chief priestess, very solemn, stripped me naked.

I had worried in advance that I might be scared – that my hands might shake, or I might shiver.

When it came to it, though, I felt strong and steady.

Dumuzi did his part well enough, grim though he was.

But I was wonderful.

"Oh, my insides!" I screamed. "Oh, my outsides!"

I writhed around on top of him as if I had been poisoned. How I roared!

"Well, well," Enki said afterwards, when he came up to give me his blessing.

"You're a good girl," my mother said later. Had she thought me a virgin before the temple rite?

I was in my copper bath, up to my neck in warm water and rose petals, and she was sitting on a stool beside it.

"You did well," she said.

"Thank you, Mother."

We held hands over the edge of my bath, and swapped our stories, always with an eye on the servants going in and out. She seemed upset still, but determined to shrug it off. "We will talk again tomorrow," she said. "But I am glad to find you so well. I'm so glad, Inanna, that you seem to be thriving here."

"I am quite well," I said, unable to meet her eye for a moment. "But, Mother, I would do anything for you to be with me, for you to be coming north with me."

"My love, so would I," she said. "But I'm not sure Dumuzi would agree."

I did my Dumuzi face, mouth turned down, nose crinkled.

"I ought to go, my darling," she said then. "I will see you in the morning. Sleep well."

She kissed my damp forehead. I look back and I realise that she was nervous. But then I had no forewarning. Only the cool of my mother's lips, and the swirl of her white skirts as she pushed open the door of the bathroom door and left.

I woke up and Enki was standing over me in the near-dark. It took me a moment to understand that something terrible was happening.

"Search everything," he said, "every box, every pillow, under the bed." Behind him I saw his *sukkal* Isimud, holding a torch aloft, and my new husband, Dumuzi, and men in armour, kicking at my lions.

I sat up in my bed, and stayed perfectly still.

They searched everything, in my bedroom and also my little dressing room and my bathroom, tipping all my things on the floor. Servants, their eyes cast down, took the lions away.

Dumuzi came over to me, not meeting my eyes. When he tried to take my *mee* of love from me, he found it would not come. He kept pulling at it, trying to get it over my wrist, but it seemed to be glued to my flesh.

"We could cut her arm off," he said to his father.

Enki looked down at the *mee*, considering for a moment. "We can take it later," he said. "Leave it for now."

Then Enki turned to me.

"No more time in the green garden," he said. "All that is over. From now until you go to Uruk, if you go to Uruk, you stay here."

"Yes, Grandfather."

When he got to the door he turned and said: "Inanna?"

"Yes?" I looked up.

"You will be lucky to survive this," he said.

Then he closed the door behind him and pulled the bolt across.

CHAPTER EIGHT

NINSHUBAR

On the day of Inanna and Dumuzi's wedding, I found myself a wall to stand on, halfway between the docks and the Temple of the Aquifer. I was not too proud to watch the comings and goings of the Anunnaki.

I saw the moon gods of Ur first, carried up from the dock on a flower-decked sedan chair, with eight burly slaves on each side of it. The moon gods were dressed in silver and white, with great crescent-shaped crowns upon their heads. They might have been brother and sister, they looked so alike. I was particularly astonished by their wings, although I knew them to be fashioned from eagle feathers. As they were carried past, the moon goddess glanced at me. She had long, brown curling hair that seemed to float around her head; she was beautiful. Her eyes, though, were wide and dark. She looked like a woman in despair. A heartbeat later her face closed, and she was only regal.

Next in the procession came Inanna, and her husband-to-be. The little goddess wore a magnificent gold crown, a bronze chest plate, ropes of huge jewels about her neck, and the same white eagle wings as her parents had been wearing. As she drew level with me, she turned her head, very slowly, and fixed me with her stare.

I was so startled by it, so transfixed, that I forgot to look at her husband, the sheep god, and then they were already gone by.

It was too late to get a place in temple, so I spent the ceremony wandering the docks, but afterwards there was a feast outside in the palace square for the servants and slaves, and to that I was invited.

Dulma, as a priestess of Nammu's temple, was sitting on the top table. I was sitting on a table some distance away, with all the temple slaves. But we all ate the same food, and it was the best food I had ever had.

I took a large chunk of venison, on the bone but so soft the flesh could be plucked off with your fingers, and I devoured it while the others stood over the food tables, still choosing. After that I ate a large pile of fish, oily and crusted with salt, and then some lamb stewed with onions and apricots.

They temple slaves all seemed to know each other, but I did not feel out of place. A woman offered me wine and said, "You are very welcome here, child of Nammu."

"Thank you," I said, holding out my cup to her.

Strong as I was, I was not accustomed to wine, and as the day turned to night, I began to feel less sure of my judgement. The eating and drinking had turned into music, dancing and more drinking, but I wanted to be home in my little cell in the temple.

I could not see Dulma in the crowd, but I knew she would not mind me leaving her, so I got up off my bench and made my way through the crowds.

I thought I knew the way out of the palace precinct, but I found myself not in the streets but in another courtyard. By the light of the stars, I could see that there were palace buildings all around the edges of the courtyard, and no obvious way through. I needed to find my way out the way I had come in. As I turned to go, I saw a bench and, for a while, I lay on it. It occurred to me after a while, lying there with my cheek on smooth, cold marble, that I was not sure how long I had been there.

I stood again, not feeling very sure on my feet. I could no longer hear the feast, and the moon had risen. I began to look again for the way I had come in.

A dark shape, in the entrance to the courtyard.

I knew at once who it was.

Enki.

There was an odd sort of glow about him, in the moonlight.

"The girl from my mother's temple," he said.

"Yes," I said. "Ninshubar." I felt for my knives, but I was not wearing them. How could I have come out with no weapons?

"You'll do," he said.

He came at me quickly, catching up one of my wrists in one hard hand.

Well, it was not the first time a man had grabbed me in the dark.

I brought my head forwards hard. My intention was to break his nose, which I find always puts men off.

But instead of connecting with Enki, I found myself flat on my face on the ground. I swung a leg round hard at him, and again, found myself kicking thin air. When I looked up, I saw him standing over me, untouched.

"Savages," Enki said.

He brought his boot down hard on my head.

CHAPTER NINE

GILGAMESH

I had Enkidu put into my bed.

    When the priestesses had gone, I went and sat on the floor next to him. I fed him some drops of water from a shell.

"I'm so sorry, Enkidu. I should not have let it be you."

"Did it work?" he said.

"Yes, it worked."

I could hardly bear to look at him with his face so distorted.

"You have made Akka very angry," he said.

"I know that."

I picked up Enkidu's bruised right hand, and held it very softly to my cheek.

Please, An, I will do anything, but let him live.

Harga brought the boy up to me in the dusk, at my command post on the battlement.

The boy was exquisite to look at, and he was dressed in the

same azure as his father wore. It had been fashioned for him into a gorgeous suit, but it was now badly stained.

"My lord Gilgamesh," the boy said, very regal.

"It is good to see you again, Enmebaragesi," I said. "I think I last saw you on that trip to the beach."

"The day we swam."

"Yes," I said. "You know I met your grandfather once, who you are named after? He came to us, not long before he died, as an ambassador."

"I did not know that, sir," he said. "But I know he grew up in Uruk, as you did."

"Yes," I said. "He grew up beneath the Anunnaki, but then he decided he wanted to build his own city, with no gods sitting above him there."

"That's Kish!" the boy said. "He built Kish."

I turned to Harga. The man was a mess of crusted blood.

"How was it?" I said to him.

"Easy enough," he said, "with everyone looking the wrong way." He came closer to me and leaned in. "They are never as clean as you hope, these things."

"They never are," I said.

In the early morning, after the men of Akkadia had pulled back into their camp, I rode out in full armour, my lion face plate pulled down, up onto the top road. There I waited, still mounted, as King Akka, in his blue robes, not even with his sword on him, rode down to meet me. He looked hollowed out, barely able to sit on his ass. His beard, normally so perfectly crimped, was straggly and dirty.

"So, this is how you fight wars, Gilgamesh."

"Enlil sent me here with forty men, and told me to hold the city. He didn't say how."

I saw that Akka had dried blood on his robes.

"Hedda is dead, did you know that?" he said.

"I did know," I said. "She wouldn't let my man take the boy."

Akka bowed his head, and then looked back up at me. "Perhaps it is best. She could not be married off, after you raped her. Who would have her?"

"It was not rape," I said. But I said nothing more. How would the details help me?

Akka shook his head, his mouth flat. "Gilgamesh, tell me that my son is safe."

"He's safe. Unharmed. You can see him up there on the wall."

Akka spun around, and as he caught sight of the blue upon the wall, a surge of life seemed to pulse through him, and he at once sat up more strongly in his saddle. With his face still fixed upon the boy, he said: "Ask what you will, and you will have it."

I said: "You were good to me in Kish, Akka, and I am sorry about Hedda. Take your army and go, and the boy goes with you."

He drew himself up and faced me once more. "Gilgamesh, there is no honour in serving these gods that you serve. You have seen how in Kish we manage to survive without them."

I lifted up my face plate. "They are my family."

"They are rotten to the core," Akka said. "The world will only be better without them."

When the soldiers of Akka had packed up the royal tents, and the wagons of Akkadia had all gone north, the farmers and their families began leaving the city of Marad for their farms and homes. It was then we heard a distant noise, a low rumble, to the south of us. The ancient walls of Marad began to shake; pebbles fell scattering down to the fields below.

At first it was only a darkness on the horizon; finally it resolved into a huge column of men, chariots, wagons.

The great army of the sky god.

"Ah, so here are our reinforcements," Harga said. "Exactly one day too late."

"We were not heroes yesterday," I said. "So, I rather think they're just on time."

Harga laughed, a strange sound. "True enough."

The army of Sumer came at us in battle formation.

First the chariots, spreading out now as the valley opened up, each pulled by two asses. Each chariot bore two men, the driver unarmed except for his daggers, the fighting man carrying throwing spears or a battle axe, or sometimes both. At the front of each chariot there was a quiver built in, holding four spare javelins, for the heat of battle.

Behind the chariots came the light infantry, the skirmishers, in their red capes and kilts, carrying their spears high. Behind them came the heavy infantry, drawn up in phalanxes, each man armed with short but heavy spears. And last came the ox-drawn wagons, and the rabble of the camp followers.

I breathed in, breathed out.

"They have the god with them," I said.

I knew the shape in the first chariot.

Enlil.

Enlil and I ate supper together, just him and me, with one candle between us, in the forecourt of his father's temple in Marad. He raised one eyebrow when I refused the wine.

"My lord," I said, "may I ask about Della, and the baby?"

He waved this question away.

"I need you to do something for me," he said. As ever he was dressed all in black: a black robe, a black hood, black gloves tied to his belt.

"Name it," I said.

"My father has agreed to give up Uruk to Enki and his son. He has gone north already to Nippur, and your father will not be long behind him. There is talk now of this son of Enki sailing north at any moment, and with the new Anunnaki at his side."

"The famous Inanna," I said.

"I have been sitting with my father," Enlil said. "It is better that it is me who hears him talking, because he talks now in and out of his sleep, and he does not seem to care who he is talking to. He has been talking about an old *mee* that he gave to the girl when she was a newborn babe. She is the goddess of love, according to the stories they tell in temple now. And indeed, when An gave it over to her, he called it a *mee* of love. But now I have heard him calling it by a different name."

"What name?"

"That doesn't matter."

"What does it do?"

He looked at me, that silver look he had when I annoyed him. "It doesn't matter what it does. What I'm concerned about is that it's now in the hands of the water gods. I want you to go south, and check on this girl, and on the *mee* too. Find out everything you can about her, and about it."

"Very well."

"My brother Enki took this girl into his keeping. There must be a reason for it. And it has never been clear to me how

Ningal produced this new Anunnaki out of nowhere. Find out everything you can, but do it quietly."

"Very well," I said again.

"But leave your men; I need them to hold on to Marad."

"I will take my manservant," I said. "But I will leave the rest."

He looked over at me, thinking. "And take Harga," he said. "Harga is always useful."

"Yes."

"And one more thing."

"Yes, my lord?"

"Keep your hands off her."

"The girl?"

"Yes, the girl. This little goddess of love. Keep your hands off her."

"It is not such a hard thing to promise," I said.

He raised his palms to the night sky. "You are dissolute, Gilgamesh. You would try to sleep with me if you were drunk enough. With a donkey. With Harga. With every girl in this city. I know what you are, Gilgamesh."

"Certainly, you seem to think you do."

He shook his head. "You did well here in Marad. You stayed sober; you kept your head. You played it well. I'm pleased. Now do this thing for me, do it well, and then you should come back to Nippur, and we will see if it can be made to work with Della."

CHAPTER TEN

INANNA

In the morning, Enki came into my rooms and sat down on my bed, one of his knees touching my leg. "Do you know what is happening, Inanna?"

"No," I said. "No one will say a word to me."

His smell was so familiar to me: of olive soap, and so clean and warm. He pushed back my hair from my forehead with one strong hand, and put his leopard eyes very close to mine.

"Your mother has stolen from me," he said. "What do you know about that?"

"Nothing. But I do not think it can be true, that she would do anything to cross you."

"All the same, she has," he said. "In fact, she has killed me, although I am not yet dead. She has murdered me. So what you do now is very important, Inanna. Do you understand that?"

"Yes, Grandfather."

Servants went in and out when he was gone. They tidied up

my things, and brought me water. No one spoke to me when I asked about my mother and father.

I shut my eyes and tried to focus on them. I could sense my father clearly. He seemed to be moving away from me. Towards Ur. Could he have left without coming to see me? Or was he being taken away against his will?

My mother I could barely get a feel of, and what I felt made no sense. It seemed as if she was below me. Far below me. But how could that be? There was only the big state room beneath my set of rooms, and below that nothing. I knew the palace well enough to know that. And why was she so faint?

In the evening, women came to dress me for dinner, as if nothing out of the ordinary was happening. I was led onto the terrace and I was seated next to Dumuzi, my new husband, although he kept his cheek turned from me. There was no sign of my mother or father.

I sat and ate, barley soup and soft cheese, some plums. No one spoke to me, but the talk of court flowed all around, as if this was any other supper in the palace. Enki, sitting opposite me, seemed cheerful enough.

"You look very holy in that saffron," he said. "I know it is your brother's colour, but it suits you well."

I pulled out my mouth into something like a smile. "You are too kind to me, my lord."

Far below me, the thing that might be my mother seemed to be growing fainter.

My husband and I travelled north to Uruk on a fleet of barges, the men rowing hard against the river. We pushed our way into a head wind, and the sails upon the masts stayed furled.

The sails had been dyed purple: that would be our colour now.

All our possessions were heaped up on the decks of the first barge. We newly-weds travelled behind on Enki's Barge of Heaven, which I had first stepped onto on the day he took me from Ur. "He's not letting us keep it," Dumuzi said. "But it makes a nice show, does it not?"

Behind us came eight military barges loaded with soldiers and their mounts. It was the morning after my fourteenth birthday, although the day had gone unmarked.

The sky above us beat thick with swifts and swallows as we sailed.

Dumuzi and I sat on wooden chairs upon the foredeck, a purple shade fluttering over us in the spring breeze. Dumuzi had a rack of new *mees* on each arm.

My husband seemed newly energised. He was the most cheerful I had ever seen him. "You know An and Lugalbanda have run Uruk for three hundred years," said Dumuzi.

I said nothing. Those were the days when I said nothing.

"But now it ends," said Dumuzi. He cast a glance at me, fanning himself. "Ugh," he said. "This sulking. Your mother is safe. She's a hostage. As you were a hostage. What is the value in a dead hostage?"

He said nothing about my father.

The fields went by, and the peasants kneeled as the barges passed, and the day grew unseasonably hot. I sat with my eyes on Dumuzi's arms, looking at his new *mees*. Was one of them my mother's *mee* of peace?

The thought grew in me as the leagues went by, and the sweat ran down my back, that my mother might in truth be dead, and although I kept my head held high, tears slipped down my cheeks.

"Look," said Dumuzi. "You didn't ask for this. My sister didn't ask for this. And I didn't ask for this. Do you think I asked for this?"

I said nothing.

"This is our job now. To hold Uruk for my father. To keep the sky gods from coming south. That's our job now. And if you want to keep your mother safe, you need to take that seriously. You need to think about the sky gods."

I didn't say anything, but I dried my eyes on my dress. It did cheer me a little, in truth, to think about the sky gods, just as my husband had suggested. To think about the king of the sky gods, my grandfather Enlil, who had gone to war once against his brother Enki, and might do so again.

Eight days on the Euphrates and then the river Warka, and then early on the ninth day, around a sweeping bend, a vast shape on the left-hand bank. I thought, *Oh, it is a cloudbank resting on the Earth*. But then the mist cleared, and the sun picked out the ramparts in gold.

Here it was: Uruk. A golden block upon the green.

The city at the heart of the world.

I stood for the approach, my hands pressed together against my chest, my bare feet apart on the cedar deck.

Closer and closer, the shudder of the oars shivering out across the river, and the walls before us resolving from the work of great giants into only countless tiny clay bricks, each fashioned by mortal hands.

We slid past reeds and lush pastures, past a small boy holding a donkey, and watching us open mouthed. Only at the last moment did I understand that there was a gap in the city walls, and that we were going to sail straight into Uruk.

"Oh!" I said, despite myself.

"Glorious, isn't it," my husband said, coming to stand beside me, with a real smile on his face.

Huge crowds had gathered for the coming of Inanna, daughter of the moon gods, and the shepherd king Dumuzi, son of Enki, by some mortal no one had heard of. God-born but not very sacred.

I was lifted down onto the White Quay, and a servant rearranged my dress as I stood there, my arms held out limp while she worked. I looked around reflexively for my lions, but of course they were not there.

"Inanna, look," Dumuzi said, looking very young for a moment. "It's Lugalbanda's boy. The soldier. You know, the one Akka took hostage."

I looked up towards the city and there he was. Standing above the kneeling crowds, on the wall at the end of the quay, with a leather-covered helmet under his arm. There he was. Sweaty and dusty, his hair damp in the sun, looking straight at me.

Just the sight of him.

Oh, my insides.

Oh, my outsides.

Oh, my heart.

There he was.

The son of Lugalbanda.

Hero of the north.

There you were.

Gilgamesh.

PART 3

"From the Great Above she opened her ear
  to the Great Below.
From the Great Above the goddess opened her
  ear to the Great Below.
From the Great Above Inanna opened her ear
  to the Great Below."

From the ancient poem known as
The Descent of Inanna

CHAPTER ONE

NINSHUBAR

When I first woke up in the blackness, I was lying on my front, my right cheek and temple on cold, wet dirt. My whole body was cold and damp beneath me. A bad smell: something was rotting.

I thought for the briefest moment that I might be dreaming, but then I tried to move and could not for the pain. I shut my eyes and I had a flash of Enki's boot coming down hard on my head; did he also kick me in the ribs?

Was I still at the palace?

When it is as dark as it can be, as black as it is in the deep caves of my country, you can lose a sense of what is real and what is dream. But I began to believe that I was awake, and that the place I was in was real. There was water dripping. Somewhere close to me, someone was whimpering.

I thought it sounded like a girl, and it may have been my eyes, but I thought I could see her glowing, just a little: a brighter space in the absolute darkness, in the shape of someone's body.

"Who is there?" I said, very quiet.

The whimpering stopped. I saw the shape turn in the darkness; something that looked like a head rose up.

"Who are *you*?" the shape said. It was a woman's voice, not a girl's.

"My name is Ninshubar."

"Are you a prisoner here?"

Prison. I had heard the word. I had had it explained to me. Things all made more sense now. "Yes, I suppose I am a prisoner. I suppose that Enki brought me here. Do you know where we are?"

"We're in the Palace of the Aquifer," she said. "Or rather, we are beneath it."

"Are you also a prisoner?"

"Yes, I suppose I am," she said.

I lay quietly then, trying to work out how to sit up without crying out.

Her name was Ningal. She said she was a goddess and a daughter of Enki. She claimed to be the mother of the young goddess Inanna, whose wedding I had just been to.

"If you are really you, then I saw you in your temple clothes," I said. "With your wings on. On your way to temple. But I did not know your name."

"You have not heard my name before?"

"There are so many goddesses," I said. "All your names sound the same. But I do know Inanna's name, and Enki's too. And I have seen both of them."

Ningal was silent.

"Where is your daughter now?"

"I don't know," she said. "I fear I have put her in terrible danger."

There was nothing dry in our clay-floored cell, no blankets or straw – nothing to keep us warm or comfortable. I was in the linen tunic I had been wearing at the feast, although it was now damp and muddy. Ningal was naked. She did have a soft shine to her, but it was a useless light; all it allowed, very dimly, was me to have a guess at where she was.

"What is this light in you?"

"It's something called *melam*. It keeps us young and helps us heal."

"I've heard about *melam*."

She put out one warm hand on to my arm. "Ninshubar, are you here to spy on me?"

I considered this. I would never spy on anyone. Unless it was part of a plan that I had. Unless there was great honour in it. But what could I say to convince Ningal of that, when she had no idea who I was?

"Ningal, it will be hard for you to judge the weight of this, but the only answer I can give you is that I do not think I have ever done anything wrong."

She laughed, a lovely sound.

"Why is that funny?" I said.

"Because I think my father Enki would say the same thing. But I tell you, Ninshubar, he is not a good man."

"I can see there is no point trying to persuade you of this. All the same, I have always done what was right."

"I am glad life has been so simple for you," she said, a little sharp.

I said nothing to that.

There was a moment's more silence, and then she said: "I'm sorry, Ninshubar. That was rude."

"If you saw me in the light, you would not have said it."

"What would I see in the light?"

"Scars," I said. "Many scars. If you always do the right thing, that is what you win for yourself. Scars, more scars, and then when your scars have scars on them, death."

"I am not as brave as you," she said.

"No one is braver than me. You should not feel bad."

Again, her lovely laugh. I put my hand out to her this time, and patted her arm.

The damp floor and walls of our cell, its exact size and all its smells, became very familiar to me. And Ningal, too, became my familiar. I learned to trust the feel of her arm, to trust that there was goodness in her, stranger that she was.

She said to me: "Ninshubar, how can you be sure that it's always right you're doing?"

"I'm only sure that I think it's the right thing, and that I have pondered what the right thing is, and then I have done what I think is the right thing. I try to take everything into account, and I make my calculations. It is not easy, and as I have told you, often all you win is suffering."

"I wish I had known you before, Ninshubar, and that you could have known my daughter. You would have been a good friend to us."

"There is still time," I said.

∽

We sat together, our arms touching, against the dripping clay wall in the blackness. I was still in a great deal of pain, although of course I did not tell the goddess.

I said: "I know what I have done to be here. I have refused to submit to him. But what is it that you did to get in here, a great goddess of Ur?"

"I took something from him that he felt to be his alone." She put her hand out and held my hand in the darkness. "I took something from my husband, too."

"So they are both angry with you. What is it that you stole?"

I thought she wasn't going to answer, but then she said: "I could never have babies with humans, like the other Anunnaki can. And you know we Anunnaki, we cannot seem to breed with each other here on Earth. When my husband and I came down here to this realm, we had our two children with us, Utu and Ereshkigal, and it should have been enough. But I began to dream of another child. And I got pregnant with Inanna."

"Why can't you breed?"

"I think it's the air," she said. "We are not used to it. Anyway, I wanted the baby. But I feared that she would die inside me. At first, I felt her kicking strongly, but as the weeks went by, her kicks grew weaker, and my belly did not grow as it should have."

"Go on," I said.

"Enki was away. So, I went to where he hides the things." She paused. "Have you ever been to the Temple of the Waves, at the edge of city here?"

"I am the protector of that temple!"

"You amaze me!"

"Only with the truth."

"Well, you will know then that there is a statue there of Nammu, the mother of the gods. Enki hides things beneath her, although he thinks no one knows. So I went in at night, and I moved the statue. It took me hours and hours to move her, but I did it. And underneath there was his *melam*, in an old bronze box. There was not much, and I knew it was everything Enki had. That he had spent years collecting it. That he had lied to everyone about it, when the sky gods came begging for it, saying he had none left. Anyway, I could have taken just a little. But I didn't. I ate all of it."

"Ah."

"I went back to Ur as if nothing had happened. But then that wasn't enough for me. So I went up into the mountains, to the place where my husband hid things in the first days. I did not think he had any *melam* left; he had sworn to me it was finished. But there was some there, and I ate that too. I ate all of it."

"And then Inanna thrived?"

"She at once began to grow."

"The miracle Anunnaki."

"Yes, but I have always known I would be found out. And now they have both found out, and they have worked out together that it was me who took all of it. So now I will be punished. Enki will torture me, to make sure all the *melam* is gone, and then he is going to kill me, Ninshubar, because really, that is what I have done to him."

"And your husband will not help you?"

"I do not think he will. And you should know too, whatever you have done, Enki is going to kill you. This is a place that people don't come back from."

I laughed at this, and then clutched at my ribs, trying to breathe through the pain.

"Ningal, this is not the first time I have been about to die. We need to work out where we are, and how to get out. Everything after that, we will work out as we go."

"Oh!" she said, almost cheerful. Her wounds had healed much faster than mine. "I do know where we are. I came down here once with Isimud once. We are in the dungeons, underneath the palace, right down deep in the Earth."

"I need to know the detail of it."

"It is a long time ago. But we came down through the guard block, along a long underground corridor, and then down some flights of stairs. With no doors leading off the stairs, as far as I can remember. Then at the bottom of the stairs, we went down another corridor, and there were cells on both sides, and at the far end there was an entrance out onto water, a passage out for small boats. And in that corridor, in the floor, there were trap doors, with prisoners under each."

I looked up at the ceiling, and for a moment I imagined I could see the smallest crack of light.

But very, very high up above us.

"Ah," I said.

She said: "Do not think I am proud of what I did here, in the first days."

But I was thinking about the trap door.

We had each taken a corner to do our private business in. It turned out the private business of goddesses smelled just as bad as mine. We had nothing to wipe ourselves on. In one of the "good corners", there was a bucket of brackish water, but that was for drinking only, not washing. There was no food at all.

It was vital to keep our bearings, and not go too close to the business corners.

"I wonder why you are in here with me," she said.

"Is it a game?" I said. "Is he playing with us?"

"If you have refused him, he will try to break you. But why put you in with me?"

"Or you in with me."

The only way we could tell the difference between day and night was that it was colder at night, or so we thought. Indeed, it was so cold that we lay close together when we tried to sleep. It was strange and rather disturbing to lie with a goddess's breasts against my back. But she was warm – warmer than she had a right to be.

"I hope she is alive," Ningal said. "I wish, I wish, I wish." She pushed her forehead against my back. "Ninshubar, please let her be alive."

"She is alive. You are alive, she is alive. What I do not know is whether my Potta is alive." I had told her all about my Potta.

"I think he is alive."

"Why?"

"These men who took you, they were not good men, but they were not the worst. You saw them hit him, knocking him out. Then they took you. Why would they want to kill him? Where was the benefit? I think they left him there."

"That doesn't make him alive."

"It makes him maybe alive."

For a long while we were silent, but then I said: "At first for a long time my plan was to steal a boat and travel slowly back down the coast, looking in at every bay for my Potta. But I began to think of how very unlikely it would be that I found him. What if I stopped at a beach, and looked around, and he was a day's run inland, getting water or food? Or what if he was many days' walk inland, travelling to try to find me?"

"You know I have barely travelled," she said. "The others went out into the world. Nammu is still out there unless she's dead.

But I clung to Eridu, and then later to Ur. I was always frightened that if I left, something might happen and I wouldn't be here for it. And then there was Inanna."

"What sort of thing might have happened?"

"When we came down from the other realm, we locked the gates behind us. But what if someone opened them again? I suppose I have never quite accepted that this is my home."

"So Heaven is your home?"

"Yes," she said. "Not everyone feels like that, of course, and it's split our family into two."

I began to starve. Ningal began to lose hold of the hope I had given her.

"I brought bad luck upon my family," she said.

"I do not believe in luck."

"Nor did I, before," she said. "But I told a lie to my grandfather, who is the king of the gods, and the telling of it has cursed me. It has brought down bad luck on me, and on Inanna."

"What was the lie?"

"That I had done nothing out of the ordinary to create Inanna."

It did not seem such a big lie to me, and I was about to say so, when with a great creak and a blinding explosion of light, the trap door above us opened.

There was a huge clattering noise, and then the light went out again. The trapdoor was again tight shut.

We groped about the floor in front of us... a bucket! A wooden bucket! It was tipped on its side. But nearby we found bread.

Sweet-smelling bread.

I divided it as exactly as I could, in the black, and we each ate our half, chewing very, very slowly in order to enjoy every crumb of it. Then for a while we felt around on the disgusting, claggy floor of our cell to make sure some bread had not been lost.

I had a plan now. The bread had restored me.

I wasn't sure of the exact nature of it, but it was a plan.

"Are you tall?" I asked her. "I think you are tall. But are you strong; have you ever fought?"

"Whatever you are going to ask of me, I am going to let you down now," she said. "The *melam* keeps me in good condition but I never use my body, not really. Only in temple for sex, or to walk about."

Had I been standing, I would have been hopping from foot to foot. How could anyone not use their body?

"We are going to practise. I want you to see if you can stand on my shoulders, and then I'll try to stand on your shoulders. We need for one of us to have our hands right up on the trap door when it opens."

"I am not going to be able to do that."

"Let's try anyway."

We crouched down together, me behind her, and I tried to climb onto her. It was like trying to climb onto a jellyfish. Next, she tried to climb onto me, but fell forwards onto her head, yelling out. "It will get easier and easier," I said, although I could not see how.

"How will we know when the trap door is going to open?" she said.

"Ningal," I said, "there was no plan, and now there is a plan. One step and then the next."

"One step and then the next," she said.

"Yes. One more thing. We must wait in absolute silence.

INANNA   217

So if there is a sound before the trap door opens again, we'll hear it. And then the next time, we'll be prepared. So no more talking, nothing."

She squeezed my hand in the dark.

"I will be quiet. But first. Ninshubar, if you escape, and I don't, will you go to my daughter? If she is alive. Go to her and tell Inanna that she should go to Ereshkigal. Her sister. My eldest daughter."

"The one in the underworld? The queen of the night?"

"Yes. Will you tell her, Ninshubar? I think Ereshkigal can help her. Inanna has a weapon on her arm, a *mee*, that we have never been able to make work, but I believe it to be important. And if anyone can get Inanna's *mee* to work, it will be Ereshkigal. She was always the cleverest of us, before things went wrong for her. Before I failed her."

"Ningal, if something happens to you, I will go to Inanna with your message. I promise you that I will do that. But it is a promise that need not be made, because we are both going to get out."

"Ninshubar, we will go and tell Inanna together. She may be in Uruk by now. You know, I wish she had someone with her who was as strong as you are. She will need help, to survive Enki."

"When we see her, together, I will see also if I can help her. I will try to help both of you."

We squeezed hands again, and then the silent waiting began.

This time, before the blinding light, we heard a scratching, and the sound of a chain against wood. Then the light. Did I see someone's legs?

Down came the bread again, and then we were back in blackness.

We ate, happy to talk again.

After that we practised, but it went no better. She could not work out how to climb up on me, even when I was kneeling down for her and telling her how, and holding on hard to her ankles. There seemed no hope at all of her balancing on me.

"I'm going to stand on you," I said. "But I'll put all of my weight against the wall, so you just need to get to your feet once I'm on."

"I'll try," she said.

We were right up against the wall: the good wall between the two good corners.

"Kneel down for me." I had my hand touching her hair, very lightly. "Now I'm going to put one foot on this shoulder and then the other on your other—"

She collapsed without any ceremony, and I found myself flailing at the wall to prevent myself standing down hard on her.

My heart skipped a beat.

"There's wood here."

"No!" she said.

We stood together, feeling together the unmistakable feel of wood, set into the wall, slick with damp and slime, and high up, but wood, not clay. It began at about the height of my ribs, and then went up and up. How had we missed it?

"It's a door!" she said. "It must be."

"It makes sense," I said. "The drop down from the trapdoor would kill people. I've been stupid."

"Me also," she said. "There must be a lower floor, below the floor where the entrance to the river is."

"We need to go round the room now, and make sure this is the only door," I said. "Don't stand in anything."

That night I said: "What is Heaven like? Is it like in the stories?"

I felt her go still. "No," she said. "It's not like in the stories."

Now we had a new plan. The door in the side of the prison cell might open. And if it did, we would escape through it.

"We have to sit next to it, one on either side of the door, all the time," I said. "That's the plan."

"And what do we do if it opens?"

"You do nothing. You just wait to be told what to do." By this time my estimation of Ningal's usefulness, in any practical situation, had sunk to an extreme low. "I'll go. I will act. You just stay exactly there until I tell you to move. It may be quick, or it may be slow, but you just sit there, exactly there, until you hear my voice telling you to move."

"Yes. I can do that."

"We need to be ready. We need to sleep in these positions now. This is how we're going to escape, with this plan. Then we will look back on this time in the dark and laugh about it, at how filthy we were and how terrible you were at trying to stand on my shoulders."

"Or being stood on," she said.

"Do not move until I tell you to. However long that takes."

"Yes," she said. "You can stop telling me now. I am as ready as a Ninshubar. Does that satisfy you?"

I'm not sure she was ready when the door did open. I think in fact that she was asleep.

But I was ready.

As with all these things, it happened quickly.

I was standing with one shoulder against the foot of the door, so when it opened, I felt it. I moved aside to allow its movement, and turned, and was momentarily blinded. But I had expected that. As soon as the door was even a hand's width open, I had my right foot up onto the sill and then I barged out, slamming my way into a man, smashing him to the floor and going down hard on top of him.

Two more men were at me then; there was a flash of metal, and something sliced my hand. I headbutted one of the men, and shoved the other into the wall. I took my foot off the first one and then stamped down hard on his head, hurting my bare foot on his helmet.

I was in a corridor. A fire bowl was alight to my left. To my right were steps up into darkness.

I could hear raised voices on my left, so without any further thought, I ran for the steps.

Up, curving round hard and narrow to the left, my hands down onto the brick steps as I scrabbled. Another corridor: men to my left, staring open-mouthed at me. To my right an open dark space. Water. It was some kind of underground river: a narrow tunnel, made of bricks.

I could not go left. There were too many men in the corridor, and I had no weapon. I could not go back down: there were more men coming up the stairs behind me.

I did my calculations. And then I leaped out into the water.

I sank down, lost my bearings. I was being swept along fast.

My foot hit brick.

I put all my power into swimming towards the wall but when

I got there, the bricks were so smooth and close-packed I couldn't get a hold of anything.

Once more I slipped under, and thought I might stay down, but a heartbeat later my face broke water. I took a deep breath, and as I did so, I caught at a lump on the wall. I dug my nails into the baked clay, and for a few heartbeats I simply clung on, gasping for air, and holding myself out of the current. The last thing I wanted was to be sucked all the way out of the river, and perhaps spat out into the sea.

My eyes adjusted. I was about fifty paces from the entrance to the dungeons. I could hear shouting from back inside. Some men came and peered out into the riverway. As they held their torches out to look down the tunnel, I kept in close to the wall, my muscles straining with the effort of it. After a few heartbeats, the torches disappeared.

When all the noise had died down, I made my way back, one handhold at a time, up to my neck in the cold water. At the entranceway into the dungeon, I wrenched myself up high, my nails scratching into the bricks, and I peered in. No one was in sight. I hoped they would all be running to the tunnel entrance, to catch me as I was flushed out.

Slowly, slowly, I pulled my bruised self out and back into the dungeons.

The tunnel inside was lit up only by one low fire bowl, the fire almost done.

There was a trap door in front of me in the brick floor with a bronze ring set into it.

I looked around. No ropes to dangle down it.

As quietly as I could, cringing at the noise I was making, I pulled at the bronze ring, and opened the trap door.

A pit of absolute black beneath, and a familiar stench.

"Ningal," I called down, low as I could.

"Yes," she said, quiet.

"Are you well?"

"Yes," she said. "They shut the door on me after you went. Are you well?"

"Yes. Look, I'm going to have to go down and come through the door to get you. So I need you to move over to my side of the door, and be ready."

"I will be ready," she said.

I shut the trap door again, quiet as I could.

I looked around. No weapons. Not even a stick. I should have taken a knife from the men; I remembered a sword on one of the men's hips, and cursed myself.

Now I must get down the stairs again and into the lower corridor. I knew it was about fifty paces back to the door from the bottom of the stairs. The question was: had they left the door unguarded? There was no way of telling without going down there to find out. If someone was there I would need to get to them, a fair way down the corridor, without them getting a spear or knife into me first.

Down I went, one step at a time, listening out with every hair on my body. One bare foot, and then another, on the damp brick steps.

One step and then the next.

Well, if you are going to do something, it is better to do it quick. I put my head round to look.

There was only the fire still burning at the other end: no one in the corridor.

I scuttled along quick as I could to our cell door, but pulled up short in front of it.

There was a messy dark patch of blood on the floor outside the cell. For the first time I looked at my left hand and saw that it was badly cut. Could it be my blood on the floor?

But the puddle of blood stretched on to the far end of the corridor. Something had been dragged down it, away from the door to the cell. Maybe it was the blood of the man I had stamped on, or the man I had pushed into the wall?

There was a heavy bronze latch on the door.

Slowly, slowly, I pulled open the door.

"Ningal," I whispered, into the blackness. I felt round to the right of the door but there was no one there.

I heard a sound, and turned.

It was Enki.

He had a woman by the hair. She had long brown curls, and he was dragging her along by them. The woman's face was slick with blood, and her legs sprawled askew as she was dragged. She was covered all over with red streaks of clay. I could not tell if she was alive or dead.

I had never seen Ningal in the light, but I knew it was her.

She was filthy, but Enki, holding her, looked very clean, and very beautiful; his *mees* gleamed in the firelight.

"You know I had forgotten she was in there when I put you in," Enki said, smiling at me. "I was drunk! How amusing to think of you together." He laughed. "Funny girl. Did you come back to save her?"

For a heartbeat I was too frightened to move or even to breathe.

But I made my calculations.

In the midst of the second heartbeat, I turned on my heel and ran. Hard.

Something heavy and hot slammed into the wall next to me as I reached the stairs, but I got onto them, scrambling on all fours.

I could hear Enki moving fast behind me.

Up the curving staircase, four steps at a time. My heart in my mouth.

Up into the high corridor, men coming at me from my left.

I went right to the underground river.

For the second time that night, I leaped out into the void, and the shock of the dark water.

CHAPTER TWO

GILGAMESH

And so upon the orders of the lord god Enlil, the three of us rode south to Uruk: me, Harga and Enkidu.

Harga rode out in front, always with his eye out for a bird or small buck along the edge of the marshes.

Enkidu and I rode side by side, through the muggy green of fields and the piled-up paths through the reed beds, and I felt a deep happiness to merely be there with him, plagued though we were by mosquitoes and other small biting things. I should have been worrying about Della, or the baby, or the reunion with my father in Uruk. Yet I felt only the settled joy that it was to ride side by side with Enkidu, talking when we felt like it, and at other times lapsing into a happy silence.

"Is Harga angry with us?" Enkidu asked.

"With me, yes, undoubtedly. I am an unending let-down to him."

"Surely not." He gave me a wink.

"You, of course, know me to be perfect. But Harga believes

that in my youth I did on one or two occasions, here or there, behave foolishly, even dishonourably."

"By in your youth, do you mean a few moons ago?"

I should have laughed; after all, he was teasing me. But I felt curiously upset by his words, ludicrous though it was of me. "I am trying to be better," I said, rather limply, and then I kicked my mule on.

When Enkidu had caught up with me, he said: "Gilgamesh, do not think I criticise you. I like you as I find you."

I nodded, but did not look at him. "I am not sure you know who I am."

"I know well enough," he said. "You are a strong wind, blowing in off the mountains."

I smiled at this. "Not everyone likes a strong wind."

"I myself like it breezy," he said.

I think I blushed at that. As I did, I saw Harga looking back at me, and knew the glance for what it was: stern disapproval. But what was it to me, more Harga disapproval, to add to the mountain of Harga disapproval I had already gathered to myself?

That night we made camp on a rocky outcrop overlooking the Euphrates. While Enkidu climbed down in the dusk to fill up all our waterskins, Harga came and sat down upon a log next to me. "What are you doing?" he said.

"What?"

"You know what. Flirting with the marsh man."

"If anything, he is flirting with me."

Harga looked then as if he wished he could abandon me once and for all. Instead he took a deep breath and said: "You Anunnaki think you can do as you like. Lie with anyone, do anything you like to anyone. But there are always consequences, Gilgamesh."

"I am not an Anunnaki," I said. "You are only Anunnaki if the *melam* flows in you. I am a mistake made by Anunnaki."

"Gilgamesh. In the marshes, to lie with another man is death. It is the same with my people. Disgrace for all, and death. Do you understand me?"

I shrugged.

"Ignore me, don't ignore me, what do I care," Harga said. "But you are going to be the death of him."

We looked down together onto the surging white of the river, and the black rocks that cut up through it, and upon Enkidu, who had begun the climb back up to us, a wide smile on his face when he saw us watching him.

"I am not ungrateful to you," I said to Harga. "He may not have been flirting, you are right. It is easy to misunderstand people, when their hearts are full of love and light."

The next day we followed the river all the way down to Uruk.

"Have you not seen your father since you ran away?" Enkidu asked. "And he is king here?"

"Yes, I ran away and have not been back," I said. "Which I regret now. And yes, my father is king here. He is also holy *sukkal* to the lord god An, which means he is the chief minister and priest of all An's lands and temples. He and An have always ruled Uruk together. Well, as much as my mother would allow them to."

"So you really did grow up with the king of the gods? I had wondered if you were exaggerating."

"I really did, Enkidu!" I said, laughing. But as I laughed, I remembered Harga's words of warning. I smoothed out my face, and said: "Let me explain how the cities of the Anunnaki work, Enkidu." I launched into a long lecture on the Sumerian city states, and their dependence on canals, that took us all the way to the riverbend, and our first sight of Uruk.

How many times have I ridden into Uruk by the elephant gates? Countless times.

And yet this time, as the great walls reared up before us, and the ziggurat beyond gleamed so white against the deep blue of the sky, my heart skipped a beat.

Enkidu walked towards the elephant gates with his head craned backwards, and his mouth open. "Is it all one piece of stone?" he said.

"No, three pieces," I said. "Each elephant is carved from one whole lump of granite, and then the centrepiece from a third."

The splendid gate was being guarded by a pack of soldiers, and I was about to declare myself when one of the men stood forwards. He looked older than the rest: a veteran.

"I cannot believe it!" he said. He dropped to one knee, on the smooth paved road, and bent his head to me. "My lord, welcome home."

Then he stood, and embraced me. I slapped him on the back as he hugged me.

"You have been gone too long, Lord Gilgamesh!" he said. He cast an experienced eye over Harga and Enkidu, before turning back to me.

"An has gone, and we are all to follow," he said, most matter-of-fact. "Before the water gods arrive."

"I must find my parents."

"Your mother took An north," the man said. "But your father is at the docks. Shall I send some men with you?"

"I think I will be safe just with these two, in my own city," I said, gesturing at Harga and Enkidu.

The guard kissed me, and embraced me again. "We have all missed you," he said. "Your father more than anyone, though."

My father was a great general, in the days when the Twelve lived in Heaven. Now as I glimpsed him for the first time in four years, standing on the city wharf in his sheepskin hunting coat, I saw that he moved like an old man now, despite all the *melam* that flowed in him.

I did not know how he would greet me, or what would he say. Would he be angry? My belly sank within me as we made our way through the soldiers towards him. But of course I should have known better.

He turned and saw me, and at once burst into tears. A moment later he had his arms around me.

"My son," he said, through his sobbing. "Welcome home."

I buried my own face into his neck, pressing my tears into his warm skin. He smelled so shockingly familiar to me, of sheep's wool, and candlewax.

After a while we separated, our faces puffed and stained with tears, and I saw that Enkidu was standing watching us, a smile on his face. Indeed, every face there was turned to us, all open and full of emotion. Except Harga's face: he looked bored and annoyed.

My father took my right hand, and raised it. "My son has come back to us!" he roared. "The wild bull of Sumer!"

The crowd burst into claps and whistles.

"Come up to the palace, my son," my father said. "And bring your friends. We are going to feed you and feed you, but first I am thinking you might want a bath."

"He's too good for you," Harga muttered at me, as we made our way into the holy precinct.

I turned on him, my fists clenched. "Do you not think I know that?"

"Easy," Harga said, leaning back from me.

Enkidu was close behind us. He put one hand out on my shoulder, and walked me on into the palace, leaving Harga to follow.

My father was still living in the palace I grew up in, but we ate venison stew together amongst packing chests.

"Dumuzi came here," he said. "With threats. It was fight or go, and An did not have it in him to fight. So your mother has taken An, and as soon as we can, we will go too."

"Is Enki really so dangerous that he can throw you from your home?"

My father put down his spoon and rubbed his face. "It kills me, Gilgamesh, to leave our people in the care of the water gods. But Enlil and An do not want a war in the south, as well as in the north." He smiled at me so warmly. "My son, I believe I can bear anything, though, now that you are here."

Before we parted that night, I said, very awkward: "Father, I am sorry. For what I have done to you. But also for all the rest of it."

He put his arms around me again, and held my head against his. "You have nothing to be sorry for, Gilgamesh. We love you just as you are."

My father had given me my old rooms to sleep in, and Enkidu had taken the little servant's room where my nurse used to sleep. I went in to check on him, smiling about at the neat leaf-patterned walls, the simple cedar bed, and the small window looking out onto the ziggurat.

He was rather large for the bed. "I cannot believe this is all mine," he said.

I laughed, until I realised he was serious.

"Where is Harga?" he said.

"We are inserting him into the royal bodyguard here, where he may be most useful to us when Dumuzi gets here."

I stood awkwardly there for a moment, looking down on him in bed, then I said: "Goodnight, then. I'd better get some proper sleep. Lots to do tomorrow."

And I left him there.

It was true that there was a lot to do. My father wanted chests of tablets of official records shifted out of the city before Dumuzi arrived, and also some personal treasures. And we were starting to move out soldiers, in small bands. If we were to hand over a city and its army to these invaders who were our close family, then it would be a very small army we would leave them with.

Enkidu and I were on the docks, overseeing the loading of a skiff, when the shouts went up, and the great horns burst into life up on the ramparts: the gods were coming now from Eridu, far sooner than anyone had expected.

I scaled up onto the wall behind the quay and helped Enkidu up after me.

The people were flooding down to see the new gods coming and who could blame them?

The great barges came through the city walls one at a time, each barge a shimmering glory: golden decks, painted prows, purple sails neatly furled. Hundreds of soldiers, too, in Enki's dark bronze chest plates.

On the second barge: the gods. The first one must be Dumuzi: tall and dark, very like his father. I had seen him at Nippur when I was a small boy, and of course he was unchanged. And then a small creature, the girl Anunnaki, dressed in the white of the moon gods, with brown skin and long, very black hair. She looked to me more like a child than a great goddess.

Soldiers picked the girl goddess up and put her down on the quay beside Dumuzi. Servant women came to pull at her robes, and arrange her temple wings.

Then without any apparent cause, the girl looked straight at me. She was some cable spans away from me, but she held my eye.

She had the blackest eyes.

I saw at once what she was.

Enlil had called her a goddess of love. But it was not love I saw. A small cold flicker went through me, of fear and premonition.

Here before me, dressed in pretty clothes but not at all disguised, was a high goddess of war.

CHAPTER THREE

INANNA

In Uruk, my new husband, Dumuzi, was a busy man. He had so many projects on the go. Where was An? He must find out. The army must be secured. Lugalbanda, An's *sukkal*, could stay on as king for now, but he must bend his knee or there would be trouble. The walls must be repaired. The canals were silted. He must have a new temple of his own, within the precincts of the White Temple, but first he needed building materials and were there enough skilled masons and brickmakers? He wanted his sister Geshtinanna brought north. How could his father be persuaded? The priests in the White Temple were duplicitous, keeping gold from him, lying about what An had taken with him.

He spent all day tramping around the city, his nose in everything, nothing beneath his notice. He gathered a retinue about him and it grew larger every day: scribes, priests, soldiers, farmers, architects. Now armourers. In the evenings at dinner, often he would eat alone with me, and he would talk and talk at me. He seemed profoundly happy to have a city of his own and

I found this new Dumuzi almost sweet. He had warmed to me since I had stopped speaking to him, and he treated me much like a friend, albeit one he had no questions for.

"You know now that I am used to it, I see you are a good match for me. You being Anunnaki, it gives me credibility. And I have power. I think that makes a good balance."

He would often give me news of my mother, since none came direct to me. "She is living in Ninhursag's compound, with your lions. And some of her servants and priestesses have come over from Ur. She eats at my father's table twice a week. Given what she did, I think she's not really got much to complain about." I did not ask what my mother had done, in her supposed attempt on Enki's life, and Dumuzi never said.

The famous White Temple that was not good enough for my husband was like nothing I had ever seen. I still remember the shock of it, although it would become as familiar to me as my own hands. There was a great climb up to it, up the huge white steps of the ziggurat, and then inside it was a field of vast columns, each four cables high and a cable wide, and each studded with gemstones of brilliant red, yellow and blue. The floor was of the smoothest marble, and the walls of the most brilliant white. A hundred narrow windows, cut high into the walls, let in shards of sparkling sunlight.

Oh, it was the glory of the ages, to stand at the grand entrance, and look down through the forest of columns to the giant cedar wood throne, which had been An's, and which would, for now, be my husband's.

It was in front of this ancient throne, on a bed that would be set up for the occasion, that we lay together once a week. I was just as wonderful as I had always been. How I roared. No one would say I was letting down the people or that the crops would rot in the fields because of how I did. Dumuzi was less grim than he had been on our wedding day: he had begun to enjoy himself.

"I know it is just the rite, that it gets under your skin sometimes when you have done it enough with someone, but I do find you attractive now, you know," he said to me at supper. "I find myself thinking about you, the shape of you, when I am out in the fields, or at night. I used to think you strangely small, and far too thin, sort of plain really. I hope that doesn't upset you; I was comparing you to Geshtinanna. But now I like the way you are made." Sometimes he would want to lie with me twice in the same ceremony.

My busy husband.

Me, I had one project.

The first time I saw Gilgamesh was from the White Quay, when he came to watch me get off the barge. I had thought my husband handsome, if you were only to look upon his skin and hair, and not examine the man within.

Gilgamesh was astonishing to me.

He had a beauty that burst out at you. That cast pallid shade upon all around him. His skin was a gleaming mahogany brown. His hair was obsidian black, with a heavy wave to it: kept long on top, but cut short at the sides and back. His eyebrows were two black arrows in flight across his gorgeous brow. His beard was dark, close cropped, as soldiers wear it to war. He had wide, strong shoulders, and narrow hips.

Oh, my outsides.

The second time I saw him he was also at a distance. He was with his wild man friend, the famous Enkidu, he of the strange wolf hair, and long wolf beard. It was said that Gilgamesh had found the wild man, close to death, in the hills near Shuruppak, and had had him taken to the temple there, to be nursed back to health.

They were walking down from the parade ground to Lugalbanda's palace, both in light leather armour, their caps in their hands, so young and strong. I saw how easy they were together, touching each other's arms as they laughed and talked. A barb of jealousy went through me, for this intimacy that I could not be part of.

How can you feel so much for someone you have only glimpsed, and at a distance?

How can a stranger, never met, never smelled, never touched, strike at you so hard?

Oh, my insides.

The third time I saw him was at a formal reception in the White Temple, with the air heavy with frankincense. The priests were still in An's colour, black, because they had not yet found themselves purple robes.

Dumuzi was sitting upon An's throne, and I was sitting on a small chair beside him, my temple wings arranged behind me.

Lugalbanda, Gilgamesh's father, and, for now, king of Uruk, approached us with his head bent.

"This is my son, Gilgamesh," he said. "He has been sent here by Enlil, as his special envoy."

At this Gilgamesh stepped forwards. He was wearing a bronze chest plate etched with a wild bull, and a helmet in the shape of a lion's head. The helmet he took off as he kneeled down before us.

"My lord and lady," he said. "I have brought presents from my lord god Enlil, who I believe may claim you both as cherished family."

Servants came forwards with two finely made cedar boxes, the wood still smelling strongly of its mother tree, and each inlaid with ivory and jade. The larger was brought over to Dumuzi, and opened; the smaller was brought to me. Inside was a pendant: a white moonstone set into gold.

I felt Gilgamesh's eyes on me. I looked up slowly, and met them.

His eyes were the richest brown, cut through with flecks of gold, and set into seashell white.

I had to look away from him, for fear my thoughts would show.

"Thank you," I said, my cheeks burning. "Does the stone have a name?"

"The Most Precious of the Moons," he said.

I looked up at him again and he caught my smile, and returned it.

Dumuzi had already set aside his box.

"You will thank Enlil for us, for these fine gifts," he said.

And then Gilgamesh was bowing and backing away into the crowd.

Oh, my heart.

The fourth time, it was at a state dinner.

It was our first formal dinner in what had been An's palace, but that was now our home.

Dumuzi arranged every detail. Not for nothing had he grown up in the Palace of the Aquifer. Everything was beautifully done, with purple cloth on every table, and hundreds of candles, and tray after tray of delicacies, and the best date wine.

On the high table there were only the four of us: me, Dumuzi, the king Lugalbanda, who had been *sukkal* to An, and Gilgamesh.

He was still damp from his bath, in blue-dyed linen trousers, and a long, matching shirt.

"You know my son, Gilgamesh," Lugalbanda said to us as we sat down. "From temple."

Gilgamesh nodded at Dumuzi, very polite. "Perhaps you remember, my lord," he said, "but we met when you were in Nippur, when I was only a boy."

Dumuzi shook his head. "No. But how is my uncle, Enlil?"

"Very well, although the war continues, and costs and costs."

"I hear you are the reason the war continues," Dumuzi said, "because of your conduct as a hostage in the court of King Akka."

Gilgamesh was still smiling, but it was a different sort of smile now, as if he was thinking about where he had put his knives.

"Cousin," I said, interrupting. "I am Inanna, Nanna and Ningal's daughter."

He turned to me, and gave me his full attention. A little shudder went through me.

"I know who you are, moon cousin!" he said. "If there is one thing about you I have not been told, I will eat this plate! Who else is the city talking about, from morning until midnight?"

I laughed, my hands clasped before me. "I have grown up feasting on your adventures."

I could feel Dumuzi's immediate irritation, pricking at me through my hind skin. "How talkative you are tonight," he said to me quietly.

"I hear you have two lions," Gilgamesh was saying. "I would give my sword to see them."

There was a little silence that shimmied round the table.

"I'm afraid my lions are in Eridu," I said, my face plain. "So I cannot show them to you."

Gilgamesh looked at Dumuzi, and then back at me.

"Will you allow me to show you around Uruk?" he said. "I grew up here, you know. Every brick here is known to me, every swimming spot, every secret passage. Let me be your guide."

"I would adore that," I said. "And I would like to swim."

Dumuzi shifted in his seat. "So, this is a new position that you occupy, is it, as envoy from Enlil to Uruk?"

"Yes, my lord," Gilgamesh said. "It was thought that with the war keeping Enlil so busy, it would be useful to have me close at hand to talk for him, and perhaps to carry messages to and fro."

Dumuzi absorbed this, tilted his face.

"I heard about what you did at the siege of Marad," Dumuzi said. "I wonder if you are proud of it."

"Have you fought in many wars?" Gilgamesh said. "Are you an expert on sieges?"

"Not so far. But then I am young, for an immortal. There is plenty of time for me to learn about sieges, in the millennia stretching before me."

Lugalbanda leaned forwards, pulling at his beard. "Another night, we must press Gilgamesh for his stories. He will tell you about the envoys of Akka, and how he first found his friend Enkidu. But tonight, my lords, I would love to hear your thoughts on the state of the temple and its lands, and what more I can do to help you settle in."

"First I would like you to tell me where An is," Dumuzi said. "And when he is to come back. We are family, and yet he seems to have fled before me. It gives a bad impression to the people."

"He has only gone north for the cool mountain air," Lugalbanda said. "The king of the gods flees no one. He is only glad that you have come north with your men, to help hold Uruk in this time of war."

"We have my father to thank for that," Dumuzi said.

Later, as we stood to go, for a moment I found myself standing close to Gilgamesh in the throng. I was so close I could feel the warmth coming off him, and smell his cedar-wood scent.

"Your father is back in Ur," he said. "But we've heard nothing of your mother."

The shock of his words, and how close he was, left me for a moment speechless.

Gathering myself, I said: "Can it be true, that my father has gone home? But without my mother?"

"I heard he was angry with your mother. Very angry." He gave a little shrug.

"He did seem upset, on my wedding day," I said.

Lugalbanda was looking over for his son.

"Goodnight, dear cousin," Gilgamesh said.

"Goodnight," I said.

As he made his way away from me through the crowd, I was not thinking about my father. Or even about my mother, who I had had no word from.

I was thinking: *I will have him.*

Come what may. I would have him.

I saw him for the fifth time the next morning.

Gilgamesh was waiting for me in the palm-lined courtyard

at the front of An's palace. He was wearing a plain white tunic, and unarmed.

He opened his arms to me. "I thought I would take a chance," he said, "and wait about for you. In case you wanted to see the city now."

I remembered Enki coming to my door, to show me the palace at Eridu. That felt like an entire lifetime ago. Three lifetimes ago.

It was the strangest, giddiest feeling, to walk out with Gilgamesh, just him and me.

I say just him and me: I had my troop of eight jailer-soldiers following me. Two had come with me from Eridu and the rest had been assigned to me in Uruk.

I had decided not to acknowledge them, since I had been allowed no say in choosing them, but Gilgamesh felt no such compunction. He lifted his chin to the captain of them, and gave him a smile I found impossible to interpret. This earned him a scowl from the curly-haired captain.

"Let's do the old quarter first," Gilgamesh said. "They say some of it is a thousand years old."

"But that was before the Anunnaki got here."

Gilgamesh laughed. He waited until we had pulled ahead of the soldiers. "The Anunnaki didn't build this city. They have done great works here. Enlarged the city. My father put up these huge siege walls. The canals, the ziggurat. But it was already a town when they got here. Or so my father tells me, and why would he lie? Who taught you your history?"

"My father. One of the Twelve also."

He laughed again. "Inanna, I know who your father is."

He led me up tiny brick steps on the inside of the city walls, and out onto the wide walkway along the top. From the city walls you could see six leagues north along the Warka, and far and wide across the sumptuous river plains, and we stood together for a while there, enjoying the slight breeze, and looking all around us.

"The old gods did their bit for us, long before the Anunnaki got here. It is they who founded Uruk. Everyone ignores what the old gods did for us. But there is no one walking here, Anunnaki aside, who does not have their blood in them. Glorious, isn't it?" he added, putting his hands out to the view.

"Glorious," I said, looking out and filling up my lungs with the air swelling up off the dark grey of the river.

It was glorious, truly glorious, the golden city, the emerald plains, the sacred river. But the truth is, it would not have been even half as glorious had I not been standing next to Gilgamesh, with his warm arm so close to mine.

"No, the old gods were here, a long time ago," he said. "They came down from Heaven, just as the Anunnaki did. Now you would think they had just disappeared off into the wildlands, from listening to the Anunnaki. But they did a lot, when it was their time."

"Where are they now, these old gods?"

He leaned down to me, and put his mouth close to my ear. "The old gods are dead, cousin. But the Anunnaki don't like us talking about gods dying. So best keep that bit to yourself."

He helped me down the steps on the inside of the ramparts, putting out one strong hand to me as I crept down towards my escort. My skin seemed to burn where he had touched me.

I saw, from the corner of my eye, Gilgamesh winking at the captain of my guard.

"Do you know him?" I said.

"His name is Harga," Gilgamesh said. "He does not have much in the way of brains, but he is a good sort." He winked again at the curly-haired captain. The captain looked back at him blank-faced.

When we were far ahead enough of my escort, I said: "Do you think they have gone to Heaven, the old gods, or do you think they have gone to the underworld, as mortals do?"

Gilgamesh stopped and looked at me. "I used to ask questions like that, and no one would ever answer them."

"My sister is in the underworld," I said. "I suppose I am sure of that."

"Yes, that is what they say," he said.

"I wonder, in a thousand years, if I will be standing here telling someone the history of this city."

Gilgamesh said nothing.

I had forgotten in the moment that he was a mortal.

"I'm sorry if that was tactless," I said.

"Inanna, I have all my life yearned for a hundred extra years, never mind a thousand. Really more for my father than for myself. But that is not your fault. You don't need to be careful in what you say to me."

As we walked on, I thought, *When I am a thousand years old, will I even remember this man?* The very thought of it, of forgetting him, was almost too difficult to bear.

The next day Dumuzi began work on his new temple, in the gardens beneath the ziggurat. I had been sent for, for the formal ground-breaking ceremony.

"I hear you have been loitering about with this boy Gilgamesh," my husband said.

He didn't bother to wait for an answer. "Carry on," he called to the priests. I considered Dumuzi's exquisitely carved nose, his fine cheekbones. It was hard to be wary of my husband, although I saw it made sense to be wary. Whatever had frightened me when I looked at Enki, this man did not have in him.

I turned back to the ceremony. They were preparing to sacrifice a white goat, before they sank the first pickaxe into the ground.

"You know Gilgamesh is a famous rapist," Dumuzi said. "They have had all sorts of problems with him in Nippur, and in Shuruppak. And then in Kish he raped Akka's sister, and started the war back up again just as it was ending. Enlil has put him with his own girl now. But they say that is only because he was forced into it. And now there are these rumours about him and the wild boy. Anyway, I don't care if you lie with him. Lie with whoever you like. What does it mean to me if you want to consort with a renowned rapist? But make sure it's in temple. Keep it proper."

"Is that where you take your sister? To temple? Is that where your father took me?"

He turned on me in what seemed like real anger, although he kept his voice down.

"Who I lie with and where is none of your business. What my father has done is in the past. You are here to do your part. If you will not do it, there will be real trouble between us, Inanna, do you understand?"

He had high spots of colour in his cheeks.

"And your mother will suffer for it," he said.

"Yes, my lord." I gave him my dove face, and was quiet. As I smiled, I thought: *One day I will make you suffer for that.*

I saw that Lugalbanda, Gilgamesh's father, was watching us, and I gave him a little bob, as a dove might make while drinking.

∽

No ground-breaking ceremony for me. I was given a second-hand temple.

It was a small, square temple, and there would have been nothing special about it, except that in the yard at the back of the temple there a grew an ancient huluppu tree, planted so long ago that people said it was there before the city. Its huge roots twisted and arched over the walls around the yard, and its great branches and green boughs thrust out triumphant above the temple, the most gorgeous sight against the gold of the city and the aquamarine sky.

"Oh," I said, seeing it for the first time.

The temple was sacred to Ninsun, Gilgamesh's mother, and one of her symbols, the eight-petalled flower, was carved over the doorway. I was told Ninsun had gone north, so she would no longer have need of a temple in this city; from today this would be sacred only to me. I wondered what Dumuzi had meant by it, to put me here, in the temple that Gilgamesh had been born in.

There were ten priestesses inside, all heavily made up and wrapped in orange, the colour of Ninsun. The tallest of them, and the first amongst them, was the chief priestess, Lilith. She came forwards and dipped her knee to me, but without much energy. The priestesses behind her kneeled, but then got up quickly, glancing at their chief.

"Lady Inanna," said Lilith. She had gleaming brown skin and soft waves of black hair, and she was very pretty in her orange.

She took me through into the sanctuary, where the temple kept its secret tablets. "My lady, first I should tell you that we do the lottery here," she said, taking a stool. "Whoever wins sleeps with the goddess."

"Oh," I said. "No." I remained standing.

Lilith raised her fine black eyebrows at me, and then stood up again. "My lady, this is your temple, and we are here to serve you. But the lady Ninsun, whose temple this has always been, has always stood forwards for the lottery. The people expect it of the first lady of the city. And besides that, our lord god Dumuzi said you would do it. The first one is in five days' time."

I unclenched my fists.

"I have only done the rites with my husband," I said, with what I hoped was a polite smile. "I would like to choose the man, if it's not my husband. That is how it was in Ur, for my mother."

"My lady, in Uruk, it will cause great upset if you break from the tradition. If you do not like it, you should go to your husband Dumuzi about it, because he has told us that this is what he expects."

She bowed her head to me, but her eyes, when she looked up, were hard.

When I came out onto the street after, Gilgamesh was waiting there, sitting very casual on a step, in an old smock of the sort slaves wear. He and my guards all looked amused, as if they'd just been laughing.

"How are you liking my mother's temple?"

This was the sixth time I saw him.

I said: "Is she angry I have it now? Are her priestesses angry with me? It was not my choice."

"My mother is not the sort to worry about some temple, and who has it. She is the great hero of her own story, and not much worried by the smaller things."

"I do like the tree," I said. "But not much else. The woman here, Lilith, has not much kindness in her."

"Write her name down, in your heart. That is what I do when people cross me, and I do not yet have a way of paying them back."

"Oh really," I said. "I had not thought of such a thing. I am not sure it is in me, to be so vengeful."

He looked at me, one eyebrow raised, to see if I was joking, and then we smiled at each other.

"Is it a long list of names you have, written on your heart?" he said.

I only smiled again at that.

"Well," he said. "I am come to walk you back safely to the palace. It seems odd to me, that they let you wander like this alone, with only these excuses for soldiers to protect you."

Once again I saw him winking at Harga, the curly-headed captain of my guard.

"I am meant to be a high goddess. Perhaps they think that eight soldiers, plus the awe in which I am held, will suffice in the way of protection."

We set off together. I walked slowly to make it last.

"Inanna, you are not meant to be a high goddess," he said. "You *are* a high goddess. Yet you act as if you have no power. As if you are only a victim in all this."

I stopped in the street and turned to him, my hands upon my hips.

"Gilgamesh, I have only one *mee* and it doesn't work. What power do I have? You know better than anyone that there is nothing much special about the gods if you strip them of their weapons."

He said: "I don't have *mees*. I don't even have *melam* in me. Do you think I have power?"

"Oh, yes," I said. "Although I am not sure why. Perhaps it is because of who your father is?"

He laughed. "How little you think of me! Of all my exploits, of my great triumphs!"

"I did not mean to slight you. I'm sure it helps that you are strong and know how to fight."

"Inanna, what I know is that there is only so much power in the world. A finite amount. Perhaps because you are a princess, you will be given some. Perhaps I will even loan you a little of mine. But the rest you will have to take."

"They want to put me to lottery in the temple," I said, turning to walk on. "To lie down with whatever farmer wins the ballot."

"That sounds very holy. We rely on the farmers."

"But if I don't want to do it, what do I do, Gilgamesh? What is my power here? Do I hide in my room, and make them drag me? Hope they don't do it?"

"What would a high goddess do? You are never going to be more of a high goddess than you are this very day. That is the thing I think you fail to realise. You will never be more holy than you are right now, walking down this street."

Dumuzi said to me, as an aside at dinner: "I am going south to fetch my sister."

"Why didn't she come here in the first place, if she was going to come this quickly?"

He looked at me, annoyed. I saw him think about not answering, but he said: "She was needed in Eridu before, but now she is free to join me. My father has written. So I am going to fetch her."

I said then, because I wanted to hear his reaction: "They are saying I must do the lottery, in my temple."

"We must fit in with local customs," he said, and smiled at me rather viciously, although I could not really see why he was so angry with me.

"I do not want to do it," I said.

"Then you will be dragged to temple, and forced down onto the bed," he said. "We must keep up appearances here."

On the morning my husband sailed south, I waited in the courtyard on my stone bench, along the path I knew that Gilgamesh always took from his father's palace to the barracks.

I was sitting there, my guards a little restless behind me, when I saw the wild man, Enkidu, walking across the courtyard. He was swinging a stone axe in one hand.

Enkidu caught my eye and for a moment looked as if he was thinking of walking on, but then he veered towards me. He was a huge man close up, very tall and also broad in the shoulder.

"Are you waiting for Gilgamesh?" he said.

"Yes, I am waiting for him." I placed my hands together neatly in my lap.

A silence grew between us, but I saw him looking at the captain of my guard, and then looking quickly down at the ground again. I looked at the ancient stone axe that he was carrying, and wondered if he was a marsh man. They are famously content with silence. And I remembered men who looked like Enkidu, standing in the royal graveyard at Ur, on the day that Amnut was buried.

When I had given up on him speaking again, Enkidu said: "I have not spoken with a god before."

"Do I disappoint?"

He seemed about to say something, but then Gilgamesh was there, smiling an odd little smile at Enkidu, and touching his elbow.

"This is the wild man Enkidu," Gilgamesh said, turning to me, and giving me a small bow. "Who they say the gods sent to me." He gave Enkidu a look I could not read.

"Yes, we've met," I said.

"I'm thinking of putting my name in for your lottery," Gilgamesh said, "if the goddess does not object."

"If I am not properly served, the crops could fail," I said. "Perhaps you are the man to serve me. How could I object?"

I noticed how the cloth lay smooth against Gilgamesh's lean belly.

"So you think I should enter?" he said. He had lovely teeth, pearl white.

"Only you can know where your duty lies," I said. But then I burst out: "Gilgamesh, how do I stop it?"

He laughed. "You must stop being so very, very careful," he said. "Is that not obvious?"

He went away, whistling, and Enkidu followed after him, with one last glance back at me on my bench.

Why was Gilgamesh whistling, when I was so unhappy?

That was the seventh time.

That afternoon, in Ninsun's temple that was now my temple, the priestesses read to me from the old clay tablets that they kept beneath the floor of the sanctuary. I should have been listening, because I liked the stories from the first days. Instead I was thinking: *What will happen if I refuse to serve these women, if I refuse to do as they ask?* Would they really have me dragged to temple?

Then there was shouting behind us, and all at once Gilgamesh was there, in the most holy of places, so large and dangerous in the tiny space. He had changed into his bronze armour, and was carrying an enormous flint axe.

My chief priestess, Lilith, leaped up. "Gilgamesh, what are you doing?"

Gilgamesh was looking at me, smiling. "Inanna, I am going to teach you that lesson that you asked for. Follow me!"

I followed him out through the small cedar door into the shaded yard beneath the huluppu tree.

"Gilgamesh," Lilith shouted, rushing out after us. "Stop it, Gilgamesh, stop this right now. What do you think you are doing?"

We stood there under the blissful shade of the old tree.

"What are you doing?" Lilith repeated. Her voice was low now, her body stiff with rage.

"I'm chopping down your tree," he said.

"This tree belongs to the gods, Gilgamesh," Lilith said. "Gilgamesh, it belongs to your mother. You must not touch it."

Gilgamesh rested the head of his flint axe down on a tree root. "Well, there is another god here, a high god, even. Let me consult with her."

He came close to me. "Goddess," he said, getting down with some difficulty, in his heavy armour, onto one knee. "I'm going to chop down this tree and make you a throne out of it, and perhaps also a bed and a new door. Shall I do it?"

I looked up at the gorgeous canopy, and regretted already its loss, but I said: "I would like a new door."

Gilgamesh stood, picked up the axe, and swung it, in a huge arc, into the ancient huluppu tree. The axe bit into the living bark with a sickening thud. Then he wrenched the axe out, and swung again.

Lilith dropped to her knees to watch him, tears streaming down her face. She turned to me.

"Inanna, this is a holy tree," she said. "The god An brought it in from the river when my great grandmother was a little girl, and it has given us good shade and fruit for a hundred years since. The lady Ninsun loved this tree above all others, and would sit here in the shade of it, and sing to us all. It is a holy tree. Inanna, tell him to stop."

"You should go to my husband Dumuzi about it," I said, "when he is back from Eridu."

I watched Gilgamesh work for a while, the sweat running off him.

He turned and said, "This is going to take a long time. And it's going to be dangerous, when it comes down. It could take down the wall."

"I would like to watch anyway."

As he cut his way steadily into the tree, I looked around me at the priestesses, and I wondered at how it was that, since that first bite of the axe, they had had no power over me.

Gilgamesh took a break from chopping, and after he had emptied his waterskin, he said: "You know, in some temples, even here, the goddess decides who will do the rite, if there is no husband there to serve her. They don't all bother with a lottery."

"Oh," I said.

"Yes," he said. "There is no reason to do a lottery; it is only custom, not law. And there are other ways of doing things. In some temples here, the priestess stands in for the goddess, and in others the goddess does the work, but she picks a different man each time, according to what is right for the world."

"What a lot of different men I will need to find, if I change the custom here," I said.

"Different men, one man, they do it differently everywhere. You must choose your own path."

Lilith was sitting on the ground, in mess of leaves and branches.

"It may not mean anything at all to you, Gilgamesh," she said, "but in this temple the lottery has always been the rule. So that any man or woman may be lifted up by the gods."

"Don't you talk to me about gods," he said, looking very angry for a moment. He smoothed his face. "Anyway, it is now up to this goddess, Lilith."

"Your mother will be angry," Lilith said, her eyes upon her lap.

"There will be no lottery," I said. "I will choose the man. This time, Gilgamesh, you will do well enough. You will serve this goddess in the next rites."

I said it boldly, but then dropped my eyes, because I felt the blood rushing to my cheeks. When I looked up again, Gilgamesh was looking down at his axe, and frowning, and I thought for a moment that he was going to refuse me. But he nodded and said: "Very well, goddess."

Eight.

The marriage rite is laid down in the tablets and upon the wall of every temple, and must be adhered to very closely if the ceremony is to have its power.

There must be a god and a goddess, or a legal stand-in for each. First the god must kiss and lick the vulva of the goddess, in a certain way and for the proper amount of time, and then he must kiss and stroke her hands and feet, her sides and back, her buttocks and the backs of her legs, in the order that is laid down. Then they must lie entwined, as one, while the hymns are sung. The congregation sing along to all of the familiar old words: he is the honey that feeds her womb; he is the holy tree; she is the field that must be ploughed and then watered.

After this the god lies upon the goddess, then she must climb on top of him and move until she has had her pleasure, and then they must lie side by side, entwined once again. Only then can he release his seed into the goddess, so that all may be right in the world.

I should have shouted and screamed, as I always had with Dumuzi, to show that there was no difference between these men who served me.

But with Gilgamesh I found myself silent.

Nine.

We met once in private, in my small room in the palace. That was the tenth time. Gilgamesh had seemed unsure, but I had pushed for it, with a new boldness.

Harga, the captain of my guard, let him in. Gilgamesh and Harga looked hard at each other, just once, as Gilgamesh passed. Whatever Harga was thinking, he said nothing.

When the door was shut, I could not quite believe it, that I had him there, all to myself. But also I felt nervous. What might Gilgamesh want, without the temple carvings to restrain him?

That time, before we lay down, he said: "Inanna, you do not know me. Perhaps you think you do, because you are young, for a god. But you do not know me. Do not be confused by what this is."

"What is it?"

"This is an affair. You are married to a god, and I am married to a god's daughter."

I had not known that. "To Enlil's daughter?"

"It does not matter who. I am bound. And you are bound. That aside, there is the difference between us that is insurmountable, because I am not an immortal. I am but a mayfly to the everlasting sun that is you. I will be dead so very soon, while you go on living. The sun cannot put all its hope into one mayfly."

"I can kiss the mayfly, though," I said. "I can warm it."

Afterwards I lay with my head upon his shoulder.

He picked up my left wrist and brought it almost to his nose, so that he could examine my *mee* closely.

"Why do you only have one *mee*, when I have seen half gods with armfuls of them?"

"This is the only one I have been given."

"And what does this one do?"

"An called it the *mee* of love. But it has never worked."

"It seems to be working on me," he said, and lifted his head to kiss it. A moment later there was a frown upon his brow, as if he regretted his own joke.

On the third morning after my husband had gone, Gilgamesh came to find me in the courtyard at the palace. I could see he had something to tell me, but that my soldiers were standing too close.

"Can you read?" he asked. "I should have asked you before."

"As well as any priestess."

"Perhaps one day I will write to you."

He paused, looking away across the yard, his head down. He looked as if he might say something else, but closed his mouth on the words. "I'd better check on my father," he said.

Then he was gone.

That was eleven, and eleven was the last time.

The next morning I learned that the king, Lugalbanda, and all his household, had left in the night, and the entire royal bodyguard with them, two hundred men. Harga, the captain of my bodyguard, was the one to give me this news.

"And the son?"

"Yes, the son too."

That day I did everything just as I always did. I thought all the time, *He will come to my door; he would not really leave without me.*

But he did not come.

My husband returned from Eridu with his sister, Geshtinanna, on his arm. He moved her into his rooms, on the far side of the palace from me. That night she sat with us at dinner, sleek and happy as an otter, and dressed in a robe so fine-spun I could see every hair on her body.

Dumuzi and Geshtinanna did not seem perturbed by the loss of Lugalbanda and his son, or even the soldiers who went north with them.

"You look tired," Dumuzi said to me. "It doesn't suit you."

"I hear Lugalbanda's son ploughed you in the temple," Geshtinanna said to me, with a hand on Dumuzi's arm.

"He was very virile," I said.

"But I hear he's gone now," she said. "They say he has a girl in Nippur that he cannot be without. A daughter of Enlil, by a priestess. They say she is the most beautiful woman in Sumer."

I was about to say something clever, but I found I could not remember what I had been going to say.

Dumuzi smiled a little then. "My father will send new guards to us."

I softened my face. "Did you see my mother, in Eridu?"

Dumuzi glanced at Geshtinanna before answering.

"No, I didn't see her, but I'm sure she's fine. I believe Ninhursag has been to see her. No doubt we will see them all when my father visits us here."

"I thought you said she was living with Ninhursag?"

"Maybe she was," he said. "She's well, Inanna."

My mind turned back to Gilgamesh.

I had seen him eleven times. But it seemed I might never see him again.

When I went back to my room that night, I sat on my bed, dressed, unmoving, my hands still in my lap, until the servants came in to light the lamps.

CHAPTER FOUR

NINSHUBAR

In the near-dark before dawn, I crawled up onto a mess of mud and reeds, somewhere along the coast to the west of Eridu. Or was I to the north? For a while I simply lay there, cold, breathing in the dank smell of the vegetation, and listening to the extraordinary rasping-barking noise all round me: almost deafening. Could this cacophony be frogs?

While I'd been in the water, I hadn't realised how much I was bleeding. Now I could see I was bleeding from so many gashes and scratches that it was hard to work out what was not bleeding. The side of my head, which had been getting better while I was in the dungeon, was now in sharp agony, as if the bone of my skull was pinching inwards. I had thought I was at sea, but when I accidentally swallowed some water, it was sweet. Was I upriver?

Eventually I got up onto my feet on the reeds and mud, keen to see what was beyond the reeds I was surrounded by, but I took one step forwards and fell into deep water again.

Whatever scrap of solid land I had been clinging to, I could no longer find.

I thrashed my way out into the open water again, trying to get clear of the reeds, and then bobbed along through patches of clear water as day broke over the marshes. The reeds were all around me and so tall that I could see nothing beyond. Would I die here, treading water, and with no idea which way to go?

Then I saw a sort of beach of mud: praise be to all the fates. To the red moon. To the spirit of the cheetah. Praise be.

I thrashed over, elbowing and kneeing my way up onto the bare mud bank. Then for a while I lay down on my front, head turned to the side, my cheek in the dankest, slipperiest mud. Only breathing. Only resting, to the deafening music of what must be all the frogs that could possibly be alive in the world.

I woke up and an old woman in black hessian was standing over me, a rope tight round her forehead, a huge bundle of reeds on her back.

"Are you dead?" she said, in Sumerian, but in an accent that I had never heard before. "Are you a ghost?"

"No, I am alive. I think I am alive."

"Are you a demon?"

"I don't think so."

She frowned down at me. "You look like a demon."

"I'm a human," I said. "Look at how I'm bleeding. Do demons bleed?"

She pondered that. "Maybe they do."

"If I am a demon, I am not a threatening demon. I am only injured and in trouble."

She looked around us, then looked back down at me.

"If you can get up and follow me, I can take you to my house. But if you try to hurt me, or steal from me, I will kill you with this knife."

She pulled a knife from beneath her wrappings: a lovely flint blade.

"You are safe with me," I said.

"A demon might say that."

"Yes, possibly."

I got up, very stiff, cold as the breeze hit me.

I followed the woman in black through the marshes, as I had once followed Dulma through the slave market.

We had not gone many steps when I saw an old wooden canoe in front of us, pulled up on the mud. The woman heaved her reeds into the bottom of it, and then pushed it onto the water.

"You get in."

She gestured for me to sit in the floor of the canoe. This I did, very nervous, though. It was a small boat, and it waggled wildly from side to side as I climbed in. I sat with my buttocks on the reeds, and my knees splayed against the sides of the canoe, a hand gripping hard on either side.

The woman was old, but once she had seen me get in, she hopped in very lightly herself, apparently with no fear of tipping us over. She pulled up a long pole that had been tucked down inside the canoe, and, balancing on a little plank, she pushed us off and out into deeper water.

I tried to reposition myself and she turned round and barked at me: "You stay still!"

After that, I stayed still, or as still as a human could while still breathing, and still casting her eyes around a little at the reeds, and grey-flecked water, and the pink-purple sky.

The old woman, meanwhile, seemed to move around very freely as she dug her pole into the water, pushing us along through the endless sea of reeds. I watched her very closely: it is always best to know how to do things.

For a long while she poled along, humming to herself a little; was she humming along with the frogs?

I sat, very uncomfortable, gripping hard, and very aware that I was far too big for this little boat. As I looked down at myself, I noticed for the first time that I still had my star of Nammu hanging around my neck.

We came at last to a strange sort of island. It was like a raft made of reeds, but with an arch-shaped structure on top. As we drew up, I saw that the structure was a simple sort of hut, made of reeds that had been bundled together. The old woman drove her canoe straight into the little island, and hopped off. On all fours, I climbed off. The island sank heavily beneath me, and I would have fallen off backwards, except the woman grabbed my wrist, pulling me forwards hard. Standing, I found that with each step I took, the reeds beneath me sank heavily, causing water to pool my feet.

"Is this a raft?"

"It is my house," she said. "You are very welcome."

I had to stoop down low to get into the hut.

Inside: heavy gloom and smoke. Rugs. A fire burning on the reed floor, between the rugs. At the far end, two round-eyed children, both naked.

"You sit," the woman said, pointing to the brightest rug.

I sat down upon this rug, looking over at the children, and them looking over at me.

The woman handed me a blanket next, and then leaned out of the doorway and with a quick and professional motion, filled up the kettle over the edge of the raft.

This she put on the fire to boil.

I was watching her and then I thought, *I must lie down now, whatever convention demands.*

I must have slept. I dreamed of the Potta, and that I was about to set out for him at last.

It was dusk when I woke. The kettle was boiling, with the woman and the children sitting around it. For a while I felt confused, and out of place. A flea appeared on my hand, directly in my eyeline, and then hopped away.

I saw the woman and children were looking at me. Out of politeness, then, I did not make any fuss about the flea that had been on my hand, or indeed about all the other fleas that now seemed to be hopping all over me.

However, I said to the old woman, perhaps sooner than I might have otherwise: "I must be on my way soon."

"Where are you going?" She was sitting in a squat, poking at a pot over the fire.

"I'm going north, I think," I said, "but perhaps I am going south."

"Eat, then, while you decide."

I smiled, my scabbed lips cracking. It took a great deal of strength not to start clawing at my body, but I did discreetly brush one flea from my left arm.

At this point the smell of the stew reached me, and overwhelmed me. Whatever it was, it smelled good: meaty and salty. I did not care what was in it: I did not want to know. If it was frogs, I would eat frogs. She saw me looking at it, and scooped some into a small clay bowl. This I took and I ate very quickly with my fingers. I did not even flinch when a flea hopped into my bowl, only scooping it up with the rest of it.

It was only after I had eaten my stew, and as I was stripping the skin from a bird claw of some kind with my teeth, that I understood they had given me all of the food.

"I'm sorry I was so greedy," I said. "I am not like myself today."

"You are our guest," she said. "Everything we have is yours. It is a delight to feed you."

As it was getting dark, an older child appeared, also naked, carrying a bundle of fish on a string. Heartbeats later the old woman was scraping fat into a pan and the fish were sizzling. I saw that the older child had a twisted foot, and walked with difficulty as he came to sit beside the cooking fire.

I felt enormously hungry once again.

"These are all for you," the old woman said.

"No. I will have none. I am already full from my stew."

This was greeted with contempt by the woman. In the end I was allowed to stop after three fish. The other three she divided out between herself and the three children.

When they had finished, I said: "Where do I do my business?"

They looked at each other. "We go out in the canoe for our private business," the woman said. "But I think it is better if you just go around the side of the hut, and do it anywhere you can. We will not judge you."

They all looked most anxious even as I clambered up, shaking off my blanket, and lumbered to the door. I was used to feeling strong and agile, and this new experience, on this wobbling raft, I found very unpleasant.

As I squatted, very nervous, at the edge of the raft, I saw nearby another raft island, with a water buffalo standing on it, looking at me through the gloaming.

"Is that your buffalo?" I said, returning, happy to have survived my expedition.

"Oh yes," the woman said. "We have several, on different islands."

In the gathering dark, she built up the fire with blocks of what looked like dried dung.

"Is it not dangerous, having a fire in here?"

"Oh yes. Very dangerous."

I pulled my blanket up around me again.

"I have never asked anyone for advice," I said. "But may I ask you for some now?"

"I am old and very wise," the woman said.

The children giggled at this, but were silenced by a frown.

"So," I said. "I have lost my son. I would have gone and looked for him before, but I did not know where to start. Last night, though, I dreamed I went looking for him at last, and when I woke and realised I had not done so, the pain was almost too much to bear."

"I see this."

"But also I have given my word to someone that I would go and find her daughter. I think the daughter is in trouble. So, my question is, should I go south, for love and honour? Or back into the heart of Sumer, for honour and trouble? What is the right thing to do, for a great hero of this world?" I said this last bit with a smile, to show her that I felt the absurdity of my words, as I sat there so dirty and not even armed.

"I think you have seen enough trouble already," the woman said. "If you could see yourself, you would agree with me. Why not stay here, live a simpler life? You are big, for this place, but we could build you a bigger island, a bigger hut. We could teach you to fish."

I waved this away. "I am a marvellous fisherwoman." I was about to go on in this vein, but then I stopped and looked again at the boy with the twisted foot.

"I am not sure I am hero enough for a life on the marshes," I said. "I'm not sure life here would be simpler for me."

"Do all heroes look like you do, where you come from?" she said. "Do they all leak so much blood?"

"In my experience," I said, "yes."

The marsh woman smiled at me, very kind.

"I think you have made your decision," she said.

CHAPTER FIVE

GILGAMESH

We left Uruk before first light, our mounts' hooves muffled with cloth, and pushed hard north.

My father had lent me one of his new animals. He called them horses, and he'd had six imported from the eastern steppes, at grotesque cost.

The stallion leaped about beneath me.

"He moves much better than a mule or a donkey, I will give you that," I called over to my father. "There's real power in him."

It was a great joy to me, to be riding along in the same train as my father; for us to be discussing a horse.

We were riding at the head of our household, strung out along a narrow pathway that snaked through heavy marshes. My father had chosen to avoid the road, lest someone in Uruk decide to chase us.

Enkidu was on the mule I had given to him after Marad, and he had to trot occasionally to keep up with my horse. Harga we had left behind in Uruk, to keep an eye on the girl.

I could tell Enkidu was sucking on something, so I dropped back to ride next to him, my new mount flashing angry teeth at his sweet-tempered mule.

"Say it, then," I said.

"You know what it is."

"The girl? Is this about her?"

"She is in love with you, and you know that."

"Girls are always in love with me, until they get to know me."

He said nothing.

"Enkidu, I barely spent any time with her!"

"You didn't have to go to her in temple, or see her in private, as I know you did. Yet you did, and you have muddled things for her."

"Inanna will survive worse than this."

"Gilgamesh," he said. "This feels wrong. You should not play with someone's heart."

There was a short silence between us, as each of us looked down at our reins. Then I said: "Enkidu, she is not some temple girl, cruelly messed about by some high lord. She is a goddess of war, whatever you may have heard of her, and a married woman. She will outlive us both by hundreds of years. Perhaps more. And besides, I have left Harga to watch over her. That is not nothing. That is something. He is tasked with her care now."

Enkidu turned his face from me and rode on ahead. I wondered if it was only concern for the girl that made him kick his mule on, or whether he was also jealous.

I had grown expert, over the years, about never thinking too hard about my conduct. When you drink, it's best not to dwell on what cannot be changed. Now as I rode along, with Enkidu's angry back ahead of me, I found myself thinking of Inanna, and her black eyes upon me, and how she had looked, sitting in bed in a sheet. I wondered now if, had it been different, had we been equals, gods both, if we could have been something together one day.

But, of course, we were not equal and never would be, and yearning after a life of the gods was something I was trying to put into my past. And what about Enkidu? How would he fit into some fantasy life where I married Inanna?

I kicked my horse on, to catch up with his mule.

"Look," I said. "When we have settled my father at Nippur, why don't we go back for her?"

"I think we should," he said, turning in his saddle. "It was wrong to leave her there like that."

Now I felt doubly punished – for what I had done to Inanna, but also for doubting his concern for her.

"Enkidu," I said. "I promise on my life that as soon as I can, I will go back for her. I will make sure she's safe."

"I think that is good," he said. "Thank you."

We stopped for the night in a small lakeside town, and my father's men requisitioned every mosquito-infested inn.

Enkidu and I were billeted on what passed as the town square, and in one of the better establishments, me being my father's son. Our inn, although double storeyed, was entirely constructed from reeds. We ate downstairs in a wide room with a big fire at the centre of it, and thick smoke hanging over our heads. Our hosts went back and forth with stew and breads, and the men of the town came to peek at us as we ate.

Afterwards we sat and each drank one cup of something a bit like beer. That is what I now allowed myself, after a long day. It was terrible beer, but we sat there in perfect peace together, as we had sat so many times, and talked about my father's splendid new horses.

Our host could not understand Sumerian, and we could not understand him, but he seemed happy to merely listen as we talked.

As it drew close to bedtime, I cannot tell you why, but a silence fell between me and Enkidu, in a way that it had never fallen before. I became alive to Enkidu's arm against mine.

When the silence had drawn on for ten minutes or so, with us each looking around, me pretending to be interested in the comings and goings of the hut, Enkidu said: "You know, Gilgamesh, there is nothing you can ask of me that I am not ready to give."

We had been given a small room in the roof space, reached via a wooden ladder, with two small beds of sorts made up on either side. There were so many fleas that, on any other night, I would have complained. That evening, though, I had nothing to complain of.

As Enkidu was about to pull off his riding shirt, I said: "Let me help you with that."

He at once turned to me, took my face in his hands, and kissed me.

And then all the rest came easy.

Afterwards we lay together hip to hip, and I said: "I should have asked sooner."

He laughed. "I could have asked. But you pursue women with such a fury, I could never be sure of you."

"Harga told me I would bring down death and disgrace upon you."

He kissed me in the darkness. "Then it will have been worth it," he said.

Enkidu woke about midnight, saying he did not feel right.

"Let's get you outside," I said.

That was easier said than done. He almost fell from the ladder, and it was dark downstairs, with people sleeping underfoot.

Out in the yard behind the hut there was a construction made of reeds over a pit, which had been pointed out to us rather proudly on our arrival. There Enkidu vomited, and emptied his guts, with me holding on to him so that he didn't topple into the stinking hole.

He leaned heavily on me as I helped him back inside. "I feel awful."

"I can see that. I've been there, as you well know."

In the morning, he seemed hard to stir, unwilling to drink water or come downstairs again. I sent word out to my father, and soon his herbalist came. The man said it was food poisoning.

At dusk my father came and put his head up into the little room. "We need to move on."

"He's not well enough to travel. But, Father, you go on; just leave us the herbalist and a few men, and we will join you in Nippur as soon as we can."

"Are you sure, Gilgamesh?" I could see from his face that he was thinking of saying something else, but did not.

"What can you do to help him by staying?" I said. "Just go."

❦

That night Enkidu seemed worse, not better.

All the same, I did not worry. How many times had I seen men sick after eating bad food, or drinking bad water?

He said to me: "Gilgamesh, I have been happy, in this time with you."

I could have said so many things, but instead I said: "Let me get you some water."

In the evening on the third day, one of my father's men came up the ladder and said: "We found this downstairs in the reeds, near where you were sitting, and we wondered if it was meant for you."

It was a small piece of clay, a neat oval, and on it, in neat little marks, it said: *For Hedda.*

"What is it?" Enkidu said.

"It's nothing," I said. "Just a bit of broken pot."

I remembered all the strangers standing near us, going in and out, on that first night when we ate and drank by the fire. Of course one of them could have been sent by Akka. I wondered if Enkidu had been the target, or whether it was me who should be lying sick.

"Sleep, Enkidu," I said. "Sleep and you will wake better."

CHAPTER SIX

INANNA

L ilith, my chief priestess as she was now, tried to make my *mee* of love work. She scratched her nails into the little marks around the edge of the dull grey bracelet, and pinched my flesh as she twisted at it.

"Is it your intention to hurt me?"

"I have never meant you any harm, my lady."

"My mother's priestesses have already tried this," I said. "It doesn't work."

Lilith let go of my wrist. "Sometimes they come alive," she said. "It happens."

One of the temple orphans came in and coughed for our attention.

"There is a girl here for you, goddess."

"Who?"

"A tall girl with very dark skin. She is very dirty. But she says she has a message for you and only you. But she is very dirty."

"Send her in," I said. "I am not afraid of dirt."

The temple orphan, who had not been with us long and had work to do on her temple etiquette, turned her head and shouted over her shoulder: "Come in, then, you!"

I have always been the smallest. First as child in a palace of grown-ups, and then as a young woman who never grew as tall as the adults around her.

This girl, though, was the tallest woman I had ever met. Imperiously tall, with hair cropped short against her shapely skull, and many scars. Scars upon scars, and over them the marks of what looked like fresh beatings. She was also very dirty, as I had been doubly warned: her cloak seemed to be largely made of caked mud. I saw, though, that she had the insignia of a temple tied around her neck on a piece of leather cord. It was an eight-pointed star, made of bone or ivory, and very white against the midnight of her skin. The sign of Nammu.

The girl had something of a swagger to her, despite the filth.

"My name is Ninshubar," she said. I could not place her accent.

"Nin-shooo-barrrr," I said.

Ninshubar stood, looking so serious that I stood up to face her. "Yes?"

"You should send the priestesses out." She waved a confident hand at Lilith and the orphan. "I have a message that is only for you."

"No," Lilith said.

"You go out," I said to Lilith. "I am not afraid of this girl."

When we were alone, I said: "Ninshubar come and sit with me." I sat down myself again, next to the fire bowl that we read tablets by.

She came over, and sat down, drawing her long legs into herself.

"Inanna, you don't know me, but I know your mother."

I nodded, my smile expectant.

"She told me her name was Ningal."

"Yes," I said, still smiling, and nodding.

My hands were prickling, and my forearms, with something like a chill.

I am a goddess of love.

"I was with her in Eridu, in a prison," Ninshubar said.

I looked at all the old scars on Ninshubar's face, and the new ones overlaid.

A goddess of love.

"I walked here, sleeping in the bush, so it was not a quick journey," Ninshubar said. "Although I cannot imagine how anyone could have done it quicker."

Love.

I remembered to breathe. "Ninshubar, tell me what you are going to tell me."

"I don't know about your father, but I think your mother may be dead."

I shut my eyes. I found I could not sense her.

I opened my eyes again, to Ninshubar's hard stare.

I said: "I have been told that my mother is in Ninhursag's compound, with my lions. That she is being well treated."

"Not when I left," Ninshubar said. "Enki was not treating her well."

Love.

"So you think she is dead?" The chill was creeping up my arms. "It is hard to kill an Anunnaki."

Ninshubar raised her shoulders, and then let them fall. "Inanna, I am very sorry, but I cannot be sure. I do not know whether she is alive or dead. But he was treating her very badly when I last saw her. I think him capable of great cruelty."

"My husband has told me so many times that she is safe."

"She was in a dungeon when I left," Ninshubar said. "Naked and bleeding."

The chill was sinking into me now.

It was a liquid, icy cold. Or was the liquid burning hot?

Pure, icy fire.

Was this rage, filling up my bones?

The *mee* upon my left wrist began to glow, a strange green light.

I am a goddess of war.

"She told me to bring you a message," Ninshubar said. "And so, I am here. But you should know that I did everything I could to bring her with me."

"What is the message?"

"She says you should go to see your sister."

War.

The *mee* tightened around my wrist.

"I should go south to rescue my mother," I said.

"Your mother said you should visit your sister. She said your sister might help you with your *mee*. Is that your *mee*?"

She was pointing at my wrist.

The ground beneath me seemed to sink in.

War.

"I need to think," I said, although my mind felt very clear, cleaned out by burning anger.

Ninshubar put one hand out onto my leg. She said: "I told your mother that I would help you if I found you. And so, I will. I will help you now, Inanna, in all that you will surely do."

"Thank you, Ninshubar," I said, and I put my both my hands

on top of hers, filthy though she was. "I will not forget what you have done."

Had Lilith done something to my *mee*? It felt different. But I knew even as I asked myself the question that it was not Lilith who had done this. It was me.

I had awakened the *mee*. Something that was in me had come alive, and now what had been only a cool metal bangle thrummed on my wrist, thrummed through me, pushing urgently, almost painfully, at the edges of my mind. I had always had a feel for the Anunnaki and their godly offspring, a knowing of where they were. Now a map of small gold sparks began to appear in my mind's eye, of where my family were. I did think I could sense my mother now, albeit faintly. And far to the south, far to the south, I saw a new spark, unfamiliar, moving north. An Anunnaki I had never felt before.

War.

My *mee* had come alive, connecting me, not just to the Anunnaki, but to all of the *melam* that flowed through the cities and the people of Sumer.

I knew now where the underworld was. I felt it true and unmistakable: a hard blue light upon the horizon. I turned my ear to it, and I could hear it calling to me.

Ninshubar was leaning over me. "Are you well, Inanna?"

"You will have to help me stand," I said. "But yes, I am quite well."

I went to dinner at the palace and took my place beside my husband. We were served heaped-up plates of river fish, fried in butter, and roast marsh fowls.

I sat, feeling calm and strong, and watched Dumuzi and Geshtinanna with new eyes. I saw the light now that flickered in them. I saw also that they did not see the difference in me, so I sat and ate, thinking over what I might say to my husband, and the sister he was in love with. I thought through, one thing after another, all the things he had told me about my mother, about how well she was in Eridu, about friends visiting her. I remembered Dumuzi standing over me, on the night of our wedding, and suggesting to his father that they cut my arm off to get my *mee*.

Dumuzi said to me: "Why are you looking at me like that? Stop it."

I shrugged at him, and continued to eat. I would need a full belly, whatever I did next, and I intended to steal food from the table, as much as I could fold up in napkins and put in my pockets.

Dumuzi shook his head at his sister, and rolled his eyes at me.

They did not deserve to be told what I was doing. But all the same I was going to tell them. I did not want it said afterwards that I had crept off, like a beaten dog.

When I had finished my food, I knew that my decision was made.

The underworld was calling to me, and I would answer its call.

I said: "Dumuzi, I am going down to the underworld, to see my sister."

He looked over at Geshtinanna. "She's gone mad."

"Nonetheless, I am going," I said.

They watched me pile some roast birds and fruit into a napkin, and some cheese and flatbreads into another. I put dried figs and apricots into my skirt pockets. Then I made my way slowly to my rooms, my guards scrambling away from their plates to follow me.

Ninshubar had bathed, or been bathed, and was now dressed in clean clothes. A long woollen smock, woollen trousers and a leather jerkin over the top, all in the rich brown of the sacred river in full flow. She looked extremely dangerous with the mud off her, and also handsome.

She seemed also to have scavenged fresh oatcakes, and she ate these lounging on my bed. I had never seen a human lounge before, not even Gilgamesh.

"So, are you going south to rescue your mother?" she said. "Or to your sister?"

"To my sister," I said. "I need to understand better what my *mee* can do, before I try to rescue my mother from Enki. And I feel it calling out to me."

"What is calling to you?"

"The Great Below," I said. "The underworld."

"I've heard of it, but what is it?"

"It is a place with many names. Some call it the underworld, others the Kur, or the Great Below, or the Dark City that no one returns from. Some call it Ganzir. You know I've never noticed, until now, how many names it has."

"And what is it?"

"It is where the dead go, when they die."

"We don't have this place in my country," she said.

The servant girls had gone, so I now dressed myself for my journey with Ninshubar watching.

First, I stripped naked. Then I put my best temple dress over my head: white, for Ur.

"A long time ago my mother asked me to submit," I said. "And for a long time, I have submitted. Just as she asked. I have said nothing when I wanted to speak. And I have done things I did not want to do. Because I gave her a promise, the sacred promise of a goddess, which can never be broken."

I tied my dress at the waist.

"Perhaps I would have died if I had not submitted. Perhaps she was right to extract such a promise from me. But the time of my promise has ended. I will no longer be submitting."

"I see that." Ninshubar nodded approvingly, her mouth full of cake. "I have never submitted to anyone," she added. "So, for what it is worth, I support you."

Next, I put on the breastplate of Ur, moulded in the finest bronze. The soldiers in my home city called those breastplates "Come, then, and try me!". They were decorated with the head of the wild bull of heaven, as he dips his horns to charge.

I could not do it up at the back.

"Let me help you," Ninshubar said. She pulled the leather strings tight and buckled it at the sides. "Why are you putting on armour?"

"When I was only a baby, the king of the gods told me that I would be the goddess of love and war," I said. "For a long time, I have tried to be only a goddess of love. Now the war is rising up in me."

"I see there is fight in you," she said, returning to my bed.

Next, I put on the necklace of lapis lazuli beads that my grandfather Enlil sent me when I was a baby. Then I looped my huge beads of ancient amber, which my father gave me in Eridu, twice around my chest. Finally, I got out my gold *shugurra*, the famous crown of the high steppe, which I had only ever worn on my wedding day.

This huge crown I put on the bed next to Ninshubar.

"That's a big crown," she said. "Where are you going, in this outfit? Are you going to temple, before we set off?"

"These are my clothes for the journey," I said.

Ninshubar looked down, frowning, at the crown. She put out one hand to feel its weight. "Is it far to the underworld?"

I shut my eyes and focused on the blue light.

"Yes, it's far. I can't tell how far."

Ninshubar now watched me open-mouthed as I opened a large cedar chest and unwrapped my wedding-day temple wings from the linen they had been stored in.

"Those too?"

"Yes, you will need to help tie them onto me."

She got up and helped wrestle the eagle-feather wings into position, tying the strings tight around my waist.

Then I put on the crown. My neck sagged a little with the weight of it.

Last of all, holding up an old copper mirror, I daubed my eyes with kohl.

"Inanna, it is nothing to me, what other people choose to wear," Ninshubar said, "but at least put on some boots." She waved down at her own boots, which ran all the way up to her knees. "Something sensible to walk in."

I looked down at the embroidered bedroom slippers that I was wearing on my feet. They were a pretty saffron yellow, with pink and green stiches on them, like little waves. I had chosen them because, of all my slippers and sandals, they seemed the most sensible.

"I intend to walk down to the Dark City like this," I said.

"Wherever it is. However far it is. This is what I am wearing. I am a high goddess, and I will dress like one."

"I am going to have to come with you," Ninshubar said. "Whether I like it or not. Otherwise, you will most certainly die."

She stood and looked around. "I have my cloak somewhere. I kept them from taking that. But I don't have a pack, or a waterskin, or any food. Or, more importantly, any weapons."

"I have some food," I said, looking about me for the robe I had worn to dinner. "I am sure we can find any other things we will need along the way."

She raised her chin, and then tipped her head to the side. "Let's go now, then," she said. "If you're going to do something, it is better to do it quick."

Outside my door, there stood the man I knew to be called Harga. I looked about but could see no one else in the corridor. I had expected my whole guard, not just this one man.

Harga and I looked at each other, him rubbing a smooth grey pebble between his thumbs.

"Are you going to temple now, goddess?" he said, looking down at my breastplate and then, with his mouth falling open a little, at my wings. "It is late for temple."

"No," I said. "I'm leaving Uruk."

I felt he was about to say something more on the subject of my outfit, but he closed his mouth on it. "I won't stop you going," he said. "Gilgamesh asked me to look out for you. So, I will. But are you sure you know what you're doing?"

"You may stand aside," I said.

He shrugged and stepped back.

"Thank you, Harga," I said.

I passed through, my wings catching at the doorway, with as much dignity as I could while pulling at my feathers, but then Ninshubar said: "Wait there, Inanna."

She was standing a little too close to Harga.

They were about the same height, nose to nose. He was heavier with muscle, and wider set, but there was something in the way Ninshubar held herself that made her look just as dangerous.

"I need your knives and your sword," she said to Harga. "We have no weapons."

Harga's left hand moved to the knife on his belt. He did not look like a man who would give up his weapons.

"Harga," I said. "We are going on a journey, and we have no weapons. We would be grateful for yours. I promise they will be returned to you, or if lost, that I will repay you in gold. That is the sacred promise of a goddess."

He looked from me to Ninshubar, and back again.

"I will give you my knives, and this axe" – he produced a copper axe from his belt buckle – "because of my orders from Gilgamesh, to do what I could for you. But I'm keeping my sword, which Enlil gave me himself."

"Thank you, Harga," I said.

Ninshubar accepted the knives and the axe but did not thank him. "What about that?" she said. She was pointing at something on his belt. "Is that a slingshot? I will take that too."

"Take the sword," he said. "But you can't have my slingshot."

She took the sword, again with no thanks.

"That man was born to serve you," she said to me as we tiptoed away down the corridor. "Is that not the law in this land, that mortals exist only to serve you? You should not be thanking people for only doing what is written down in your law."

I walked ahead through the dark streets. The moon was obscured by cloud but in my mind's eye the underworld called to me, bright and strong.

Ninshubar followed on behind me, swinging Harga's axe in her right hand.

As we made our way up to the main city gates, we saw by the light of a fire bowl that the guard was asleep in his chair.

I kept on walking, not looking back at Ninshubar, out into the fields, heading east.

Since Gilgamesh had left me, I had felt empty, and lost. Aware of the pain, yes, but it had been a distant, shapeless pain. I had had no plan. No way forwards.

Now my anger lit up a path before me, streaking out across the river plains. It lit up my heart and it lit up the *mee* upon my wrist.

I would go down to the Great Below, and I would speak to my sister, Ereshkigal. And then I would understand what power was, and how to take it for myself, so that if I ever had a daughter of my own, no one could take her from me.

War.

"So, you know your way to this place, even if you don't know how far it is?" Ninshubar said.

"I've never been there," I said. "But my *mee* is guiding me."

"I've seen the tricks that *mees* can do," she said. "Your grandfather Enki was kind enough to show me some of them."

"Did he hurt you?" I said, turning back to look at her.

She gave a little shrug. "There are always repercussions, if you refuse to submit to someone."

"He hurt me," I said. "Although I did submit."

"Well, I am sorry for that," she said.

As the skyline brightened, we crossed a wide meadow. Far away in the gloom I thought I saw a leopard, looking at us a long while with its head dipped, before it slipped away. Behind us, in the city, we could hear dogs, and shouting, floating to us in snatches on the wind.

"Should we run?" I asked.

Ninshubar made a scoffing noise. "You are wearing a crown! And slippers!" She laughed, a happy laugh. "Wings!" She could not stop chortling to herself.

"I am happy to so please you," I said. "I have never until now been a figure of fun."

"Wings!" she said, and laughed again.

CHAPTER SEVEN

GILGAMESH

For four long days, Enkidu hovered between life and death.
The herbalist said to me: "If it is poison... if he has been poisoned... then it is very late now to treat him. But I will try."

We forced pastes down his throat and carried him down to the hearth so that medicinal smoke could be blown over him. We sat him up against the central post of the hut, and the priests of the village came to say their prayers over him and bang their drums. When I could see that he did not understand what was happening, and was frightened by it, I had him carried back upstairs to our loft.

For a long time after Enkidu stopped speaking, I could still hear him breathe. It took a long time after that until he stopped breathing, and for all of it I sat with him, as I had sat with him in Marad. I thought about all the things I had never said to him, and moments I had let go by.

"I love you, Enkidu," I said. But I did not know if he could hear me.

After I was sure Enkidu was dead, I lay down in his bed with him, and held him.

I realised I did not know what the traditions of his people were. I did not know if he would rather be buried, or left out in the mountains for the birds, or something else entirely.

After a long time, the tavern keeper came halfway up the ladder. I saw by his gesticulations that he wanted to know if I wanted any food or water. I could see, also, he wanted to ask about Enkidu, but for now, he did not.

For long periods I must have slept.

I became aware that Enkidu was very cold, except where I had been holding him tight.

I pressed my mouth against his silken hair, and breathed the smell of him off his neck.

He was already going stiff.

How did I not know what he would have wanted?

I woke up with my face covered in tears. The pillow beneath me was soaked, and Enkidu very cold.

For a while I got up. I climbed down into an empty hall, found a bucket of water, and drank. But then I climbed back up to the sleep space. I realised I could not get back into bed with Enkidu: suddenly he was apart from me. Instead, I covered him up to the neck with a blanket, arranged his hair and beard so that he was tidy, and then lay across from him in my own bed.

A long time later, a different voice on the ladder.

"My lord, you are needed downstairs." I recognised the voice: one of Enlil's men.

"No. I don't want to come."

"The god is here," the man said. "Come downstairs."

I went down just as I was, down the cane ladder. Enlil was sitting cross legged on an old rug, the tavern keeper next to him. I went over and sat with them.

Enlil put one heavy hand onto my knee, and then we sat there a while together, watching the dung fire.

"Your father would have come, I am very sure, but he is at the front."

I nodded.

"They say your servant died seven days ago."

"I don't know."

"You have been with his body for seven days and seven nights."

"Perhaps."

"Do you blame yourself for his death?"

"I am entirely to blame. It was punishment for what I did in Kish. Enkidu was not in Kish. How can I not blame myself?"

Enlil passed me a cup of water, and I found I was thirsty, and drank it down in one.

"What is your intention now, Gilgamesh? Is it your intention now to pass over with him?"

"I am going to go north, and kill Akka."

The lord god Enlil leaned over and put his arms around me, and for a while I sat with my forehead on his shoulder.

"We will punish Akka, but first let us bury Enkidu," he said.

Enkidu was put on a wagon, tightly bound in linen strips, and wrapped in a rug. He had started to smell, and I felt shame that I had allowed that to happen to him.

I travelled next to him, lying down on my back on some sacks, my face to the sky. Enlil rode next to the wagon.

The road wove through farmland and open grassland. I watched ducks fly in formation overhead. I said: "Have you ever felt this? That you do not have it in you to go on?"

"I feel it every day," Enlil said. "I am not my brother Enki, so in love with life that I would kill to get more of it. But I go on."

"Why?"

"Duty," he said. "It is my duty to go on."

"Duty to who?"

He looked over at me, I think quite astonished. "To my family," he said. "To you, Gilgamesh. To Ninlil. To all of you."

"I had not realised."

"And guilt too," Enlil said, his face turned away from me. "I go on out of guilt."

I woke lying on my side, shaking back and forth as the wagon moved, with my back to Enkidu. Enlil was still riding alongside, his hood very black against the brilliance of the sky.

He said: "It is a great sadness to me, that we ran out of *melam*, before you came along. We have all loved you so much, young fool though you may have been. For a long time we kept hunting for it."

I shut my eyes. "What does it matter what happens to me, or

even to you? What does it matter what happens to the Anunnaki?"

"It would be worse without us," Enlil said. "Men like Akka have forgotten that."

At the outskirts of the Holy City, Enlil put up one hand and our small convoy drew to a halt.

"You should get up now and get on your horse," he said. He had a tight look about him. "She will be waiting for you. She has had the baby. You have a son. His name is Shara."

I did not want to get up, but I got up.

"I will take Enkidu's body to my temple, for him to be prepared. Do you have an idea on ceremony? A ceremony for a city man, or for a marsh man... what do you want for him?"

"I want him buried like family," I said.

He nodded. "I will have them dig a grave in the royal graveyard. You can come and see it all, make sure it is right, but first go home."

"Thank you, Enlil."

"I feel your grief, Gilgamesh. And I know what it is to feel guilty. How dead it can make you feel. But you must stand up now for your wife and son."

"Yes," I said. "I know."

He leaned over to touch my hair. "Just pretend to be alive," he said. "After a while it will almost be true."

My wife, Della, was standing on the steps of the Blue House, holding our newborn son to her chest.

I found myself standing and only looking at them, with no words in me.

I thought: *How I wish Enkidu could see him.*

"Are you not going to kiss me hello?" she said. "And kiss your son?"

I found myself walking past them, and into the palace.

When I was in my bath, she came and found me again, this time without the baby. I could see that she had dressed up carefully for me, and she had painted her eyes with kohl and the shining powder they make from seashells. She stood and looked down on me with her delicate hands clasped before her.

"I hear you lay with the little goddess girl in Uruk."

"Yes." I shut my eyes and sank deeper into the water.

"And not just in temple, but in secret."

"Yes."

"They say Enlil found you in bed with your servant's body. You had been lying with his corpse for seven days and seven nights. Is that true? That the body had begun to stink, and you were still lying with it?"

If I could have thought of a single thing to say that might have made her feel better, I would have said it.

I met with Enlil, in the same room where he had told me I would marry his daughter.

As I stood before his desk, he said: "I have asked that they carve his likeness, a statue, in the cedar wood you sent me from the forest."

"Do you have his likeness?"

"They have his body. And they will ask you if the likeness is true enough, before it is finished."

"I would like that." I sat down upon the chair that had been set out for me. "He saved my life in that forest."

"I did not know that."

I nodded, and then we looked at each other.

He said: "I have been thinking that we should set up a temple for you here. There are precedents. And we could set up his statue there."

I nodded.

"Will you write the lament?" he said.

"Yes."

"Will you read it?"

"I will try."

"I will finish it for you, if you cannot go on."

"Thank you, Enlil."

Afterwards he took me to his temple, to look at the grave goods, that had been set out for the people to look at.

Upon a great table, carved from *elammaku* wood, there sat the most beautiful objects, of the rarest woods, the most intensely coloured inlays, the finest workmanship. And gold – so much gold. I was looking closely at a double-edged dagger, the hilt inlaid with lapis lazuli, when I realised that I had won it as booty, in my first battle against the northerners, and given it as a gift to Enlil.

I looked up at the god and he said: "Yes, all of these things you won in battle, and gave to me. And now I pass them to Enkidu, so that he may live in comfort in the underworld, and be reminded every day of you."

I put my hand to his arm, and spoke quietly so that the priests would not hear: "Enlil, will I see him again?"

He drew back from me a little. "You know the stories."

"Are they true, Uncle?"

He turned his full face to me, and was for a moment silent. "They are true, Gilgamesh. We will make the sacrifices, and he will be well cared for in Ganzir. And you will see him on the other side."

"Thank you, Enlil," I said. I held on to his hand. "Thank you for all you are doing, when I have done nothing to deserve or expect it from you."

"And yet we love you," he said. "And always will."

The royal cemetery at Nippur was at the edge of the city, standing upon open plain. The graveyard stood guarded by only a thin line of palm trees, and in the distance, the ice-capped mountains.

I had thought it would only be me and Enlil at the ceremony, as much as I had thought about it at all, but as I followed Enkidu's bier from the temple to the graveyard, I saw that the cemetery was thronged with people. Priests, priestesses, the ordinary people of Nippur, and down in the grave pit: my family, all dressed in simple robes of undyed linen.

They stood in two short rows, flanking the marble tomb.

On the right stood An, the king of all the gods, wearing a bronze mask in the shape of a bull. He leaned upon the arm of my mother, who I had thought to be far away, in the summer palace. Who I had not seen for so long. She gave me her softest smile.

On the left: the lord god Enlil, king of the sky gods, and the leader of Sumer's great armies. Next to him, his wife Ninlil, who I had not seen in public in two years. She looked very small next to him, her black eyes huge beneath her hood.

I went to stand between them all at the entrance to the marble grave, and watched as the priests laid down Enkidu's body on the flower-covered table that had been set out ready.

It was time for me to say my lament.

"May the sacred river mourn you," I said, looking down upon the sprays of rosemary and thyme on his linen-wrapped chest.

Tears began to pour down my cheeks, and I thought for a moment I could not go on. But there would not be another funeral for Enkidu.

My mother came to stand beside me, in a shock of sweet jasmine perfume, so familiar to me. She put her hand on my arm. "Your tears are a blessing, Gilgamesh," she said. "Do not fear the shedding of them."

And so somehow I went on, with my mother holding my arm tight.

"May the pure Euphrates mourn you," I said. "Whose waters we walked beside, in our vigour."

At the end, I turned to his corpse and said: "Goodbye, my love."

I might have thrown myself onto him then, but Enlil came forwards to help my mother, and each pressed kisses into my cheeks.

Afterwards they helped me hack off my hair, with the double-edged dagger that would soon be placed in the tomb with Enkidu. And not long after, they sealed his grave over, and we began to fill in the pit.

Enlil called me to his temple the day after the funeral. He was in the tablet chamber: a small room lit by fire bowls, hidden away behind his statue. He waved away his scribes.

"Have you thought about what you are going to do?"

I sat down in the chair opposite him. "I want to punish Akka. But I gave a promise to Enkidu, just before he died, that I would go back for the girl Inanna."

"Who you lay with, although I begged you not to."

"Yes."

He gave out a heavy sigh. "Gilgamesh, I think instead you should spend some time here. Live quietly for a while. Come hunting with me, hold your baby, get to know your wife. Spend time with your mother, who you have not seen for so long. Live in peace for a while, before you ride out into battle again."

"Della hates me."

He made a scoffing noise. "What does Della know about love or hate? She is a child still. You could win her over in minutes if you chose to."

I could not find anything in me to say. I felt only emptiness, where my joy and small thoughts and wishes and dreams had all been.

Enlil was still looking at me.

"If you go after Akka, you will die," he said. "That vengeance must wait. Inanna, you do not need to worry about. She is an Anunnaki. She will survive. Think about yourself now, Gilgamesh, and your new family."

"I will try," I said, trying to make my face into a smile for him.

"My father loves you so much. And he has asked to see you. Why don't you spend some time with him? He is a good man to be with, when you truly do not know which way to go."

"Thank you, Enlil," I said. "I will do that."

He came round to me, and I stood, and let him put his arms around me.

"We have always loved you so much, Gilgamesh," he said. "And we love you still. You are not alone."

I nodded against his shoulder, and there was a part of me that felt grateful to him. But his embrace did not comfort me. Indeed, I could not see then how I would ever feel comfort again.

So I sat with An, the king of the gods, in the afternoons. Enkidu's funeral had been too much for him, and now he lay in a strip of sunlight, and sometimes he spoke, and sometimes he shut his eyes and I saw that he was dreaming. With his mask off, I saw that all the youth was gone from him. He no longer looked like an Anunnaki: he looked instead like any other dying man.

"You think that if you live long enough, your heart will harden," he said to me. "But it is not always like that. Now I remember the great grief of my youth, when my mother died, and it is still fresh to me. It is a knife, twisting in my heart, twisting, and twisting. So, I know what it is like to be you today."

I nodded, but said nothing. An had not killed his mother, as I had killed Enkidu, so to me the two things did not seem to be the same.

Only two servants were allowed near An now. "They will pass over when I pass over," he said. Other than that, only the Anunnaki were allowed inside – and me, of course.

"It's a long time since a god died in this realm," An said. "I must die very quietly."

Sometimes he would seem not to remember me at all, and then a moment later be entirely present. "Did you see the girl, in Uruk?"

"I did, lord god."

"You know I saw her as a newborn baby. Even then, she reminded me of Enlil, that soul of black fire."

"Now you say it, I do see the resemblance. That hint of razed cities and a land scorched."

We both smiled at that.

"Yes, she's serious," An said. "Even as a baby, she was serious."

In the day they would carry his bed out into his courtyard. It had a low stoop all around the sides for shade, painted black and white.

"They are all worried about you," An said. "It would be a dream for him if he had *melam* to give you."

"*Melam* cannot cure what ails me."

I am not sure he heard me.

He said: "What a thing it is, for us to be reduced to this, unable to help someone we love so much. Or even to save ourselves."

"Will I see him again?" I said.

An turned to me, but frowned.

"Enkidu," I said. "You were at his funeral."

He shut his eyes. "Gilgamesh, the stories are not for you. They are not for us."

"Are you saying I won't see him? That Enlil lied?"

A long pause, so that I thought he would not answer.

"We are too few to survive here without the stories. Enki and Nammu always said it. That only the stories could keep us alive."

He opened his eyes and tried to reach for his water; I moved at once to help hold the cup to his mouth.

"Is that my answer?" I said. "Are you saying I will not see him?"

"I think you need to walk the world," An said. "Go out and find your own path. Find for yourself how to be a hero in this realm. Find a way to forgive yourself." He took another sip, and then waved the cup away. "I have an idea for where you should begin your journey. You know, in the first days, things went wrong for the Anunnaki, and some of the things we had were lost."

"I didn't know that, my lord. What happened?"

"The Kur was not made to withstand such a descent. So our things were scattered."

"By the Kur, do you mean the thunderbird, my lord?"

"Yes, we called it that." For a while he went silent, but then he said: "There is a man called Uta-napishti; have you heard of him?"

"The hero of the Great Flood."

"Yes. He is on the far side of the world now, but he may know where there is *melam*."

"I'm not sure that I want it now," I said. "I'm not sure what I want."

I found my hand abruptly gripped tight between his two ancient hands. "I want it," he said. "I want the *melam*. I'm not ready yet, to give up. I want you to find it for me."

He released my hand, and lay back on his pillows. "After the flood he went through the secret passage beneath Mount Mashu, to the far side of the world. And it is said he found a source of *melam* there. That is what I have been told."

"I'll go and look for you," I said. "Just tell me where to head."

"Enlil's man Harga knows the way."

"He's not here. He's with the girl Inanna."

"Enlil, then. He will tell you. He is the one who helped them through the mountain, when they were afraid to stay here, and perhaps face more floods."

I put on my hunting outfit: wool beneath, thin leather over. I took an axe, my bronze sword, my bow and a quiver of arrows. A pack of food and a camel-felt cloak.

"Where are you going?" Della said.

I put my hands on her shoulders, and kissed her forehead.

"I need to go somewhere, for An. But I will come back."

Then I walked past her and out onto the street.

CHAPTER EIGHT

NINSHUBAR

What a creature Inanna was as she walked so very slowly to the underworld.

Like a little owl, very fierce.

She walked ahead of me, and I had to take unnaturally short steps in order not to outstrip her. Her outfit was ludicrous, and yet there was something quite magnificent about her huge crown, and wide wings, against the gorgeous pink of the dawn, and the glory of the open river lands. The crown must have been heavy for her, but she did not turn. She kept going, through fields, through grass, across rough ground, in her thin slippers and huge wings.

I had another feeling too, hard to put into words.

When I was in my own country, I knew my place. The world arched over and around me. Everything I did was of import. I was connected to everyone and everything, even when everyone and everything was trying to kill me.

Since I had been in Sumer, I had felt myself only to be a small thing, at the edges of the world. What I did, what I said, what did that matter in this great land?

But now, walking behind Inanna, who was still not much more than a stranger to me, I thought: *This is the centre of the world, right here.*

I was once more connected to everything around me, to everything that would now happen.

And more than that.

Where this one walked, I would follow. I felt it in my bones.

With all these weighty thoughts swirling around my head, it had not occurred to me that Inanna was anything but the most reliable guide to the underworld, a map made of living flesh.

But then, at midday on the first day of our journey, we came to a large canal, lying directly in our path.

"We have to cross it," she said, looking up at me expectantly, with one hand up to support her crown.

I in turn looked expectantly at the canal. It seemed very deep, impossible to see the bottom of. Too wide to jump. It seemed to go on endlessly in both directions, and with no sign of a bridge.

"I am a marvellous swimmer," I said. "I could swim you over. I'm guessing you don't swim?"

"I have swum," she said.

"I misjudged you!"

"Well, I have floated a little. Always with someone's hand beneath my belly. But never out of my depth. I think I might sink in this."

"Certainly, you would, in that crown," I said, with just a little sharpness in me. It came to me, in a blast of remembrance, how useless the girl's mother had been.

I looked again left and right, somewhat exasperated. "We can't go around. We have no idea how long it will take. So, we swim. I'll take all your things across first, and then I'll come back for you, and I'll help you over."

The heat of the day was beginning in earnest as I put her crown, assorted jewellery, armour and pretty slippers into my cloak. I stripped, and added my boots and weapons to the bundle, keeping on only my tunic. I looked up to find Inanna standing naked before me, holding out her dress to me. She looked very small and thin, standing naked in open countryside. She had bee-sting breasts, and bony hips, and her pubic hair was very black against her sapling-brown skin. "Are you not worried someone will see you?" I said.

"I perform naked in temple," she said. "It is nothing to me."

I added her dress to my now mighty bundle, and tied it up tight.

"I will just carry the wings above my head," I said. "Although I think, really, we should be just leaving them here, for all the use they are doing us. But I am not complaining. It is not ideal. But I will carry them for you if it is important."

"It is important. Thank you," she said, looking out over the canal.

Very slowly, my bundle and the wings in my arms, I began to climb down into the black and oily water of the canal.

I am famously brave. But all the same, it was unpleasant. "Ugh," I said, despite myself. "It's slimy. It's horrible. It's cold. Ugh!"

One moment I had my backside on the bank, and my feet in the water, and then abruptly, because I could not use my hands to help myself, I fell, straight down like a stone, my bundle clutched to me. I came up gasping, holding up the sodden and heavy bundle and wings, desperately treading water. "It's freezing!"

"Can you put your feet down?" She stood peering down at me from the bank, naked and still very dry.

"No, I can't." I turned onto my back, abandoning all efforts to keep our things dry, and kicked my way over to the far side of the canal. There I pushed the wings, already battered, and the awkward bundle, now soaked, onto the grassy bank, and then laboriously pulled myself out, gasping. I had a flashback as I did, remembering the marshland north of Eridu, and trying to find dry land there, and the feeling that I might drown simply out of exhaustion before I could find something hard to stand on.

I sat, looked over at Inanna, trying to catch my breath. My ribs still didn't feel right, from when Enki attacked me.

Inanna was standing there watching me, but then she turned, her attention caught.

As if in a dreamscape, a little canoe came floating between us. A little boy, also naked, very brown, sat at the helm, his eyes upon Inanna. Where had the boy appeared from?

"Goddess," he said. "I saw you coming. May I help you over the canal?"

"Oh!" said Inanna. "I would like that. I would bless you. I do bless you."

The boy, with a grace born of long practice, in one motion wedged the little boat up close to where Inanna stood. "Step in, my lady."

Inanna was able to step in quite neatly, and in such a queenly manner that she might have been dressed in the finest cloth. I saw the face she gave him: a soft face, like a dove.

Moments later, they were across, the boy's biceps working.

Inanna stepped out warm and dry onto the bank next to me.

"Not a drop on me!" she said.

It was impossible not to feel just a little bad-tempered.

"I have nothing precious to give you as a thank you," she said to the little boy.

"You owe me nothing at all, goddess. Serving you is reward enough." He let go of the bank, and drifted off downstream, his back to the current, his lovely eyes still turned on us.

"All hail Inanna," he shouted, from a safe distance.

"Oh, my heart," she said, smiling. "What a lovely child. But I think it's my *mee* that attracted him to me."

I stood, picking riverweed off my thighs.

"Well, we are over," I said, and began to unpack my bundle.

For five long days we crossed the river lands, sometimes wading, waist high, through flowing water, or marsh. Sometimes picking our way around bogs, or crossing canals. When all the palace food had gone, I got a knife into a passing river rat, and we ate it raw, since there was no firewood to roast it over.

"I am grateful to be eating," Inanna said, chewing very seriously on a small bone, "but I do prefer river rat cooked."

"Even dogs prefer it cooked," I said.

"Although I am not sure I have eaten river rat before," she added.

On the sixth morning, we saw a herd of thin-striped gazelles, grazing in the distance, and stopped for a while to watch them.

"I was a great hunter, in my own land," I said. "I was a great runner."

"I do not doubt it," Inanna said.

I sensed a change coming in the landscape, and sure enough that afternoon we saw hills, rising slow and gentle, ahead of us.

"Inanna, what do you think you will find in the underworld?"

"I don't know," she said. "But I feel it calling to me. Before my *mee* began to work, the underworld was only an idea to me, a story. But now I know it is important to me and my people. I am connected to it. My *melam* speaks to it, not just my *mee*."

It was not obvious until we got close, but as we pressed on through the day, we realised there was bush ahead: bush that we must get through, if we were to reach the hills beyond.

At first the bush was thin, but soon enough it thickened, and to make progress we had to squeeze between vines and under low-hanging branches.

Two large vultures seemed to be monitoring our progress, hopping between branches far above us.

Inanna said: "It's my *mee*. I think it is attracting things to me. All these animals and insects."

She had begun the journey slow: now, she was a great deal slower. Sometimes she would waste even more time by stooping down to exclaim over some crawling thing.

I was carrying her wings by then, as well as all her other things, and it was becoming difficult not to worry that we might never, ever clear the jungle.

"You will be a thousand years old before we make it even to the foothills," I said eventually, although I hoped not unkindly.

"Oh, I am slow, I'm sorry."

We were whispering; the close jungle seemed to demand it.

A large biting insect landed on my cheek, and I slapped it off. "Why is nothing biting you? Is it the *melam*?"

She pulled up, turned to look at me. "Yes, insects have never bitten me. Although they would feast upon my friend Amnut."

It was then I heard it. I listened, intently, for a few heartbeats. "Do you hear that?"

"Like a roaring?"

"Yes."

We pushed on through the bush, and then, abruptly, it gave way to open sky.

And an enormous, roaring river.

Not just a canal. This was a great river of the Earth. Indeed, it could only be the Tigris, which I had heard much of, but, of course, never seen.

"Did you know this was here?" I said.

"No," she said. "I've never been out here. Although now you say it, I knew that that it was here in theory. I knew it was to the east of Uruk. And I suppose, had I been thinking differently, I might have guessed we would meet it before we got to the mountains. That it would lie between Uruk and the underworld. Yes, you know, it would make sense that it would be here."

"That's good," I said. "That this makes sense."

There was no obvious crossing place in sight. Only the astonishing stretch of the water, with trees and vines all along on either side. Huge turquoise butterflies, the size of singing birds, lifted up off the trees as we stood and watched.

I had a downcast moment. No little boy could help us with this river. But even so, it was good to have that smell in my nose and lungs, the good and thrilling smell of a clean and daring river.

"It's very beautiful," I said. "And what fresh air. If I was alone, I would just wade in."

Strong as I was, could I swim across, dragging another with me?

"Perhaps we could find something to float across on," she said, but she did not seem overly confident in what she said, and I, certainly, had no confidence at all in her plan. The more I looked at the river, the faster the water seemed to run.

"I think we do need to get across," she said. "We need to climb up those hills that we saw before. I am certain it is this way." I had begun to recognise the look she had when she was communing with her *mee* – a sort of thoughtful absence.

"I am a great swimmer," I said. "I swim like a dolphin. But this is dangerous. Even if I get across, I may not get across with you in tow."

"I think perhaps we should stay here tonight," she said.

She sat, trying to be no trouble, as I gathered wood and made a fire.

Everything was just a little damp, there in the wet jungle at the edge of the world. I was attacked by waves of biting things, and as I slapped at my skin, I could not help throwing some rather vicious looks at Inanna, who sat entirely serene.

"I suppose it must be my *melam*," she said, nodding.

With the fire lit, though, and smoke blowing on me, my mood eased.

We ate the last of the river rat, unsavoury as it was, and as we chewed, we looked out together as a stag came down to drink on the far side of the river. He kept his eyes on us, even as he waded into the water, to drink and then to eat river weed.

Inanna shut her eyes, opened them. She seemed ill at ease. Soon after she lay down and I put my cloak over her. I could see that she was not herself.

"Ninshubar," she said. "I feel a dread mounting in me."

"What is it you dread?"

She looked at me, almost desperate. "It might be this *mee*. It's working now, but it has only just begun to show itself to me. And it's connected to what lies ahead of us."

"We will work it out," I said.

"Perhaps, perhaps. But I feel it is a darkness that is pulling me there."

"Inanna, you will feel better in the morning."

In the very early morning, we stood again upon the bank of the great river, looking out over the great surging of the water. The mist floated only an arm's length above our heads.

I could not see how we were going to get over, but I was glad at least that Inanna's mood seemed to have lifted.

"Perhaps I could swim it," she said, turning a hopeful face up to me.

I was about to scoff, when, over the far bank, shadows appeared in the mist.

Elephants!

They all saw us, at the same moment we saw them. We were all, I think, equally shocked.

"Put your hands up," Inanna said, "to show you have no weapons. To show we are here in peace." This we both did.

The elephants dipped their trunks to drink, but they were all watching us as they did. At the centre of the group there was one much larger than the rest, with long, ivory tusks, and I felt her eye on me the hardest.

"Have you seen an elephant before?" I said. "We have them in my country, you know."

"One was brought to Ur, but we couldn't keep it alive. We were very sad when it died."

"They are my mother's spirit animal. Very, very dangerous."

"Ninshubar, I need to concentrate." She put her hand out on my arm, so that I would not be offended by this.

The largest of the elephants waded into the water.

She seemed to be looking at Inanna.

"I think she wants to help me," Inanna said. "She is coming to me."

We both stood and stared as the elephant kept on coming towards us, until she was swimming, her trunk raised before her.

"It's my *mee*," Inanna said.

I had my heart in my mouth as the elephant began to be pushed downriver. She turned into the current, and kept swimming, only her trunk and the top of her head visible. Twice she disappeared entirely from view, and Inanna grabbed at my left wrist, holding my skin so tightly it was painful. Twice the elephant appeared again, her trunk and then her head breaching the water.

Long and agonising heartbeats passed before she reached the safety of the shallow water upon our side of the river, and got her feet down. Finally, her sides heaving, she rose up to tower over us.

What a sight she was, close up. Her huge body was a slick black with river water, and her tusks looked very bright against the darkness of her flesh.

"Very, very dangerous," I said, my hands moving for my weapons.

"Ninshubar, there is no need for that," Inanna said. "She is here to help us cross the river."

Very reluctantly, I put Harga's knife away, and then his axe.

The elephant lifted her trunk a little, and made a low sound that we could only just hear. The elephants on the other side of the river stamped their feet and flapped their ears.

"I will go first," I said. "Then you come to me."

I got down into the Tigris, feeling silt below my bare feet. I was surprised by how cold and fast the water was, even so close to the riverbank.

I made my way over to the elephant very carefully, feeling my foothold each time before the next step, to be sure I wasn't about to be taken by the water. Then I was there, beneath her, enveloped in her musky scent. I put one hand on her great leathery shoulder, and kept on looking up at her. She turned a huge brown eye to me, watching me, but she made no attempt to shrug me off.

"She is here for you, you are right," I said. "Inanna, what a witch you have turned out to be. Now are you going to come and get on her? I will help you up."

She was only in her dress; she looked about her for the rest of her things.

"I will go back for everything," I said. "You just come to me."

Inanna turned around to climb in, her hands on the bank. Then she waded slowly over to me, her eyes wide with alarm. "How cold it is! And how fast!"

Finally, I caught her by the hands. She was up to her waist, looking up at the elephant.

"She's so beautiful."

"Inanna, I do beg you to hurry," I said.

The elephant curled her trunk around, and seemed to smell Inanna, touching her neck and cheeks very gently. Inanna stood stock still for this treatment.

"I think if I stepped onto one of her tusks, I could climb up her," Inanna said.

Of that I was doubtful.

"You just let me hold you, and I will help you up on her."

There was then something of a tussle as Inanna tried to climb onto a tusk, and the elephant and I struggled to help her. But soon enough, with the help of the elephant, I finally managed to push her up.

For a while Inanna simply lay on top of the elephant's head, her legs and arms akimbo, her face in the animal's back.

"I am up," she said. "But I think if I move, I might fall."

By this time, I was getting cold, and feeling that if it was not for the elephant standing in my path, I might already have been swept away.

"You wait there, just like that, and I will get our things."

I waded back out, and shoved everything we had into my cloak-bundle, including my boots. There was no time for ceremony, and Inanna's extraordinary eagle wings were shoved in with the rest.

"Inanna, I am going to climb up too," I said, ploughing back into the river.

"She will not hurt you," Inanna said, from her face-down position on the elephant's back.

As quick as I could, I slung my bundle over my shoulder, and I heaved my way up onto the elephant, standing on her left tusk to push myself up high. I had to push Inanna out of the way, and bully her into a sitting position, all very hard while I was trying to carry a bundle with a gold crown in it.

Once I was up, however, I felt quite triumphant. I had a marvellous view across the river to the other elephants. They were in the water, and all looked alarmed by what was happening.

"She is very nervous," Inanna said. "But she is brave. She will take us over now."

I put my arms around Inanna's waist, and gripped her narrow hips with my thighs. "I'll keep you on."

The low cloud had lifted, and now with the sky over Sumer lit up pink with the flames of dawn, the elephant carried us over the river, first wading, and then, for a magical period, swimming, the river water flowing up over our thighs.

Such glory!

There were a few moments when I was worried, when the water caught at us, and I had to hunch over Inanna, grabbing at the elephant's ears, so that the mighty river could not drag us away. But then the elephant was wading again, up strong onto the bank. All the elephants came up to surround her, and we saw now for the first time that one amongst them was newborn, and still covered in wisps of hair.

Our elephant stood still, breathing heavily, as I first climbed down, dropping easily to the ground, and then as I helped Inanna clamber down.

We both stood there then, looking up at the elephant.

"Thank you, elephant," I said.

"Yes, thank you," said Inanna. "Bless you." She put one small hand out onto the elephant's side, and the animal seemed to shudder. A heartbeat later, the whole herd moved off, far quieter than I had expected, and was gone into the green of the jungle.

We walked on a few paces, the sun beginning to dry us.

I burst out: "I have ridden an elephant! And it isn't even breakfast time yet! Imagine what might happen before lunch!"

Again, we faced dense bush, but Inanna was certain of the way. I led us forwards therefore, now and again hacking at something with an axe, and by the time the sun was hot enough to worry us, the bush was thinning and we were climbing upwards, gently but surely, onto grassland. In the distance we spied low hills, the tops rocky red.

I told Inanna stories to cheer her along, of the people in my country, at what they would think about the slippers. I told her also about the long run, and how I had lost my Potta, although I tried to make the story a light one. I told her about the sacred running words: *One step and then the next.*

After a long period of thoughtful silence, she said: "Ninshubar, when I was a baby, it was said in the temples that I would one day be Queen of Heaven and Earth."

"And you surely will be," I said, smiling.

"Yes, I do believe I will be," she said, with no smile on her. "And when it happens, when I do become Queen of Heaven and Earth, we will go and find your Potta boy, this boy who you adopted, and bring him back here to Sumer."

I nodded, but said nothing, turning my face to scan the land.

She stopped, turning to me, her hands out. "This is a sacred promise, Ninshubar. The undying promise of a god. When I am crowned Queen of Heaven and Earth, we will leave at once to fetch your Potta."

I had that strange feeling I had had when I first saw her in Enki's temple: a lurching feeling inside me.

"We will find your Potta," she said.

She turned and walked on.

First her steps, and then my steps, following on behind her.

It was cold that night. We lay together in a dell, out of the wind, with me behind and my cloak looped over her, so that it kept us both covered. She was strangely warm to hold, just as her mother had been. For a while, a set of owls kept us awake.

"What a noise," I said.

"It's the *mee* again. I can feel it calling to them."

"Tell me more about this underworld of yours. I thought you could only get there if you were dead."

"My family, the Anunnaki, they come and go. In the stories, anyway. I am told that Enki has been there. Enlil too. And others, I think. I wish I had asked my mother now."

∽

In the morning we woke both very cold. We had nothing left to eat.

"I should go hunting," I said.

"I think we should keep walking. If you don't mind walking hungry."

I made a scoffing noise. "I have walked hungry before this. I was thinking only of you." In fact, I was ravenous, but if Inanna could bear it, then so could I.

We had thought we were climbing into mountains, but the foothills brought us only up onto a plateau that stretched to the horizon. The flat was studded here or there with rocks, a few lone and stunted oak trees and, between, bouncy moss.

We walked all day, her first, stepping around large clumps of moss, and tiptoeing around small ponds, and me trying not to trip over her by walking at a normal speed.

As dusk approached, we came to tumbling stream, and both drank our fill from it. I drank more than was comfortable, in an effort to stave off my hunger.

"I had never drunk from a stream before we set out on this journey," Inanna said. She was wiping her face and hands dry on what had once been her white dress.

"I am thinking now there is a long list of things you have never done."

We sat on a broad grey rock, our faces to the setting sun, and talked about the food we would eat if we could choose to eat anything. "I would be happy with just a bowl of radishes," she said.

"Or what about a little grilled lamb," I said. "With just some salt and lemon on it."

"And maybe some flatbreads, and soft cheese mixed with garlic and salt to dip them in."

"And the smallest piece of hard cheese, with a little honey on it," I said.

After that we lay down, absurdly hungry, in my cloak.

"What are we going to do in the underworld?" I said.

"I think it will be just me that goes in," she said. "I don't think you will be able to cross, or not alive."

"I suppose I'll wait at the gates, then, for you. There are gates, yes?"

"There is a gatekeeper," she said. "So yes, I think, gates. Seven gates, in the stories."

Later, before we slept, I said: "Do the Anunnaki go there when they die, or do they never die?"

"I don't know if the Anunnaki go there, or if they go back to Heaven, where they came from. We never talked about it, at home. I realise that everything I thought was clear and certain was nothing of the sort."

"Where I come from, the person's spirit goes up into the sky when they die. Everyone goes up, there is no price for it, and everyone is free up there. That is the law in my land, and I think it is the law in all the lands where the Anunnaki do not rule."

"I only know about these lands, and what they say here. They say the underworld is a bad place unless you have great riches to take with you when you die. If you are poor, and you are buried with nothing, then it is very bad for you down there."

"It's not much to look forward to."

"No," she said. "But it means that the people work hard."

The next day I felt faint with hunger, strong as I was, but I saw she suffered less than I did, and so we set off again without stopping to hunt. After the morning's walking, the ground began to rise, and soon we could see mountains. By the afternoon, we were on a mountain path, winding between stacked-up boulders and clumps of cacti.

In the cool air, we climbed higher and higher, and as we tracked our way upwards, an eagle zigged and zagged very low over our heads. I looked up and smiled at it. I saw Inanna watching it, unsmiling.

And then, as the sun set, there on the path before us stood a small stone hut, with smoke coming out of the chimney. I had never been so happy to see something. "There will be food," I said. "I can already smell it."

A man came out of the hut and stood to watch us as we approached. He was dressed in a plain linen smock, and he had grey hair and a grey beard. It was strangely hard to tell how old he was.

"Welcome, strangers," he called, when we were close enough to call to. He sounded like an Anunnaki, although he did not have the look of one.

"You are welcome here," he said, and raised both hands, to show us he was carrying no weapons.

I put my axe back into my belt loop, but I kept a hand on each of my knives.

"I would like my crown, please," Inanna said. "And all my other things."

Setting my bundle down on the path, I helped her into it all: the chest plate, the jewellery, the wings, now bedraggled and broken, and finally the crown.

Only when she was in her full temple wear did she walk on to the hut.

As we drew close, the man gave us a little bow, and then disappeared through the door. "Follow me, follow me," he called.

Inside the hut it was neat and simple, with a small table and three chairs in front of the fire, and a bed along one wall. It smelled of hay, and fresh baked bread. There was a half loft above us, full of sacks of what looked like grain.

The old man gave us clay cups of water, and then put a copper pot over the fire to boil. "You two look as if you've been walking," he said, very politely.

We both nodded, and put our cups out for more water.

"You have the look of a goddess," he said to Inanna, "in that very fine outfit you are wearing."

"Yes," she said, pulling at her muddy dress to make it lie flat on her lap.

"It is rare," he said, "to see visitors here. People have forgotten that Ganzir is a real place."

He got up and brought down a wooden box from a shelf, took off the neat-fitting lid and offered us some sticky-looking honey cakes, each one rolled in sesame seeds.

We two women fell upon them.

"I was thinking what to make for your dinner, what might tempt your palates," he said. "But I see now that you will not be difficult to feed."

When I had eaten more than my fair share of the cakes, I paused for a while, and looked around at the sweet-smelling room. I noticed how everything had its place, very precise.

Inanna took off her crown, and put it on the rough-hewn table.

"I won't be staying for dinner," she said. "I am the goddess Inanna. And this is my friend, Ninshubar, a warrior from the south."

Our host nodded.

"I would like some dinner," I put in, "even if Inanna does not."

The old man ignored me, and instead pointed at Inanna's *mee*. "You are wearing a weapon of the Anunnaki."

"I am an Anunnaki," she said.

"I have been told there are twelve."

"Now there is a thirteenth."

I turned and looked at the man properly and I saw that he was not as old as I had thought.

"Now you must tell us who you are," Inanna said.

"My name is Neti. I am the gatekeeper to the Kur. If you wish to go on from here, then you will have to come with me."

"I've heard of you," I said. "In the temple stories. You are the gatekeeper to the underworld."

"I am."

Neti had a different look to him now. Had he changed his robe, while we were eating our cakes?

"What do you know about Ganzir, Inanna?" he said.

"I've heard my mother use the word," she said. "My mother Ningal."

"I know Ningal," he said. He got down a jar, and poured the two of us some date wine, very oily on the tongue.

"Up behind this house, there's a ridge, and over the ridge there's a hidden valley, and its name is the Valley of Ganzir. In the bottom of the valley there's a lake, and next to it is a huge rock that they call the Kur, which means 'the rock from the sky'. And that is where the entrance to the underworld is."

"But you live here?" I said.

"In the first days, the Anunnaki used to go back and forth from the Kur, and the people became curious, and they would come and try to get into it. So, the gods put me here, to watch over the valley, and keep the unwanted out."

"Were you here when Enki came?" Inanna asked.

"Yes, I was here." Neti smiled. "Anyone who wants to go on from here, they must go on with me."

"I do wish to go on," Inanna said. "I would like to go on now."

"What about me?" I said.

"You go this far, but not further," Neti said. "This hut is for those who wait. I will take Inanna on, and if she returns, she will come and meet you here. You will be comfortable; the bed is clean. There is plenty of food, if you look for it, and there is a good stream nearby."

I turned to Inanna.

She took my hands in hers, and said: "Ninshubar, if I'm not back in a few days, let's say three days, please go and get help."

"Who from? What kind of help?"

"I don't know," she said. "But my family know about the Kur. Try my grandfather Enlil. Or Lugalbanda. I believe they are together in Nippur. There is Dumuzi. He is after all my husband. I believe my own father might be in Ur, although since he seems to have done nothing to help my mother, I cannot know if he will help me."

She paused a few long heartbeats, and then said: "I think Enki will know how to get in here. He may be the person who could help you."

"I have just fought my way out of his dungeon."

"He's been here, and he got back. Who knows what he knows, or what he has that could help me?"

"If he chooses to help you."

"It may be worth trying," she said. "If something goes wrong."

"Do you think something might go wrong?"

She turned her bottomless eyes to me. "I am walking into darkness. I do not know what I will find there."

"And what do I tell your family you are doing down there?"

"Tell them I have gone to see my sister. Tell them whatever you need to."

She put the gold crown of the steppes onto her head, and then she and Neti set off up through the gathering dark onto the ridgeway, leaving me standing there outside the stone hut.

I called after them: "Neti, how is that the dead get into the underworld? Do they have to come out here like this? Do their ghosts fly here? How does that work?"

Neti stopped walking and turned back to me. "The Anunnaki are in charge of the stories," he said. "I am only in charge of the gates."

"Go on then, never mind," I said, waving them off with one hand.

And on they went up the hill, her looking small and vulnerable, with the darkness creeping up at them fast.

CHAPTER NINE

INANNA

From the lip of the crater, I looked down on Ganzir for the first time.

It was a huge crater, perhaps a league across. At its centre lay a perfectly round lake. Behind the lake, stretching from one side of the crater to the other, was a long, bulbous ridge of rock, a swirl of dark reds and dark yellows, getting darker and more shadowed by the moment.

"That is the Kur," Neti said.

He did not need to tell me. The rock thrummed blue to me, flickering at me in the evening light.

"It's from the sky," Neti said.

"And the gate is inside the rock from the sky?"

"Seven gates," he said. "There are seven gates into the underworld."

As we made our way down, the slope turned to scree, and I had to take off my torn slippers, and place them in my pocket, for fear I might fall over.

"How do you decide who goes in?" I said.

"Only the Anunnaki go in, only the Twelve," he said. "But Ereshkigal has banned them all from entering."

He stopped, as if thinking something over, looking down at the ground. "But I do not think I have to stop you. Moreover, I do not think I can."

"But what about the dead?" I said.

"You can't go in if you are dead," he said, looking at me as if I was losing my mind. "Or not without special permissions."

I stood for a moment, frowning after him, but then kept on following him.

As we crossed the grassy bottom of the crater, I understood how huge the rock from the sky was. Close up it towered over me, five cables high. I went up to it, cautious, and put out one hand to it – and felt it vibrate at my touch. I shut my eyes and for a moment saw a woman in emerald-green standing before me. I opened my eyes and all sense of her had gone.

"It's over here," said Neti.

He was standing next to a round outline in the rock: a neat circle. Had I been alone, I would not have seen it in the dusk. The shape began about at the height of his head, and curved round to just above his feet.

"This is the first gate," said Neti, with one hand upon the rock, exactly in the middle of the circle. "Anything that is valuable, that you might want back, you should leave here."

I took my crown off.

Oh, the instant relief!

"This is valuable, very valuable," I said. "Is there somewhere I can leave it?"

"You can just leave it here on the ground. No one will take it. No one else can come this close."

I put the crown down on the grass to the left of the round gate, although reluctantly. As I was bending over, there was a high-pitched sound. The perfectly round door had disappeared, leaving only a perfectly round hole in the rock.

Within: darkness.

"In we go," Neti said.

I stepped closer to Neti and the rock, and peered inside.

"Neti, I'm confused," I said. "This rock is from the sky. Is this the Thunderbird, which the Anunnaki came down from Heaven in?"

"Certainly, they were in it, when it fell from the sky," he said.

"So the Kur is also the Thunderbird. I had not understood that."

"I am not in charge of the stories," Neti said.

I was about to touch my hand to the edge of the entranceway, when Neti said, in a different voice: "Touch nothing!"

I withdrew my hand.

"It's better you don't touch anything in here, when you don't know what anything does," he said.

"As you wish."

I peered inside the Kur, and saw only a dark, damp space, smelling of wet and cold. It looked as if everything inside was made of a metallic rock.

"In we go," Neti said again.

I had to lift my dress up to step through the round doorway, and onto the damp floor beyond. My wings caught at the edges of the gate, and I had to turn and tug at them to get inside.

It was a small cold space, lit only by the last of the light outside. Neti got in next to me, and we were forced to stand close to each other, my wings jamming against the walls.

Neti leaned over, then, and touched something. The gate to the outside at once snapped shut, and in the same moment a blue light burst into life above our heads. I only then understood that I was standing pressed against a second gate, a dark circle shape in the grey.

I also noticed that Neti had no smell at all.

"Neti, does Ereshkigal know I am here?"

"Yes."

"Is she happy I am here?"

He hesitated. "No. She is very unhappy."

"Why?"

"She thinks you have come to steal from her."

"Oh," I said. "Tell her I am not here to steal anything."

"She thinks you are not who you say you are. She does not believe there is another Anunnaki. She thinks you might be An, or Enlil."

"Tell her that Ningal had a baby, and I am that baby."

Neti looked very unhappy himself now. "She doesn't care what I say. She only sees that I am letting you in. She thinks that the Anunnaki are no longer allowed in. That she has made sure of that. But you see I have to let you in. I cannot do anything except help you. Because you have the marks of the Anunnaki upon you, and you are not on the list of the banned."

"What now, then?" I said, impatient to get out of that strange, blue-lit hole.

"Nobody told me there was another Anunnaki," Neti said, but perhaps only to himself.

He then pressed one hand to the centre of the second gate, and it disappeared: beyond seemed to be an even smaller space, with another round door opposite it. Before we went through it, he said: "You have to take off everything else you are wearing,

and leave it in this room before you go through this next gate."
He pushed at the wall behind him, and where there had only been
flat wall, now a large drawer slid open. "You cannot go through the
second gate until you are completely naked."

"I'm not taking off my *mee*," I said. "It doesn't come off." With
some difficulty, I undressed, dropping my breastplate and clothes
and jewellery into the dark grey drawer. My wings I pushed
in last.

"The *mee* is part of the Kur," he said. "It will be well looked after
here. You cannot go further with your *mee* on." He pointed to a
shelf above the drawer that I did not think had been there before.

"It does not come off," I said, pulling at my *mee* of love to show
him that it was too tight to pull off.

To my complete surprise, it slipped off easily. "Oh!" I said.

I placed it carefully down on the little shelf. I suppose I had
thought I would feel different without it, but nothing seemed to
have changed: the Kur still thrummed blue to me.

"You have to get into the next room alone now," Neti said.
"I will see you on the other side."

I went through gate two, into a small space with nothing to
break up the dark metallic rock of the walls. Neti shut the door
behind me. There was a moment of pitch black, and them a red
light filled the second space. A moment later, a deluge of hot water
fell upon me, and then before I could get my breath, a searing
wind howled around me, almost knocking me to my knees. I stood
there braced against each wall, until the wind died away.

"Neti, what is this?" I shouted.

Only when the air was still again did a door open. It was hard
for me to be sure now, having been spun around, but it seemed
to me that this was a different door – that this was the third gate
I was going through.

Neti was standing on the other side, in a larger space, blue-lit and also empty of adornment. "I hope it wasn't a shock."

"It is over," I said, although my hands were still shaking, and my hair seemed to have lifted into a cloud around my head.

"This is gate four now, and gate five just on the other side," he said. "Nothing happens between these gates. You have been cleaned now and there will be no more cleaning. But you have to shut gate four behind you, before you can open gate five, do you understand? It creates a break between the realms, when both doors are shut. But I cannot go further. I stay here."

"I understand," I said.

"On the other side of gate five, there is a room, and you will see a door in front of you. That is gate six. Only those of pure Anunnaki lineage can enter gate six. I think the gate will let you through, because you seem to me to be Anunnaki, but I cannot be sure. The gate, though, it will make sure. It cannot be mistaken. After that you are in the Kur. If you want to go onwards and find Ereshkigal, you must go through the seventh gate, and find her in the Dark City. But I would strongly recommend against that. Once you are beyond the seventh gate, only Ereshkigal can decide if you will come out again."

"This is very complicated," I said. "Is this all really necessary, to go from one room to another, and another and another, and for what reason?"

Neti spread his hands in apology. He was wearing different clothes from the clothes he had been wearing in the world outside the Kur. He was now in a slim-fitting all-in-one outfit, with trousers instead of a skirt, and I had to lean against a wall as I took this in, feeling that I might be drunk from the wine I'd had in the hut.

"Mistress, the rules of the Kur, on entering and exiting, are very strict, and must be adhered to very exactly. There is the protocol of entry and the protocol of exit. There cannot be exceptions to the sequence of events and actions that are set down, and that has always been the case. No one can change what is laid down. That way disaster would lie."

"Yes, yes," I said. "So, if I get through the seventh gate, then I am in the underworld? And that is where Ereshkigal will be?"

"The seventh gate takes you to an in-between place, between the realms. And that is where the Dark City is, and your sister's temple." He waggled his head a little. "It would be better not to enter. You do risk being trapped."

"Is it true she can leave, if she wants to?" I remembered Enki telling me that, on our voyage from Ur to Eridu.

"The other Anunnaki sealed her in. But then she sealed them out." He wrung his hands. "She does not like me speaking to you like this."

I opened up gate four for myself, pushing my hand into the centre of the circle, and then jumping back as it snapped open. As before there was darkness beyond, and then a moment later, blue light. I gave one last glance at Neti, and then stepped through into the tiny space, the gate instantly closing behind me.

For a moment I only stood there, in the small empty space between gates four and five, waiting for something to happen. Was something going to happen? And then gate five sprang open.

Again, a room carved from this rock that was almost like a metal, and blue light, and a new round gate opposite me: gate six. This one was marked with strange signs that reminded me of writing, but with characters I did not recognise. I took a step forwards towards the gate when a woman's voice rang out, as if from all around me, echoing back and forth in the blue-lit space.

"Whoever you are, go back," said the woman. "You are not welcome here." It was a rough voice. It must surely be Ereshkigal. Was she in pain?

When the voice had stopped, I said: "Ereshkigal?" I turned my head, looking for her, even in the ceiling. "Ereshkigal? Sister?"

There was a short pause.

"I have no sister," she said. "Whoever you are, go back. Open up the gate behind you, and go back. If you keep going as you are going, you are going to die. I will not let you through."

I stopped looking around me, and looked instead at gate six. Was Ereshkigal on the other side?

"I mean no one any harm," I said. "My parents are Nanna and Ningal. You do not know me, but I know about you. I come here sent by Ningal, our mother. She is in trouble, Ereshkigal, and needs our help."

There was another pause.

"Whoever you are, come through gate six, and you will die."

Then the voice stopped, and the room was very quiet. For the first time, I felt how far away I was from the outside, and with no understanding, even, over whether I could go back. I had to breathe deeply to overcome a sudden overwhelming sense of being trapped.

I reached out for gate six and it snapped open.

I stepped through it into darkness, and instantly stood bathed in red light.

This was a much bigger space, with several shapes in the walls that might have been doors or gates. It was warm too, and very dry after the gates on the way in. All of the doors were round and plain, unmarked. But one was bigger than all the others, and marked as gate six had been, and this I knew, without needed to be told, was the seventh gate.

I went over and put my hand on the seventh gate. It felt curiously warm. A gentle buzz and a click, and it disappeared.

The gate was perfectly round. Inside: blackness. I could see nothing in there at all. But a strange smell came at me out of the dark, an incongruous smell: the smell of a forest floor, and with it a sense of dampness and cool.

I kneeled down and put my hand in, very cautiously, only for my fingers to disappear from sight as soon as they crossed the threshold.

I pulled my hand away, rattled, and rubbed at my fingers, to make sure they were all really there.

It came to me that I should look behind the other doors before I committed to the seventh gate. I went over and touched a door at random and it snapped open upon another room. It looked like a string of rooms, in fact, one leading to the next. They seemed to be full of strange boxes, odd shapes, all piled up in the deep gloom. A strong sense of foreboding stopped me taking a step inside.

I turned around to find the seventh gate still open, with its gaping yawn of black.

I knew what Ninshubar would do. I knew what Gilgamesh would do. They would walk straight in. But for a moment I only stood there, gathering myself.

I could sense nothing ahead of me: the strong feelings of connection to the Kur that I had felt as we walked across Sumer... none of that lay before me. Through the seventh gate lay only blankness.

Well.

I am not afraid.

I put one bare foot in, and watched it seem to disappear as it crossed the threshold. Well, waiting wouldn't make it better, so I stepped straight through and down.

The damp stone beneath me tipped, righted, and I found myself on my hands and knees. Above me: stars. What looked like stars. Very dim stars. And the fresh and surprising smell of a forest. I stayed crouched on the stone as I tried to understand where I was.

By the soft silver light of these stars, it seemed that I was on a thin stone bridge, leading off into blackness, and with blackness below and to each side. The bridge was just a little wider than me, and with no handrails to prevent me plummeting to what I felt must be certain death. I forced myself to look down properly, leaning very carefully over the edge, but could see only blackness beneath. Yet I had a sense of a great drop.

The forest air was still, damp, but every now and again a gust of cool fresh air hit me, confusingly, as if there was a window open onto the outside, and close to me.

I stood up, very, very slowly, turned around so carefully – and almost fell.

I could only see the thin narrow bridge stretching away behind me. There was no sign at all of the seventh gate, which I had only moments before tumbled through. The gate that I was certain I had not moved away from. A huge wave of vertigo hit me, and very, very slowly, I dropped to all fours again. I felt it was imperative that I remembered which way I had been facing when I first came through the gate, so then I carefully edged around to face the way I had originally been facing. Or so I hoped.

I crawled forwards, carefully. Slowly at first, and then as time passed, more quickly, although the rough rock of the bridge was hard on my bare knees. Eventually I stood, cautious, and began to walk. I tried to keep my feet, as far as I could tell in the starlight, exactly in the centre of the bridge.

On I went, and nothing changed. The bridge stretched out in front of me through the starry sky, and behind me looked just the same, unchanging. Eventually I grew bored of creeping and more confident of not falling. I began to walk quite casually along this strange highway through the stars. The place had a dreamlike quality, and it was hard to understand if I was being careless, or if on some level I could not understand, this was all just for play.

After a time I found impossible to measure, the walkway began to curve gently downwards and to the right. And then, with a surge of relief, I saw smudged light far below and in front of me. I walked on, just a little faster. It was a city, far below me, a lake of sparkling lights.

So here it was, the Dark City. The famous Dark City from so many poems.

It was real!

I tried to suppress the lurching anxiety that rose up in me. I could see no way back. I couldn't stay where I was. So, I must go on. My choice had been made. Onwards, and downwards.

On I walked, and slowly the walkway broadened, flattened, and then became a stone-paved road, smoother and drier underfoot. Around me in the blackness I thought I could make out trees, and then low buildings. Was I on the ground now, and if so, where was this ground?

That was when I saw something.

A movement, somewhere in the dark to my right.

For the first time, I felt very vulnerable.

Again, a flicker of movement.

Even only half-glimpsed, there was something wrong with the movement. What was out there in the darkness? I thought about the demons in the temple stories.

I began to go much faster, almost to scurry. The buildings grew up thicker, closer to the road. Dark windows looked down on me. And here or there, in the dark – something. The smell now was not of the forest, but of something rotting.

Finally, the road bent to my right and I saw in the distance, over crooked rooftops, what must be Ereshkigal's palace: a dark confection of spiralling towers against the misty, black sky.

The road I was on turned into a promenade, with dark statues lining the way. Strange demons, carved in black stone, leered down at me in the gloom. And here or there – something.

The palace reared up at me far sooner than I had expected. Suddenly there were huge stone steps in front of me, too large to be built for human legs, and high up at the top of the steps I saw hazy white light, spilling out from the doors of the palace.

Up I climbed, on my hands and knees, struggling to get from one step to the next.

At the top I delayed. I could not see through the doors; they stood open only a crack. But then two strange shapes appeared on either side of them. I shrank back from them. They looked like men, but they were bent over, wizened, and nonsensical to my eyes in the dusk light, as if they had too many hands and ears.

With their strange scuttling movement, they pulled open the doors for me.

I am not afraid.

I walked forwards into a vast room, a forest of columns, each one inlaid with a dark stone that might have been obsidian, and a pale type of ivory that might have been simply bone. The roof, high over me, was painted black, and the floor below was made of stone, but covered in a drift of pale grey dust, oddly slippery in feel. The dust sifted up between my toes as I walked.

This great room reminded me of An's throne room in the White Temple, except where everything there was sunlight and colour, here everything was only in shades of grey and black.

As I made my way down the colonnade, I saw that at the far end of the room, in a pool of darkness, there stood a huge throne, and on it, a shape.

The shape, I was almost certain, was making a noise. The sound of an animal whimpering.

It was my sister.

I had dreamed for many years of one day meeting her, of what I would say to her, and what she would say to me.

"Ereshkigal," I said quietly. "It is me, Inanna. Your sister."

The whimpering stopped.

I edged forwards, small step by small step, unsure of what might be underfoot as the dust drifts grew thicker across the stone floor. Now around me there seemed to be benches, although moments before there had been none. Some of the benches were empty, some crowded with hooded figures, human-like perhaps, but too small to be human, and, sometimes, too large. The smell of death grew stronger, and I shut my mouth to keep out the dust that now fell like snow upon my head.

So here was my sister, once a child of Ur.

I could almost see in her, almost, the shape of our mother, but she was grossly bloated. Was she pregnant? Her features seemed to slide into each other.

"Sister," I said.

Ereshkigal's eyes, bulging strangely, appeared from beneath her cloud of dark hair.

And then it happened very quickly.

"Seize her!" my sister screamed. "She is going to kill me!"

All the scuttling creatures, creatures with no faces, but too many legs and arms, all the creatures on the benches and from behind the columns, all of them came rushing at me.

As the first demon threw itself at me, I thought: *It will not touch me.*

It landed on me hard, knocking me over onto the dust-covered floor. Two others were on me a moment later.

I thought: *But they will not hurt me.*

The first demon smashed its scaly face into my nose, and pain exploded through my head.

Then they were all upon me, a great wave of them, clawing and gouging at my bare skin. I was crushed into the floor by the weight of their writhing, wet flesh.

I heard screaming.

It was me screaming.

There was a moment of disconnection, my brain thinking, *They will not really damage me, all will be well*, but then their fangs were coming away with mouthfuls of my flesh.

From beneath the writhing mass, I glimpsed that from every door behind the throne, from behind every column, more monsters were pouring, bigger creatures, dark and shining.

"Ereshkigal," I tried say, when for a moment my mouth was uncovered. But the monsters were choking me, smothering me, crushing me, in stench and blood.

Moments only, of blinding, obliterating pain.

And then the darkness.

CHAPTER TEN

GILGAMESH

And so I journeyed to the far side of the world.

I remember passing desert men: thin, shifting pole-shapes on the horizon. They walked with their heads turned to me.

My father had told me to stay away from the desert men. They worship the scorpion: they do not worship the Anunnaki.

I remember running out of water.

I was attacked by a lion. I thought in the night, *It is only a nightmare.* But I woke with my mules gone, and blood all over me, and a lioness lying dead beside me upon the sand.

Perhaps that night, perhaps the night after, I dreamed of a monster with fire blazing out from its claws.

The monster said: "Gilgamesh, where are you wandering to? The life you seek, you will never find."

The next day, in the light, I thought, *I am going to die out here. Is this what I want?*

I was hungry, but the hunger was nothing, compared to the thirst.

I walked. I was barefoot. When had I taken off my boots?

For a while I sat down, with the warming sun on my face. After that I got up on my hands and knees, pressing my palms down into the red sand, but I could not find a way to stand up.

I was looking down at the sand, thinking, *So many colours in it, when you look closely,* when I became aware, with a shocking start, that I was not alone.

A group of men had formed a loose circle around me. Some stood, one foot up against a knee, leaning on staffs. Others had squatted down to watch me. All were wrapped in black robes and with black turbans upon their heads.

They had hard brown faces and thick black brows.

I tried to speak, but found my throat and mouth were too dry to make noise.

I realised I was dressed only in a raw lion skin and that I was covered in old blood. My weapons, pack and boots were nowhere to be seen.

"He is a demon," one of the desert men said, in passable Sumerian.

The others nodded, contemplative.

I pointed at my throat. "Water," I said, but so quiet, through my cracked lips, that I could not be sure that they could hear me. "Water."

"I think he is a lion," another man said. "But he has taken off his lion skin, and this is what is inside. This is the demon, inside the lion."

The first man shook his head. "To me he looks like a demon who has killed a lion and is wearing its skin," he said. "He is from the nether world. He has emerged, and found the lion and killed it, and now he is here."

For a while I put my hands down in front of me, then I rested my head on the sand in front of me, my bare buttocks in the air. "I am a man," I said to the sand. But they seemed not to hear me.

A new noise: an animal. I turned my head: dark hooves. A man swung off the animal. He was wearing red trousers under his desert wrappings. "What are you all doing? Pick this man up and take him back to the camp."

"He's a demon," someone said.

"He's a Sumerian," the man in the red trousers said. "Find out what something is worth, you fools, before you let it die."

My captor's name was Uptu and he was a great man up there in the high desert. He was out on the plain with fifty men, to hunt the lion that lived there, and when he was not hunting, he lived in a tent that King Akka himself would have thought splendid.

In this tapestry-lined tent, I was given my fill of water, and then they took away my foul and uncured lion skin, wiped me clean, and put me in a long black robe. Only then was I allowed to sit down on the woollen rug at the centre of the tent.

Uptu prepared us a drink of mountain tea while the other men squatted around the edge of the tent. The tea was scalding hot and sweet, mildly bitter. I drank it down, but at once he poured me another cup. Only when I had forced down three cups did Uptu hunt around for other cups, and hand them around to the other men. Finally, he sat down cross-legged in front of me, with his own tea, and sipped at it. Since he said nothing, I said nothing.

When everyone had drunk their tea, a young boy came in with a large tray heaped with grilled meat, flatbreads and fried green okra, heavily spiced.

Uptu nodded at me, and then handed me a small clay plate.

"Thank you," I said. I heaped my plate high.

"Now you are our guest," he said. "You are under my protection. No harm will come to you here in my camp. Any man who harms you here will die horribly, and afterwards I will eat his private parts and his eyeballs." All the men around us nodded at this.

"Good," I said, eating steadily. "Thank you."

I ate a second full plate, and then a third one.

After that the other men came forwards to shovel meat and breads onto their own plates. These they took back to their corners of the tent and, squatting down again, they all ate very intently.

"Everything is very good," I said. "Delicious."

"I am a king out here in the desert," he said. "Everything I have is good."

"Indeed," I said, looking around at the rugs, and the elaborate calfskin tent. "My name is Gilgamesh."

"Are you the famous Gilgamesh, the mortal child of gods?"

"I am surprised you have heard of me, out here."

"What language am I talking to you in? We are not barbarians. We have our own towns out here, you know. We trade. We know what happens in Sumer, and how it fights its wars, and what its gods can do. But tell me why you are in the desert."

"I am heading for Mashu, the twin-peaked mountain."

"That is our mountain. We guard it."

"Do mountains need guarding?"

We regarded each other for a moment in silence.

"I think you know that this one is special," he said. "This one has a way through it, through the dark, to the land on the other side. If you want to walk another way, it will take you a full month to walk around. So yes, this mountain we guard. And people pay us to pass through."

"I am going through the mountain," I said.

"If you have gold, you will. This is how we get our gold, to pay for our animals, and these fine rugs you sit on, and to buy brides who are worth more than all these rugs, and all our animals. All these men you see here are married to princesses. Because of this mountain."

"I have gold."

He smiled. "Where are you hiding this gold, Gilgamesh? Because we did not see it on you when we found you in the desert."

"The gold I have is a long way away."

Uptu sat up straight, and wiped his hands on a cloth.

"That is a problem for you, although we will be very glad for you to stay with us while you rest and recover your strength. My boys are curing your lion skin for you, by the way. It will be better to wear when the raw meat has been stripped of it, and the hide treated properly."

"Thank you, Uptu. That is very kind."

"I would do anything for a guest."

We looked at each other, both sipping our tea.

"Anything but let me through your passage?"

"Once you leave this camp you will not be my guest. You will be a guest friend. No one will harm you, who knows what you are to me. But even guest friends must part with gold when trading is underway."

"What will you do if I just walk on, and find my way to the passage, and go through it?"

"We will slaughter you," he said. "And then cut you into small pieces, to stop you going to the underworld you believe in, and to show you we are serious men who do not issue warnings and then fail to follow through on them."

"And you will not accept one lion skin as the payment?"

Uptu shrugged. "We have lion skins. Many lion skins. Better than the one you brought."

I looked about me. Well. It was this, or home again, having never really tried.

I said: "Uptu, I challenge you."

"You seek to amuse me," he said.

"I challenge you. I do not know your ways here, but in my country, in matters like this, you can challenge a man to a fight to the death. Or sometimes, if someone is too scared to fight, we settle these things on a hunt. First to kill is the winner. That sort of thing."

"I do not think you will find a man here who is scared to fight," Uptu said.

"That's good to know. Because I will fight any or all of you for the right to pass through this passage of yours. Let the gods decide, through my mortal flesh, what is the right thing to happen here. Are you too frightened to fight me yourself, Uptu? I am happy to fight a younger substitute. Name anyone and I will stand up with them."

"You were not so cocky when we found you."

"Take away water from a man, and he wilts. But you have given me water and I thank you for that water. And now I am challenging you to a fight to the death, if you will not let me through this passageway, as I have asked you to. As I believe, as my host, you should be obliged to. Why is this passageway yours? It was made by the gods of Sumer. They have told me this themselves. Now you take it for yourself, taking gold for passage. You are all brigands here. Not men of honour. You are thieves of the desert. Little scorpions that steal and sting."

"It will be my pleasure to kill you," Uptu said, getting up. "Since you are so very, very anxious to be dead already."

I saw the change in him: a sharpening. The men of the desert will kill over a small insult, and then go back to their food. This was not such an extraordinary thing we were engaged in. All the same, I looked around, and saw that everyone was much more cheerful.

We stood out on the desert, five cords apart, facing each other. I took off the robe they had given me. I did not want to fight naked, but I did not want to give him anything to grab.

The scorpion men stood around us in a large circle, all whooping, all heavily armed. Uptu took off his weapons, and threw them, very elegantly, to the boy. He took off his robe too, but underneath he had on a long woollen smock, and his red trousers, and these he seemed happy to fight in.

How old was he? Twenty-five? He looked in good condition: lean, but very strong.

For the first time, and rather late, I had a moment of profound doubt. The odds here were not in my favour. Was this really how I wanted my life to end?

"You look nervous, Gilgamesh," he called over. "Are you having second thoughts? If you do not want to fight, you don't have to. We will put you down quickly, like a dog with a broken leg. There will be no shame in that, for a creature like you."

The crowd liked this; the whoops grew louder, and they all clapped and laughed.

"I think he is frightened," the boy said. "See how his penis is all shrivelled up with fear!"

All of them laughed so hard at this that they had to clutch themselves and wipe tears from their faces.

I breathed in, breathed out.

Then I sat down on the ground, cross-legged, my head hanging.

The crowd began jeering and screaming at me.

Uptu approached me but carefully, looking to see what I was up to.

"I feel sick and dizzy," I said. "Just give me a moment."

He came right up close, still wary.

"I think I must be sick," I said. I retched and retched, and then up came a vile little dribble of vomit. As I coughed it out, I began to urinate, yellow liquid dribbling and disappearing into dry sand.

"What is this?" Uptu said.

He peered hard at me, and then he turned his attention just for a moment to the crowd. With my urine still flowing, I instantly launched myself forwards at his legs. I bit down hard, as hard as I could, on the sinews at the back of his right ankle, crunching through flesh and sinew and cartilage, till my teeth hit bone.

Uptu went down like an axe falling, face down, screaming.

I swarmed over him on all fours and before he could turn to get at me, I grabbed his head in my arms and twisted as hard as I could.

One loud crack and he was dead.

The men in the circle fell silent.

"I want my lion skin back," I said.

The boy led me through the desert and up to the mountain.

"Was he your father?"

"My uncle."

"I'm sorry."

"He should not have fallen for such an obvious trick."

The desert sand turned to rubble and then rose up over mounds of rock. Soon we walked in a land of stone and twisted, ancient trees.

He said: "You know you could be the chief of our people now. You have won that right, until someone else challenges you."

"Do you think they would challenge me?"

"Certainly, they would, if you stayed. And you would die very quickly. You cannot act the fool and piss on the ground, and think to win that way twice."

"Tricks never work twice."

"There is honour in the kill, however you do it. But I myself would not like to rely on tricks when I am the king here."

He waved at me to follow him up the side of a boulder. He pointed south. There amidst the sand and rock, I saw the outline of the skeleton of a great round ship, long beached in this dry place.

"The Great Flood came up to here," the boy said. "We all clustered in the higher land – I am too young to remember it, but I have been told. Then Uta-napishti came with this boat and with other boats too. And he asked to be let through. We said no, and for a while there was a standoff. But then your god Enlil came, in a boat of his own. And he took them through the mountain. Most of the boats we chopped into pieces, and sold as relics, for good luck. But that one we leave as a reminder, of how high the water came."

I looked up at the twin peaks of Mashu, the great mountain bull, and its grey horns of rock, piercing the sky.

"What is it you seek, on the far side of the mountain?" the boy asked.

"The secret to immortality."

"For a man who wants to live a long time, you are going about it a strange way."

"Yes," I said. "I know that."

The entrance to the mountain passage looked like the entrance to an ordinary cave.

"It is a long walk through," the boy said. "And there is no light at all. It takes a whole day, or a whole night. It doesn't matter if it's day or night when you are inside."

"Have you been through?"

"No but I have heard the men talking of it. People get frightened, and turn round and come out. I have heard it's twelve hours through if you keep walking fast. And if you don't get lost. They say that sometimes people never come out."

"Well, I am going in."

"You are brave, for a Sumerian," the boy said.

"Thank you for showing me the way." I was noticing for the first time all the bruises on him, new ones on top of old. "You could come with me. See the world on the other side."

"I think you will die in this mountain," he said. Then with a last nod to me, he went off downhill. Soon enough he was only a small dark shape, moving off quickly into the desert.

The passage through the mountain narrowed quickly and within a minute I was in pitch darkness, feeling my way.

Enlil had said: "Keep a solid wall to your left, and you will not go wrong, but just keep going, long after you think you have gone wrong somehow."

The boy had called me brave. Now I had to be brave. If bravery is to keep going when you cannot see anything. When all you can smell is the rock and the wet. When you feel that you are going mad, and the whole mountain is going to come crashing down on you.

Did they dig this out, the gods? How was the wall so smooth, and the floor of the passageway so flat?

When I had gone on so long it must have been hours, I sat for a while, resting my back against the wall, desperate to rest but also desperate not to get spun around, and, the gods forbid, end up going back the way I had come.

I began to see things in the dark. Faces flickering, shapes resolving. A man's face, becoming a woman's face, becoming a lion's roar.

How could I have been walking so long, straight through the heart of a mountain? I was thirsty again, and also hungry. It was hotter than it had been, and that only added to how parched I felt.

I remembered going back up to the sleeping space in the loft, after Enlil had come for me. Going back up to get Enkidu's body ready for the strangers who were going to come up and get him. How as I moved him onto his side, to tidy his clothes, a maggot fell from one of his nostrils. I had a rush of shame, thinking about that maggot.

Then I was hit with no warning by a towering wave of grief. I had not cried since the funeral. But now I found myself weeping and weeping, there all alone in the absolute black.

CHAPTER ELEVEN

ERESHKIGAL

My demons hung her body on a hook, on the wall behind my throne.

The *gallas* lifted her up high and then pulled her down hard. The metal hook pierced her throat and then curved up through her brain and out of one dead eye with the most delightful crunch and splurch.

It gave me a sort of peace, looking at her. A distraction from my pain. For whole hours, my eyes stopped itching, and I could breathe easier, and my heart was steady.

Where life had been, where love and anger and laughter had been, now there was this animal carcass. Rotting meat on a hook. There was only so much her *melam* could do. It could not fix this, not here in my temple of death.

It made me feel differently, more kindly, towards my own crooked limbs, and swollen gut.

As the evening prayers began, the dust of the dead began to fall heavier. It began to settle on the corpse.

I became transfixed by the blood-matted hair, and the jagged wounds. By the bulging gleam of exposed fat, the splintered bones, the blue skin, this ordinary meat horror, crusting over black. As I sat watching, I saw for the first time something moving inside the corpse, a flicker of new life in the blackening flesh.

The worms of the underworld were going to work on the body of the goddess Inanna. What had once been a priestess of Heaven was now meat to be chewed through. To be gobbled down. Just as I was only meat for the baby that ate me up from the inside.

She was theirs now, this false sister, and I found that very beautiful.

PART 4

"No one at all sees Death,
No one at all sees the face of Death,
No one at all hears the voice of Death,
Death so savage, who hacks men down."

From *The Epic of Gilgamesh*

CHAPTER ONE

NINSHUBAR

Neti had told me to wait quietly in the hut. It was not in my nature to be obedient, but I went in there on my first night, and I thought, *I will just put my head down*.

Down went my head, onto blankets that smelled of soap. And that was it for me. I look back in shame at this. How did I go to sleep like that, without even making sure of the area?

The next day I was up at dawn, and I stood most happily in front of the hut, with the morning light blazing out over the mountains behind me, and the river plains in the distance before me, and the sweetest, coolest air upon my face. I could have foraged then for food in the hut, but as I listened to the mountain and its noises in the early light, it came to me that it was the perfect morning for a hunt, perhaps for something bigger and more delicious than a river rat. Also, I thought it would not be a bad thing to have an idea of where I was, and what the land was like.

Back in the hut, I stripped down and bound my breasts with the long, soft piece of leather that I had been using to tie up my cloak.

I cursed myself for not having a bow with me. But I had my knives, and sword and axe, taken from Inanna's guard. I could improvise some sort of spear. Although I would be hunting, I did have just one honey cake, before I ventured out in earnest.

What a place, what a view. Neti's stone hut was tucked with its back against a rocky escarpment, but it looked out across a high plateau of fine green grass, and then beyond, across islands of piled-up rocks, down onto the great plateau, and then below that the river plain, a great patchwork of green and blue, here or there with a puff of the whitest cloud hanging over it in the early cool. To my right, to the north, there were mountains: real mountains, blue in this light; wrapped in trees until a certain height, and then raw stone pushing up into the sky. To the south, I thought I could see open water, although it might have been more land, shrouded in mist.

I was simply standing there, absorbing all this, when I caught just the smallest movement to my left. I did not react, other than to steady my chin a little. But I did my calculations. I was almost certain it was a man. And that he was hiding from me in the rocks to my left. The more I thought about it, the more I thought I knew him.

Well, if you are going to do something, it is better to do it quick.

I ran as fast as anyone possibly could have at the rocks to the left of me, a bronze knife in each hand. When I was two paces away, the man rose up.

Wearing a heavy leather coat.

He had both hands in the air above his head.

I saw at once that he did not intend to fight me, and also that it was the bodyguard, the one who had been standing outside Inanna's rooms.

"Harga?" I said.

"So it would seem," he said.

He looked to be alone, although I could not be sure of it. He had a bow across his back, and a quiver of arrows. Also, at his belt, the slingshot he had refused to hand over to me.

I had not looked at him properly in the palace corridor – only at his weapons. Now I saw that he was a strong man. Twice my age, perhaps, but not too old to fight. He had thick black curls that sprang up from his head, and skin that had seen many years of hard sun. He had long, narrow eyes, and a clean-shaved chin.

"What are you doing here?" I said, lowering my weapons.

He put his hands down. "Gilgamesh told me to watch Inanna."

"Did he?"

"Have you tried getting closer to the Kur?"

So: he was all business.

"I've only been here a short time," I said.

"As have I," he said. "Come this way. There is something you should see."

We made our way up the slope together, both of us looking at each other carefully.

Only a few paces from the hut, Neti appeared. One heartbeat there was only air, and the next there he was.

This was secret business. Shamans' business.

Neti now stood directly in our path. He was wearing a simple cloak, as a farmer might wear, and old-fashioned sandals, but I could see that there was something strangely clean about him, now he was standing in daylight.

"This far but not further," he said, one firm palm held out to us.

I looked at Harga. He tipped his head to the right, and we both walked right.

Neti appeared in front of us again, one hard hand held out to us. "This far but not further," he said.

I tried to walk right at him, intending to lift him out of my way, but I found I could not. I could walk right up to his palm, but I could not reach out to touch him, and nor could I take one step further. Movement forwards was simply no longer possible for me.

"You can do that as often as you like, but it doesn't change," said Harga.

I took a step back from Neti, and breathed easier.

"Neti, what is this?"

"This far but not further," he said. He did not seem the same to me as he had the previous evening, when he had been so friendly, and communicative.

"Neti, do you know me?" I said.

"This far, but not further," said Neti. I wasn't sure any more that he was looking directly at me.

"It's like this all the way around," Harga said. "In a big circle around whatever's up there."

I felt overwhelmed by this dark business with Neti. But also embarrassed. How had this old man, Harga, already learned all this, while I had been sprawled out in bed?

"There are cakes in the hut," I said. It was not much to throw at him, but for now it was all I had.

Harga was in theory unremarkable and so it is hard to say exactly why I found him so annoying.

We spent three long days together, waiting, in that place. He was a practical man, a hunter, a fire starter, a doer. I could see that he would fight, if it was necessary. What was there to be annoyed by? And yet.

If I really had to narrow it down to just one thing, it would be that there was nothing at all that this man was not better at. After even only a short while, even though I am famously free of jealousy and other pettiness, it began to scratch at my nerves. When we hunted rabbits, it would be his trap that got the rabbit. Once he killed a duck with a pebble from his slingshot, even though I had told him that it was impossible that he could do it. When we brought down a little mountain deer, which I did not know the proper name of, it was Harga who got the arrow into it, and then who knew of the history of this particular kind of deer, and how best to cook it. Afterwards, when he was skinning it, he showed me a little trick he had to make it easier to pull the skin off whole. He knew that I might be interested, he said, having seen how I had skinned a rabbit earlier.

"Thank you," I said.

On the third night I said to him: "Tomorrow, if Neti does not come to us, we must find our way in to get her."

But in the morning, I was woken by knocking. I expected Harga, but it was Neti, the dawn sky behind him.

Harga only then appeared, his black curls wild upon his head, wrapped in a blanket.

"Where is she?" I said to Neti.

The gatekeeper wrung his hands together. He seemed entirely present now – his full self.

"Inanna is dead," he said, in an apologetic sort of way.

"I've been told to tell you that," he added. "And, also, to tell you that there is nothing you can do about it."

CHAPTER TWO

GILGAMESH

I lost time there, in the black heart of the mountain.

I thought about my father, who I had let down so badly. I thought about my wife, Della, who deserved better. I thought about Enkidu, and how he had looked at me.

Once so long ago I had said to him, "I am not sure you know who I am."

And he had said to me: "I know well enough."

I thought about the black eyes of the goddess on me, as she looked up at me from the White Quay at Uruk.

At some point I stood, and kept on walking through the mountain.

When I had been in there perhaps a week, perhaps a month, perhaps a year, or perhaps only a few hours, when I had fainted against the wall so many times, but each time come to, and walked on, only terrified above all things that I had started going the wrong way, finally, I saw light in the distance.

I walked on, the light growing brighter, my forehead crinkling up at the harshness of it.

I emerged, blinking, into a heaven. A green forest, mossy-floored, with a stream cascading through it. It was like a garden, a perfect garden.

I drank from the stream, scooping it up in my hands, and it was the sweetest water, as sweet as the water in the cedar forest.

Then I stood in the stream to wash the mud, and sweat, and blood off me. I could not tell what was my blood, and what was Uptu's. There was nothing I could do about my twisted and filthy lion-skin loincloth, but the rest of me I could scrub new. Last of all I dipped in my shorn head, and rubbed it clean with sand from the bottom of the stream.

Behind me up high I could see rocky grey crags, eagles soaring. Far below, I could see what looked like a river plain and a strip of seashore. And... was that a building? Where there was a building, there might be food.

I set off at once, still wet from the stream.

As I dropped down through the woods towards the sea, I saw that the building was fashioned from stone, and looked much like a tavern, with a high stone wall around it, and smoke coming from its chimney. It stood with its foundations on the rocks at the back of a long, wave-battered pebbled beach. Might there be food cooking beneath that chimney? I sped up.

When I was close enough to make out the seabirds perched along the stone roof, I saw movement: someone disappearing inside the gate. A woman? She looked as if she was wearing a long cloak, and perhaps a veil.

By the time I got there, the large wooden gate was bolted against me. I looked around; would I have to climb up and over to get in? The drystone wall was about a cord and a half high and it looked solid; I wasn't sure I could get much of a hold on it if I tried to climb.

"Mistress of the house," I called. "Will you open up? I am only looking to get food."

"Go away!" She sounded Sumerian.

I looked down, remembering afresh my disgraceful lion skin, and that I was otherwise naked.

"My lady, I may look strange, but I am less mad than I look. I've come through the mountain from Sumer. Will you let me in? I have no weapons, and mean no one any harm."

"Just go away!"

"If you will not open up and feed me, will you at least tell me where to find Uta-napishti? He was a Sumerian man, and he came through this way with many others, sometime after the Great Flood. I'm told he came through the mountain, but I know no more than that. My father-in-law, Enlil, and my patron, the god An, they have sent me here to find him."

I looked up to find a head staring down at me, over the top of the wall. It belonged to an old woman, wearing an ancient, embroidered veil. "Come in, then," she said.

It was indeed a tavern, if not a busy one. The woman fed me yellow cheese and bread with dried fruit in it, and watched me eat it in the smoky gloom.

"My name is Shiduri," she said.

"And mine is Gilgamesh."

"I am going to guess you are the famous Gilgamesh. You know we hear of you even here, at the far edge of the world. Boats come in, and I feed them in return for news. Is it true you are friends with a wild man named Enkidu?"

I ate for a while. "He's dead," I said.

"I am sorry, Gilgamesh, because I do know about grief," she said. "So, what do you want with Uta-napishti?"

"Have you heard of *melam*?"

"I may look old to you, but I am even older than I look. Yes, I know what *melam* is. I was married to the man you seek, and when he found *melam*, he gave me some."

"Do you know where he found it?"

She shook her head. "Uta found it out in the ocean. I wasn't with him when they found it. So you will need to go and find him on his island, if you want to look for it."

She helped me to more food, and poured me more wine. "I cannot take you to the island. Only the stone men can go back and forth across the Waters of Death."

"How far is it?"

"A few leagues out to sea. You can see it on a sunny day, when the sky is completely clear. They say it has fine forests, fine pastures, clean water, and the seas around it boil with fish. But first you need to cross the Waters of Death."

"But the stone men are happy to cross these waters?"

"If you give them gold, yes. Do you have gold?"

I shrugged at that. "Why aren't you with them on the island, Shiduri? If they are your people."

She gave me a sort of smile. "Uta and I lost our children, in the Great Flood. And our marriage did not survive it. So in the end he went over to the island, and I chose to stay here, and be mostly alone."

I lived in the inn for the next few days, and the old woman pointed out to me the comings and the goings of the stone men.

They wore their wild curls long down their backs, although their faces were shaved, and they wore close-fitting leather trousers and caps made of sealskin. They looked like serious men who would not run from bad weather or a fight.

They came in their boats most days, pulled them up high on the sand, and went up in groups to the garden in the foothills below the mountain. There they gathered fruits and pinecones, or sometimes they would fell a tree, and bring the wood down as planks. Sometimes they fished in the lagoon behind the beach, or stood in the shallows as the surf came in, spearing stray turtles or rays if they came too close.

I stood on the old woman's spying stone, which let you peep over the wall, to watch their movements.

"You keep your head low, Gilgamesh," she called from inside the hut. "If they decide to come up here, I cannot turn them away. And they will very likely kill you, just for being here."

"But they allow you to live here?"

"They tried to kill me, but I came back to life. Now sometimes one of them will hurt me, but most of them are wary of me."

"Why are they called the stone men?"

"That's how they kill. Those bags on their hips are full of the smoothest, roundest beach stones. They fire them out of slingshots, and I assure you, they are deadly. It's how they bring down deer, as well as their enemies."

"I'll keep my head down," I said.

Shiduri had no weapons of war, but she had an axe. A good stone axe, of good flint, glued with black pitch into good oak, and then bound with gut.

I said: "Will you give me this axe?"

"You have no way of paying me for the food and wine and beer you have already drunk. Never mind the bed you sleep in. How are you going to pay me for this axe?"

"Loan me the axe, then. And you know what your payment is. Your payment is my company."

I tried to give her my old smile, but it felt strange upon my face.

"If you ever do learn to smile again, and put some flesh on those bones. And if the scars of frostbite, and too much sun too, ever heal upon you. If all that happens, then no doubt old women will feed you and host you for free and shower axes upon you."

I laughed. "Do I look so terrible?"

"Your face is sunken, your cheeks are hollow, your mood is wretched, your heart is full of nothing but sorrow. Yes, you look terrible, Gilgamesh. You look terrible, you sound terrible. You are terrible. But I do see that there was great beauty in you. That there was once."

I laughed again.

"It is good to hear you laugh," she said. "I will lend you my axe."

The stone men came the next day.

"They are walking this way," Shiduri said, standing on her spy stone. "They are quick to violence. They may kill you."

"How many?" I said. I was standing behind the gate, with the shaft of Shiduri's axe gripped tightly between my hands.

"Six are walking this way. But I think the boy they had with them is missing. And maybe another. What is your plan now, Gilgamesh?"

"Let me get up and look."

I peeked out over the wall and saw a group of stone men making their way along the path at the back of the beach. The leader of the group was a boulder of a man, and he wore a dappled black and white sealskin. In one hand he carried a sling, and in the other a bag of what must be pebbles. I ducked down behind the wall again, and Shiduri took back her place.

"Yes, I think there are two missing," I said. "When they get close, close enough for the slingshot, you make sure you get down."

She rolled her eyes at me. "I know about slingshots. I know that the hard way. Tell me, what is your plan?"

"My plan is to get over to the island in their boat."

"You will need them to cooperate with you, then, because it's a big boat, and it's the kind of sea you need to know very well, and even then, you will no doubt drown."

"All of that I got from 'the Waters of Death'," I said.

She got down off her stone. "If I stay up there, they will see me looking, and become suspicious."

For some moments we stood and looked at each other in silence, but soon enough a stone man began bellowing through the gate at us.

"Shiduri, we know you have a man in there. My people are not blind. They see him creeping around in your yard, back and forth to the wash house."

She stood up on the stone again. "I can have a man here if I want to. I can have anyone I like here. Who are you to tell me who I can give a bed to in my tavern?"

"You can have stone men in here. Or traders who visit with our permission. That we agreed to. But not strangers from the mountain. And we can tell you what to do now that you have built your house on our land."

Another voice: "Open up the gates, old woman."

"Get down," I whispered, and pulled at her skirts. She got down quickly.

Then I raised my voice, for the men over the wall. "Can we negotiate?"

"What do you want?" the first stone man shouted back.

"I want to go over the Waters of Death, to the island, to see Uta-napishti, my forebear. I would like you to take me there in your boat, since I am told you are expert mariners, and you are my best chance of getting there. What would be your price for taking me there?"

They conferred quietly.

"We'll do it," the voice said. "For two small pieces of silver."

"That's a good price," I said.

"They are trying to trick you," the old woman whispered. "They intend to rob you and perhaps kill you."

"Oh really?" I whispered back. "Are you saying these men of violence may be untrustworthy? Thank the gods you are here to warn me."

"So come out and talk," a stone man called. "We could take you over to the island now, if you wanted."

"We would like you to back well off first," I called. "Just while we get to know each other."

"All right, we are all backing off," the voice shouted. "We are backing off," he said again, obviously further away.

"They will have left someone behind to kill us with his stones," Shiduri whispered.

"Woman, how stupid do you think I am? I am not a newborn puppy, with my eyes still shut. Of course they have left someone behind."

"Gilgamesh, I am trying to help you, a total stranger who I owe nothing to. There is no need to take a tone with me."

We both stood there for a while, listening.

"How are you with weapons?" I said.

"What does it matter?"

"I'm trying to think of a way out of here that doesn't end up with that boy dead."

A boy's voice: "I can hear you! I can hear what you're saying!"

"Can you?" I called back.

"I don't want to die either. But my father said to get you."

For a while we two stayed quiet inside, and he stayed quiet outside.

"I wonder if this counts as a siege," I said, remembering a different time.

The old woman only frowned at me.

"It's a siege," the boy shouted. "You are inside something, and I'm the enemy forces outside, trying to get in. And there's a wall."

I had a flash of sadness for this squalid situation, for this boy now assuredly going to die too. And for Enkidu, standing on the wall at Marad, such a short time ago, in his terrible saucepan-helmet.

"Boy! This is going to end badly for you. Can I persuade you to accept a trade? My life, for a trade? There is honour in a trade, surely?"

"I don't think there's honour in a trade. My father said to get you; that's where the honour lies."

"But that was when it was a trick," I said. "When I wasn't meant to know you were there. But now I do know. So, your plan has gone wrong."

There was a short silence.

"True enough," he said.

"Why don't you run over and get them, and tell them I'm on to you all, and bring them back. Then if anyone is going to get killed, it'll be one of the adults. I hate killing children; I always have."

"I'll run off, then, and get them."

There was a clattering sound from about where he had been talking from.

"Is he just pretending?" the woman said.

"I think so." I sighed deeply.

"I think this is more like a stand-off than a siege," I called to the boy.

He was quiet for a while. Finally, he said: "Did you know I was still here?"

"Yes," I said.

I heard the unmistakable sound of the adults returning: voices, their feet, rocks tumbling down the path behind them.

"They knew I was out here," the boy said. Then there was a *pwaf* sound and an "Ugh!", as if someone had been hit around the head.

"We saw the boy when you were coming up here," I called. "It was a terrible trick."

As I said this, a new and worrisome thought came to me. Could someone climb into the yard from the other side of the hut, out of my sightline? Was this all a ruse? I couldn't remember now the lay of the land there. I lifted my eyebrows at the old woman, and gestured back towards the hut with my head. She nodded, picked up a rock from the ground and began creeping away towards the door. She pointed at her right ear and then the door, and nodded.

What? I mouthed.

There's someone inside! she mouthed back.

I lifted my axe, and nodded.

"What's with the stones?" I called out, in what I hoped sounded a cheerful manner. "Are you cavemen? Why not arrows?"

"Stones are better," came back a voice I had not heard before.

"They're not better," I said. "The range is so short! If I had arrows now, I would not have let you get this near the hut, and things would be very different. I could have come out and picked you all off before you even knew I was here."

"But you run out of the arrows!" It was the boy, sounding perky enough. "There are always more stones, especially if you're always looking out for them."

I heard a scuffling noise inside the hut, as if someone had tripped on something.

I called out: "Well, I do know a man who likes stones and a slingshot: a nasty piece of work called Harga. But he always carries a bow and an arrow too, because he is not entirely stupid."

The scuffling noise inside the hut stopped.

The crowd outside fell silent for some long moments.

"Is he a big man?" one of them called over the wall.

"Who?" I said. My mind was whirring. Were they talking about the man in the hut?

"This Harga you speak of. What does he look like?"

I stood up straighter, raising my eyebrows at the old woman. She shrugged back at me.

I shouted out: "The Harga I know looks like a piece of leather. But uglier. Black curls. A sly man, always plotting. If you put him alone in a cupboard, he would plot against the cupboard. That is the Harga that I know."

"Is he still alive, this Harga you speak of?"

"He was when I last saw him. In Sumer. Which was not long ago."

"How do you know this Harga?"

"He serves the god Enlil," I said. "That's how I met him."

At this the men on the far side of the wall all burst into laughter. A moment later, a happy face appeared from inside the doorway of the old woman's hut. "Can you really know Harga?" the man said, putting away his weapons. "I cannot believe it!"

I noticed for the first time that the black curls these stone men sported were not so different from the curls that Harga was so proud of.

The man from the hut pulled open the gate and peered out. "Lads, down weapons!" he called. He looked around at the woman, nodded to her, turned back to me, all warmth and humour. "Any enemy of Harga is a friend to the stone men," he said. "You are welcome in our land!"

CHAPTER THREE

NINSHUBAR

In the beginning, I did not believe it.

"Is Inanna dead," I said to the gatekeeper, "or were you only told to tell us that?"

"She is dead," Neti said. "Ereshkigal had her executed without trial. I am sorry to tell you this, Ninshubar, because it seems you were fond of the young goddess."

"Let me past," I said.

"No," he said. "This far but not further."

I went to push past him, but found I could not.

"You two must leave now," he said, with his polite smile.

Harga stepped forwards, his hand touching my arm.

"Can she really not be saved?" he said. A good question.

"That I cannot tell you," Neti said. "I am not in charge of the stories. I am only in charge of the gates."

I collected all my things from the hut and tied my cloak around my shoulders. Then Harga and I consulted, standing well away from Neti.

"Inanna told me to go and get help if she did not come out. She gave me a list of gods to ask for help. At the time I thought she was talking only for talking's sake."

"You think the gods can fix this?"

"Her family, the Anunnaki, they go in and out of that place. I think the rules are different for them."

"That is true on many counts."

We looked at each other.

"I have my orders from the goddess," I said. "There is no point dwelling on what might or might not have happened to her. I am going to ask the Anunnaki to help her, as she asked me to. I can think of no better plan than the terrible plan she left me with."

"This is the sort of business that I absolutely hate," Harga said.

"You do not need to come with me. If your orders were only to watch her."

"Gilgamesh told me to keep the girl alive."

"Inanna never mentioned Gilgamesh. He is not on the list of people who might help her."

"They are cousins."

Harga began throwing a pebble from one hand to the other.

"I'll stick with you for now," he said. "Until I see which way this thing is going."

"You are quite the hero."

"Heroes die," Harga said.

Inanna had said to go to her grandfather Enlil, and also Lugalbanda, in the north, and then Dumuzi, her husband, in Uruk, then her father in Ur, perhaps, and then Enki in Eridu, in that order. And I had said to her, "Oh yes, oh yes." But I had no idea at all how to get to any of these places, except perhaps Uruk. If I headed west, perhaps I would not be far off it? Perhaps I could even retrace our steps. But how to get to Nippur, which I had only heard of a handful of times?

I led our party for the first few minutes, striking out confidently to the northwest.

But then Harga said: "If we are going to Nippur first, I know the way to Nippur. And this is not the way to Nippur."

"Lead, then, if you insist upon it." I stood aside to let him pass.

As we walked down the mountain, veering off to the north, he turned his head to me, quite cheerful, and said: "You know, I used to live in Nippur, when I first came to Sumer. It is my home, really. I could probably lead us there blindfolded, if was pushed to it."

"I did not know that."

Oh but of course, if we were going to Nippur, Harga would be able to lead us there blindfolded. Of course he would.

We walked out onto the spine of a ridgeway that flowed down towards the plains, with long slopes of scree tumbling away to either side of us. Monstrous eagles kept watch over our procession of two.

Sometimes the walking was easy, along bare rock. At other times we had to pick our way around thickets and sheer rock faces. When it was almost dusk, we were finally down off the ridge, and the land was flat before us. It was a strange landscape, quite flat, thick moss underfoot, and with no obvious shelter ahead. I knew full well that we were both tired and hungry, although neither of us had said anything to the other.

It was Harga who pulled up first. "Better we stay in the rocks for the night," he said. "A lot of leopards here. Better we have something to the back of us, and to make a fire with."

The light was going quickly as we made our way back to the ridgeway.

I was walking slightly ahead of Harga when a man in a cloak and headdress rose up at me. He had a stone knife in his hand.

I balanced for a moment on my left foot, mid-flight, and then in one easy move, I took the knife from my attacker, and held it to his throat. "Give me everything you have," I said.

I looked back rather triumphant towards Harga, only to see that he also had a man by the throat, and another on the floor behind him.

"Do you need help?" I called.

"No, no, I have them," Harga said.

We searched them, being careful of any rearing up of their courage. Mine had a waterskin, with some water in it, and some flatbread, wrapped in linen, and the chert knife, which I gave back to him, and some green onions. One of Harga's had cheese and dried meat.

"Praise be to the red moon," I said, gathering it all up together in a cloth.

We watched our assailants limp off across the tundra.

"You have quick eyes," Harga said.

I was careful not to show that I was pleased by that, as we sat down to share the food.

It was five days of walking from there to Nippur, two days across the tundra, sometimes making our way around jewel-like lakes, and then three more days after dropping down onto the fertile plain of the two rivers.

At night, up high, it was often close to freezing.

Harga and I could have slept close, on those cold nights. Instead we hunkered down on opposite sides of the fire, with our backs to each other.

In the day it was searing hot, once we were on the plains, but we were in the water so much, crossing canals and rivers, that I did not mind it too much.

Then one morning, there was Nippur, the most sacred city on Earth, with its famous clay-brick ziggurat that even I had heard of. It was strange to me, after Uruk and Eridu, that the city had no great city walls around it.

"Do they not need to defend themselves here?"

"No one would attack the Holy City," Harga said. "Even Akka used to come here to pray, before the war, whatever he says now about not needing the gods."

The open farmland around us gave way to reed-thatched houses, then villages. The muddy track we were on became something approaching a road, with a colonnade of date palms running along each side.

Although there were no walls around Nippur, we soon came upon a gang of soldiers, sitting on wood and leather camp chairs, and strung out over the road. Despite the sweltering heat of the day, they had a fire going on one side, with some birds roasting on it.

I saw that they expected us to stop.

"I am here on behalf of the goddess Inanna," I said to the soldier closest to me. "You must tell Enlil I am here, and let me in."

"You don't look like you know any gods," the man said.

"And yet I do, and I am here to see Enlil, on Inanna's orders. He may well kill you just for this very short delay and if he does not kill you, it is very possible that I will."

This might have gone on for some time, but Harga stepped

forwards. He ignored the man I was talking to, and lifted his chin to the crew by the fire.

"It's me," he said. "We're going past."

The man in front of me stood up and moved his chair.

"Easy, Harga," he said. "No need for any fuss."

I looked very suspiciously at Harga after this, as we made our way towards the six-storey precinct at the heart of the city.

"Are you Gilgamesh's man, or Enlil's?"

"I'm more scared of Enlil, if that answers you," he said.

I could tell he had more to say.

"What?" I said.

"He has been good to me, Enlil. Like a father. So it is wrong to say only that I fear him."

The great lord god of the sky, Enlil, was out in the fields to the east of the city, his sleeves rolled up. I had heard that he was a worker. He was looking at some drawings sketched out in the sandy earth, with a group of men around him. He had on a simple linen dress, but bound at the waist with a gold chain, and three *mees* around each arm and one around his neck.

"What?" he said, looking up. "Oh, Harga. I was not expecting you."

He looked over at me then, with no smile.

"You don't kneel for gods where you come from?" he said.

"No, we don't," I said. "What of it?"

Enlil turned and gave me his full attention, hands on his hips. He had a hard, grey look to him. "But you wear my mother's mark upon you?"

"I do," I said. "I serve in her temple."

"This will not be good news," Enlil said.

Harga passed me into the care of the chief steward of Enlil's palace. The steward passed me on to an elderly female servant, who showed me to a small courtyard.

There a little girl brought me water to clean myself and wash my clothes, and she gave me a strip of cloth to wrap myself in as I waited for the sun to dry them.

The courtyard had a sheltered verandah along one side, and a bench in the shade there. On a small table next to the bench, the little girl set out water, bread and cheese for me.

All of this I fell upon, and then after I had eaten, I lay down upon the bench.

I woke up and a small girl was standing over me, dark against the bright of the sky. I at first thought it was the little girl who had fed me. But then the girl's face came into focus, and I saw that she was not in fact a girl.

I swung my legs over, and sat up.

The woman was strangely small and smooth-skinned, but I saw now by her *mees*, but also by the way she held herself, that she was a goddess and very ancient. She had on only a plain black dress, with no elaborate stitching of the kind the gods favour. Her eyes, dark and round, seemed too big for her face.

"I came to look at you," she said. "I am Ninlil."

"Well, I am something to look at," I said. I did not feel as nonchalant as I sounded. She made me shiver, this little doll of a goddess.

"I am Enlil's wife," she said. "But I am his second wife. So, I am only step-grandmother to your mistress Inanna."

"She's not my mistress," I said.

Without warning, Ninlil sat down next to me, and put both her small hands onto my arm. "They will not help Inanna," she said, her huge eyes fixed upon mine. "You will find no help here."

"Because they have no way to help her?"

"They will tell you that."

I removed her hands from my arm. "Talk to me plainly, goddess. I won't get you into trouble."

She laughed. "I won't get into trouble. No one believes anything I say."

"Well, I will listen to you, at least."

She leaned in and whispered to me. "Inanna is An's weapon. Against Enki."

As she spoke, a door opened and there was Harga, just as dirty as he'd been earlier, but carrying a large pack.

He dipped his head to the goddess. "Ninlil."

The goddess stood, bowed her head to Harga, and then hurried away past him out of the courtyard, without even a glance of goodbye at me.

"There's no help here for us," Harga said, "so it's Uruk next, if you want us to go on with your plan."

Harga seemed curiously serious as we made our way south along the river. I thought about asking for his thoughts but after a while he said: "You do not know my master, Gilgamesh, but things have gone wrong for him. A friend of his, of ours, has died. And I am sorry for it."

"I'm sorry, Harga," I said. "So did you see Gilgamesh, in Nippur?"

"I only saw Enlil. And he said that once he had tools that could have helped us, but now the only Anunnaki who might have the power to help us is his brother Enki. Or perhaps Dumuzi, if Enki has passed the tools on to him."

"And he's happy you keep going with me, on this strange quest?"

"He wants to know what is happening, so yes. You know, for what it's worth, Ninshubar, I think Enlil would help her if he had any way to do it. He's loyal to his family."

"I wonder," I said. But I did not repeat what Ninlil had said. *An's weapon*, I thought to myself.

Harga said: "You know I have grown fond of Gilgamesh over the years. Idiot that he is. I fear that the loss of his friend..."

"What?"

"I fear it will break him."

I knew that it was a long way to Uruk, but Harga was sure of how to get there, and we were on road now, or a road of sorts, following rutted tracks that wound through pasture land and over small wooden bridges. So close to the river, it was muggy and hot even in the early morning.

"You work hard for these gods," I said to Harga.

"They pay me in gold."

"Yet you sleep in ditches, and under trees."

"Not tonight I won't," he said. "There's a tavern up ahead. But anyway, I have a lot of gold. And on the other side, when I pass over, that means a better life."

"Is that right?"

"If you go over empty-handed, into the underworld, you suffer for it."

"But it is better with gold?"

"It's better," he said. "Not good. It is still the underworld. But better. There's a difference, maybe only a small difference. But you know when you are somewhere for eternity, then small differences will matter."

Around a bend in the river: Uruk, with its vast yellow-brick walls. We took shelter some distance from the ramparts, beneath the shade of a huluppu tree.

"Dumuzi doesn't know us," I said. "So, I think we just go in and ask him to help her. Keep it simple."

"He doesn't know you, but he may have heard about a woman looking like you appearing in the city before Inanna left. You are distinctive-looking."

"Thank you."

"Lepers can be distinctive-looking," he said. "Also, although I have never been formally introduced to the man, I have often been in his presence, as captain of his wife's bodyguard. I am very well-known besides to everyone he keeps about him."

"So, you think it is too dangerous for us to approach him? What is your plan, then?"

"I have no better plan."

I had never seen the north gate before: a huge stone arch, held up by two stone elephants.

Here people were moving freely in and out of the gates, and no one stopped us as we made our way in, odd a pair as we no doubt were.

I had seen Uruk on the day I met Inanna, but I had been focused so intently on getting to her that I had not paused to look about me at the city. Now I walked open mouthed along the canal that cut through the city, gawking up at the white of the ziggurat, and the huge walls that surrounded it all. "To think I thought Eridu impressive!" I said.

We came to a halt at a set of wooden gates, ornately carved.

"We are here to see the god Dumuzi," Harga called, "who is king here. We have news of his wife, Inanna."

A small square opened in the door and a face appeared, looking hard at Harga.

"Aren't you Gilgamesh's man?"

"I know him," Harga said.

"Come on in, then, will you?"

We were taken to a small room in the barracks. There we waited, each sitting on a small stool. Many heartbeats passed before a soldier came in and crooked his head at Harga; the two of them went out, leaving me alone on my stool. I was not sure what was happening, but I felt relieved to see the friendly way in which they were all treating Harga.

After a long while a man in a tall copper helmet came into the room. "I'll take you for some food now," he said, his smile warm.

I stood, smiling back, and as I did, the man punched me in the stomach.

I went down like a sack upon the tile floor. Then he brought his foot down hard upon my head.

CHAPTER FOUR

GILGAMESH

All of the stone men crammed into the front room of Shiduri's hut, in the highest spirits.

Shiduri served out stew and flatbreads, throwing the odd sour look at me.

The man who had broken into the hut was the leader of these stone men, and his name was Urshanabi.

"More beer!" said Urshanabi, waving his cup at Shiduri. Then he said: "So sorry, Gilgamesh, do go on. Is Harga a great man in your country? Surely he must be a great man, for you to know him at all."

"Harga is an assassin and a spy, a soldier for the god Enlil, although for a while now he has marched with me. But no, he is not a great man. He is a servant. Even the word 'assassin' makes him sound grander than he is."

For this I was thoroughly clapped, my back slapped.

For a moment I thought about adding a word in Harga's defence. After all, he had saved my life more than once. But then looking around at the stone men's bright faces, I reconsidered.

They wanted to know everything that I knew about Harga, from the first moment I had heard anything of him, to the last, and lingering in particular detail on anything personal I knew about him, and anything I had ever seen him do in a fight. They wanted also to know anything I could possibly tell them about Harga telling tales on me to the god.

"He was always a sneak!" Urshanabi said. "A liar and a thief and a sneak."

"I wish I had met him," the boy said, gulping down his beer. "But he ran away from here before I was born."

"When you go back through the passage, maybe we will come with you," Urshanabi said. "We will come with you and kill Harga for you."

"That's very kind of you," I said. "Really it is. But I need to get over to the island first, to ask some questions of Uta-napishti. After that, I would relish a journey with you, and to see you kill Harga. Or die trying at least."

They all laughed uproariously at that. Urshanabi said: "Gilgamesh, we will take you over to the island this afternoon. You can do your business with the witch people. Then we will bring you back here and we will talk about this passage."

"Is it not dangerous, this journey?"

"You are with stone men now. You need not fear anything!"

Shiduri would not come.

"But surely you would be safer over there, with your people?" I said. "Safer from men like these stone men?"

"I made my choice a long time ago," she said.

"Is he a bad man, then, Uta-napishti?"

She shook her head. "He was a good man. But I kept grieving, and he moved on. He wanted more children. More life. More. It was unfair to force him to watch me grieving, year after year. So I stayed here, when they moved over to the island."

"Why did you take the *melam*, if you had had enough of life?"

She laughed. "I thought it would cure me of my grief!"

"But it did not?"

"It did not," she said.

I put my arms around her, and for a moment we stood with our foreheads on each other's shoulders.

"The pain must have got easier, though?" I said.

"Not yet," she said.

She raised one flat palm to me as we made our way to the boat.

"Are you not afraid of these Waters of Death?" I said to the stone men as we pulled and pushed the boat down into the water.

"It was the god Enlil who called them that, to keep people away," Urshanabi said. "We call this the strait."

"Ah," I said.

The stone men rowed at first and then when it became very shallow over the reef, they poled us along with long shafts of pine. The white-hot sun beat down hard upon us, and wave after wave of flying fish, a rain of silver, came cascading into the boat.

In the distance, gathering slowly, a pine-covered island: white cliffs. Closer and I could see stone huts, chimneys puffing smoke. Gardens cut out of the forest, lines with clothes drying. I put out my hand to the mirror-flat sea, and let it trail in the warm and silky water.

We headed into a beach of small grey stones, of the sort the stone men might kill with. A row of fishing boats was pulled up at the top of the beach above the tide line, and in front of the boats, people were gathering.

One tall thin man stood out in front of them, a hand raised to shade his eyes as he watched us come in. I knew immediately it was Uta-napishti.

He came down towards the surf as we grew close.

He was wrapped in a sealskin cloak, his head bound like a scorpion man, in a rolled-up headdress. Even across the water, I knew at once who he reminded me of: the god Enlil. The same look of granite, worn down by rain.

"Who are you?" he called out to us. He had a deep and powerful voice; the sea seemed to ripple before him. "What are you doing here? You have no business here, stone men."

"We bring you a visitor," Urshanabi called. "A Sumerian."

Uta-napishti led us up to a long stone chieftain's hut, thatched, with a wooden door at each end. The large door at the front had a small door set into it, and this we now stooped through. Inside it was dark; a fire burned at the centre of the room, and over it hung a large bronze pot.

"You are all welcome here," said Uta-napishti.

A woman came in and began to stoke the fire as we settled down to sit around it.

When the leaves had steeped, and the tea had been poured out into clay cups, and everyone had a cup, then Uta-napishti said to me: "You are a prince of Sumer, Gilgamesh. I know who you are, although you were not yet born when I left. So, what is it that has brought you here, looking as you do, so thin, so ravaged, wearing only that lion skin?"

I looked about at the stone men, at the villagers clustered outside the doors to the hall.

"There is a rumour that you have a source of *melam*."

"Who told you that?"

"The god An," I said. "Enlil believed it also."

He smiled. "I did find *melam*, but it's all gone. A long time ago." He did not have the look of a liar about him.

"Would you show me where you found it, perhaps, so that I can look for more?"

"And why would I do that, Gilgamesh?"

"I was sent here by Enlil, who saved you, when the flood came. Perhaps I thought you might be grateful."

"Hah!" he said. "Is that what they told you? That Enlil saved us?"

"It's what they teach in temple. That when the Great Flood was coming, Enlil told you to build boats, and you did, and so you were able to rescue your people. And then Enlil led you through the mountain, to a place of safety."

He laughed. "Come for a walk with me, Gilgamesh."

We walked up through the sparse pines, with two fish eagles wheeling above us.

"Enlil is my father; did you know that?" he said.

"I did not." But he did have the look of Enlil to him; I had seen that even from the boat.

"He was worried that his wife might not like him having a baby with another woman. His wife is strange in the head. So he sent me off to Shuruppak, to be brought up there."

"I know Shuruppak."

"I became a master boat builder. Over the years, Enlil visited me many times, and then one day he came and said he wanted me to build a great fleet. So that he could go to war against his brother, Enki, who they suspected of hoarding *melam*. Then the Great Flood came. There was not much time, but we put everyone we could upon the ships."

"And you ended up at Mount Mashu?"

"Yes. The waters took us there, and dumped us. Enlil found us, and brought us through the mountain. That I must thank him for. But the ships were never meant for us mortals, and he did not warn me about the flood. Indeed, I believe he may have caused it, somehow, in his war against his brother."

"So you found the *melam* after you got here?"

"We found strange things in the water near here, when we were out fishing. Strange objects, made of metal, and with bottles inside. Inside one we found *melam*. Some I took, some I took over to Shiduri, the rest I gave out to the other survivors of the Great Flood. But then it was all gone. For a long time, young boys used to try to dive down to the wreckage of whatever it is down there, to try to find more of it. But too many of them died in the trying, so we stopped them doing it."

"Will you tell me where to go, so that I might try? I have been sent here by An. I cannot leave without trying."

"I will tell you," he said. "But you know, the goddess Nammu was here, perhaps a year after the deluge."

"I did not know that. No one in Sumer has seen her since time out of mind."

"She was here. She even walked in these woods with me, and stayed in one of our huts for many weeks. She went out every day to the place where the metal objects are, and the boys watched her diving down, and staying down for many hours. But she always came up empty-handed."

"All the same, I would like to try for myself."

He lifted both hands to the sky. "The stone men can show you, then. I will tell them where to take you."

As he walked me back down to the boat, Uta-napishti said: "Gilgamesh, even if you do find it, it is not a small thing to take the *melam*. To set yourself apart from all other humans. Now when children are born here, I cannot celebrate. It breaks my heart that I will soon watch them die. That they are so vibrant, so very present, and then all of a sudden nothing is there! Not a day goes by when I do not regret taking the *melam*."

"I have seen my own father suffer, watching me grow up, and knowing he could not help me. But the *melam* would not only be for me."

Before we parted, I said: "Why would Enlil lie about the flood, and what happened? Why would he lie about your part in it?"

Uta-napishti laughed. "It's all lies, Gilgamesh. Everything we are told about the Anunnaki. It's all stories. Stories designed to keep them in power, and that is all. I learned that as a boy, and it is time you learned it too."

"Is the afterlife only a story?"

"All of it," he said. "It is time to grow up, Gilgamesh. It is time to write your own story. A true story, which you can be proud of."

The stone men leaned as one over the front of the boat, looking down into the light that spun up from the turquoise depths. The boat leaned over dangerously as they did so.

"This is it," Urshanabi said. "This is where they said it would be, and I can see something down there in the water."

They helped me tie stones to my ankles. It was a gorgeous day, the sea so incredibly clear, the sky so blue, the smell of the water so fresh, a lovely wind. How I would have loved to just go for a simple swim today! But instead it was this.

"You make sure you can untie these ropes," Urshanabi said. "Show me how you can undo them. It will be harder down there in the dark when you are fighting for breath."

I nodded. I stood naked on the edge of the boat. I had a large stone, about the size of a kettle, tied to each foot. A third, about twice as large, Urshanabi now passed to me, grunting as he heaved it into my arms.

"We will hold up your foot stones while you jump, then let them go either side of you as you go in. When you get to the bottom, drop the big stone, and the foot stones should hold you down there while you work."

"Very well," I said.

With them holding my foot stones out over the water for me, I stepped out into the air.

And went down like a boulder off a cliff.

I had to fight the urge not to panic.

I had to fight to keep from breathing out, or in, or from trying to thrash my way back to the mirror surface above.

Below, a dark shape.

Then I was there, a foot down, the sand resolving beneath me; the shape was hard, dark metal, a mass of it. I dropped the large stone, and then crouched down in the gloom to touch the object.

It was metal, strangely clean and smooth even after all these years, not a scrap of weed or coral on it. It seemed to be submerged in the sandy bottom, only a triangle of metal poking up. I ran my hands over it, but could not find any way into it.

Already my lungs were exploding: I could not stay down much longer.

I went to untie my left foot; the rope slipped off easily.

I went to untie my right foot; it would not undo.

I was going to die down there.

I knew I must not panic. That panic would kill me. And yet it was rising up in me and I did not know how to stop it.

My fingers just kept fumbling over the rope; it would not come. I would have to swim up with the stone still tied to me.

I grabbed the stone up, and tried to kick away from the bottom. But instead of hitting sand, my foot hit metal – pain.

I felt that my eyes were failing; everything went black. I was heading for the surface, but suddenly hit sand again. A lump – something in my hindbrain made me grab it. Then I was kicking madly, my rock in one hand, and the slippery unknown object in the other.

Kicking, blindly. Was that the surface above?

Intense pain in my lungs, splitting pain behind my eyes.

Silver, undulating, just above me.

I broke through, grasping, holding my objects aloft. Sank.

Again, I was drowning.

Moments later strong arms lifted me aloft, and up into the boat. I vomited water, then lay back, looking up at the clear blue sky, and the stone men's grinning faces and curls, and relishing the good dry plentiful magical air, heaving it into me.

"You have got something!" the boy said. "Is it a bottle?"

Urshanabi untied the remaining rope from my ankle. "You took your time, Gilgamesh. We wondered if you ever planned to come back."

I could not yet speak, but my sight was clearing. The panic was fading.

"Let me take that stone from you," Urshanabi said. I realised I was clutching it to my chest. I passed it to him.

So.

In my right hand: a metal container of some kind. A dark grey metal.

I sat up properly. "Has anyone got a cloth?"

I dried the metal container carefully. It was almost exactly the length of my hand, smooth, cylindrical, and with what looked like a stone stopper for a lid. Then I dried my hands very carefully, and then dried the cylinder again. The stone men sat and watched me most intently; they allowed the boat simply to drift.

"Where was it?" Urshanabi said.

"Just in the sand, near the object. It was just by chance I felt it there and grabbed it."

"Are you going to open it, then?" the boy said.

They were all leaning forwards, so eager to see.

I twisted at the stopper, very, very careful. It didn't budge.

"Let me do it," Urshanabi said. "I can open anything."

"I'll do it," I said.

I twisted harder. Nothing.

I gripped the bottle between my bare knees, and tried again. Had it moved just a little?

I gripped it hard in my left hand, and twisted the top as hard as I could in my right. As I did so, it flew up into the air.

The bottle went one way, the stopper another; a thin stream of black powder slicked out across the water.

Just like that, it was over.

"Oh," the boy said. "I'm so sorry, Gilgamesh."

I watched the bottle tumbling down into the depths, over and over on itself. The powder had long since disappeared into the blue.

"Was that the stuff you were after?" Urshanabi said.

"I think so."

"The gods like to play tricks on us," he said. "They like to give us hope so that it is worse after."

The stone men all looked so stricken.

I began to laugh.

"There are no gods," I said. "We are the ones who play tricks on ourselves."

And then I could not stop laughing.

After a while, I realised I was crying.

Urshanabi came to sit next to me as I sobbed, one hand upon my shoulder.

"Have you searched for this medicine for a long time?" he said.

"I'm not sad about the medicine." I wiped the tears from my face, but they kept flowing.

I put my hand on Urshanabi's hand. "We have so few moments," I said. "Already I have wasted so many of them."

"Will you keep diving? Will you try again?"

"I'm going to go home now," I said. "I need to be a man now, and not only half a god."

I looked around at their upset faces.

"My friends," I said. "You are good men, and I thank you for your help today. Now, I need to get to Uruk. There is a woman there that I ought to be getting back to."

That cheered them all up. "What kind of woman?" the boy said.

"Does it matter?" I said. "So, can you take me? Could we sail there? Or do I need to walk through the dark once more?"

Urshanabi looked up at the sun, and then put one finger up into the wind. "We can have you at Ur in four days if we stay well out from the shore," he said. "Maybe another week or ten days to get upriver, against the current."

"I can pay you," I said. "I have gold if you can take me to it."

"The stone men are heroes, not mercenaries," he said. "We will come just to see it. To see the far side of the world. And to kill Harga."

"I am glad I met you," I said, and as they set their sails, I looked back only once at the smooth and silky water, and the dark shape that lay beneath it.

CHAPTER FIVE

NINSHUBAR

And so for the second time in my life, I woke up in prison.

It took a while to work it out, but then I saw Harga, lying in the straw on the other side of the cell. I knew that my head injury was bad because I felt very strongly that to move my skull in any way might lead to disaster. But from what I could glimpse of Harga, his injuries might be worse.

I am a cheerful woman. Brave too. I do not think anything else has ever been said of me. But lying there, the blood trickling down from my hair into my right eye, I did for a while feel close to despair. I shut my eyes for a while, and tried to simply breathe, and calm myself.

It was a small room with thick clay-brick walls. From where I lay, I could see a small, high window and solid blue sky beyond.

The secret in these situations is to do your calculations, and then you make a plan. But for now, I had no plan in my mind, beyond hoping that the pain in my head would fade.

I could not tell if Harga was breathing.

"Harga?"

Nothing.

"Harga!"

But he didn't move.

Later in the dark I heard him saying something.

"What is it?" I said.

"They kill prisoners in the morning here."

"You think they are going to kill us?"

"They always do it in the mornings," he said.

In the morning, I was still alive, and Harga was still breathing.

"They did not come for us," I said.

I managed to push myself up into a sitting position. The room swirled about me as I did so.

I crawled over to Harga, and sat myself down next to him. I moved his head into my lap, and tried to rub the worst of the blood off his face and chest, so I could see what damage lay underneath. His right eye was too swollen to open.

"I'm alive," he said, both eyes still shut.

"Well, they did not come for us," I said. "What have they done to you?"

"Hit me. In the face. In the guts. To find out what we were doing here."

"You know, I thought we would see Dumuzi. I thought we would put our case to him."

"He came to watch me tortured. So I had my chance to make our case."

"What did you tell them?"

"Everything. Did they not torture you?"

"They only beat me, and then dumped me in here with you."

I sat in silence for a while, one hand upon his hot forehead, the other in his curls.

"How do they kill you here?" I said.

"They push you off the walls, with a rope round your neck. So that the people can see from the town."

"A quick death."

He opened up his one good eye, and looked at me: "Not always."

That night we lay close together, me behind him, one arm wrapped gently over him.

"I would have liked to have gone home again," he said. He had not been able to move from where they had thrown him, and I now sat in a puddle of his urine, but I did not mind it.

"To your home in Nippur?"

"No, to my homeland. I left there as a young boy. My father was not a good man, and so when Enlil said, 'Come with me to Sumer,' I came. But since then I've wondered if any of my family are alive, and if I ought to have stayed, to protect others from my father."

"Are there people who would still want to see you?"

"Maybe not. Is there anything you wish you had done?"

"I have no need of such musings," I said, "because I am going to get us out of here."

"I wonder you can even sit up."

"You will see."

In the morning, the pain in my head was worse. I had taken some beatings, since leaving the Temple of the Waves for the last time. The attack on me by Enki, in the palace courtyard. Fighting to get out of the prison cell beneath the palace. Now this. I wondered if all the beatings I had taken had combined to weaken my skull. But then the pain in my right arm, and the piercing aches in my lower back, were not much better. Over and above all that, I had not had anything to drink for what felt like an age. And as anyone who has been really thirsty will tell you: there is nothing worse than thirst.

"Still alive," I said. But there was no answer from Harga.

He was lying very still, although I could feel him breathing. Sometimes if they hit you too many times in the guts, you die of it after, and there's nothing that can be done.

And then I heard something, and gripped Harga hard.

There were footsteps outside our cell, and low voices. Were they coming to kill us?

The door opened with a hard push and all at once there were men in the room, feet all around me, hands beneath my arms, pulling me away from Harga.

I had no strength left to struggle with.

But something in my hindbrain told me: these were not soldiers.

"Fucking Harga," a foreign voice said. "Not much left for us to kill."

A Sumerian answered him, in the same palace accent that Inanna spoke in: "Well, let's get him out of here while he's still at least partly alive. Then you can kill him at your leisure later."

Harga spoke, although it was more like a croak: "I'm not dead yet, you stone fuckers."

A face appeared before me: a beautiful young man, with short dark hair and a neatly trimmed beard, and jet-black brows, straight as arrows. He was clean and sweet-smelling too, with eyes that seemed to glitter with their own light.

"Who are you?" he said, peering closely at me. "Are you with Harga?"

I tried to speak, but made no words.

He was peering at my neck. "She has the sign of Nammu on her," he said. He looked up at his friends. "We should take her too." He turned back to me: "I am Gilgamesh."

I had heard of the hero Gilgamesh, in temple stories, and in the markets of Eridu. I had heard of him also from Harga.

No one had told me he would be beautiful.

"Water," I said.

With a man on each side of me, and hard hands beneath my armpits, I was half dragged and half pushed downstairs and along corridors. Twice a soldier emerged into our path only to be struck down by one of our party.

From a dark basement we climbed down into a dark tunnel, and then through caves, with Gilgamesh ahead of us. At last we emerged onto a sandy river beach.

"My father and I built these barracks," Gilgamesh said. "When I was only a boy. So I know all the secret ways in and out."

Before us stood a wooden boat, its sails collapsed, pulled up on the sand.

Harga and I were set down with our backs against the boat.

Gilgamesh squatted down before us: "Harga, when we heard from the guards you were a prisoner here, how could I not act? After all you have done for me."

Harga nodded, but did not speak.

"We'll get you somewhere safe," Gilgamesh said. "But then we need to say farewell to you. I need to find the goddess Inanna, and I'm told she's gone into the mountains."

He stood up before Harga had time to answer.

"Gilgamesh," I said.

He kneeled back down to look at me. "What is it?"

"We know where the goddess is," I said. "We were with her, only days ago."

Gilgamesh's face split into a wide grin.

He turned to Harga. "Can this be so?"

Harga nodded. "We should reminisce later, my lord. They will soon realise we are missing, and be after us."

Gilgamesh's grin faded. "How good it is to see you again, Harga," he said.

CHAPTER SIX

INANNA

I was standing by the great river, in the shade of a huluppu tree. A woman was sitting on a rock not too far from me, with her feet dangling into the waters. She had golden curls, and she was wearing strange clothes, emerald green in colour, and with curious flaps and buttons.

Did I know her?

She said: "You've been knocked about. I'm sorry about that. People think we heal and that's it. But one never forgets the pain. Sometimes you're never the same because of it."

I looked down at myself, but I seemed clean and well. I was wearing a plain linen smock, and my feet looked pretty and clean.

The woman said: "Inanna, you need to keep moving. Or you will be lost between the realms."

I felt no sense of worry.

"I am not afraid," I said.

"I am making my way towards you," she said. "But I cannot get there as quickly as I would like."

"There's no hurry," I said. "I'm happy sitting here."

"Inanna, no, you need to keep moving."

The woman smelled like roses. I had my head in her lap. The brilliant green cloth she was wearing was strangely slippery against my cheek.

She pushed my hair from my forehead, and smiled down at me.

"Do you know who I am?"

"You are Nammu."

"Who gave you the master *mee*?"

"You mean my *mee* of love?"

"I think you know which *mee* I mean."

"An gave it to me when I was a baby."

"I had thought it was lost. Do you know what it is?"

"It connects me."

"I did know about you, Inanna. Word did reach me. But I was slow to see what you might unlock."

"I am the thirteenth Anunnaki," I said.

She pressed her bright red lips to my forehead.

"You are too close to the darkness, Inanna. You need to come back to the light."

I was lying on my side, beside a long, thin pit of fire. Two lions were tied up in the fire pit, one behind the other in a sad little row. Each worked its feet as if it was trying to walk but could make no progress. The flames were licking at their paws, but they did not seem to be in pain.

I thought, *That is cruel; someone should cut them free.*

Yet I felt no sense of urgency.

∞

I was in my rooms in Uruk; I shut my eyes, and I was beside the river once more.

Nammu was there, next to me, on one bank of the river. On the far side of the river, I could see a man, dressed in strange black armour, with a black hood pulled up over his face.

I felt heat and turned. The lions were still in the fire pit, still moving their feet as if they were walking. It struck me now that they were going to burn alive.

I said to the woman in green: "Free them! We must free them! Or we must kill them. How can we let them burn alive?"

But she only looked at me, as if nothing was wrong. "Inanna," she said. "Who do you think is burning? Who do you think is on the fire?"

CHAPTER SEVEN

GILGAMESH

Ninshubar was the tallest woman I had ever met. I am a tall man, but it's possible she was as tall as me. Tall and strong, and with a great air of certainty to her, even injured, and even with the filth of a prison cell on her. Indeed, she was more than certain: she was imperious.

She spent all her time in the boat watching me, watching the stone men, weighing us. I caught her eye, to see if I could put some pink into her dark cheeks, but instead of blushing, she at once leaned forwards towards me, holding my stare in the most unnerving manner, as if she was very ready to hit me.

I found myself leaning backwards, away from her.

When I got him alone, I said to Harga: "Who is this woman?"

He considered this question for some time, in the infuriating way that he had, and then finally said: "She can hunt and track."

"You are an enraging person," I said.

The stone men hung on our words to each other. They had not seen Harga since he was a scrap of a boy. Since then he had grown up in the minds of their people as a snake of a man, an absconder, a liar, perhaps many things worse.

Now they were profoundly put out by this version of Harga that they had found themselves with. An injured man, making no complaint at what he suffered. A hardened soldier, much fussed over by this extraordinary woman, and, indeed, by me. And a man who seemed to have been acting with great honour in all that had just befallen him. All of it was baffling and unsettling to them.

On the other hand, they were delighted, enthralled even, by Ninshubar. Everything she did made them smile and clap.

She bound up her own head wound, and very soon was steady on her feet. They watched her dive into the river and swim alongside us, even with hippos bulging along the banks. They watched her fish, and sharpen her knives, and they admired how she sprawled out to rest when it was her turn to lie down in the sails.

"The women are better in your country," Urshanabi said.

"Not all of our women are like this," I said.

Harga nodded at that, in stern agreement.

On the fifth day, in the early morning, the river around us burst up with small, pink dolphins. I was sitting at the helm, with only Harga awake near me.

"I'm sorry about Enkidu," he said.

"Thank you, Harga."

"He was a man you could count on."

"Yes." I nodded to myself, looking out over the water. "I wonder where he is now."

"Do you not believe in the afterlife, my lord?"

"I want to believe it."

I looked over at Harga. He was so battered still, and his eye had still not opened. "How old are you, Harga?"

"Old enough to worry about these things."

Ninshubar grimaced as the Temple of the Aquifer rose up above the marshes.

"I am here in this city so often," she said. "You would think I liked it. I am hither and thither. I am the great traveller of Sumer. And yet always I am returning to Eridu."

I laughed at this, very good natured, only to earn a hard scowl from her.

"It is my first time at Eridu," Harga said. "So for once you can be the one who knows it all."

She threw him a smile for that.

Were they friends, these two? Could anyone truly be a friend of Harga, when he only had disapproval to serve out?

What had he done to win her smiles when I was worth only scowls?

Coming up with a plan had proved contentious. Harga believed himself the best military planner and he favoured going in alone to confront Enki, while we all stayed out of the way. Ninshubar had a different plan, with herself at the heart of it, and would not consider leaving without rescuing Inanna's mother.

Each of their plans I vetoed. I then set out my own: Harga, Ninshubar and all but one of the stone men would take the boat past Eridu to a beach south of the city, and they would wait for us there. Meanwhile Urshanabi and I would enter the city, and find our way to Enki. After all, I had met Enki before, and was family to him.

"It is a terrible plan," Ninshubar said.

"You may very well think so," I said. "But this is a military expedition, and I am a general in the army of the sky gods."

"How is this a military expedition?" Harga said.

"Well, I am here, and you are my deputy, and you are here, so I think the military nature of this is really quite self-evident," I said.

Fortunately, the stone men had no ideas at all, now that killing Harga seemed to be off the table.

In the end, running out of time, we settled upon my plan. I would have liked to have had Harga with me; he was always useful. But he was still slow on his feet after his beating at Uruk, and his eye was not yet better. I certainly could not take Ninshubar. She seemed to have recovered from the rigours of her captivity, but she had not long ago fled Enki's dungeons, and was a woman who would be easily recognised.

And so we would divide, but be quickly reunited.

Quickly in, and quickly out.

"We will see you all at the meeting place," I said to them, as Urshanabi and I climbed out onto a beach north of the city.

"All will be well. I know Enki," I called out to them. But I was thinking, *But I do know Enki*.

We watched as Ninshubar leaned over to whisper something to Harga as the boat slipped away from us to the south.

"Are they together?" Urshanabi said to me.

We were walking along the river and past the city boundary stone.

"Harga and Ninshubar?" I said. I found myself affronted by the very idea of it. "She is a warrior princess. And he is an old man. He must be over thirty. And he has the look of a toad about him. He is a servant. They cannot be together." Although the more I thought about it, the less unlikely it seemed. Had they not been travelling the land together? These things can happen when you are out upon the road with someone. I pushed away the thought of Enkidu, riding ahead of me.

Urshanabi said: "Harga is less like a toad than I remember him. Also he is less like a stone man now, and more like one of you."

We were a strange sight, at the gates to the city.

"I am Gilgamesh," I said, holding out my arms to the guards' post over the gates. "Do you know me?"

All six men on guard took turns to look down at us from the peephole.

I know I must have looked strange, kitted out as I was with weapons stolen, albeit fairly, from stone men on the far side of the world. And I was dressed in fighting leathers that Urshanabi had lent me, and helped sew to fit. But all the same I am a child of the Anunnaki, and I have a look to me that cannot be mistaken.

The man I guessed to be the captain said: "Say something to prove who you are."

"I know the names of Inanna's lions," I said. "I know that her mother the moon goddess is a prisoner in this city. I know that the men of Eridu ran screaming from my father in the first war of the gods. Shall I keep shouting things out?"

They let us in, and we were led through the streets to the palace. For a long while we sat upon an old cedar bench, in the stoop of a palace courtyard, with me wishing I had brought water. Eventually a figure appeared: Isimud, *sukkal* of Enki. I had not seen him since I was six years old, but he was not a man to be forgot.

"Follow me, then," he said.

He led us through the baking precincts, to a long stone wall with a small blue door set into it. He pushed it open: a rectangle of verdant green lay within. I had to stoop to enter. Isimud did not follow us, but instead closed the door upon us, shutting us inside.

We followed the small stone path through the trees and flowering bushes, and there, beside a pond, we found Enki.

He was sitting on the edge of the water, feeding some fish. On each side of him sat a full-grown lion. The lions looked up at us with their narrow yellow eyes, but then tipped their faces back down to the fish.

Isimud had let us keep our weapons, and so we stood here now before the lord of wisdom heavy with axes, knives and swords, and of course Urshanabi's stone-throwing assemblage.

When I had first met him, many years before, Enki had seemed more alive to me than any of the other Anunnaki. Now he seemed emptied out, and older, though it was hard to say why I might think so. He waved for us to sit down on a marble bench set back from the pond.

"I recognise you, son of Lugalbanda. But who is this lump you have with you?" He lifted a forefinger at my stone man friend.

"This lump's name is Urshanabi," he said. "He is a great prince in the land of the stone men, over past Mount Mashu."

"Did An send you there, hunting *melam*?"

"He did, my lord."

"You were wasting your time. There may be scraps there but no more. Nammu went and emptied it out years ago."

He swung his legs around, lifting his right leg to move it, and as he did the lions moved so that each remained by his side. "There is water for you there, and fruit," he said, pointing to a table in the hard shade. Urshanabi leaped up to fetch us each water and plums.

"Did you come to tell me travelling stories, Gilgamesh?"

"No, my lord, I came here to tell you that the goddess Inanna, your son's wife, has gone down into the underworld, and is said to be dead now, at the hands of her sister."

What had been tired in Enki was at once gone. He leaned forwards.

"I heard she had gone mad, and gone wandering off into the wilderness. Does my son know of this?"

"He was told. But he remains in Uruk. And Inanna remains lost in the underworld."

Enki rubbed at the lions' ears, one hand on each of their heads. "This is very strange," he said. "Very strange. Stranger still that it should be you, son of Lugalbanda, coming to me with this story. Were you with her when she entered the underworld? Tell me all that you know, and leave nothing out."

I thought about leaving things out, about not mentioning Ninshubar, but there seemed little point in half-truths now that I was sitting before the god. "I think you know the woman they call Ninshubar?" I said.

Enki pulled back his lips from his teeth, just as I have seen a leopard do. "I think I know the woman you speak of," he said. "Do go on."

When I had told him all that I knew, and eaten more plums, and finished his jug of water, Enki said: "I will help you, son of Lugalbanda. Follow me."

We followed him out of the walled garden, and its emerald light.

"Why will you help us?" I asked, genuinely curious.

"I do not wish the death of any Anunnaki," he said. "There are too few of us already."

I found that hard to believe. I knew that Enki had spent years stealing *melam* from his relatives. But ah well.

"And I am interested in how the underworld might have changed Inanna," Enki went on. "It always changes you."

"It has already changed Inanna," I said. "She's dead."

"We will see," said Enki. "She is Anunnaki."

"You think she can be saved?"

He shrugged, turning to me, the lions turning with him. I realised for the first time: these must be Inanna's famous cubs! Of course they would now be full grown.

"Inanna may survive, she may not," Enki said. "It will be interesting if she does. Let's see how Enlil likes it when Inanna returns with the knowledge of what the underworld really is."

"And what is that?"

"That's Anunnaki business, Gilgamesh."

Together we climbed down the steps that led to the exit from the palace. I saw how Enki struggled, just a little, with the steps.

"What's your interest in this, Gilgamesh?" he said. "Have you fallen for this girl? Or are you here on behalf of Enlil?"

"I am here on behalf of me."

Enki laughed. "Now that I do believe."

We walked through empty streets with the lord of wisdom, his *sukkal* and a phalanx of his personal guard walking behind.

"I shouldn't be showing you the way to one of my hiding places," Enki said, "but then my hiding places don't seem to be as secret as they used to be."

Finally, all hot and sweating, we reached a small temple at the edge of the city, with crinkle-cut waves along its walls. I saw the mark of Nammu upon the door – the same mark that Ninshubar wore around her neck. "Welcome to the Temple of the Waves," Enki said.

Inside there was only deep gloom, until my eyes adjusted. An elderly priestess crept out of the dark, bending low to the god. Only then did I see the statue of the goddess, very ancient, but extraordinary work, very lifelike.

"Help me move the statue," Enki said.

"My lord!" the priestess burst out, but then she bowed lower, and backed away.

The statue did not look like it had ever been moved, but between me and Urshanabi, and two of Isimud's boys, we found a way to shift it sideways over the dirt of the floor, all of us anxious not to harm her ancient paint.

Beneath the place where the statue had been standing, there was a hole in the floor, and in there, a clutch of metal boxes.

The priestess came forwards, open-mouthed, to look down upon it with us.

Enki reached down and took out a dark grey box.

"Come on," he said, leading us through the holy of holies to a small dirt yard beyond. He took a seat on a pillow in the shade there, and fiddled with the box until it opened.

Out came two black beads, very shiny, made of some kind of rock.

"These have names," Enki said. "Very ancient names. Kurgurrah and Galatur."

I looked closely at them, but they looked like nothing more than simple obsidian beads.

"The way I remember it," Enki said, "is that the Kurgurrah looks more blue in the light."

As I looked at them, the two beads rose up, and then sat very still in the air between me and the god.

"These may look like simple things to you, but they are not," he said.

"They do not look simple to me."

"You must be quiet now so that I can talk to them." He shut his eyes for a while, with the flies hovering before him.

Then the leopard eyes were open again. "These little flies, they can pass through the gates to the underworld, and then back, without troubling the gatekeeper. These flies, well, even in Heaven, when they were made, they were something to have. Although I have not had much use for them here."

The two beads moved a little, and as they moved I saw one of them had some blue in it.

"They were my mother's, you know, in the before times," Enki said.

"What are they?"

"They are like a cross between a *mee* and a demon," Enki said. "But they will do you no harm. They will only do what I ask of them."

"So what will they do for Inanna?"

"They will try to save her, and bring her back to this realm," he said. "You take them to the Kur, as close as you can, and release them. That's all you need to do."

He put the flies in the box, and handed it to me. "I did send them in once before, to try to reason with Ereshkigal…" He trailed off. "Come back and tell me how it goes. And bring me those two flies back."

"And that's a god?" Urshanabi said as we picked out way out of the city.

"He is a god in this land."

"He seemed like a man to me, a rich man, with magic tricks, but a man."

"He's hundreds of years old," I said. "He has that black stuff in his veins that you made me throw into the sea."

That he laughed at. But then he said: "Uta-napishti has the black stuff; so does Shiduri. And they are not gods."

"We call Enki a god," I said. "He's what passes for a god in Sumer. A powerful one, even."

"These are strange sorts of gods," he said.

"What kind do you have, in the land of the stone men?"

"Invisible ones, which come in the night and leave clues. Ghostly ones, which dance in the fire when you're drunk. The usual gods."

"I think they had those gods here too, until my family came."

We were an hour's walk from the meeting place, but the time went quickly. Perhaps these demon-flies were not the answer, but I had seen them float in the air. They were something, indeed. And we had survived a visit to Enki. All in all, I felt quite triumphant as we made our way through the sand dunes to the beach where the boat would be. I began to craft in my mind the story of our trip to Eridu, so that it might strike the most awe into the hearts of both Harga and Ninshubar.

As we emerged from the dunes, we at once saw the boat pulled up upon gleaming white sand, and, next to it, five stone men.

I knew at once that something was wrong.

Urshanabi's first mate came hurrying forwards. "Harga and the woman would not come with us. As soon as you were out of sight, they forced us to drop them beside the city walls."

"Where did they go? What are they doing?"

He shrugged. "They said they would meet us here. They said they would be back before you, and you would never know."

I breathed in, breathed out.

"We should just go," I said to them. But as I said it, I realised I had no idea at all as to how to find my way to the underworld. And these stone men would not know either.

"What could they be doing?" Urshanabi said to me.

It came to me then, with a settled certainty. Ninshubar had gone back for Ningal, and Harga had followed her. Endangering all of us, and Inanna too.

We sat in the scrubby shade, waiting, and sweating. Twice I walked down to the sea, stripped off my leathers, and plunged in, just to be cool for a few minutes after.

Waiting.

Until we had been waiting too long.

"They would be here by now if they were not in trouble." I stood up, arranging my weapons upon me. "I will go back for them."

"I will come with you," Urshanabi said, and then all the other stone men stood forwards.

"You come with me, just in case," I said to Urshanabi. "But the rest of you should guard the boat."

"What has it come to, that I am going to rescue Harga?" Urshanabi said.

Then we struck out into the beating heat once more.

We walked through the low bush that led to the western walls of the city.

"What are you thinking?" Urshanabi said.

"I'm thinking we head back to Nammu's temple. Do you remember the necklace that Ninshubar wears? That is the mark of Nammu. So perhaps that old priestess can help us. The only other place I can think to go to is the palace, because the dungeons are there and that might be where Inanna's mother is being held. But I cannot see how we will make our way in there, great heroes though we are."

"The temple first, then," he said.

We entered the city by the small gate next to the Temple of the Waves, and were about to climb the steps and enter, when we heard the shouting and the sound of men in armour running.

The two of us turned as one to look down the sun-bleached, dusty street, and all at once time seemed to slow, as it always does for me in battle.

Harga and a naked woman were running towards us, with Ninshubar hanging between them, apparently unconscious. Three cords behind them came Isimud, running, with soldiers behind.

I at once broke into a sprint, running straight past Harga and the women, straight at the heart of the action.

"Just go, just go," I shouted at Harga as I wove past him, and then I came to a hard stop in front of Isimud, my axes in my hands.

The men of Eridu likewise came to a hard stop in front of me, filling up the street. Urshanabi was close behind me, with his slingshot in his hands.

"Isimud," I said, giving him my most heroic smile. "Isimud! What are you doing chasing my friends?"

It was a narrow street, and we were standing perhaps two cords apart. Isimud, slim though he was, had a hardness to him that could not be mistaken, which only comes with killing. He had knives on his belt, and in his raised right hand, a bronze-tipped spear. His men behind had their swords out.

"Gilgamesh, stand aside," Isimud said. "My lord Enki has sent you on with his blessing. We have no quarrel with you. But your friends have taken someone who does not have permission to leave the city."

"The naked woman?"

"That is the goddess Ningal," he said. "She stays here."

I glanced around and saw Harga and the woman who must be Ningal leaning over Ninshubar. They had laid her out on the steps of the temple. Why weren't they running, while they had the chance?

"So, if I agree to hand over Ningal, you will let the rest of us go?"

"Yes," he said. "Enki wants you to take the flies north and succeed in your mission."

"Ah," I said. "Well, no. I do not agree to hand over the goddess."

"Are you going to fight us all, Gilgamesh?" Isimud said. He took a step forwards. As he did, I saw more men of Eridu coming along the street to join Isimud's gang. Perhaps another ten of them. And behind us, the sound of more drawing up.

"I will fight you all," I said. "And slay you all. I have never been beaten in battle, as all the cities in Sumer know very well. I will slay all your men, and I will put you down for a while, although perhaps the *melam* will mend you."

I raised my axes. "Prepare to die, men of Eridu," I shouted. I knew that I must look most glorious as I stood there, and very deadly.

All the same, I could not quite at that moment think of anything that was going to save me. I'm good in a fight, because I never stand on ceremony. And when I do stand on ceremony, it is only ever a trick. But there is not much two men can do against thirty, in a narrow street and at close quarters, and with all heavily armed.

"If you do not stand down, we will kill you both," Isimud said.

The soldiers all looked at me, and raised their weapons.

"Enough!" I shouted, lowering my axes. "Enough!"

Everyone, momentarily, was still again, expectant.

"I just need to tell you something," I said.

I glanced at Urshanabi, and he glanced back at me, his eyebrows raised. I glanced around me, at the closed windows and doorways, and back at the Temple of the Waves, but still I could not see a way out for us.

So this was it. This is where I would die. This humble street. This was my last stand.

"At least will you give my father a message?" I said to Isimud.

"Enough time-wasting," he said, and lifted his spear to throw it.

I thought I might have had another moment to try to say something else, but then his arm came down hard and the spear was in the air.

I at once released both my axes, but had no time to go for my sword.

Then, just for a moment, it was as if time itself had stopped.

Isimud's spear hung in the air, only an arm's length from my face. My axes hung in the air upon either side of it, and Urshanabi's deadly stone, just released, lay motionless before him, moving neither up nor down. We men were also motionless, our mouths open, and a moment later a curious chill fell upon us, a vast cooling of the air.

A woman stepped out between us, wearing an emerald-green robe that clung to her as if wet. She had golden curls, twisting and gleaming down her back, and skin the colour of polished cedar. When she turned her sapphire eyes upon me, I knew her at once.

It was Nammu, queen of the gods, who had once been An's wife, but had not been seen for fifty years. She looked exactly like her statue, unchanged.

As she turned to look over at Isimud, our weapons fell from the air onto the sand.

"No more fighting," she said.

Everyone put away their weapons; all eyes lay on the goddess. Nammu looked back to where Ningal was tending to Ninshubar. I saw Ningal look up at the mother goddess, but I could not read the look they gave each other.

Then Nammu turned back to me. "Take your friends and go," she said. "I do not need Ningal here."

I took a step backwards, my eyes still on Isimud.

"You will not be pursued, Gilgamesh," the goddess said. "Take the demons to Inanna. Set the goddess free."

The goddess Nammu had said we would not be pursued. But we could not count on that.

I took half of Ninshubar's weight, and Urshanabi the other half, and we ran through the bush towards the place where we had left the boat and the stone men, with Harga and Ningal behind us. Ninshubar was indeed unconscious; she was also bleeding heavily from a gaping scalp wound, and also from her eyes and mouth. I had seen enough people dying to know she did not have much time left.

I had a thousand words of recrimination in my mouth, ready to hurl at Harga, but I knew it would only slow us, so I only ran on, silent, my right side straining from the effort of carrying Ninshubar's limp but very large body.

"To the boat!" I shouted as we made the beach, and at once the stone men scrambled towards it, and began dragging it down the beach. We laid Ninshubar in there, on the folded sails, and then made our way out to sea as fast as we could, two on every oar.

When we were far enough out from what was only an empty beach still, I took what felt like my first breath in hours, and sipped some water from my waterskin. Ningal was sitting with Ninshubar. "Give me your knife, Gilgamesh," she said.

I passed over a blade.

Ningal cut at her wrist, and then put the flowing blood to Ninshubar's mouth. "My blood will keep her alive for a while."

I looked about me at this strange collection of people I found myself with. The six stone men, and Harga of course, once a stone man, and with the same wild curls, but now sadly battered. He sat with Ninshubar's head in his lap – Ninshubar, who had been so very alive so recently, now lying at the edge of death. And this strange naked goddess Ningal, who I knew I had met when I was a boy, but who did not spark any memories in me without her temple finery on her.

"Urshanabi," I said. "You are a great man. But the time has come for us to part. Drop us along the coast just a little, out of sight of Eridu, and then you should head home. I will have to send you the gold I promised you."

"That I refused," he said.

"But I will send it all the same, just as soon as we are done rescuing Inanna."

"You will still need us," he said.

"This goddess will help us now," I said. "But once again, I do thank you. I'm only sorry that your hopes of killing Harga have been confounded."

A short time later, we waded ashore with Ninshubar, and turned to wave at the stone men.

I felt a lurch of sadness to be seeing the last of such friendly faces.

Urshanabi called back to me across the water.

"This is a strange and terrible place!" he said. "You would be wise to leave with us."

"I have never been wise!" I called back as the water opened up between us. "No one can accuse me of it!"

We spent the night on the beach they left us on, just the four of us now. Every hour or so, Ningal, dressed in an old leather jerkin given to us by the stone men, cut at her wrist, and gave more blood to Ninshubar before it healed. I woke to find Ninshubar sitting up, her eyes open.

Ningal crouched down in front of Ninshubar, and kissed her nose. "You came back for me," she said. "You are a great hero."

"I told you I was," Ninshubar said. She glanced at me, and then looked around at our little camp amongst the bushes. "Where is Harga?"

"He's getting water," Ningal said.

"I should not have let him come with me," Ninshubar said. "But he refused to let me go alone."

"He saved you," Ningal said. "I could not have carried you away alone."

"We should go," I said. "It's a long walk to the mountains."

I walked with Harga, carrying his small pack for him, because he was so slow.

"As soon as you were gone, she said she was going back for Ningal," he said. "So I went with her. She said she knew a way into the dungeons, through a tunnel that leads in off the marshes. So we went in, and made our way into the dungeons. Ningal was there, just as she said. But on the way out it got messy."

"It is never as clean as you hope," I said.

"We killed two or three of them, but then one of them got her in the head and then the lungs. I cannot believe she is up and walking."

We both looked ahead to Ninshubar, who walked with the goddess's hand in the small of her back. We had only been going a few hours, but already she looked as if she was going to collapse. As we watched her, she wiped blood from her mouth, and for a moment stopped walking, struggling to breathe.

"She's dying," Harga said. "The blood of the goddess makes her walk, but her wounds aren't healing."

We made slow progress, even with the goddess cutting her wrist every hour to feed Ninshubar her blood.

Ningal had been walking with Ninshubar. But then Harga said: "I will take her." After that he walked every step of the way with his arm around Ninshubar's waist, holding on tight to her ribs. When we stopped, he would help her sit down, and when she slept, she slept with her head upon his shoulder.

"We should not be pushing on like this," he said, on the second morning. "It is going to kill her."

Ningal and I came to crouch beside him. Ninshubar seemed to be unconscious, with her head upon his thigh.

Ningal said: "What do you suggest? We could send Gilgamesh on alone, with the flies, but he does not know the way, and it is certain to delay him. We may lose our chance to save Inanna."

"My worry," I said, "is that I may somehow need Ningal's help when I get there. But I am happy to push on alone, if that is best for Ninshubar."

We were all silent then.

"Harga, if she is going to die, she will die whether we push on, or we stay here," Ningal said finally. "I am sorry to say it, because I love her too, but it's true."

"Rest might save her," Harga said, his mouth flat. "Just rest might be what she needs."

"She needs *melam*," Ningal said. "And I believe that I ate all the last of it when I had Inanna in my womb. I am very sorry for that, but that is what I did."

Another long silence, with all of us watching Ninshubar, and the slight rise and fall of her chest. "We all go on, then," Harga said.

That afternoon we began climbing into higher ground, and through rocky valleys.

Ninshubar spoke only once that day. She seemed to come to, as she was walking, and she said to Harga: "I'm too heavy to be leaning on you like this."

He said to her: "It is nothing to me. You are as light as an eagle feather."

"You lie very badly," she said, and almost smiled. But then her eyes almost shut, and she seemed gone again, only alive enough to put one foot in front of the next.

On the evening of the sixth day, we reached a rock-strewn plateau, and then, with its back to a grassy slope, a low stone hut.

An old man was sitting out on a rock in front of the hut. It was hard to focus on his features, in the gloom of the near-dusk.

Ningal stepped forwards. "Hello, Neti," she said.

"You bring those things no closer," the old man said to me. "The Kur does not want them here."

"What do you mean, old man?" I said.

"The demons that you have in your pocket."

"Ah," I said, pulling the box out of my coat. I opened it up, meaning to pick the beads out, but the flies came instantly to life, hovering just over my head.

"Do you mean these demons?" I said.

In a blink, as everyone turned to look at them, the flies had gone. Had I seen them streaming over the horizon?

In a blank moment, the old man had gone too.

"Let's get Ninshubar into the hut," Ningal said.

We laid her down in the old man's neat little bed. I thought of Enkidu, and how young he had looked, as he lay dying. Until the very end, I had hoped that he would touch a low, and then begin to rise up again.

Harga sat himself down in the chair next to the bed, and shut his eyes.

"There are always honey cakes here," Ningal said. "I will fetch them."

"Honey cakes won't save her," Harga said.

CHAPTER EIGHT

ERESHKIGAL

*W*hen we first came down from Heaven, the dazzling sunlight blinded us. I do not think we ever got over it, of the shock of Earthlight. Our vision returned but with it came the gaudy blues and greens that are Earth's true colours. And the noise! The screeching birds and crashing waves, clawing at our nerves. The air itself was an assault upon us, renewed at every breath. For a long time, we did not know if we could survive.

A great spasm of pain went through me, from my groin to my chest.

I found myself leaning over my desk, my stylus still in my hand, gasping for air, and sobbing.

"My lady?"

It was my little priest-demon, the one with the ear in the middle of his forehead.

"My lady, can I help you?"

I shook my head, tears streaming down my face. My clay

tablet was getting wet; I tried to wipe away the moisture with my sleeve.

"Are you writing your history, my queen?"

I nodded at him, and wiped at my face.

The little priest-demon was shifting from foot to foot.

"Is there anything else?" I said.

At this the priest-demon bowed, his eared forehead almost touching the flagstone floor of my bedchamber.

"My lady, we have visitors."

For a moment, my pain was forgotten. "*More* visitors?" I put down my stylus. "It is only a few weeks since the girl came!"

"Yes," he said, looking up at me, but staying low. "It is two men, this time. Men of a sort."

"What sort?"

"A strange sort," he said. "They are in your temple, my lady, and they seem very interested in the body of the goddess."

With some difficulty, I pushed myself to my feet.

"I will see these strange sort of men," I said.

The dust of the dead fell heavy as I made my way to my throne room.

I saw that my demons were all there, their eyes bright in the dark alcoves and underneath the benches.

And here, too, my new visitors.

The visitors bent low from the waist as I sat myself up on my blackthorn throne.

They wore long dark cloaks and hoods pulled down low over their faces; they were more like shadows than men. One seemed more blue, and one seemed more black.

Of course I knew very well what they were.

Behind them, there was Neti, whose job it was to keep out creatures like the flies.

"Mistress, do you know us?" the blue shadowman said.

"No," I said. "I have never seen you before."

The shadowmen both bowed again.

"We thought you might recognise us," the blue one said, "from when we were here before."

"No," I said. "Now state your business."

The shadowmen had their eyes upon the rotting body of the goddess. The corpse was dry now, furred and dark grey in colour.

I was about to speak again, when Neti said: "I did not let them in!"

"You will be spoken to and punished later, Neti," I said.

But then with no warning the pain came for me again.

Through the pain, I became aware of the shadowmen, looming over me.

I realised I was on the floor.

The blue man said: "My lady, we can help you, with this pain you are suffering."

I pulled my knees up to my chest, and rolled over onto my side in the dust.

"No one can help me," I said.

The blue man kneeled down beside me.

"Ereshkigal, we can help you. All we ask is that you let us tend to the body of Inanna. Let us see what we can do for your sister. And in return, we will make your pain go away."

"I don't know," I said, sobbing. "I can't be sure what is right."

The black man kneeled down next to his shadow brother. "There is no pain we cannot touch," he said.

"Did Enki send you?" I said.

"Does it matter who sent us?" said the blue man. "We could hear your screams all the way from the gates."

"I haven't been screaming," I said.

"My lady," the blue man said, "we beg you to let us help."

CHAPTER NINE

INANNA

I was sitting upon a rock at the edge of the river, with my feet in the soft, cool water. The man in black armour was standing on the other side of the river, up to his knees in the water.

"You can come across," I called to him. "It is not deep."

As he began to wade deeper into the water, coming ever closer to me, I caught a glimpse of his face, beneath his black hood. I saw that he was Anunnaki, although I had never seen his face before.

Nammu was beside me, sweet-smelling, touching my arm. "It is time to leave this place now, Inanna," she said. "All is good here."

I rose up to consciousness through a thick soup of all flavours and textures of pain.

When I could open my eyes, there were two dark shapes hovering over me. The shapes resolved into men, or not quite men, something in between, in dark grey cloaks. I shut my eyes again.

I could not make my mouth work, but I could feel tears sliding down sideways from each eye and into my hair. I began to breathe harder. A rising panic.

"You're safe." A man's voice.

That did not feel true.

"Just breathe, breathe steady. The pain will lessen. Just breathe."

A moment, an age.

For a time, I was sitting up, propped up by the shadowmen.

They were holding something to my mouth, and I sipped. Cool and sweet on my tongue.

I thought I heard a woman's voice, and crying, but it might have been me.

"Inanna, we are going to move you again. We need to straighten your legs."

Unbearable pain.

Blessed dark.

I opened my eyes, just a crack, and the two shadowmen were there, one very black, although indistinct, the other dark but with a shimmer of blue.

"Inanna, you are doing well," the blue one said. "Very well. Just lie still, and your *melam* will do the work now. Very soon you will begin to feel something like yourself."

Behind them I could see a woman, oddly twisted in her chair –
a wild bush of a head. She had her face in her hands.

For a moment I thought the two shadowmen were only tiny
dark spots in the air, but then they were men again.

"I am Kurgurrah," said the blue one, "and this is Galatur. We
have been sent here by the god Enki to bring you up to the world
again. We are helping you. Trust us. Feel safe. I know this is very
painful, but you are doing very, very well."

"I have dreamed of her," I said, but I do not think I said it out
loud. I shut my eyes again.

I was breathing shallow and fast. The pain in my head felt too
much to bear. Again, Kurgurrah's voice, reassuring. "My lady, we
have been gathering up all the very tiny pieces of your skull that
had been scattered around and we had not noticed were missing
before. We think now your head will heal properly."

The woman's voice, familiar to me, further away: "I think there
is still some brain here."

In my dreams, one of the men said: "I wonder what she has
been doing, while she was lost in the dark."

"Do you worry, brother?"

"I do worry. I worry that Nammu has been working on
her."

I could not understand them. Were they talking about me?

I woke, and heard them talking, the two shadowmen and the
twisted woman.

"Lady Ereshkigal, we are destroyed by your beauty, by your blinding glory," Kurgurrah was saying. "If you would let us take this girl up to the world again, it would help her heal more quickly."

The other shadowman said: "The dust here, falling so heavily, makes it much harder for us to work on her wounds."

"No."

Galatur again: "My lady, the baby that is inside you, it is harming you. You will feel better without it."

"Will it be dead, if you take it out?"

"Mistress," said Kurgurrah. "This baby was dead before you got here. It has been dead a very, very long time. You will feel much better without it inside you. It is making you very sick."

The woman began sobbing. "I can't do it."

Kurgurrah said: "Mistress, it is no longer a baby. Let us relieve your pain. It will take us only moments."

"Maybe," she said. "I'm so tired. Oh, perhaps."

"Open your mouth, then," Galatur said. "We need to go inside you."

I must have slept. It might have been hours. It might have been days.

"My lady, you are looking a little better." It was Kurgurrah.

I opened my left eye just a fraction, shut it again. I'd been moved; I was on some sort of bed now, and this wasn't the throne room any more.

"We do hope you are feeling better," said Kurgurrah. "Because you are looking a lot less grey, a lot less mottled, almost alive in fact."

I felt groggy; I felt pain. But yes, it was not as bad as it had been.

I opened both my eyes.

The shadowmen were standing next to my bed, their hands behind their backs. Ereshkigal was sitting in the far corner of the room, looking more like a heap of clothes upon the floor than a person.

I tried to speak, but my throat was burning agony when I tried.

"Better not speak yet," said Kurgurrah. "Your throat was badly injured, and it will take a while longer to heal. But you are fortunate, in having so much *melam* in you. We have never seen so much in one person. It is quite something! Your blood flows almost black."

Galatur leaned forwards. "I think you are probably confused, so let us tell you what has happened. You were attacked by Queen Ereshkigal's demons, badly battered, your head quite badly damaged, and you died, and then you were hung on a hook, so that caused more damage. And then when we tried to get you off the hook, your body fell onto marble and one of your legs broke rather nastily. So there has been a lot to fix."

"Also," Kurgurrah said, "you should know that you were dead for many days. Many, many days. And the worms that seem to live down here now, they had had time to infest you, and they caused a deal of damage on top of everything else that was done. And some things they ate so much of, it has been very difficult to make them whole again."

"But you are growing strong and well again," said Galatur. "All is good. All is well. There is no need now to feel anxious about what you are feeling. Only know that your body, and your *melam*, they are doing their work."

Ereshkigal looked up, her head emerging from her furs: "She still looks wrong."

Kurgurrah turned a polite smile towards my sister. "Her head is not quite knitted yet, mistress," he said. "It needs to find its shape again."

"*Her* head is not right either," Galatur said, but quietly, so that only Kurgurrah and I could hear.

I swung my legs over the side of the bed, pushed myself up. Everything was jerky, unnatural.

I looked down and saw that my belly and thighs were coated in a crust of dust and blood. I was in a long, oblong room; the walls were clad in dark stone.

"Help me get up," I said.

Later I sat at the round table with the three of them. I wore an aged and scratchy fur, of some long-dead creature. I sipped at strange-smelling water, out of a heavy metal cup, and picked at strange black cheese. It tasted like an old blue cheese, but sour and rotted.

Everything hurt, even my fingernails, even the fur against my skin.

"I want to go now," I said. "I don't want to be here any more. You must all help me get out."

The shadowmen shifted in their ebony chairs. Kurgurrah said: "Mistress, we would like nothing more than to take you out, but Ereshkigal holds the keys to the gates. Although she could not stop you getting in, it seems she has full control over who gets out." He made a strange sort of laugh. "It seems even we cannot leave without her permission!"

"Which we had not expected," Galatur said. "She has been tampering with this world."

All I could see of Ereshkigal was the top of her head, resting on the table, and her shuddering shoulders.

"Oh, just sit up, Ereshkigal," I said. "Face me."

She shook her mop of hair, and made a moaning sound. "I didn't mean them to kill you," she said. "I thought it was a trick. I thought it was An."

"Let's just go," I said to the shadowmen. "You can help me get out. Let's just leave her and go."

"We have tried leaving with you already, my lady," Kurgurrah said. "On several occasions, I should add. We have been carrying you back and forth, yet to no avail."

"While you were not yourself," said Galatur.

"We have given up on removing you," Kurgurrah said. "The queen here has many demons, and the most deadly of them she calls *gallas*, and these *gallas* were very insistent that we stayed here, all three of us. They insist now that we do not even leave this room."

Galatur said: "You should know, my lady, that we were warriors, in the other realm. But our powers are restricted in this place."

The weight of my own body became too much for me.

"I'm going back to bed," I said. "Please talk to this woman and force her to free me."

"We are already fully committed to that as a course of action," Kurgurrah said. "We will not let our efforts dwindle."

I woke up and Ereshkigal was sitting on a small wooden chair next to my bed. With her hair pulled back from her face, she did have the look of our mother, although so bloated and warped.

The feeling that I was not in pain, or not in the pain I had been, filled me with something like giddy relief.

"Is this the underworld, sister?"

"It's a place between the two worlds," she said. "A city along the road."

She put out one claw-like hand and touched it to my arm, as if unsure what my skin would feel like. Her calloused touch was strangely cold.

"So all the dead people, they are further on, are they? Further down the road? Do they pass this way?"

"What dead people?" my sister said, as if my question made no sense.

"The dead people who have come down from Earth."

"It is only me here, Inanna, and the Kur, and the *gallas*, and all my demons here, although I do not know if you have seen one yet. They sometimes hide. No, I do not think I have seen a dead person here, except you, when you were on your hook."

I wondered which of us was being difficult.

I thought about my friend Amnut. I thought about her father, and her mother, and all the people who had lain down in the pit that day.

"Ereshkigal, do the dead not come here, when their mortal bodies die? Are they somewhere else? Is this not the same underworld that is spoken of in the world of light?"

"The dead don't come here," she said. "I don't think they go anywhere, do they? They're just dead."

I sat myself up. "But, Ereshkigal, all those people out there, toiling for the Anunnaki, so that they will have riches to bring over with them... is that all for nothing?"

"I think it's for the good, isn't it?" she said. For a moment she looked quite haughty; I could imagine her as she must have once been. "But you know I was not in charge of the stories. That was Enki, and Nammu."

I still could not understand it.

"Ereshkigal, is there another underworld somewhere, another Dark City? Somewhere else the dead go, which has the same name, perhaps? Am I misunderstanding something? Or are we just in the wrong room here?"

She seemed to consider this.

"I think I would know if there were dead people here," she said. "But maybe there are and no one ever told me. No one ever comes to see me here. So perhaps it is just another secret from me."

She began weeping again, and put her forehead down on my bed.

Kurgurrah and Galatur made their presence known. A discreet cough, and they edged forwards.

"Ereshkigal, glorious queen of the night, they would all come, all of the Anunnaki," Galatur said, "if only you would let them in. It is difficult for them to come and see you, when you have made sure Neti will never let them through the gates." He sounded close to showing his anger.

At this I sat up.

"Enough," I said. "Sister, I need to leave. I need to help our mother. So what I will do is this: I will leave, but I will send down a replacement."

Ereshkigal went still for a moment, and then looked up at me.

"I will make sure my replacement is to your tastes," I said. "Someone who will be the best possible servant to you."

Kurgurrah stepped forwards, his face tipped to one side, as if about to intervene, but then Ereshkigal sat herself up.

"I would like a proper servant," she said. "I have my demons, and I love them, but I would like a servant who could serve me in my temple."

We regarded each other.

"In the rites, I mean." She raised one dark eyebrow, for emphasis.

"I will send you such a servant," I said.

Very quickly it was time to go.

I had no things to gather. No bags to pack.

But I could not quite leave, not when I still could not understand.

"Ereshkigal, what is the underworld, if it is not where the dead go? What is this realm we are halfway to here? What would I find, if I walked down the road here?"

"Our home," she said. "We are halfway to our home, here. The place that we came from, before we came to Earth."

She began crying again. "How I wish I could get back there."

Kurgurrah stepped forwards, bowing his head to me. "My lady, if we may, it may be wise to hurry along now, while we still have the queen's full permission to leave. In my experience of such moments, things can change so quickly."

I put one hand down onto Ereshkigal's back. She felt damp, oddly cold. I gave her a pat. I found I felt no animosity to her, strange as that may sound.

She looked up at me, sniffing. "I have this for you," she said, taking something out of a pocket. A small pot, very black. I took it from her, somewhat suspicious.

"It doesn't work for me any more," she said. "But it's *melam*."

I said: "Sister, do you know why my mother sent me to you? Surely it cannot be for this when I have *melam* already?"

She gave a sly laugh. "What she wanted me to do, I have already done." She smiled, and shook her head.

"I thank you, sister, despite what has happened," I said. "I hope you can find some peace, with the companion I send down to you."

"Send me a god," she said. "But I don't want an Anunnaki. I am sick of the Anunnaki, and their bottomless pit of lies."

"On that one thing we can agree," I said.

I followed the shadowmen out of the oblong room and into the throne room. My right leg dragged a little; I could not pick my foot up properly. I saw Kurgurrah casting a glance down at my leg as I limped forwards; I saw him catching Galatur's eye.

In the throne room, creatures slithered and scuttled just out of sight. But two large demons came forwards. They were tall, and shaped like men. They wore hooded robes, like men, and gloves and boots, heavily carved, of some ancient substance, just as men might wear. But their faces, in the deep shadow of their hoods, were not the faces of men: they seemed to be carved from solid silver.

One of these creatures carried a silver sceptre, of the kind that a royal minister might carry, although he looked nothing like a minister. The other carried a mace, as a soldier might, although he did not look like a soldier.

"These *gallas* will accompany us upwards," said Kurgurrah. "And they will bring your replacement down. It is all agreed, so let us all hurry along now."

Again he cast a glance at the way I was walking.

"What are these things?" I said.

"They are like demons," said Kurgurrah. "They are part of the Kur, but they can move around on their own. They can come in here, to the Dark City, and they can come out with us into the world. We were creatures of high value, when the Anunnaki lived in Heaven, but these *gallas* were worth far more, I do admit it. How wonderful that they are still working."

Galatur said: "Inanna, you should know that we will not escape these creatures. We must give them a suitable substitute, of the sort you have promised, or they will bring you back here."

"These *gallas* do not eat, or drink," Kurgurrah said. "They will not accept gifts, or bribes. They will only do as they have been ordered. And if that means tearing a wife from her husband's arms, or a child from its mother, they will do it. Believe me, they will not turn from their task until it is done. And they are very powerful."

"They will have their substitute," I said.

Kurgurrah ushered us all out of the throne room, and into the dark streets beyond. "As quick as you like, then, all," he said. "Before she changes her mind again."

I walked through the Dark City, naked, as I had walked in.

When I breathed, my lungs scratched against my heart. Every step was pain. Had they put me back together exactly as I had been before?

In my hand I carried the little black pot that my sister had given me, since I had no pocket to put it in.

Kurgurrah and Galatur walked in front of me, shadowmen.

Behind me, so unnatural and inhuman, came my sister's *gallas*.

We climbed the long narrow walkway, up and through the stars.

"My lady, may we help you?" Kurgurrah said.

"I am quite well," I said.

This time the walk seemed to take hours. But then I saw the seventh gate ahead of the shadowmen.

They stood aside, balancing precariously on the edge of the walkway, to allow me to approach the gate first.

It opened at once for me, as did each after. My four companions crowded in after me through each gate, as if anxious not to be left behind.

As gate two opened, there was Neti in the tiny space, neat in a dark blue suit.

I took one step forwards, leaving the *gallas* and the shadowmen crushed between gates two and three.

Neti was holding out my *mee* to me. I slipped it onto my left wrist and straight away I felt the difference, a thin vibration through my bones: a surge of power and connection. I leaned against the metal wall for a few moments to steady myself.

I looked hard at Neti. "What have you done to it? Why is my *mee* different?"

"The master *mee* was almost dead, you know," he said. "But the Kur has revived it."

My possessions were still in the drawer where I had left them. With my strange audience watching, I clambered into what had once been a white temple dress. I pulled my stained old yellow slippers out of the pocket, and put them on. The little black pot from Ereshkigal went into a pocket. The precious jewels, and chest plate, and wings, I left there in the Kur.

The final gate, and then we were all out in the dazzling sunlight. Had the world always been so bright?

A sudden charge of wellbeing went through me. My leg felt less awkward.

(Inanna?)

I looked around, but there was nothing. No sign of who could have spoken.

The *gallas* stepped heavy on the grass, their silver strong and bright in the sun. But Kurgurrah and Galatur seemed to flicker now, as if they were only ghosts and had no real substance.

On the ground where I had left it was my crown.

"Your woman-servant is waiting for you, in the hut," Neti said.

"Ninshubar," I said. I had not given her a thought.

"I am sure they will all be glad to see you."

I said: "Neti. Why did you call this the master *mee*?"

I held out my wrist to him.

"That's its name on the manifest," he said. "A very nasty weapon, in the wrong hands."

"Not a *mee* of love, then, as I was told."

"You can use it for that," Neti said, his hands spread wide. "I have seen it used for that. But other things also. You can take control of other *mees*, as I'm sure you have already sensed. If you are close enough. And control of those wearing the *mees*. A very nasty weapon." He shook his head. "You know the Kur had thought it missing. It is always good to find out that the things on the manifest are safe."

The peaks of the mountains were picked out in gold in the sunlight as we cleared the ridge and made our way down towards the hut.

About fifty cords from the hut, I saw a man, sitting on a rock.

"Hah!" I said, stopping. I put my hands upon my hips. "Hah!"

It was Gilgamesh.

He looked so gleaming and yet so casual; he might have been sitting on a bench in the palace precinct at Uruk.

He was thinner. Much thinner. But he looked well.

"Your mouth is hanging open," he called. "But it is me who should be astonished. Who are these companions of yours?"

He got up and came so close to me, so luminous, and so full of vibrant cheer, that I felt at once his old magic working on me.

I waved at my odd new friends.

"These are *gallas*, demons of the underworld. And these others, these are Kurgurrah and Galatur."

The two shadowmen seemed to be struggling now, flicking in and out of existence, sometimes men, sometime more like two small flies.

"Mistress," Kurgurrah said. "It takes a great deal of energy to maintain these forms outside the Kur. Energy that you may regret having wasted later. We wonder if we might travel in a somewhat lazier fashion, perhaps in the metal box your friend has in his pocket?"

"Oh yes," said Gilgamesh, reaching for it.

At this, the flies both dropped like stones to the earth; I looked down and where the shadowmen had been standing, now there were only two shining beads of black rock, lying upon the mossy mountain grass.

"I'll get them," said Gilgamesh, kneeling down and carefully picking them up. Then he looked up at me. "You look dreadful, Inanna."

"Why are you here?" I said. "How are you here?"

He took a deep breath in, and then a deep breath out. "You'd better come into the hut," he said. "I have good news for you, but also bad."

I turned to face the hut and as I did, I felt the dipping, the pulling in of the world, that marked a great well of *melam*. I knew at once it was her.

I began scrabbling down the slope. "Is she here?" I shouted back to him, my bad leg forgotten. "Is she here?"

"Yes!" he called. "Wait for me."

My mother was coming out of the hut as I made it to the front door. She put her arms around me, and held me.

We stood together for some minutes, each with tears rolling down our cheeks. Then a man appeared from inside the hut. It took me a moment to place him: it was Harga, the captain of my guard in Uruk.

"What are you doing here?" I said. "Did I not leave you behind in Uruk?" I turned to Gilgamesh. "Where is Ninshubar? What has happened?"

Inside Neti's hut, I sat down on the floor next to Ninshubar, who was no longer conscious.

With the others watching on, I kissed her limp left hand.

"Mother, I have something that could help her," I said. I got out my pot of *melam*. "I had thought I would give it to you, Gilgamesh. Because I know the burden you carry. But perhaps there is enough for more than one."

I handed the pot to my mother. "What do you think? Ereshkigal gave it to me."

My mother opened it, very careful. "There is only enough for Ninshubar. She is very close to death."

"Will it save her?" I said.

"It should do more than that," Ningal said.

"Then do it," Gilgamesh said. "Do it. Give it to her."

"I am sorry, Gilgamesh," I said. "That you cannot join your parents."

He shrugged, and gave me a cheerful wink.

"Give her the *melam*," he said, "before it's too late."

CHAPTER TEN

NINSHUBAR

I woke up on my back in Neti's hut, in smoky half-light.

Inanna was sitting on a stool beside the bed. She had tears streaming down her face.

"Inanna, what is it?"

"It's your scars," she wept. "They are all gone."

I must have slept again.

I opened my eyes again.

Harga was sitting with me, his narrow, yellow-green eyes very bright in the gloom of the hut.

"Harga, I feel strange," I said.

He put one warm hand out to me, and rested it on my forehead.

Then Inanna came forwards to stand over us, and he took his hand away.

"I don't know what will happen now," Inanna said. "I think you might feel worse, before you feel better."

"You don't need to worry about me," I said. "This was not my first beating."

"It is not the beating they are worried about," Harga said. "It is the medicine they have given you for it."

Then the darkness came for me once more.

It was worse than any beating I had had before. Much worse.

When the pain was too much, I talked to Inanna. "What was the underworld like? Is it like in the stories?"

"No. It is not like in the stories."

"That's what your mother said to me, about Heaven. That it was not like in the stories."

"She is here, you know," Inanna said. "You rescued her."

Later I said to Inanna: "Do you remember being dead?"

"I remember waking up. I remember the pain."

"Do you remember your promise about my Potta?"

"I remember."

"I release you from it. When you are Queen of Heaven and Earth, as you surely will be, you cannot be running around the world looking for lost boys. I will go alone if you will let me. But I will come back to you."

"Ninshubar, I am not yet a queen of Uruk, never mind of all of the Earth, never mind Heaven. There will be time to talk about this."

"I would love to show you my country," I said.

One morning I woke up and I felt strong. Strangely strong. I saw that Ningal was with me, dressed in an oversized leather tunic.

She looked very pretty and well, with her long brown curls tumbling over her shoulders.

"What have you done to me?" I said.

"We gave you some *melam*," she said.

Inanna came forwards. "I am sorry we could not ask you first," she said.

I sat up, amazed by how easy my body felt. "I am strong," I said to both of them.

I emerged from the hut, and found it to be early morning. Harga and Gilgamesh were chopping wood; they both turned to look at me.

And then all at once two monsters sprang forwards at me.

They were like tall humans, but with featureless faces made from some metal that might have been silver, if it had not had a strange green sheen to it. They had eyes that were only dark holes in their metal faces. I saw that they were killers, and my hands moved for my weapons, but I had none.

One of the monsters carried a sword. This he pointed at me, and said: "This one will do. She is a god, although newborn."

"No, I will not do," I said.

Gilgamesh laughed out loud at this. "Easy there, Ninshubar. These monsters are our monsters."

Inanna stepped between me and the metal creatures.

"My husband, Dumuzi, will be the sacrifice," she said to them. "He will take my place. It is all decided already." She turned to me. "Ninshubar, I have promised to send someone down to the underworld in my place, and it will be my husband. So now we will go and get him."

"I wonder if the people will think it fair," Gilgamesh said to Inanna. "They think you and Dumuzi very much in love, and that he has treated you well. You are folk heroes, to the common folk."

Inanna looked at him, and then at me. "That is in the past now," she said. "What people think, what people don't think. I will decide what is fair now."

"A high goddess," Gilgamesh said.

"Yes," Inanna said.

She looked around at each of us. Ningal was at the door to the hut; Harga was standing by the wood pile, an axe hanging from his right hand.

"It's time to go," Inanna said.

I felt different in my body as I paced on. I had not understood that it was not only scars I had been carrying. I was also carrying long-term damage. Parts of me that ached at night, or when I walked too long, but I never thought to remark on. The piece of my skull that never seemed quite right. The headaches in the night. The pain in my shoulder, so humdrum, that was always with me, that made me throw differently. All that was gone. With every step, with every hour of sleep, with every breath, I was more than I had been. I felt a kind of uplift in every part of me.

Time and time again I felt Gilgamesh looking at me when he thought my attention was elsewhere. "How well you look," he said, smiling at me.

Harga watched me too, but said nothing.

Word began to run ahead of us as we started to pass farms and villages. Word of the little goddess returning to Uruk, of her mother the moon goddess with her, of the hero Gilgamesh in her retinue, and of these two living weapons that were with us, demons from the depths of the underworld.

We entered the city through the leopard gates to the south.

The people came out onto the streets, or leaned out of windows, but they stayed silent. The sun flashed off the demons of the underworld as we passed through the squares and markets on our way to the great precinct of the gods.

I had expected to find Dumuzi there. Instead, when our strange procession had found its way up the ziggurat and onto the smooth marble floors of the White Temple, we found, sitting on the cedar-wood throne, a large round man, dressed in bright yellow.

"Sister," he said to Inanna. He did not get up. "Mother," he said to Ningal.

Inanna walked barefoot ahead of us, down the great avenue of columns that ran down the centre of the temple.

"Get off my throne, Utu," she said.

"It's your throne now, is it, sister?" he said. "The *gallas* do not make you a queen."

"Perhaps they do," Inanna said.

The *galla* with the sword said: "We will accept this one." It pointed its sword at Utu.

Inanna stopped in front of the throne, and looked up at her brother. "I have to send a god to the underworld, to take my place. It is a deal that I have made with our sister. These demons say they will accept you. Do you want to go to the underworld, Utu?"

I was glad to see him recoil from her.

"Where is my husband?" she said.

Utu got down off the throne, no longer looking sure of himself. "Dumuzi has gone, sister," he said. "The *gallas* were seen, as you made your way here. And he chose to flee. I think perhaps he regretted not having helped you, when you were dead in the Great Below."

When the ancient throne was empty, Inanna took her place on it, her feet dangling. She looked very small and plain, in her old white dress. And yet she looked like she belonged there.

"I do not want to fight you, Inanna, or have any unpleasantness," Utu said. "But I must insist that you leave Dumuzi alone. I do not think the boy has done anything wrong, other than marry you as his father told him to."

"Why are you here, Utu?" she said. "And why do you speak for my husband? What are the water gods to you?"

Utu had a funny look to him now, as if he had forgotten what he was going to say, or where he was. He looked about him, and then sat down on a stool that was meant for a priest.

"Inanna, I did not know that you could be saved. Or I would have come to help you. I have nothing against you, sister."

"I know."

The *galla* with the mace came forwards. "We will take this one," it said.

"No," she said. "It will be my husband who takes my place. He is the price of my release. I have already decided on it."

Gilgamesh and Harga went out to find Dumuzi.

"I do love a hunt," Gilgamesh said.

They took the army with them, and they fanned out across the plains of the two rivers.

Word came: Dumuzi's sister, Geshtinanna, had been found hiding in a friend's house.

Soldiers tortured her. I am told they poured molten tar over her vulva. But she did not give her brother up.

"Was Gilgamesh there?" Inanna said.

"I do not believe so."

"Well, she will heal," Inanna said. "Although she may never recover."

I had thought she would be angry with the men who did it, but she said no more about it.

Uruk stood aghast, holding its breath. The people stayed huddled in their compounds. An was gone, and their king of three hundred years with him. The sheep god, so recently elevated, had run for his life. The great god of the sun, Utu, was said to be crying in his bedchambers.

And now here was this small goddess with the blackest eyes, calling herself the queen.

We walked through empty streets: me, Inanna and, behind us, the silver monsters.

Inanna walked with slow and careful steps, looking at each quiet doorway with great seriousness, as if it might be about to open.

"When they find my husband, it will not be over," she said. "Enki will come north to punish me, and to free Dumuzi."

"Do you want my advice?" I said. "Because this is the sort of thing I excel at."

She smiled up at me. "You excel at everything."

"I am capable," I said. "Yes. But in matters of war, I excel."

"Is this war, then, now?" she said.

"When you send Dumuzi down into hell, then it will be war. As I think you well know."

"Advise me, then," she said.

We had emerged out into the great square beside the temple precinct, which on a normal day would be thronging with people, but now stood empty but for a few stray dogs.

We sat down together on a granite bench, and the *gallas* took up position in front of us, back to back.

I said: "You cannot be queen of Uruk while Enki can come north at any time and put you in your place."

"But it is thanks to him I am here, and alive. He did not need to send the flies."

"All the same," I said.

We walked on after that, to the temple where I had first met Inanna. The priestesses, dressed in a brilliant orange, got down onto their knees, and then rested their foreheads on the floor of the temple, as Inanna looked down on them.

"They did not always kneel for me," she said.

"There is a difference in you," I said.

"Yes," she said. "I feel the difference."

Inanna had taken Dumuzi's rooms in the holy palace: four floors of rooms, with steps down from each, opening at the lowest level onto a magical courtyard, with a pool. The pool was open to the sky, and decorated with colourful mosaics. "I would not take his rooms," she said, "except I know how much my lions will like it here. They love to paddle."

Inanna's rooms were connected, by a door and also a gate, to adjoining rooms that had once been Geshtinanna's.

Those adjoining rooms Inanna gave to me.

I for some time paced around in them, when I was first alone there, before trying out the enormous, and very soft, bed.

I remembered my thin sleeping mat in the dry season camp in my country, lying so close to the rest of my family that I had to be careful when I turned over.

One morning, early, Inanna came to see me in my marvellous rooms. I awoke to find her sitting on the end of my bed. The *gallas* were behind her, silent, but watchful.

"How silently you all creep about," I said, embarrassed not to have heard them coming.

"I am sorry that I did not give you a choice, about the *melam*," Inanna said. "I have separated you from other humans, and you will learn the cost of that, as I have done."

"Inanna, I would be dead otherwise, and it is done. I have only thanks for you. Well, and also questions."

"Yes?"

"Am I a god now?"

"We call Isimud a god, and I am told that he was human, before Enki gave him *melam*. And he has lived a hundred years now, and still looked strong when I last saw him. I also know that you will be able to use *mees* now, if we can find you some."

"I will begin by taking Dumuzi's," I said.

"There is something else, though," she said, "that will be your choice. Yours only to make. Ninshubar, do you know what a *sukkal* is?"

Lilith, Inanna's chief priestess, had never seen the ceremony done. But Ningal remembered, having seen it done for Isimud.

The ceremony took place in the White Temple. It made me smile, standing there before the altar, how I had once thought the Temple of the Waves to be a wonder of the world.

"Will this be your temple now?" I said.

"Until I have time to build a bigger one," she said.

She was wearing purple. She had decided to keep the colour, since Dumuzi would not be needing it.

"It has a regal look to it," I said. "Very queenly."

"I agree."

Lilith appeared then, carrying the clay totems of Inanna's new queenship: an eight-pointed star, an eight-petalled blossom and a knot fashioned from reeds. They would be the marks of her temple now.

"I chose the sign of Nammu for you, Ninshubar," Inanna said. "And the blossom for Ninsun, and my time in her temple. And last of all the knot of reeds, because it is my mother's totem."

"Good choices," I said.

Then Ningal came forwards, with the bronze mask of the bull in her hands.

She helped put it over Inanna's head, and fasten it at the back, and then stepped back.

Inanna was too small for the mask, but she was nonetheless transformed by it. She did not look like a human thing when she turned to me to start the ceremony.

"You have to kneel down," she said.

I kneeled.

"Ninshubar, in Heaven, the greatest of the Anunnaki take a *sukkal*," she said. All the priestesses were ranged behind her, all in purple.

Lilith handed Inanna a long flint blade.

"Ninshubar," she said. "An Anunnaki and their *sukkal*, they are two bound as one. If you become my *sukkal*, you will slay demons for me. You will vanquish gods. You will serve at my side until the world ends. It is not a thing done lightly."

She held out her left wrist over the granite altar, and drew the copper blade across it; a shocking amount of blood began to spurt out.

"You have to put some of my blood in your mouth," she said.

Not knowing what else to do, I stood up, took hold of her bleeding wrist and put it to my mouth. The blood had a hard, metallic taste to it.

"If you serve as my *sukkal*," she said, "I will make you a great queen. A great queen in history. You will roll in silver; you will own vast estates. You will have palaces, and slaves, and glory, like no *sukkal* has ever had."

"I don't care about palaces, and silver," I said.

She ignored this. "But you will never be free. You will serve me until you die."

I kneeled down again, and watched, in the silence that followed, how quickly her wound closed and healed.

"You have to stand now," she said. "Do you see Lugalbanda kneeling, or Isimud? A *sukkal* kneels for no one."

Geshtinanna refused to give up her brother, but not all of Dumuzi's friends were so steadfast; not all of them had *melam* to help them heal. Soon enough we heard that he was in the low desert mountains to the west of us.

Gilgamesh, Harga and the army came in from the east, but only stopped to eat before moving on. This time Inanna and I went out with them, her going ahead in a chariot, with the *gallas* either side of the wheels. I was offered a mount, but said I was happy to walk.

I tried to speak to Harga as he rode out of the city, but although he returned my smile, he pushed on his mule and was quickly gone.

We crossed the Euphrates at its widest and shallowest point, and by the second evening we were in the hilltop town of Arali, which was said to be famous for its honey and its mountain teas. Now it would be famous for something else.

We had talked over what we would do when we found him. But when the time came, our choices were taken from us.

It was late afternoon. A shout went up from a soldier, who was looking over the reed fence of a pigsty.

A man stood up: it was Dumuzi, appearing before us as if from nowhere, and to everyone's entire surprise. I suppose he had been lying down, hiding from us.

I had a glimpse, very brief, of him looking dishevelled. He was dressed like a farmer.

He put his hands out to Inanna. "Inanna, I'm sorry," he said. "I should have told you about your mother. I was wrong not to."

"Yes," she said. She looked at him with no expression on her face. "But also you offered to cut my hand off. Do you remember? And you threatened me. You threatened my mother."

"I'm sorry," he said. "I was wrong."

"You said you would make my mother suffer."

Inanna turned to the *gallas*.

They were standing motionless behind her.

"This one will do," she said to the demons.

In a heartbeat the first *galla* was over the reed fence, in a blur of silver. It sank one of its metal arms into one of Dumuzi's legs.

He was already screaming, blood pouring off him, when the second *galla* went streaming over the fence, and sank its metal arms into his back.

Dumuzi went limp between them, the blood gushing from his wounds, as we all stood frozen, only looking on.

"We accept this man as the sacrifice," the *galla* with the sword said. It leaned over and pulled Dumuzi's *mees* off, from one arm and then the other.

These it threw down on the ground.

Then, so quickly, the demons, with Dumuzi slung between them, were gone.

I looked about me – at Inanna, looking down at the *mees*. At Gilgamesh, his sword drawn but now hanging useless. At Harga, a pebble in one hand, the slingshot in the other. At the soldiers behind them, standing open-mouthed.

"Praise be to the Queen of Uruk," Gilgamesh said. His voice carried well.

"Praise be," I said, smiling at Inanna. I stepped forwards to collect Dumuzi's *mees* from the mud.

Inanna watched me with her hands folded before her.

"Some triumphs there is no joy in," she said.

Afterwards, in Uruk, I brought Geshtinanna to Inanna. The woman seemed broken in spirit, although she bore no physical scars.

"She wants to share her brother's punishment," I said to Inanna. "So he does half a year in the underworld, then she the next half year, and then they swap again, and keep swapping. They will never be together again, but they will each spend half their time out in the light. Ereshkigal will always have one of them with her, a god to serve her. Well, that's her suggestion."

"Ereshkigal will not agree."

Geshtinanna dropped down onto her knees on the marble of the White Temple. She raised her hands to Inanna. "Goddess, if Ereshkigal will agree, will you?"

"Oh, I don't care," Inanna said. She looked up at me. "This girl is nothing in this," she said. "Do as you see fit."

Afterwards I went to find Harga. He was in the general barracks mess, where the common soldiers ate. He looked up at me when I appeared at the doorway. "Yes?"

He was wearing the new bronze sword that Inanna had had made for him, in honour of the sacred promise she had made him on the night I took his weapons from him.

"May I speak with you?" I said.

He looked about at his fellow soldiers, and then back at me. "All right," he said.

"I meant alone."

And so he followed me, with no enthusiasm, out into the yard, and we sat down together on a bench beneath the stoop. "What is it?" he said, not looking at me.

"You saved my life in Eridu," I said. "I would like to thank you for that."

He stood up. "I accept your thanks."

I stood too. "Harga will you not sit with me?"

He sat down again. "Ninshubar," he said. "I am glad you are alive. What more is there to say?"

"I thought we had become friends." I sat down next to him.

"You do not know me," he said. "We are acquaintances. That is all."

"I do not feel that."

He stood again, and looked down on me.

"Ninshubar, if you want me to speak plainly, I will speak plainly. There is an ocean between us now, where before there was perhaps only a stream."

"I am a wonderful swimmer," I said.

"You look younger every day. You shine with the god light. Your arms are heavy with *mees*, great weapons that could kill me in an instant. This is an ocean."

"I do not believe it has to be."

He said: "Ninshubar, I will be dead soon. How many mortal men do you know, in Sumer, who have lived past forty? And I am already thirty-five. Find someone who can walk beside you."

He gave me one last look, and then walked back into the barracks.

I felt a strange sensation upon my right cheek, along the line of my nose.

A tear.

I rubbed it hard away.

CHAPTER ELEVEN

GILGAMESH

After the demons took Dumuzi, I was not alone with Inanna again until we were in Uruk.

We sat together on the bench where I had once sat waiting for her, when she was the child bride of Dumuzi, and had no say over who was in her guard.

"I'm sorry I left you," I said. "With no warning. The whole time we were riding away, Enkidu scolded me for that."

After I had said his name, I found myself looking at my sandals, and there was a long silence between us.

"Is that why you came to rescue me?" she said. "For Enkidu?"

"Yes," I said.

She moved herself just a fraction further away from me. "I would like you to be my king here," she said, "as your father was king for An."

"I would like nothing more," I said, "than to be king of my own city. But I was asked by the god Enlil to try to make it right with my family, with my wife and my baby son."

"Oh," she said.

"And when I was on the far side of the world, I realised that it should not be for someone else to ask me to do the right thing for my family. So, I am going to try with them."

"Yes."

"As I should always have done, from the time I got her with child."

I felt her turn to me, and take in a breath.

I met her eye.

"Bring your wife and your son here, then, and take the palace," she said. "Everything done properly."

We sat there a while together, I think each not knowing what to say next. It came back to me very clearly then, the rite in her temple, when she was so silent, and I had thought I might be crushing her. And how it was with her, just the two of us, back in her room.

She said: "Gilgamesh, if you do not want to be king here, then I will not try to persuade you. But I will not ask anything improper of you. You can bring your family here with honour."

"Thank you, Inanna," I said. "I'll go and talk to them in Nippur, and see where their hearts lie."

She looked down at her lap. "You do not feel it, what I feel," she said. "But I suppose that is just as well."

"We barely know each other," I said.

She nodded, her eyes still upon her lap.

"Go and talk to your family," she said. "And I hope you will return here to be crowned."

"I will take Harga," I said.

"Harga is always useful," she said, reminding me very strongly of Enlil as she said it, the words all turned the same way, and with the same dark look.

"I am not sure how long it will last, this reformation of my character," I said.

"I did not mind the old you," she said, her black eyes on me.

She smiled at me, then, her seriousness gone for a moment.

I thought about asking her about the underworld, about what she had seen there. About Enkidu. I almost said the words, but then thought, *Now is not the right time.*

Instead I picked up her left hand and kissed it. Just that one kiss. And she nodded again, and a moment later stood, and left me.

CHAPTER TWELVE

INANNA

I dreamed I was standing on a wall, and a man came walking up to me, in black armour, and a black cloak. I thought he was going to kiss me, but instead, with no warning, he pushed me hard.

I fell from the wall, my mouth open in shock.

"Inanna."

It was dark. Night-time. Ninshubar was in my bedroom, holding up a candle. Something was wrong.

"It's an earthquake," she said. "Come with me."

She took me by the hand, and led me down through my rooms. As we walked, the floor seemed to move beneath me, dust falling from the ceiling. For a moment we stopped still, holding on to each other.

"Come, let's get outside," she said.

In the courtyard, we sat down on the edge of the pool, with our feet in the cold water.

"Nothing can fall on us here," she said.

The earth moved again; we heard roof tiles falling, and shouting.

"Does this happen often, here?" Ninshubar said.

"No. Never."

"It happens in my country," she said. "Never so hard, and never for so long, but it happens."

"No, this is very strange," I said.

I shut my eyes, and followed the bright lines out to the Anunnaki, and out to the Kur, far to the east. Something was different. But what? I could not make it out.

"Are you well, Inanna?" Ninshubar said.

"I am quite well," I said. "I am just shaking off a dream."

Had I dreamed of that dark stranger before? I could not be sure.

When daylight came, we went from house to house, with my mother too, making sure no one had been buried, or trapped, or hurt.

In the early evening, my mother said: "Inanna, if you are going to go, you should go. You should go quickly."

"It's a bad time to be leaving."

"There is never a good time to do the hard things," she said. "I do not want you to go, but if you are going to go, go now. I will hold the city, until Gilgamesh returns."

"Your mother is right," Ninshubar said. "If you are going to do something, it is better to do it quick."

We left at dawn the next day. Just me, and Ninshubar, and the four boys who manned the temple skiff.

"This is the fastest boat in Sumer," I told Ninshubar.

"It is the fastest boat in the world," one of the boys said. He then blushed very deeply, for having spoken uninvited.

I gave him a smile.

"It is the fastest boat in the world," I said. "And it is death to delay it. So we should be in Uruk in two days and two nights, if the wind stays with us. I wonder if he already knows about Dumuzi."

"Let's hope the wind favours us, then," Ninshubar said. "Because it would be better if he did not."

It was time to go into battle with Enki.

Ninshubar was right. How could I be a great goddess if, at any time of his choosing, my grandfather could come and take from me my safety, my happiness, my city, even my mother?

So now we sat on a plank in the tiny boat, as it bent over in the wind, me in a dress and plain cloak, and Ninshubar, my *sukkal*, in fine-mesh armour, and a copper helmet on her head, and with the gleam in her eye that the *melam* gives you.

"So let me hear your plan," Ninshubar said.

"First we will crush Enki and then we will rescue my lions," I said. "And then we will steal Enki's great arsenal of weapons. And then I will truly be queen of Uruk."

"If you kill Enki, you will be queen of all the Earth," Ninshubar said. "I'm not sure about the Heaven bit."

"I don't need to kill him," I said. "Only to humiliate him, and steal his arsenal. I will leave him with his life. That will be my thank you to him, for his help with the flies."

"If you think that wise," Ninshubar said.

"Have you ever killed someone?"

"Not yet," she said. "But, Inanna, whatever you decide, I will follow you."

I touched her arm. "When Uruk is secure, we will go and fetch your Potta, in honour of the promise I refused to be released from."

"Will you be Queen of Heaven and Earth then?" she said.

"I will be close enough to it."

I stood up then, holding on to Ninshubar's shoulder with one hand, and a rope in the other.

I lifted my voice up to the fields, and the marshes, and the glorious blue sky.

"I am coming for you, Enki," I shouted. "I am coming for you!"

Now was the time for the gods of war.

CHAPTER THIRTEEN

ERESHKIGAL

I was a beautiful princess, when I lived in Heaven, and everyone loved me. I was the cleverest of all the children. And I was the only child in the palace who had a flying animal. When I went out flying on it, it would swoop from cloud to cloud.

I could not remember the name of the flying animal. How could I have forgotten it?

I sat there for so long, trying to remember, that when I came to myself, my hand and my clay tablet were covered in dust. The dust of the dead, mixed with dust from the earthquake.

A short knock at the door, and Dumuzi appeared.

"You should come," he said.

"I am writing my history."

He rolled his eyes. "You have a visitor," he said. "Your demons are beside themselves."

"Another visitor!"

"Yes!" he said. "Another visitor. So leave your stupid tablet, and come and see."

"I had no guests at all for more than eighty years. Then my sister, and then the shadowmen, and then you, and now another!"

"Your demons don't like him," Dumuzi said. "I think they're hiding."

I pushed myself up to my feet, careful not to wrench my back. "I wonder if he caused the earthquake," I said.

Dumuzi tipped his head to one side, thinking. "Yes, it does seem strange that he should come so soon after."

I stumbled over some broken masonry on the way to the throne room, stubbing a toe hard. For some time I had to lean against the cold stone wall of the corridor, waiting for the pain to pass.

With some reluctance, Dumuzi came back for me, and put out his arm to me.

"There's rubble everywhere," he said. "Your demons should be clearing it up, not hiding in corners." But he slowed his steps so that I could keep up with him.

And so I was on Dumuzi's arm when I entered the throne room.

The stranger was sitting on a bench.

He was wearing black armour, and a long black cape. He had the markings of the Anunnaki. But he was not one of the Thirteen.

I had not seen armour like his for four hundred years.

Not since the time before.

꩜

My visitor had not come from the realm of light.

He had come through different gates, and from a different realm.

"You do not know me, Ereshkigal," the dark stranger said. "But I know you."

END OF BOOK ONE

SOME NOTES ABOUT THE BOOK

This book is a retelling of the *Epic of Gilgamesh*, which is often said to be the oldest piece of literature in existence. Gilgamesh himself is often described as the first literary hero.

A very long time ago, in what is now modern Iraq, the stories that now make up the epic were recorded on clay tablets, in a script called cuneiform. These must have been popular stories, because they were collected in royal libraries, and at some point strung together to form the epic. This epic persisted as civilisations rose and fell in the Mesopotamian region.

Sumer is the first civilisation known to have blossomed in the region and indeed anywhere in the world. Its people, the Sumerians, spoke a language with no known origin, and it is unclear where they first came from. Later came the Akkadians and the Babylonians and many others. All of these peoples knew about Gilgamesh. Schoolchildren, in ancient times, were made to copy out stories about him.

Thousands of years later, copies of the epic, or the stories that it is made up of, were dug up by archaeologists, because it turns out clay tablets are a superb way to store information. Cuneiform can be used to write in different languages, and some of the stories were written in Sumerian, others in later languages.

The oldest copies of Gilgamesh stories found are from about 2000 BC, but the story was perhaps already old by the time it was written down, in the same way that the *Odyssey* was already probably ancient before being recorded in writing in Ancient Greece.

The goddess Inanna does play an important role in the epic of Gilgamesh, but as is obvious from the title, it is really all about Gilgamesh. This novel, however, is not only based on his epic. It is also a retelling of two important Mesopotamian myths in which the goddess Inanna is the big star: the myth of Inanna and Dumuzi, and the story of Inanna's descent into the underworld.

Could these extraordinary stories about Inanna predate the epic of Gilgamesh, making Inanna, in fact, the very first character in literature? Quite possibly.

For the purposes of this book, I've also thrown in scraps of other Mesopotamian writings, including "Inanna and the Huluppu Tree", and "The Envoys of Akka", of which only some lines still exist.

A lot of this book, however, just to warn you, is simply made up.

So were Inanna, Gilgamesh and Ninshubar "real" people who walked about the land in ancient Sumer in 4,000 BC, when my story is set?

It's quite possible that Gilgamesh actually was a real, living man, and even a real king of Uruk, just as he is in the epic. It's claimed that he probably lived in around 2,700 BC, but it could have been earlier, or later. Many things, with Sumer, right at the beginning of recorded history, cannot be known for sure.

Inanna, I am going to guess, was never a real person. But she was certainly a vastly important deity in the Sumerian pantheon, and she is said to have later morphed into, or inspired, the goddess Ishtar, and then later Aphrodite, and then Venus – making her arguably the longest-lived female deity in recorded history.

Ninshubar does not have myths of her own, or none that have yet been found. She is largely only ever mentioned, in Mesopotamian literature, in her role as Inanna's trusty right-hand woman. Later in history Ninshubar appears to have been redrawn as a man, but in the oldest stories, she was a woman.

For this novel, I have largely invented the backstories of these three characters. I have seen Ninshubar referred to as a "queen from the east", for example, but in this book I have her as an ordinary woman from somewhere close to modern Mombasa, until fate intervenes.

I have also found myself obliged to stray quite far at times from the myths that inspired these characters.

Mesopotamian myths are vivid, bold, shocking, wonderful… but they are also short, fragmentary and deliberately repetitive – perhaps they were sung? They also differ wildly in age, contradict each other, and are often baffling, and they tend to offer little useful explanation of anyone's motivation, at least from a modern standpoint. So I ended up picking and choosing from them according to what felt right for my characters as they grew upon the page.

What of the other characters in the novel? Many are from the mythological or historical record. Enkidu, Lilith, King Akka and all of the Anunnaki, for example, have their names recorded upon clay tablets for one reason or another.

Other characters are purely fictional. My beloved Harga, for example, is made up. Amnut is also made up, but she was inspired by a real person in history. In real life a girl with a silver ribbon on her body was found in a mass grave that was discovered and excavated at Ur in the 1930s.

So is this book historical fiction, as well as a mythological fantasy? The answer of course is no, given that I have near-immortals walking around the place. But I have tried to stay broadly true, in spirit at least, to what we know of the region in ancient times, because otherwise, why bother to set the book in a real place, and base it on ancient stories?

For this reason, many of the objects in this book, such as Enki's table base made up of a ram standing with its feet in a tree of some sort, are real. That "ram in a thicket", as it is known, is on display at the British Museum in London. My description of Enlil's army as it arrives at Marad is taken from images captured on the museum's so-called Standard of Ur.

As far as we know, the Mesopotamians invented the wheel, chariots, writing, bricks, canals, the basis of how we measure time, paved streets, beer, sailing boats and much, much more, and I have felt free to scatter their accomplishments through this book, even if, strictly speaking, they wouldn't all have been present and correct in 4,000 BC.

Some things are just made up because I was tying myself up in knots trying to be historical. For example: my measurement of distance in this novel is a nonsense. Cables, cords, leagues… all made up at least in the way I am using them here.

On some subjects, meanwhile, I have gone down deep rabbit holes in my concern for accuracy, however irrelevant it might seem to anyone else. For example, could I give my characters horses to ride on? On the Standard of Ur, the horse-like animals shown with the army do not look like modern horses. They are perhaps a cross between donkeys and a species of wild ass now extinct. And yet in Asia, in about 3,500 BC, people were domesticating the wild horse. Surely my characters deserved to ride horses! Mules and donkeys just didn't feel as glorious and heroic to me. In the end I have used a mixture of donkeys, mules, onagers (wild asses) and some actual horses. In my story I claim that the horses have been imported by Lugalbanda, Gilgamesh's father, at great cost. Well, perhaps the Sumerians did have some horses, and we just haven't dug them up yet!

Is this book also science fiction? Well, a tiny bit. But only because when you read the myths of ancient Mesopotamia, it's hard not to see some science fiction there. I am not alone in this view, as you will quickly discover if you google "the Anunnaki". Indeed, the myths about them have spawned a strong industry in the arena of "the Sumerian gods were aliens".

Although I do not believe that the Anunnaki were aliens, it is very easy to see how people might decide upon such a thing, given that the myths are stuffed with talk of "thunderbirds" coming down from the sky and so on.

For the purposes of this novel, I have leaned into this alien-conspiracy heritage a little simply because I instinctively prefer my gods' powers to be based in some sort of science, however notional, rather than old-fashioned magic. My Anunnaki have a backstory as creatures from "another realm" – read into that what you will – and technology from that distant realm in the form of weapons (their *mees*) and the strange black stuff (*melam*) that gives them immortality. Sumerian scholars will tell you that the *mees* were aspects of civilisation, not weapons. The word *melam*, meanwhile, is a word associated with the look or the clothing of the gods, not some magical stuff that ran through their blood. But this is above all else... a novel.

Speaking of science: clay tablets are still being dug up in Iraq. But also, modern science is allowing us to gain new insight into tablets that were dug up a long time ago, but until now have been too damaged and also too numerous to translate. As I write this, an international project is working to digitally record the tablets already in our museums, so that an artificial intelligence can have a good, hard look at them. All of this means that at any moment an entirely new story about Inanna, Gilgamesh or Ninshubar might be unearthed.

The map at the front of this book is of course a guess at the truth. The cartographer who very kindly drew it for me had to approximate the course of the rivers in 4,000 BC and also the ancient coastline. He also at my request left off the cities of ancient Sumer that I did not include in my story, but he did try to ensure that the distances between the cities actually shown are correct. The one outright piece of fiction on the map is the presence of the cedar forest. The site of that forest has been much debated in the years since *The Epic of Gilgamesh* was written, with some saying it lay in the Zagros Mountains, and others in Lebanon. But it probably did not lie on the flat land between the two rivers. Probably!

If you are interested in reading more about Inanna, please may I recommend to you the marvellous *Inanna: Queen of Heaven and Earth* by Diane Wolkstein and Samuel Noah Kramer? It was this beautifully written book, and the way it pieces together the stories about Inanna into a sequence about a girl growing up, that inspired me to write this novel.

For more on Gilgamesh, I recommend *The Epic of Gilgamesh* as translated by Andrew George.

If you are interested in reading about Sumerian society more generally, I recommend *The Sumerians* by Samuel Noah Kramer, *Daily Life in Ancient Mesopotamia* by Karen Rhea Nemet-Nejat and *The Sumerians: A History from Beginning to End* by Henry Freeman.

If you can find it, Sir Leonard Woolley's book *Ur: The First Phases*, about his dig there, is small but astonishing, with beautiful pictures of his finds.

For a wonderful glimpse of the marshes of Iraq as they might have been even in very ancient history, I recommend *The Marsh Arabs* by Wilfred Thesiger, and Gavin Maxwell's *A Reed Shaken by the Wind*. It was these two books that inspired Ninshubar's brief journey into the marshes near Eridu.

ACKNOWLEDGEMENTS

Thank you to Elle, fellow founder of Fight Club, an extremely exclusive novel-writing club (membership: two). I would never have finished a novel without Fight Club.

Thank you to my son Aldo, my first reader.

Thank you to Richard T. Kelly, my tutor at the Faber Academy in London. When I was moaning to him rather wetly about having committed to multiple first-person perspectives, and had I bitten off more than I could chew, he threw out: "Oh just go for it." Very obediently, I did just that.

Thank you to all my fellow Faber Academy students from the class of September 2021: Laura, Veronika, Susie, Wilhelmina, Emilia, Ed, Francesca, Elizabeth, Adam, Natalie, Katharine and Jo. What a blast you have all been!

Thank you to all my other readers over the past three years: Esther, Chloe, Blue, Sapphire, Richard, Michael, Melanie and Clementine.

Thank you to my brother-in-law, the cartographer Tim Absalom, for the map of Sumer.

Thank you to my mother, for handing down to me her passion for archaeology.

Thank you to my agent, Ian Drury, for picking me out of his slush pile, and my publisher, Daniel Carpenter at Titan, for buying this book and also editing it.

And finally thank you to my husband, Jon, for being just the best.

READING GROUP DISCUSSION GUIDE

1. How do Inanna, Gilgamesh and Ninshubar's backgrounds and upbringing impact the ways in which they each view the world?

2. The Anunnaki receive their power through their *mees* and *melam*, and their abilities and gifts are based on the hoarding and collecting of them. What does this tell us about privilege and power?

3. How familiar were you with the *Epic of Gilgamesh*, or indeed the lesser-known epic poem *The Descent of Inanna*, before reading this book?

4. The breaking of traditions is a key theme throughout the book. How do each of the characters break from tradition and how does it affect them?

5. Both Gilgamesh and Inanna enter into marriages during the course of the novel. How do their experiences differ?

6. How does Inanna's near-immortality affect the way she experiences the passing of time? How does the author capture this?

7. The food of the gods and the humans, the dinners they have and the conversations over food are hugely important to the

novel. What is the political impact of food and eating in the book?

8.   Would you take *melam* if you were offered it? How might it change your perspective on the world?

9.   In her notes about the book, the author discusses how she has blended historical truth, the existing myths and her own invented fiction to create the story. How effective is this?

10. All three main characters end up in absolute blackness. What do they each learn in their climb back to the light?

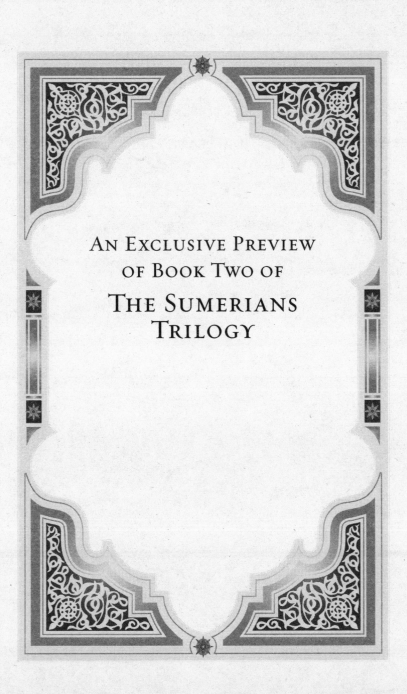

AN EXCLUSIVE PREVIEW
OF BOOK TWO OF

THE SUMERIANS
TRILOGY

CHAPTER ONE

MARDUK

In the city of Kish.
Nine months before Inanna's
return from the underworld...

I was in with the royal ladies, cleaning up after the most elderly of their dogs, when the news swept through the court.

The hero Gilgamesh had been captured in battle.

Taken prisoner by King Akka himself, on the banks of the Tigris, and brought to Kish with his hands and feet bound, slung over the back of a mule.

The lion of Uruk was *here*, in the palace!

For some long minutes, I leaned upon my mop, ears straining for every detail of the hero's capture. Only when I felt royal eyes falling upon me did I return, most reluctantly, to my mopping.

The dog had done its sloppy business all over a mosaic: a beautiful scene of a goddess in a chariot, being pulled along by lions. I was in truth spreading the muck around, rather than cleaning it up, but I had no ambition at all to be good at mopping.

Indeed, it was important to do unpleasant jobs badly, in order never to be asked again.

Hedda, the king's sister, came to stand in the way of my mop, with a very wheedling look to her. "Marduk, go and find out what you can," she said. She was a small creature, lightly made, and handsome in her blue velvet.

"Go yourself," I said. "I must clean up after your dog." I began to mop with some vigour around her tiny, slippered feet. It was my firm policy to resist all orders given to me, unless either bribed or threatened with violence.

"Please, Marduk," she said, stepping back to protect her slippers from me. "At least find out if he is going to live." She gave me her most winning smile. "I will pay you in fresh figs," she said. "I know how much you like them."

"I will go," I said. "But I want cheese with my figs."

Mop in one hand, sloshing bucket in the other, I made my way, circuitously, to the palace kitchens. On my way I gathered fragments of intelligence.

It was said that the hero Gilgamesh had been captured alongside a man called Harga, and that this man Harga had immediately been sent south with a ransom message for Gilgamesh's father, Lugalbanda. Gilgamesh himself was badly wounded, and had been carried in unconscious over the back of his mule. Some said he would not survive the night. Others said he had fallen in the Tigris, and almost drowned, shortly before his capture.

It was my intention to pass unobserved through the kitchens, on my way to the palace gardens, where I hoped to find my friends. But as I slipped through the gloom and heat of the bakery, Biluda, the head of the king's household, loomed up before me.

"Where in all of Akkadia have you been?" he said. "I have sent out five messages for you to come here at once, and yet no one could find you." He was wearing his formal household robes: a brilliant blue, embroidered all over with kingfishers, the totem of the king.

"I was clearing up dog mess," I said. "As you told me to." I held out to him my filthy mop, and quarter-filled bucket.

"You have heard the news, I presume?"

"I have been working."

"Of that I am fairly doubtful," he said. "However. We have a Sumerian prince here as our guest, and I would like you to take him some necessaries."

"I heard he was dying."

"Not presently," Biluda said. "Although he is much dented." He pointed one long but crooked finger at the flour-covered kneading table, on which stood a glass, and a large clay jug. "You will take these to the captive, and then tell him you will come back to him with a robe after."

I put down my bucket, and leaned upon my mop. "Why me?"

"Marduk, you are a slave, not a prince of this household. I have told you to take these two things to the captive, so take these two things to the captive."

"You are a slave; I am a slave. I do not see what that has to do with it."

"I am the chief slave, who can have you whipped, so just take these to the captive, Marduk, before I lose my temper!"

"But why not go yourself?"

Biluda smoothed down his long, grey beard, and then, in a low voice, he said: "He likes pretty boys; that is what they say."

"And?"

"You are a pretty boy. Perhaps he will say something interesting to you, if you take him his water." He shut his mouth hard flat on that, as he did when he was getting angry.

"There is no need to be cross about it," I said. "I only ask 'Why me?', when you say I cannot be trusted with anything."

"I think I can trust you to take a glass of water to a man," he said. "That is, if I can only persuade you to do it."

"And what sort of interesting thing might he say?"

Biluda clawed out his fingers at me, as if about to strangle me. "Men forget themselves when someone takes their fancy. You would not know that, being so high-minded."

"All right, I'll take the water," I said. "I would like to see this great hero of Sumer."

I put my head around the door. The lion of Uruk lay on his back on a small, wooden bed. He was bare-chested, but with a sheet pulled up over his hips. Black hair, brown skin and very bright eyes. His throat looked bruised, and he had a belly wound that ought to have been bandaged.

All the same he looked very dark, and powerful, and gleaming, against the simple white linen of his bedding. A lion of man, indeed.

"My lord, may I check on you?"

"Certainly," he said. A deep voice, and an accent that felt oddly familiar to me, although I could not quite place it.

I began to make my way into the room, the glass and jug held out before me, only to be hit with the full force of his dazzling smile.

It occurred to me for the first time that the lion of Uruk might be dangerous.

Of course I did not have a weapon; slaves do not carry weapons. I could cut his throat with the glass, if I could smash it

on something. Or perhaps just hit him with the jug. I had killed
a man, in Egypt, with only my thumbs, but that man was not a
seasoned soldier, as Gilgamesh most certainly was.

"Do you know how I got here?" Gilgamesh said, still searing
me with his smile.

"You passed out entirely, my lord," I said. "They had to carry
you from your mule."

I could see, from the way he was holding himself, that he was
thinking about getting out of bed. I took two steps backwards.

"They thought you would be thirsty, my lord, after having
slept so long," I said, "and I am to bring you a robe and to tell
you that as soon as you are recovered, the king hopes to see you
at dinner."

All the tension seemed to drain out of him.

His dropped his blistering smile.

"What does that mean, at dinner?" he said.

When I had safely delivered the water to the hero Gilgamesh, I went
back out into the corridor. Biluda was lying in wait for me there.

"What did he say?" he whispered.

"He was interested in dinner," I said. "I think he's very hungry."

"And what else?"

"He asked after his man Harga."

"That's all?"

"That's all. Perhaps he finds me less pretty than you do."

Biluda, looking hugely irritated, handed me a linen robe. It
looked much like the slave's smock that I was wearing, except of
course it was very much cleaner.

"Go back in," he whispered. "And this time ask him about the
war, that kind of thing."

"I think that would be very odd. He will guess I have been told to do it."

"And yet you are a slave, and just this once you will do as you are asked, Marduk."

"I will take him the robe. But I'm not going to ask about the war."

Gilgamesh was lying with his eyes shut, as if asleep, when I went back in. A line from an old temple poem came to me: *The sleeping and the dead, how alike they are.*

I was about to back out, but he said: "No, come, come." He turned his face to me. "I am only resting." He had one hand upon his belly.

I made my way cautiously forwards, to drop the linen robe at the foot of his bed. "For you to wear," I said.

"What are you?" he said. "A prince? A spy?"

"A slave."

"Ah! How do they treat their slaves, in Kish?"

"Better than the slave trader who brought me here."

"There are no good slave traders," Gilgamesh said. "That's what my father says. It brutalises your spirit, to buy and sell men like animals."

"Perhaps your father could stop men from selling each other," I said, "since he is a god, or so it is said."

Another flash of the hero's smile. "Quite right," he said. "Come, sit down a moment. Where are you from? I've never seen anyone so pale before, or with such red hair."

After a moment's hesitation, I sat down on the hero's narrow bed, being careful not to sit too close to his feet. "Do you know it is rude to ask a slave where he is from?"

Gilgamesh laughed, clutching at his belly. "I think I have been told that, and forgotten it."

"I was taken from my family when I was very young," I said. "But I remember snow along a shoreline. Since then I have met people who say there are people like me in the far north." I shrugged.

"And then you were brought here?"

"I have been all over," I said. "Most recently I was in Egypt." I pulled up my left sleeve, to show him the brand of a lion-headed eagle on my arm. "That is the sign of the temple at Abydos. Have you heard of Abydos?"

"Only that it's a holy place."

"It's an evil place," I said.

"You talk a lot, for a slave."

"I am not a good slave," I said. "I have disappointed all my owners."

Gilgamesh propped himself up a little, wincing as he did it. "You have more spirit in you than most slaves of my acquaintance."

I moved over a little, to avoid his foot, which had moved against me beneath the sheet.

"I will have the spirit beaten out of me soon enough." I paused for a moment. Well, what harm would it do to speak it? "My plan is to escape."

"Where will you go?"

"To find my mother."

"In the far north?"

"My adopted mother. Somewhere south of Egypt."

Gilgamesh moved as if to sit up, and then lay flat again, grimacing. "I would like to eat at the king's table tonight. But I am not sure I can dress myself with my shoulder as it is. Will you help me with that robe there?"

"No," I said. "Dress yourself."

Gilgamesh frowned for a moment, and then laughed. "You're a terrible slave!"

"It is not my intention to become a good one."

"Hah!" he said. "Tell me your name, terrible slave boy."

"Marduk," I said. "That's what they called me in Egypt."

"A strange name."

"It means 'dragon's breath', in Egyptian."

"Because of your hair," he said.

"You are a thinker, then," I said, "not only a soldier."

He rolled his eyes at that. "Do you remember your real name?"

"I think I used to. Sometimes I think I dream and it is there, but then I wake and it's gone. But my adopted mother called me the Potta. So that is how I think of myself."

We smiled at each other.

For just that one heartbeat, we were only two men, alone on a bed together, rather close, and with him naked under his sheet.

I stood at once to go, but, at the door, turned to look back at him. I had a foolish rush of sympathy for him, for how battered he was, for how low he had been brought. Also sadness, because our paths, having crossed this once, were so unlikely to ever cross again.

"Good hunting to you, Gilgamesh," I said. "Hero turned captive, who was once the lion of Uruk!"

"I hope to see you again," he said.

"Let it be out in the world, then," I said. "With us both free."

I raised one palm at him, and then not knowing what else to say or do, I left.

"Good hunting to you too, Marduk," Gilgamesh called after me. "Marduk the terrible slave boy, who was once called the Potta!"

ABOUT THE AUTHOR

EMILY H. WILSON is the editor of *New Scientist*. She has previously worked as a journalist at the *Guardian*, the *Daily Mail* and the *Mirror*. Born in Brighton, England, but raised in Lesotho and Seychelles, she has a degree in chemistry from the University of Bristol. She lives in Dorset, England, with her husband, sons and dog, Argos. Her website is emilyhwilson.com, she is on Instagram at emilyhwilson1 and she tweets @emilyhwilson

ARCH-CONSPIRATOR

BY VERONICA ROTH

Outside the last city on Earth, the planet is a wasteland. Without the Archive, where the genes of the dead are stored, humanity will end.

Antigone's parents – Oedipus and Jocasta – are dead. Passing into the Archive should be cause for celebration, but with her militant uncle Kreon rising to claim her father's vacant throne, all Antigone feels is rage.

When he welcomes her and her siblings into his mansion, Antigone sees it for what it really is: a gilded cage, where she is a captive as well as a guest.

But her uncle will soon learn that no cage is unbreakable. And neither is he.

A PORTRAIT IN SHADOW

BY NICOLE JARVIS

When Artemisia arrives in Florence seeking a haven for her art, the powerful all-male Accademia, self-proclaimed gatekeepers of Florence's magical art world, refuse her.

Alone and fighting for recognition, Artemisia makes allies such as Galileo and the influential Cristina de' Medici, as well as the charming, wealthy Francesco Maria Maringhi.

When scandal erupts, Artemisia must choose between revenge and her dream of creating a legacy that will span the generations.

For more fantastic fiction, author events,
exclusive excerpts, competitions, limited editions and more

VISIT OUR WEBSITE
titanbooks.com

LIKE US ON FACEBOOK
facebook.com/titanbooks

FOLLOW US ON TWITTER AND INSTAGRAM
@TitanBooks

EMAIL US
readerfeedback@titanemail.com